*Every journey to success*

*starts by taking the first step*

# The Storm Legacy:

*Deceitful Skies*

**Zach Thorn**

# The Storm Legacy:
# Deceitful Skies

# Prologue

The Chinook's roar vibrated through Devin's bones, a physical assault that rattled his teeth inside his helmet. He tightened his grip on his M4, the cool metal familiar against his gloves, and scanned the desolate landscape unfolding below—a blur of dun-colored rock and dust stretching across Afghanistan. Sweat plastered Manny's short, dark hair to his forehead beneath his own helmet; he adjusted the strap, his gaze fixed grimly on the horizon.

Deep in contested territory, the mission was straightforward: extract a high-value target from a village nestled in the unforgiving terrain. The vibrations of the helicopter were the only constant in the tense air, punctuated by the rhythmic thump of the blades and the occasional burst of static from the radio headset.

A sudden, violent lurch threw them against their restraints. The engine sputtered, choked. Warning lights flared across the instrument panel like angry red eyes. The pilot's voice, strained, cut through the static, "We're hit! Going down!".

Instinct took over. Devin and Manny braced, muscles coiling as the world outside dissolved into a sickening vortex of dust and spinning sky. The helicopter slammed into the rocky ground, skidding, tearing metal screaming before shuddering to a halt—a mangled wreck. Disoriented, senses assaulted, they scrambled from the wreckage, the adrenaline momentarily masking any injuries.

Figures emerged from the swirling dust—enemy fighters, weapons leveled. The air exploded with gunfire. Devin and Manny instinctively found each other's backs, reacting in concert, their movements honed by shared battles. Rifles barked, brass ejecting as they sought cover behind a crumbling mud-brick wall, the sharp smell of cordite stinging Devin's nostrils, mingling with the metallic tang of blood.

"Heavy fire!" Manny yelled over the din. "Need an egress, Dev!".

Devin scanned the chaos, spotting a narrow alleyway between two structures. "There! Alley!" he shouted, pointing. "Move!".

They broke cover, sprinting across the open ground, rounds kicking up dirt at their heels. Reaching the narrow passage offered a sliver of safety. But shadows shifted within the alley. A Taliban fighter lunged out, AK-47 rising, his face a mask of fury.

The world compressed. Devin saw the sunlight glint off the worn barrel, the fighter's focused intent. This was it.

A hard shove sent Devin sprawling into the dust. Manny had pushed him clear as the AK erupted, bullets tearing through the space Devin had occupied a heartbeat before.

"Dev!" Manny shouted, already moving towards him, checking for wounds.

"I'm good," Devin gasped, scrambling up, adrenaline surging through him. He looked at Manny, his chest tight with a gratitude that went deeper than words. "Appreciate it, brother," he managed, his voice rough. "You saved my ass".

Manny grinned, clapping him on the shoulder. "Always, Dev".

They exchanged a look—a connection forged in shared danger, tested and proven once again.

RING! RING! RING!

The phone's insistent pierce cut through the nightmare. Devin jolted upright in bed, sweat cooling on his skin, his heart hammering against his ribs. He sucked in a breath, lungs burning, the phantom firefight still echoing in his ears.

His hand trembled as he reached for the phone on the nightstand.

"Hello?" he croaked, his voice rough.

"Devin?" A familiar voice, thick with tears, came through the line. "It's your mother. Devin, your father... he's gone".

The words slammed into him, the dream dissolving as the brutal fact settled in his gut. He sat, the phone slipping from his suddenly numb fingers, the silence in the room amplifying the crushing weight of the news.

Three years. Three years of silence, of pride, of calls unreturned. Now, the door was slammed shut, locked forever. Regret surged, a choking flood of unspoken words, missed chances. Why hadn't he called? Why let anger fester? He wanted to snatch back time, erase the years of distance, but the chance was gone. The love, always there beneath the resentment, now had nowhere to go.

Tears stung his eyes, but he blinked them back reflexively. Family first. Be strong. His father's voice, a phantom echo in his mind. He was the rock, the responsible one, the one who never broke. But alone in the darkness, the grief felt immense, threatening to buckle him.

The bedroom door creaked open. Manny shuffled in, hair tousled, eyes bleary with sleep.

"Dev?" he mumbled, voice thick. "What's going on? Phone ringing off the hook...". He yawned, stretching, then his gaze fell on Devin, on the discarded phone, and his sleepy posture shifted, alertness replacing confusion. "Who was that?".

Devin looked up, meeting his friend's questioning gaze. The words wouldn't form, lodged somewhere painful and tight in his throat. He shook his head, unable to speak, the unshed tears finally spilling over. Manny's expression morphed instantly from sleepy curiosity to alarm. He crossed the room quickly, sitting on the edge of the bed, his hand gripping Devin's shoulder. "Dev, what is it? What happened?".

Devin dragged in a breath. "It's... Dad," he choked out, the name cracking. "He's gone, Man".

The words hung between them. Manny's eyes widened, his grip tightening instinctively. A flicker of memory crossed his face—Mr. Jones's booming laugh, the easy way he'd welcomed Manny into their home, treated him like another son. Especially after... Manny's own past intruded, the screech of tires, his mother gone, his own father's subsequent spiral, and the Joneses taking him in, offering shelter from that storm. Mr. Jones had been a steady presence, a second father figure. The loss felt sharp, personal, layering onto old wounds.

Manny pulled Devin into a hug, a solid, grounding presence. They clung to each other, the nightmare, the phone call, the weight of the world outside momentarily receding. In the shared silence, in the comfort of a bond forged through fire and loss, they faced this together, as they always had. And beneath the grief, a quiet resolve began to form—to honor the man they'd both lost, to face whatever came next.

# Chapter 1

# Deceitful Greetings

The low slant of the late afternoon sun stretched shadows like grasping fingers across the manicured lawns of Center Street. An autumn crispness had settled over Jim Thorpe, turning the maples lining the road to fiery crimson and deep gold—colors that felt jarringly vibrant against the pall that had settled over Devin since the news came three days ago. October 23rd. Each mile closer to the old Queen Anne Victorian at 218 tightened the vise around Devin's chest. Three years. Wasted in silence he couldn't take back.

The Range Rover slid silently to the curb before the house. "Seems quiet," Manny observed from the driver's seat, nodding towards an unfamiliar sedan parked further down the block.

Devin extricated his tall frame from the passenger seat, the fine wool of his Armani suit feeling alien against the backdrop of the aging house. Its porches sagged slightly, paint peeling near the ornate trim—a neglect that resonated uncomfortably within him. *Strong. For Mom.* The thought was a mantra against the ache in his throat.

They walked up the familiar flagstone path. The heavy oak front door stood slightly ajar. Devin pushed it open, stepping into the cool quiet. The scent of lemon oil and dried roses instantly transported him, yet the air felt thin, charged with an unnerving emptiness. Muffled voices drifted from the living room doorway to their left. Devin met Manny's gaze, a silent question passing between them, before moving towards the sound. His mother, Annabelle, sat huddled on the floral sofa, seeming somehow diminished within its cushions. The usual light in her eyes was drowned in red-rimmed exhaustion, and loose strands of silvery-grey hair had escaped their usual neat twist. Across from her, a stranger occupied one of the wingback chairs—late forties perhaps, with a receding hairline, watchful eyes, and clad in a trench coat that looked as weary as its owner. The man's voice was low, steady. "...difficult, Mrs. Jones, I understand. Initial reports suggested cardiac arrest, but the final toxicology came back this afternoon. Potent, fast-acting toxin found in his bloodstream. I'm afraid the Mayor's death is officially a homicide".

Annabelle gasped, a hand fluttering to her mouth.

Devin stepped fully into the room then, Manny a solid presence just behind him. "Mom?".

Annabelle looked up, startled, tears spilling freely as she saw him. "Devin! Manny!" She surged up, rushing into Devin's arms, burying her face against his suit jacket. "They... they said...".

The man in the trench coat rose, his sharp eyes taking in Devin's height, the expensive suit, the air of command that clung to him even now.

"Detective Davis, Carbon County Sheriff's Department," he said, his voice carrying the unmistakable weight of long, hard days. "My apologies for your loss, Mr. Jones. And for the timing of this news".

Devin held his mother close, the detective's words echoing – Homicide. Toxin. A cold dread coiled deep in his gut. "Devin Jones," he replied, his voice tight, meeting Davis's gaze squarely. "This is Manuel Rivera". He kept one arm around his mother. "I run Echelon Axiom Global, security firm out of New York. If my father was murdered, Detective, EAG resources are at your disposal".

Davis gave a slow nod, his expression unreadable. "Appreciated, Mr. Jones. Your father's position... complicates things. Civilian assistance needs clearance, but thank you." He hesitated. "Official cause is homicide. We're pursuing leads discreetly. Again, my condolences." He gave Annabelle a brief, sympathetic glance, nodded once to Devin and Manny, and saw himself out.

The heavy front door clicked shut, leaving a thick, vibrating silence. Annabelle clung to Devin, her quiet sobs shaking her small frame. "Murdered... Devin, who?".

Devin held her tighter, his own mind grappling with the impossible question. "I don't know, Mom. But we'll find out. I promise".

Manny stepped forward, placing a gentle hand on Annabelle's shoulder. "We're here, Mrs. J. Anything you need". After a moment, he cleared his throat softly. "Alright, I need to run out, pick something up," he said, his glance meeting Devin's. "Won't be long. Hang tight". He squeezed Annabelle's shoulder again before heading out.

Devin guided his mother back to the sofa, sitting beside her, letting her cry, the detective's brutal confirmation settling over them like a shroud. Just as her sobs quieted slightly, a sharp, insistent Bang, bang, bang! hammered against the front door, startling them both. It wasn't a friendly knock. Devin's head snapped up, senses instantly on high alert. He moved towards the foyer, Detective Davis's words adding a chilling weight to the aggressive sound. He opened the door.

Brad Ewing filled the frame, his hulking presence instantly familiar, though the usual smirk was absent, replaced by a look of surprise that seemed almost genuine. Beside him, Kaitlyn looked small, polished, her composure a stark contrast to the raw grief within the house.

"Devin," Brad said, his blue eyes lacking their usual arrogance but holding an intensity Devin remembered well. "Man... heard about your dad. Kaitlyn told me... couldn't believe it." He paused. "Tough news. Really tough".

Devin kept his own expression carefully neutral, the word homicide pulsing in his mind, coloring Brad's sudden appearance with suspicion. "Brad," he replied evenly. "Thanks for coming".

Brad ran a hand through his styled blonde hair. "Yeah, well... condolences, obviously," he gestured vaguely, his broad shoulders seeming to test the limits of his jacket. "Your father... carried a lot for this town. Always involved." He shook his head, his weathered face

attempting thoughtfulness. "Pressure gets to everyone, I guess. Some burdens... especially when you're dealing with certain elements...".
Certain elements. The phrase snagged. Devin kept his voice level. "I appreciate that, Brad". "Come in. Mom would appreciate the thought". Brad's strained expression returned. "Of course," he said, his eyes flicking past Devin to where Annabelle stood silently in the hallway, a fragile statue of grief. He gestured to Kaitlyn. "Come on, sweetheart".
As Brad stepped past, his large frame crowding the space, Kaitlyn moved forward. For just an instant, as Brad's back was turned, her smile flickered, revealing a shadow of something—weariness? distaste?—before her mask clicked back into place. She stepped close, not for a handshake, but enveloping Devin in a hug, her vibrant blonde hair brushing his cheek, the scent of expensive perfume suddenly cloying.
"Devin," she whispered, her voice husky against his ear, "I'm so sorry". He felt himself stiffen as her arms tightened around his neck. "You look good, Devin. Really good".
He pulled back slightly, the warmth of her embrace feeling inappropriate, wrong, given the detective's news, given Brad. He met her eyes – sympathy seemed to sparkle there, but was there something else beneath it? "Thanks, Kaitlyn," he murmured, stepping clear.
Brad cleared his throat loudly from the living room doorway. "Well, shall we?" Impatience and possession laced his tone.
Devin's mind raced – *Homicide. Toxin. Brad. Certain elements.* He gestured towards the living room. "Yes, of course".

They settled into the room, the air thick with unspoken things. Devin sat beside Annabelle on the sofa; Brad and Kaitlyn took the armchairs. The only sound was the soft crackle from the fireplace. Brad leaned back, crossing his legs, the smugness fully returning now that he was seated. "You know, Devin," he began, his voice expansive, "your father and I, we talked quite a bit over the years. Spent a lot of time together, actually". Devin simply raised an eyebrow, saying nothing. Beside him, Annabelle shifted, her posture stiffening.

"Yeah," Brad went on, seemingly unaware or perhaps enjoying the reaction. "Golfed up at Blue Mountain often enough. John swung okay, for an older fella. Talked shop. Town business, investments..." He waved a hand vaguely. "Coffee, too. Most mornings, Sunrise Diner. Same booth. Creature of habit, your dad".

Devin's jaw tightened. Golf? Daily coffee? His father had never mentioned spending regular time with Brad. The narrative felt forced, false, a constructed intimacy that grated against Devin's raw grief and burgeoning suspicion.

"Fascinating man," Brad continued, his gaze sweeping the mantelpiece photos. "A pillar. Handled things. Knew how to deal with... difficult situations, difficult people. Pulled the right strings". He paused, glancing at Devin, a slight, condescending smile playing on his lips. "Takes a certain kind of man for that world. Not everyone's cut out for it. Some run off, play CEO, forget their roots".

The dig landed, sharp and precise, but Devin kept his expression impassive. Alibi? Or boasting? Was Brad hinting at knowledge of the murder, the 'difficult situations'?.

"He loved this town," Brad added, his tone attempting softness but the arrogance underneath remained. "Tried to do right, even if it meant... making tough calls. Stepped on toes, sure. Leadership, right?".

Kaitlyn stirred in her chair, her gaze fixed determinedly on her lap.

"Good man, your father," Brad concluded, the attempted sincerity transparently false now. "Complex. Dealt with a lot".

Kaitlyn reached out then, her touch light on Devin's arm. "He was so proud of you, Devin," she whispered. Her voice, unlike Brad's, carried a ring of truth that resonated. "Really proud".

"Thank you, Kaitlyn," Devin managed, the genuine sympathy a brief anchor in the swirling tension.

Brad nodded, the smug grin snapping back into place far too quickly. "Well, Devin," he said, pushing himself up from the armchair, his voice dripping condescension, "good seeing you. Still the intense kid, huh? Never quite fit".

Devin's jaw clenched hard. He rose slowly, meeting Brad's gaze across the room, the silence stretching. "Thanks for stopping by, Brad," he said, his voice dangerously quiet, each word precise. "Mom and I appreciate it".

Brad chuckled, a flicker of malice in his eyes. "Of course. Wouldn't want to upset the grieving son." He turned, paused at the doorway. "Anything I can do. Anything at all." He looked back, his gaze locking onto Devin's, turning sharp, predatory. "After all," he added, his voice dropping to a low, menacing whisper meant only for Devin, "we wouldn't want anything else to happen to this family, would we?".

The threat landed, raw and chilling, amplifying the detective's confirmation tenfold. Devin felt his muscles coil, ready to react, fists tightening at his sides.

Kaitlyn quickly put a hand on Brad's arm. "Come on, honey," she urged, her voice firm beneath the soothing tone, pulling him towards the front door. "Let's give them space".

Brad hesitated, his eyes locked with Devin's in a silent, charged challenge, before turning with a final smirk and following Kaitlyn out.

The click of the front door closing echoed in the sudden vacuum left by Brad and Kaitlyn. Devin stood motionless in the living room, the low thrum of adrenaline fading, leaving behind the cold residue of Brad's veiled threat. He turned towards the sofa where his mother sat, pale, her hands trembling in her lap, eyes wide with a fear that seemed distinct from her grief. The detective's confirmation—homicide—resonated with chilling clarity now.

Before Devin could find words, the front door opened again. He stiffened, turning sharply, but it was only Manny stepping inside, followed closely by Rachel. Manny juggled several large paper bags, the savory aroma of garlic and soy sauce momentarily cutting through the house's heavy atmosphere.

Rachel's gaze found Devin immediately as she entered the living room, her usual energy slightly muted. Auburn hair pulled back efficiently, her hazel-green eyes narrowed slightly with concern as she registered his stance, the almost palpable tension in the room.

"Devin," she breathed, crossing the room quickly.

He met her halfway, instinctively pulling her into an embrace, the simple, familiar warmth of her a needed anchor. "Came as soon as Manny called," she murmured against his chest.

He held her for a moment, letting the solid reality of her presence push back the swirling darkness. "Glad you're here, Rach," he said, his voice rough.

Manny entered the living room, setting the bags bulging with takeout containers on a side table. "Figured food might help," he said, then offered Annabelle a respectful smile that softened the lines of weariness around his own eyes. "Mrs. J, Rachel insisted".

Annabelle offered a tremulous smile in return. "Oh, that's... very kind, dear. Thank you, Rachel." The sight of Rachel seemed to steady her slightly.

"Of course, Mrs. J," Rachel replied, stepping back from Devin but keeping a hand lightly on his arm, her concern still evident. "Manny told me... about the detective".

They moved towards the dining room, the scent of the food following them. Devin helped his mother into a chair before taking one himself. Unpacking the cartons—lo mein, broccoli beef, kung pao chicken—felt like performing normal actions in an entirely different reality. The familiar ritual was strained, dissonant.

Rachel looked from Devin to Annabelle, her expression serious. "Manny said... the detective confirmed it? It was really... homicide?".

Annabelle nodded, fresh tears welling. "They found... something. A toxin".

Devin elaborated, keeping his voice low. "Davis confirmed it just before Manny left. Positive tox screen. Didn't give details, just said it changes the investigation". He paused, glancing at Manny. "You missed Brad Ewing by about ten minutes".

Manny's head came up sharply. "Brad? Here? What the hell did he want?".

"Condolences," Devin said, the word tasting bitter. He quickly recounted Brad's performance—the fabricated closeness with his father, the feigned sympathy layered over condescending jabs, the talk of "difficult people" and "certain elements," culminating in the thinly veiled threat whispered on the way out.

Manny let out a low whistle, his knuckles white where he gripped a takeout carton. "Right after the detective leaves? Saying crap like that? Smells rotten. Like he knows something, or he's part of it".

"Exactly," Devin agreed. "With Dad murdered, and Brad acting like that... we can't just wait for the Sheriff's department." He looked directly at Manny. "I want EAG analysts digging into Brad now, Manny. Financials, associates, comms—everything. We run our own investigation".

Manny gave a grim nod. "Done. I'll get Kate on it first thing. We'll see what he's hiding".

Rachel listened intently, her reporter's focus evident in her sharp gaze. "Devin," she began, her voice hesitant, revealing an internal conflict, "when this breaks—Mayor Jones murdered, someone like Brad possibly involved... it's huge. Gary, my editor..." She met Devin's gaze. "I'll have to cover it. Objectively, of course, but I can't sit on this".

The air grew tense again. "Can't you hold off, Rach?" Devin asked, frustration tightening his voice. "Just until we know more?".

"I wish I could," Rachel said earnestly. "But it's the job. Potential homicide, public figures, possible corruption... the story exists whether I write it or not".

"Story?" Annabelle cried out suddenly, pushing her plate away so forcefully a carton tipped over. Her face crumpled. "My husband is dead! Murdered! And you're talking about investigations, suspects... turning his death into a story?" Her voice broke. "He's not even buried! Can't we just... grieve? Without... all this?". She buried her face in her hands, shoulders shaking.

"Oh, Mom, Mrs. J, we're so sorry," Devin and Rachel said quickly, guilt washing over them.

"She's right," Manny murmured. "Apologies, Mrs. J. We got carried away".

Devin moved to his mother's side, resting a hand on her shoulder. "Mom, sorry. You're right." He looked at her pale, exhausted face. "It's too much. Why don't you go upstairs? Try and rest?".

Annabelle nodded, wiping at her eyes with a trembling hand. "Yes. I think... I need to".

"Let me help you, Mrs. J," Rachel offered, starting to rise.

Annabelle shook her head, pushing herself slowly, wearily to her feet. "No, dear. Thank you. I just... need a minute alone". She gave Devin's hand a fragile squeeze, then turned and walked slowly towards the hall staircase, leaving the three friends sitting amidst the cooling food in a heavy, uncomfortable silence.

As Annabelle's footsteps receded upstairs, the silence in the dining room felt thick, weighted. The half-eaten Chinese food seemed incongruous against the backdrop of grief and suspicion. Manny, after a moment, quietly got up and headed towards the living room; the muted flicker and sound of the television starting up drifted back a moment later.

In the kitchen, Devin and Rachel began clearing the table, the familiar, mundane task of scraping plates and rinsing dishes becoming a silent, shared ritual. The easy camaraderie they usually shared felt replaced by a quiet strain, the day's revelations—homicide, Brad's menace, Rachel's journalistic dilemma—settling between them. They worked without speaking, the clink of porcelain and the rush of water filling the silence for several minutes.

Suddenly, a loud clatter-crash from the backyard shattered the quiet. Devin froze, exchanging an instantly alert look with Rachel.

"What was that?" Rachel whispered.

"Stay put," Devin murmured, quickly drying his hands on a dish towel. He moved to the back door off the kitchen, the one leading to the small wooden deck. Easing it open, he stepped out into the cool night air, scanning the darkness. Moonlight faintly illuminated the yard, revealing the metal trash cans lying overturned near the wood line at the property's edge. Nothing else seemed disturbed. No figures in the shadows, no hidden movements. Raccoons, most likely, drawn by the discarded food. Still, the noise set his already frayed nerves on edge. He listened intently for another moment before stepping back inside, securing the deadbolt.

"Just the trash cans," he reported quietly to Rachel, though the explanation felt thin. "Probably raccoons".

They finished the dishes, the silence returning, comfortable in its familiarity, yet still underscored by the day's tensions. Devin found himself watching Rachel as she stacked plates, noticing the faint lines of strain around her eyes, appreciating her steady presence. As they dried the last pan, Devin gestured towards the living room.

"Want to join Manny? Watch TV?" he asked, the question feeling slightly forced, an attempt to bridge the silence.

Rachel hesitated, her eyes meeting his for a moment, the earlier discussion about her reporting still a subtle barrier. "Actually," she said softly, "I think I'll head up. It's been... a long day".

Devin nodded, trying to hide a flicker of disappointment. "Yeah, okay," he said, aiming for casualness. "Get some rest".

"Good night, Devin," Rachel whispered. Her eyes held his for a fraction longer than necessary before she turned towards the stairs.

"Night, Rachel," he replied, his voice low.

He watched her ascend, her silhouette disappearing into the dim upper hallway, the faint trace of her perfume lingering. He forcefully pushed away the thought of their complicated history, the undercurrents always present between them. Not the time. Turning, he headed towards the living room to join Manny.

He found Manny slouched on the couch, engrossed in the flickering screen. Explosions bloomed silently, followed by the dissonant soundtrack of Coppola's "Apocalypse Now". The eerie light played across Manny's face.

"Seriously?" Devin asked, arching an eyebrow as he sank into the worn leather armchair opposite the couch. "This? Tonight?".

Manny offered a wry, tired smirk without looking away from the screen. "Brando, man. Besides," he finally glanced over, "kinda fits the mood, doesn't it?".

Devin watched the chaotic river scenes for a moment. "Damn. This movie... takes you back." He paused, the energy shifting between them. "Remember Leatherneck? That mess on the road to Kandahar?".

Manny's smirk evaporated, replaced by a shadow in his eyes. He nodded slowly, gaze returning to the screen but focused inward now. "How could I forget?".

"Four vehicles," Devin murmured, the memory surfacing unwanted but sharp. "Rolling like we owned the road... until we didn't".

"Yeah, with that transport full of civvies hitched to us," Manny added, his voice low. "Shoulda known. Too quiet out there".

"Told Johnson to keep his eyes open..." Devin trailed off, shaking his head faintly. "Made no difference. Soon as we hit that gorge pass...".

"Boom," Manny said softly, the word landing like a stone. "RPG took out lead Humvee. Then Three went up. Saw Wilson crawling out...".

"Hit the dirt," Devin picked up, the shared memory creating its own cadence. "Covering the transport. Miller took rounds but stayed up. Tough kid".

"Trying to shield those civvies... firefight erupting all around".

"Perimeter," Manny nodded, his gaze distant. "Sun dropping fast. They were everywhere".

"Back-to-back on that slope..."

The memory flared, visceral—dust, smoke, the cacophony, the heat...

...A sharp crack echoed off the rock walls, and Manny cried out, stumbling back, his hand flying to his side.

"Manny!" Devin yelled, scrambling towards him, a cold fist clenching around his heart.

Manny clutched his side, pain twisting his features. "Hit, Dev," he gasped, sinking to his knees.

Devin dropped beside him, ripping at the clasps on Manny's flak jacket, his fingers clumsy with adrenaline. "Where? Talk to me, where?".

"Side... ribs..." Manny groaned, breath hitching.

Devin found it—an ugly tear in the fabric, blood welling dark and fast. He shoved his palm against it, trying desperately to slow the flow. "Hold on, brother," Devin pleaded, his voice choked. "Just hold on".

But the odds were stacked against them—pinned down, outnumbered, and now Manny bleeding out. A cold wave threatened to pull Devin under, but he fought it back, scanning the battlefield for any sliver of hope.

Just then, a dark shape arced through the air from the shadows below, landing near the transport truck. The subsequent blast was deafening, ripping through the gorge, followed by terrified screams cut abruptly short. When the dust and smoke cleared slightly, Devin saw them—three crumpled shapes on the ground near the truck. Johnson. Diaz. Evans. Gone.

A surge of raw fury burned through Devin. He grabbed Manny's arm, hauling him towards a deeper cluster of boulders. "Move!" he gritted out. "Gotta move now!". He half-dragged Manny, who was fading, towards a narrow crevice, shoving them both into the slight protection it offered. Huddled there, the gunfire still intense, Devin felt the cold grip of despair tighten again. They were losing. He couldn't stop it.

Then, a new sound sliced through the din—whop-whop-whop. Devin looked up, hope surging through him like a physical shock. Two AH-64 Apaches banked hard around the ridgeline, nose-down, weapons pods already swiveling, searchlights stabbing into the darkness.

Rockets streaked, cannons hammered, unleashing a storm of fire onto the insurgent positions below. The answering gunfire faltered, sputtered, then died as fighters scattered, seeking refuge from the aerial onslaught. Devin looked down at Manny, pale and weak, but his eyes were open. "We're gonna make it, brother," Devin whispered, relief washing through him, hot and fierce. "We're gonna make it".

The Apaches circled, raining fire, providing cover as the quick reaction force arrived on the ground. Medics swarmed the wounded. Devin helped Manny stumble towards the waiting medevac helicopter, his own body screaming with exhaustion, the images of the firefight burning behind his eyes.

As they lifted off, leaving the chaos below, Devin looked back. The burning wreckage of the Humvees illuminated the gorge, casting flickering light on the still forms of his fallen comrades. He closed his eyes against the sight, a single hot tear escaping, tracing a path through the grime on his cheek. Survival had come at a bitter cost.

The roar of the helicopter faded slowly, replaced by the discordant sounds of gunfire and dialogue from the television screen. The quiet of the living room felt heavy, thick with the phantom scent of dust and smoke.

Devin dragged a hand down his face, his gaze lost somewhere beyond the flickering images, seeing not Vietnam, but the harsh, unforgiving rocks of Afghanistan. "Still see their faces," he confessed, his voice rough. "Johnson, Diaz, Evans... Miller barely made it out. Just kids, man".

Manny nodded slowly, his gaze distant. He shifted on the couch, his hand moving unconsciously towards his side, where the ghost of pain lingered. "I know," he murmured, his voice almost swallowed by the room's quiet. "Hear 'em sometimes. Dreams." He didn't look at Devin, his voice dropping lower. "That grenade... shoulda been me...".

Devin's hand landed firmly on Manny's shoulder, a solid, grounding weight. "No, brother," he said, his voice steady, forcing Manny to meet his eye. "We did everything we could." He held Manny's gaze. "We survived. Came home". The words felt incomplete, a truth acknowledged in the slight shadow that crossed Devin's eyes before he looked away.

Manny looked down, tracing the seam on the worn couch cushion with a finger. "Left pieces back there, though, huh?" he asked quietly.

Devin didn't answer right away. The silence stretched, filled only by the movie's violence. He leaned his head back against the armchair, eyes closing briefly. "Yeah," he finally breathed out, the word barely audible. "We did".

They sat in silence for a long moment, the ignored film playing on. The air between them was charged with the shared weight of what they'd seen, what they'd done, the indelible marks left behind.

Then, Manny straightened, taking a deeper breath, his focus seeming to return to the present. He looked directly at Devin. "But we're here now," he said, a trace of the familiar resilience hardening his voice, his posture shifting. "Together. That counts".

Devin opened his eyes, meeting his friend's steady gaze. He saw the exhaustion warring with the resolve, likely seeing the same reflection in his own expression. He offered a small, weary nod, feeling a fraction of the tension ease from his shoulders. "You're right," he said, managing a faint smile that didn't quite banish the shadows from his eyes. "We're here".

They held the look for another moment, anchored together not just by time, but by the storms weathered, the losses endured. The unspoken understanding of facing whatever lay ahead settled between them, heavy but absolute.

# Chapter 2

# Gathering Shadows

*Twisted metal, burning fuel, the choking grit of dust—the crash site assaulted Devin's senses. The Chinook lay broken on its side, smoke pouring from the ruptured fuselage into the acrid air. Face smeared with dirt, Devin scanned the wreckage. "Manny, sitrep to KAF," he ordered, his voice raspy. "Down two clicks south, heavily engaged".*

*Manny nodded grimly, ducking behind a jagged piece of metal, radio already crackling as he relayed their position. Gunfire hammered the air, echoing off the barren hills. The surviving marines fought with disciplined fury, outnumbered but holding their ground. Devin directed fire, trying to maintain order in the chaos, then spotted movement—Taliban fighters attempting an eastern flank.*

*"Manny, take point!" he yelled. "Push 'em back!".*

*Manny moved instantly, leading a small squad, their combined fire driving the attackers back into the rocks, but more seemed to materialize from the landscape itself.*

BEEP! BEEP! BEEP!

The alarm's shriek ripped Devin from the firefight. His eyes flew open, heart hammering, the phantom surge of adrenaline slow to ebb. He slapped the alarm clock silent. Quiet pressed in, heavy and absolute. Outside, dawn painted the sky in streaks of pink and orange, but the light filtering through the window felt brittle, harsh.

He lay still, breathing, letting the weight of the past day settle back over him. Homicide. Not a heart attack. Brad's smug face, his thinly veiled threats. The conversation with Manny last night, dredging up Leatherneck's ghosts. And Rachel... the unavoidable static now crackling between them over a story she felt compelled to write. Sleep had been a battlefield of fragmented images, offering no peace.

Swinging his legs over the side of the bed, the cool shock of the floorboards jolted him fully awake. His body ached, his mind felt thick, clogged. He stumbled towards the bathroom, thoughts of EAG reports and pending meetings intruding—he shoved them aside. Not now.

Cold water on his face did little to cut through the bone-deep exhaustion. Stepping out of the bathroom, he almost ran straight into Rachel emerging from the guest room opposite his. Already dressed, auburn hair pulled back, she steadied herself against the doorframe.

"Whoa," she said, her hazel-green eyes quickly taking in his disheveled state. "Rough night?".

He managed a tight nod, rubbing his face. "Something like that. Coffee?".

Her expression was sympathetic, but the easy warmth they usually shared felt... muted. Guarded. She stepped aside. "Already brewing. Sounds like your mom's up too".

"Thanks, Rach," he mumbled, heading for the stairs. The interaction felt stilted, careful. He couldn't analyze it now. *Coffee first.*

He descended the stairs, the rich aroma of coffee and frying bacon growing stronger, pulling him towards the kitchen.

He found Annabelle at the stove, tending to the sizzling bacon, a stack of golden pancakes already waiting on a platter nearby. Her movements had the practiced ease of decades in this kitchen, but Devin noticed the tension tightening her shoulders, the slight tremor in her hand as she reached for the coffee pot.

"Morning, Mom," he said, leaning against the doorframe as she poured coffee into a mug for him. "How are you doing?".

Annabelle turned, her smile faint, not quite reaching eyes shadowed with exhaustion. "Getting by, I suppose," she replied, her voice soft, lacking its usual resonance. "It's just... the quiet is loud, you know?". Her gaze drifted past him, towards the window overlooking the backyard, a profound sadness washing over her features.

Devin nodded, the familiar morning sounds of the house now feeling muted, amplifying his own hollow sense of loss. He stepped closer, resting a hand gently on her shoulder. "I know, Mom."

They stood that way for a silent moment, the shared grief an almost physical presence between them.

"He talked about you constantly, Devin," Annabelle said suddenly, her voice thickening as she turned back to the stove, maybe a little too quickly. "Always bragging... even about the trouble you boys used to find".

A small, involuntary chuckle escaped Devin, the memory a brief flicker of warmth. "Yeah, I remember.". A faint smile touched his lips. "Pretty sure he wasn't bragging after we swapped the old mayors' portraits with Looney Tunes characters, though".

Annabelle's lips curved, a genuine smile this time, though fleeting. "No, he certainly wasn't. But," she conceded, poking at the bacon, "he admired your audacity, even then".

With the memories momentarily stirring a lighter, though still poignant, atmosphere, Annabelle turned slightly from the bacon, wiping her hands on her apron. "So, dear, amidst everything, how are things with Echelon Axiom? It must be incredibly demanding."

Devin leaned against the counter. "It is. Busier than ever, to be honest. We've landed four new government contracts in the past six months, which is keeping everyone flat out. Plus, I have meetings overseas coming up soon to explore establishing some additional field offices." He added with a slight sigh, "And we're also navigating some rather... entitled clients who seem to think they need a small army for every minor task."

Annabelle nodded, a mixture of pride and concern in her expression. "It sounds like a lot to carry, especially now."

Just then, Rachel appeared in the dining area entryway, looking more put-together than she had upstairs. "Morning," she said softly, taking a seat at the large oak table.

"Morning, Rachel," Annabelle and Devin replied in near unison. Annabelle placed a plate laden with pancakes onto the table but remained standing, turning back to wipe absently at the already gleaming countertop.

A moment later, Manny appeared at the bottom of the stairs, hair sticking out at odd angles, eyes still half-closed. "Mornin'," he mumbled, navigating by scent towards the coffee pot in the kitchen. He returned holding a steaming mug like a lifeline and sank into the chair opposite Rachel. "Smells great, Mrs. J," he offered, his voice gravelly with sleep. Annabelle gave a noncommittal hum, her attention fixed on the counter she was polishing.

Manny took a long swallow of coffee. As the heat hit him, his posture straightened slightly, eyes focusing. He looked across at Devin. "Hey, called Kate last night after... everything." He lowered his voice. "Put her team on Brad Ewing, like we talked about. Told her I want a preliminary workup by noon".

Devin nodded. "Good. The faster, the better".

"Yeah," Manny continued, swirling the dark liquid in his mug. "And while I had her, she mentioned a flagged email. Potential new client request. Big money, long-term detail, but wants a one-night preliminary this Halloween." He frowned faintly. "CEO of... Mercury something?

International? Kate flagged it as vague, though looked legit on the surface. Said the details are in the EAG inbox. Told her to run full background anyway".

Annabelle froze at the counter, her back ramrod straight, knuckles white where she gripped its edge.

Rachel looked up from her pancakes, a spark of professional interest in her eyes at the mention of a high-profile security need. "Mercury International?" she mused. "Financial sector, maybe? Rings a bell." She paused, her expression clouding over, the initial curiosity replaced by a frown. "Funny how it works, isn't it? Some CEO needs bodyguards for a Halloween party..." Her voice gained a sharp edge, reflecting recent experiences. "...while families I just saw can't get clean water, forget protection from bombs. Kids..." She stopped, shaking her head slightly, and pushed her plate away, appetite clearly gone. "Sorry. The contrast just... hits hard sometimes. All these resources poured into protecting wealth while...".

The unspoken comparison filled the space. Annabelle turned abruptly from the counter and began rearranging the perfectly aligned silverware on the table, her gaze averted.

"Rach..." Devin started gently, but Manny interjected, his gaze flicking towards Annabelle's tense back.

"Right," Manny said, clearing his throat. "Speaking of resources, Dev, we need another vehicle. Can't all fit in the Rover if we have to split up. Need something less... attention-grabbing".

Devin nodded, grateful for the pivot. "Yeah. Good call. Something low-key".

"Heading to the rental place?" Rachel asked, seeming eager for a concrete task. "Mind if I tag along? Need to grab a few things".

Annabelle turned then, extending a small, folded note. "Actually, Devin, while you're out... could you get these?" Her voice was quiet, tight with held-back emotion.

Devin took the list, noting her avoidance of his concerned glance. "Of course, Mom. Got it".

Manny pushed back his chair. "Alright. Let's hit the road." He glanced from Annabelle back to Devin and Rachel. "I'll grab my keys". He headed for the entryway, leaving Devin and Rachel to gather their things, the air still thick with Rachel's sharp comparison and Annabelle's quiet distress.

Manny handled the Range Rover smoothly through the familiar streets of Jim Thorpe. An initial, comfortable silence settled in the car. Rachel gazed out the passenger window at the passing Victorian architecture, while Devin, in the back, felt the familiar bittersweet pang of nostalgia looking at his hometown.

"Remember trying to build that raft for the Lehigh?" Devin asked suddenly, a faint smile touching his lips.

Manny chuckled, eyes flicking to the rearview mirror. "How could I forget? Your 'unsinkable' masterpiece went down ten feet from the bank. We walked home dripping mud and picking off leeches".

Rachel laughed, turning in her seat. "And Mrs. J grounded you for a week!".

"Yeah," Devin conceded with a headshake. "Not my finest engineering moment".

Silence fell again for a few blocks, the shared memory a brief respite.

Then, the unmistakable opening chords of The Killers' "Mr. Brightside" filled the car – their unofficial high school anthem. Almost automatically, they started singing along, a moment of shared history briefly eclipsing the present tension.

As the song faded, the atmosphere shifted back instantly. Manny's eyes returned to the rearview mirror, his expression tightening almost imperceptibly. He checked it again a block later.

"What's up?" Devin asked quietly from the back, catching the subtle shift.

Manny kept his eyes on the mirror. "Maybe nothing. Dark sedan, Crown Vic maybe. Picked us up right after we left Center Street." His voice was low, clipped. "Pretty sure it's the same one parked down the block yesterday when we arrived".

Rachel twisted slightly in her seat. "Hard to see inside. Tinted windows".

Devin leaned forward. "Okay. Next left, Manny. Loop Washington, come back onto Broadway. Let's see if they stick".

Manny nodded grimly, executing the turn. The easy nostalgia evaporated, replaced by sharp alertness. As they completed the loop and turned back onto Broadway, the dark sedan mirrored their turn, maintaining distance, its purpose now clear.

"Definitely a tail," Manny confirmed, his voice flat.

"Okay," Devin said, running through scenarios. "Doesn't guarantee hostile. Could be Davis keeping tabs after the homicide ruling".

"Or Brad's people making good on his threat," Rachel added quietly, the possibility settling heavily in the car.

"Or someone else entirely," Manny muttered. "Point is, we're being watched. Let's stick to the rental plan, see if they follow us in or keep rolling. Stay sharp".

Manny signaled and turned into the small lot of KGT Rentals. All three watched the street intently. The dark sedan slowed as it passed the entrance, the driver hidden behind the tint, then accelerated down the road, continuing on its way.

"Didn't follow," Rachel noted, a touch of relief in her voice, though the unease remained.

"Doesn't mean they're gone," Devin cautioned, scanning the street before opening his door. "Could be circling. Let's move fast".

They climbed out of the Range Rover, the shared laughter over the old song dying quickly, replaced by a sharp, watchful tension. The rental lot was small, the selection sparse.

"Not much to choose from," Manny commented, his gaze sweeping the available vehicles then flicking back to the street.

Devin's eyes landed on a dark gray GMC Sierra pickup in a corner. Solid, anonymous. "That one," he pointed. "Less likely to draw attention".

Rachel managed a small smile that didn't quite ease the strain around her eyes. "Rugged. On brand".

Devin gave a quick nod, appreciating the attempt, though his own focus remained outward. "Let's hope." They signaled the lone attendant, completed the necessary paperwork with curt efficiency, the mundane process feeling strangely disconnected from the reality of their situation. As Devin finished signing, Manny clapped him on the shoulder.

"Alright, grocery run's on you two," Manny said, his tone aiming for casual but falling slightly short. "I'm taking the Rover. Need to call Kate, let her know about our potential shadow." He looked from Devin to Rachel. "Eyes open. Stay out of trouble".

"You too, Manny," Devin replied, returning the clap, the simple words resonating with unspoken weight.

Manny climbed back into his Range Rover, offered a final, quick nod, and pulled out of the lot, deliberately heading in the opposite direction the sedan had taken. Devin and Rachel watched him go for a beat, then turned towards the Sierra.

"So," Devin said, unlocking the truck, his voice low as he glanced towards the road one last time, "Market first?".

Rachel nodded, her own eyes scanning the street. "Yeah. Stick to the plan. But let's not linger".

Devin offered a tight grin that didn't reach his eyes. "Sounds good." He slid behind the wheel, Rachel climbing in beside him. As they pulled the Sierra out onto the road, the sensation of being watched, of unseen threats lurking just beneath the town's familiar surface, prickled Devin's skin.

He found a parking spot near the entrance of Grocery & More and killed the engine. The tension from the tail still hummed between them, a low frequency beneath the surface, but they had tasks to complete.

The automatic doors slid open, admitting them into the brightly lit bustle of the market. The aroma of baking bread, the bright pyramids of apples and oranges, the low murmur of shoppers—it was a thin layer of normalcy stretched taut over the churning uncertainty beneath.

"Okay," Devin said, pulling out Annabelle's folded list. "Supply run. You grab your things, Rach? I'll handle Mom's list. Meet back by the snack aisle, ten minutes?".

Rachel nodded, seeming to appreciate the focus. "Sounds good. And Devin? Don't buy all the jerky". She gave a small smile before heading towards the pharmacy section.

Devin grabbed a cart, the wheels squeaking slightly, and started down the aisles, moving with the efficiency of long habit. Milk, eggs, bread, coffee—the basics. He tossed in jerky and a couple of bags of chips without thinking—fuel, simple comfort.

Turning into the snack aisle, pushing the slightly unsteady cart, he saw Rachel near the far end, comparing labels on pretzel bags. He started towards her, ready to head out, when a familiar voice boomed from the next aisle over.

"Devin! Well, I'll be! Good to see you home, son!".

Devin turned. Coach Miller, his old high school football coach, beamed as he strode towards them, looking exactly the same—tall, broad, with an easy command that Devin remembered well.

"Coach!" Devin replied, a genuine smile briefly relaxing his tense features. The sight of a familiar, uncomplicated face was an unexpected relief. "Great to see you".

Coach Miller clapped a heavy hand on Devin's shoulder, his broad grin softening into sympathy. "Awful sorry about your father, Devin," he said, his voice gruff but kind. "John was a great man. Did a lot for this town." He shook his head, a thoughtful frown appearing. "Hard to believe. You know," he lowered his voice slightly, "he seemed... distracted, the last couple months. More than usual. Even missed the homecoming game. Wasn't like John to skip that".

Devin's fleeting smile tightened. Distracted. Off. The words echoed his mother's observations, the detective's hints, now underscored by the stark reality of homicide. "Yeah," Devin kept his voice carefully level. "It's... sudden. Thanks, Coach. Appreciate it".

Coach Miller's gaze shifted past Devin as Rachel approached. "Rachel! Look at you!" he boomed, grin returning. "Good to see you too! Keeping this one in line, are you?". He gave Devin a knowing wink.

Devin felt a slight flush creep up his neck. Rachel smoothly tucked her arm through Devin's. "Just catching up, Coach," she said easily. "Nice seeing you".

Coach Miller chuckled, enjoying their brief awkwardness. "Right, right. Old friends." He squeezed Devin's shoulder again. "Take care," he said, his expression turning serious. "And Devin? Your father was damn proud of you. Never forget it".

With a final wave, the Coach headed towards the checkout lanes. His innocent observation about Devin's father landed like a stone, adding another disturbing piece to the puzzle.

They quickly finished their shopping, the checkout process feeling jarringly mundane. Grabbing the plastic grocery bags, they walked back through the automatic doors into the parking lot.

As they neared the gray Sierra, Devin stopped abruptly, his grip tightening on the bags. "Hold up," he muttered, his gaze fixed on the area near the adjacent McCoy's Cold Beer distributor.

Two men stood near the entrance, not drinking, just... present. Unfamiliar. Their dark jackets seemed too heavy for the mild day. They weren't relaxed; their postures were stiff, their attention directed outward, scanning the parking lot with an intensity that felt wrong. They weren't waiting for buddies to grab a six-pack.

Rachel followed his gaze, her brow furrowing. "Who are they?" she whispered.

"No idea," Devin replied, his voice low, assessing them. The way they stood, angled slightly away from each other but eyes constantly sweeping, felt practiced. Guarded. "They don't belong".

They paused by the truck, Devin making a show of rearranging the bags in the bed, using the moment to observe. The two men exchanged a few quiet words, heads dipped together, faces lost in shadow. One checked his watch, then scanned the lot again, his gaze sliding past Devin and Rachel without lingering, continuing its sweep. An air of coiled tension radiated from them.

"Waiting for someone," Rachel commented quietly, her reporter's analysis kicking in. "And trying very hard not to look like it".

"Yeah," Devin agreed. The tailing sedan, Brad's visit and barely veiled threat, the detective's confirmation, the Coach's observation... his mind flashed through the sequence. It felt connected. "They're not here for beer." The unease intensified, prickling the back of his neck.

After another minute, as if on a silent cue, the two men shared a brief, curt nod. They turned sharply and walked quickly towards a dark, non-descript sedan parked further down the row – the same one? Impossible to be sure – got in, and drove off without looking back. The departure felt as abrupt and unsettling as their presence.

Devin met Rachel's gaze, a heavy understanding passing between them. The simple grocery run had just become another data point suggesting trouble had firmly arrived in Jim Thorpe.

"Okay, that wasn't normal," Rachel remarked, watching the sedan disappear, a thoughtful frown creasing her brow. "Who were they waiting for? Why here?".

"Good questions," Devin agreed, the unease hardening into certainty in his gut. He shook his head slightly. "First the tail, now this. Feels like things are heating up".

He looked at Rachel again, the earlier awkwardness gone, replaced by shared concern, by the familiar glint of focus in her eyes. "Definitely more going on here than just a funeral," he said grimly.

Rachel nodded, her apprehension visibly warring with the pull of an unfolding story. "Seems like it," she agreed, tossing her own bags onto the floor of the truck cab.

Hundreds of miles from the rolling hills of Pennsylvania, the view from the sixth floor of Echelon Axiom Global's Manhattan headquarters was a panorama of steel and glass under a descending sun. Inside Kate's office, the air conditioning hummed softly, a world away from Jim Thorpe's damp autumn air. Sunlight caught the sharp angles of her glass desk but didn't seem to warm the cool precision of the room. Kate sat centered in her chair, posture straight, a secure headset nestled against her dark hair. Her focus seemed directed outward at the city sprawl, but her attention was entirely on the voice in her ear.

"Yes, Mr. Grant," she confirmed, her tone even, modulated. "The initial deployment, Halloween. Thirteen personnel, Tier Two operators, specialized event security. Confirmed. Team leader Adam Tinison is former military with countless details of high value clients."

She paused, listening. Her left hand rested flat on the desk, motionless save for the faint indentation her thumb made on the smooth surface. "The separate access point for your principal guests... understood. Expedited entry is feasible. EAG maintains the perimeter; internal intervention only occurs under direct threat protocols. Your guest list remains private, provided the outer cordon holds."

Another pause. She remained outwardly relaxed, controlled. "And the extension—limited surveillance, rapid response capability through November fifth—is approved. The revised fee schedule is acceptable." She made a quick notation on a digital pad, the stylus moving with quiet efficiency. "The asset retrieval component for the primary event... it deviates from standard threat mitigation, Mr. Grant. EAG doesn't typically recover client property. However, considering the contract's scope and duration, we'll allocate the necessary resources for that contingency." Her eyes flickered toward a secondary monitor displaying encrypted network traffic—a fleeting shift, immediately corrected as her gaze returned to the window.

"Of course," Kate continued, her rhythm uninterrupted. "Precise coordination is essential for both phases. We require access details and clearance codes twenty-four hours prior to initial deployment... Encrypted transfer, naturally... Excellent."

She listened for a final moment. A barely perceptible tightening at the corner of her mouth was the only outward sign as the call concluded.

"Agreed, Mr. Grant. The full contract, reflecting the extended duration and terms, will be dispatched via secure courier tomorrow. Echelon Axiom is prepared to ensure the success and security of your engagement."

"Understood. Goodbye."

Kate disconnected the call with a precise click. She held the stillness for another second before slowly lifting the headset, placing it onto its charging stand with care. She drew a long, slow breath and released it quietly, her expression unchanging as she continued to survey the vast city below.

# Chapter 3

# A Legacy Honored

Inside Ewing Automotive, the plush carpet muffled the frantic click-click-click of Brad Ewing's pen against his polished mahogany desk. Sunlight flooded the spacious office, illuminating dust motes dancing in the air, but Brad's attention was welded to the phone receiver crushed against his ear, his knuckles strained white.

"...Yes, Sir. Understood," Brad forced the words out, his voice tight, the usual arrogance replaced by a raw nervousness. "I just... when I saw him back...".

The voice on the other end sliced through his explanation, cold, flat, utterly devoid of inflection. "You thought? Your function is not to think, Ewing. It was certainly not to engage Jones or indulge in adolescent power plays. His return was factored. Your... initiative... was reckless. It risked compromising the objective. Do not interfere again. Is that clear?".

Brad swallowed hard, the sound loud in his own ears. "Yes, Sir. Crystal clear. Won't happen again".

"See that it doesn't". The line went dead.

Brad slammed the phone down, the plastic cracking against the cradle, the sound sharp in the cavernous office. He shoved a hand through his hair, his face flushed beneath the tan. *Damn Jones.* Always complicating things. He glared out the window at the rows of gleaming cars, resentment momentarily flaring brighter than the fear coiling in his gut.

Meanwhile, across town, the newly acquired gray GMC Sierra turned into the driveway at 218 Center Street. Devin cut the engine. The silence that fell felt heavier than before, thick with the residue of the market encounter. He and Rachel retrieved the groceries from the truck bed and headed inside.

The house felt marginally less desolate with Manny's Range Rover parked out front. They found him in the kitchen, leaning against the counter, nursing a coffee mug.

"Hey," Manny greeted them, nodding at the bags. "Supply run go okay?".

"Mostly," Devin replied, setting the bags down. "Ran into Coach Miller. And saw a couple of guys watching McCoy's who didn't belong".

"Watching? How so?" Manny straightened up, instantly focused.

Rachel described the two men as Devin began unpacking the groceries—their deliberate stillness, the way they scanned the lot, their abrupt departure in the dark sedan. "Definitely waiting for someone," she concluded. "Looked completely out of place".

Manny frowned. "Add it to the pile. I heard back from Kate after I left you." He took a sip of coffee. "Mixed report on Brad. On the surface? Looks clean. Standard books, owns the dealership, minor tax stuff years ago, nothing glaring".

"And the other shoe?" Devin prompted, pausing with the milk carton in his hand.

"The other shoe could bury him," Manny clarified. "Kate said his personal finances show massive cash flow spikes over the last few years. Millions, unexplained. But," he leaned forward slightly, lowering his voice, "when cross-referenced with Ewing Automotive's official books... it washes clean. Somehow. Dealership profits are way out of line for this area. Smells like heavy laundering, but the books are cooked expertly. Hard to pin down without an inside source or a full forensic audit".

"Laundering..." Devin considered it. The word resonated, fitting somehow with Brad's too-polished veneer, the slightly-too-large lifestyle for a small-town dealer. "Okay. Keep Kate's team on it. There's definitely fire under that smoke".

They finished putting the groceries away, the conversation defaulting to safer territory, trying to patch over the tension with forced normalcy.

They moved into the living room, Devin and Rachel filling Manny in on the details of the men outside the market.

"...just watching," Rachel was saying, sinking into an armchair. "Then vanished. Poof".

Devin added, "Felt like they were waiting for a meet. Think it was the same car from earlier?".

"Could be," Manny shrugged, settling onto the couch. "Or just the town's usual weirdness dialing up".

Just as Devin started to voice another theory, the front door opened and closed softly. Annabelle appeared in the living room doorway. Her posture seemed composed, her hands clasped before her, but the deep sadness in her eyes was inescapable.

"I just spoke with Martha Porter," she said, her voice quiet but clear, cutting through their low conversation. "It seems some people from town have organized an informal get-together tonight. To honor John." She paused, her gaze drifting towards the fireplace mantle. "It's down at The Underground Escape. Starting around eight, she said."

"Are you thinking of going, Mom?" Devin asked gently.

Annabelle gave a faint, weary shake of her head. "No, Devin. I don't believe I will." She looked directly at him, then included Manny and Rachel in her gaze. "Thank you for asking, but... places like that, especially when people have had a few drinks..." She hesitated, choosing her words carefully. "Sometimes, memories get blurred, tongues get loose. People don't always consider the feelings of others, or... or the full truth of things. I think I'd rather stay here tonight. Remember him quietly."

She offered them a fragile smile that didn't quite reach her eyes. "You three should go if you feel up to it, represent the family if you like. But I... I think I'll just head upstairs and rest for a while." She turned towards the staircase without waiting for a reply.

Manny watched her ascend, worry tightening the lines around his eyes. Once her footsteps faded above, he turned to Devin and Rachel. "Man," he sighed, running a hand through his dark hair. "This is... heavy." He hesitated. "So... should we go? To The Underground? Like she said, represent? See what the mood is?"

Rachel nodded slowly, her expression thoughtful. "It might be good to show our faces. Hear what people are saying, maybe get a sense of things beyond... well, beyond Brad."

Devin considered it. His mother's subtle warning about loose tongues and blurred truths resonated with the unease coiling in his gut. The house felt heavy, suffocating. Staying here felt like hiding, while going to the place where the town was remembering his father, even with the potential for uncomfortable encounters, felt necessary. "Yeah," he finally agreed, the word decisive. "Okay. We should be there. Let's go."

They moved quickly then, heading upstairs – Devin to his old room, Manny to the guest room that had practically become his over the years, Rachel to the one across the hall – shedding their day clothes for something more appropriate for the evening gathering.

Minutes later, they met back in the entryway. Devin grabbed the keys to the rented Sierra. "Better take the truck," he said. "Rover stands out too much, Manny".

Manny nodded. They stepped out onto the porch. The air had cooled noticeably, carrying the damp scent of fallen leaves. As they walked towards the driveway where the Sierra sat beside Manny's Range Rover, Devin's eyes automatically scanned Center Street.

His gaze snagged, then froze. Down the block, parked just within the dim yellow halo of a streetlight, sat a dark sedan. Low light obscured details, but the silhouette... it felt unnervingly familiar.

"Heads up," Devin murmured, tilting his head subtly towards the car. Manny and Rachel glanced down the street, their movements casual but instantly alert. A look passed between them – grim recognition, unspoken question. The same car? Still watching?

"Son of a bitch," Manny muttered, almost inaudible.

"Still going?" Rachel asked Devin quietly, her hand drifting towards her pocket, towards her phone.

Devin stared at the sedan, a muscle twitching in his jaw. After a long beat, he turned decisively towards the Sierra. "Yeah," he said curtly. "Let's go." They wouldn't let unseen watchers trap them in the house.

They climbed into the Sierra, Devin behind the wheel. The truck's cab felt smaller, more confining than the Range Rover. He pulled out of the driveway, deliberately turning away from the direction of the parked sedan, his eyes flicking to the rearview mirror instinctively. The sedan remained stationary. But the awareness of unseen eyes, the knowledge that someone was out there, settled between them like a fourth passenger.

The drive through Jim Thorpe's quiet, lamp-lit streets felt different now. The familiar charm of the Victorian architecture seemed overlaid with a subtle menace.

"Need gas," Devin noted, the fuel indicator light blinking insistently as they approached the Hillside on Susquehanna Street.

He pulled the Sierra under the bright fluorescent lights of the gas station canopy. While Devin started the pump, Manny and Rachel headed into the convenience store, the automatic doors whispering open.

Inside, Rachel grabbed a coffee from the self-serve station, the caffeine a necessity now. Manny picked up a couple of waters.

At the counter, the cashier offered a tired smile. "Busy night?".

"Something like that," Rachel replied vaguely.

They paid and stepped back out just as Devin screwed the gas cap back on. "Ready?" he asked, taking the offered coffee from Rachel with a grateful nod.

"Let's hit it," Manny said, injecting a forced energy into his voice.

They continued the drive, the silence stretching now, heavy and tense. They passed the darkened Bingham Graham Opera House, then turned onto Broadway. The relative liveliness of the downtown strip – restaurants still serving, lights spilling from pub windows – did little to dispel the weight that had settled over them.

Finally, Devin pulled the Sierra into a parking spot near the Mountainside Inn. Downstairs, through the basement-level windows of The Underground Escape, warm light spilled out, accompanied by the low, muffled thrum of music and conversation. It promised noise, distraction, perhaps a brief escape from the grim realities pressing in.

They got out of the truck, instinctively scanning the street one last time before heading towards the bar's entrance, steeling themselves for the noise and the crowd, hoping to find a temporary oblivion within.

The heavy door of The Underground Escape groaned inward, releasing a blast of warm air. The usual scents of stale beer and fried onions seemed overlaid tonight by the lower, more subdued hum of a specific gathering rather than random Wednesday night revelry. A simple, hand-lettered sign hung slightly askew behind the bar: "Remembering John Jones." Dim bulbs cast long shadows across the worn floorboards, illuminating clusters of townspeople – some raising glasses, others talking in hushed, earnest tones, their faces reflecting a mix of sorrow and remembrance. The place was packed, a testament to the man they were honoring, the air thick with shared history and palpable grief, yet still underscored by the baseline noise of the bar.

Devin, Manny, and Rachel stepped inside, the door sighing shut behind them. The sudden immersion was jarring after the tense silence of the drive. They scanned the room, recognizing many faces from around town, clearly present for the informal tribute Annabelle had mentioned just before heading upstairs.

They navigated through the groups, offering brief nods but aiming for distance, eventually claiming a high-top table in a slightly less crowded corner near the back. Sliding onto the stools felt less like shedding armor and more like bracing themselves. The weight of the day – the homicide confirmation, Brad's menacing visit, Annabelle's quiet warning about loose tongues – made the need for a drink sharp and immediate, a way to fortify themselves before navigating the evening's emotional currents. A waitress materialized quickly through the throng. Whiskey for Manny, beers for Devin and Rachel.

As they waited, the door creaked open again. Devin glanced up automatically, muscles tightening. Brad Ewing entered, Kaitlyn a polished accessory beside him. Brad's eyes swept the room, slid over their table without a flicker of recognition, and then he guided Kaitlyn towards the far end of the bar, snagging two empty stools. He pointedly kept his back to them.

"Would you look at that," Manny muttered into his glass as the waitress set down their drinks. "Mr. Invisible".

"Maybe threatening grieving people takes all his charm," Rachel said, her voice dry as she took a sip of beer. Her eyes narrowed slightly, watching Brad lean over the bar to order. "Still... seeing him makes my teeth ache". Devin took a long swallow of his beer, the cold liquid doing little to cool the anger Brad always seemed to ignite just beneath his skin. Seeing him there, acting as if yesterday hadn't happened... "Speaking of Brad being a world-class prick," Devin said, keeping his voice low, "remember the Lehigh Valley Mall? Food court?".

Rachel grimaced. "Don't remind me. Trying to study for finals." She shook her head. "Him and his usual crew, acting like they owned the place, circling".

Manny leaned back on his stool. "And then we rolled up. Never seen you go from zero to sixty that fast, Dev. Pure murder-face".

"You just stared him down," Rachel recalled, looking at Devin. "He only backed off 'cause you two showed".

Devin shrugged, the memory sharp: *Brad's sneering face inches from Rachel's, Manny stepping up beside Devin, the deliberate shoulder check from Brad, the taunt—"Scared, Jones?"—then the sharp snap of Devin's control, the satisfying crunch of knuckle hitting jawbone, the ensuing chaos.* "Someone had to," Devin repeated quietly. "It got messy".

"Messy?" Manny grinned faintly. "Place looked like a tornado hit it. Pretty sure Jake Thompson got introduced to an Auntie Anne's pretzel tray".

Rachel shuddered slightly. "That was really the start of it, wasn't it? The real war".

They fell silent, the memory heavy between them in the dim bar. Even The Underground seemed to hold those ghosts. Eventually, Manny raised his glass. "To old friends," he said, his voice holding a complex warmth, "and getting through the bad blood". They clinked glasses, a silent agreement to let the memory settle.

They deliberately shifted the conversation, talking about anything else, letting the bar noise and the alcohol begin to smooth the ragged edges of the past few days. Across the room, Brad, several drinks down already, seemed to be losing his earlier pretense of ignoring them. His voice got louder. He kept glancing towards their table, a visible mixture of irritation and arrogance tightening his features. Finally, tossing back the rest of his drink, he slid off his stool and started weaving through the tables towards them, leaving Kaitlyn sitting alone at the bar. The familiar, unpleasant smirk was firmly back in place.

"Ah, hell," Manny sighed. "Showtime".

Brad stopped beside their table, leaning down, the scent of whiskey rolling off him. "Well, well, well," he drawled. "Look who decided to crawl out. Prodigal son and his fan club". His eyes locked onto Devin. "Couldn't stay away, Jones?".

Devin met his gaze, keeping his face impassive. "Catching up, Brad".

"With the welcoming committee?" Brad sneered, flicking his eyes towards Manny and Rachel. "Still collecting strays?".

Manny's hand tightened around his glass. Devin gave a minute shake of his head. Not here.

"Small town, Brad," Devin said steadily. "Bound to run into people". He paused, letting a slight, challenging smile touch his lips. "Speaking of which, saw some interesting types hanging out by McCoy's earlier. Keeping good company these days?". He lifted his glass slightly.

Brad's smirk wavered, just for an instant, his eyes narrowing as the implication hit home. A flicker of unease, quickly masked by rising anger. He leaned closer, his voice dropping to a menacing whisper. "Maybe you should be more careful, Jones". He paused, eyes glinting. "Wouldn't wanna end up like dear old Dad".

The words, blunt, brutal, referencing the murder—hit Devin like a physical blow. The carefully constructed dam of control inside him shattered.

"You son of a bitch!" he roared, shoving his stool back, surging to his feet, blind fury washing over him.

"Devin, no!" Manny was there instantly, grabbing his arm, hauling him back just as Devin lunged towards Brad. "Not here! Think!".

The physical restraint, Manny's urgent voice—they pierced the red haze. Devin blinked, the dimly lit bar swimming back into focus. Rachel's shocked face. Manny's iron grip. He sucked in a ragged breath, his body trembling with adrenaline and rage. Almost lost it.

He started to pull back, to regain control, but Brad, face contorted in a vicious sneer, reacted wildly, snatching a half-empty beer bottle from a nearby table and swinging it hard. Pain exploded against Devin's temple as glass shattered. Stars burst behind his eyes, warm blood instantly slicking his skin.

Pure instinct fired. As Brad lunged again, thrusting the jagged bottleneck forward, Devin ducked under it, the glass whistling past his ear. He pivoted, ignoring the blinding throb in his head, and drove his fist straight into Brad's jaw. The crack echoed, sharp and sickening.

Brad crumpled backward, hitting the floor hard, the broken bottle skittering across the worn wood. Gasps and shouts erupted from nearby tables.

Devin stood over him, breathing heavily, blood dripping from his temple, knuckles stinging. His gaze felt like ice. Ignoring the sudden hush and the stares, he deliberately turned, walked back to his stool, sat down, and picked up his half-finished beer, taking a long, deliberate swallow.

Manny and Rachel stared, momentarily speechless.

"Well," Rachel finally breathed, her voice unsteady, "that escalated...".

Devin wiped blood from his temple with the back of his hand. He looked at his friends, his expression hardening into cold resolve. "Sometimes," he said, his voice low but steady, "you draw a line". He met their eyes. "No one threatens my family. Not Brad. Not again".

Manny slowly nodded, a grim understanding in his eyes. He raised his glass slightly. "Damn right," he said quietly. "To drawing lines".

Rachel watched them both, the reporter in her undoubtedly connecting dots, seeing the shape of the story forming. "This," she murmured, almost to herself, "is definitely going to be complicated".

The ambient noise of the bar slowly started to filter back in, though nervous glances still flickered towards their table. The uneasy peace was broken. Battle lines were drawn.

They finished their drinks in a charged silence, the earlier attempt at finding refuge impossible now. Devin's head throbbed. Brad wouldn't let this go. There would be fallout. But looking at Manny, at Rachel, their presence solid beside him, Devin felt the anger cool slightly, replaced by a cold determination. He was ready.

Finally, Rachel checked her watch. "It's late," she said quietly. "Funeral's tomorrow. We should go".

Devin nodded. "Yeah. Time". He pushed back his stool.

Manny raised his glass one last time. "To tomorrow," he said, his eyes meeting theirs, grim but resolute. "Whatever it brings".

They touched glasses briefly. Stepping back out into the cool night air felt like surfacing from deep water. The quiet street seemed deceptively peaceful after the explosion inside. They walked towards the Sierra, the unspoken knowledge that the storm had truly broken hanging heavy between them. They had each other. For now, it had to be enough.

# Chapter 4

# Trials of Grief

The grandfather clock in the hallway chimed the half-hour—8:30 AM—the sound echoing in the quiet house. It was the morning of the funeral, the air outside crisp and clear, the autumn sunlight sharp against the window panes, a stark contrast to the somber task ahead. Devin, already dressed in his suit, stood staring out the living room window, lost in thought, while Manny and Rachel waited quietly nearby.

The front door opened and closed softly. Annabelle entered the living room, already wearing her coat, her posture radiating a fragile determination beneath the deep sadness that still shadowed her eyes.

"Alright," she announced, her voice quiet but firm, breaking the heavy silence. "It's time. We need to leave for the service at O'Donnell's Funeral Home now. The burial at Immaculate Conception will follow directly after".

Devin turned from the window, the finality of her words hitting him like a physical weight. The need for answers, the suspicions swirling around his father's death, had to be pushed aside. Today was about honoring his father, supporting his mother.

"Right," Devin said, his voice subdued, meeting his mother's gaze. "Okay. Let's go."

Manny and Rachel stood, their expressions reflecting the solemnity of the moment. This task required a different kind of fortitude. Devin went upstairs briefly to check on his mother one last time before they left. He found Annabelle in her bedroom, standing motionless before the open closet, staring at the simple black dress she had chosen.

"Need help, Mom?" he asked softly from the doorway.

She turned, a flicker of gratitude in her weary eyes. "Oh, Devin," her voice was thin. "I just... thank you, dear. I'm ready".

He stepped closer, putting an arm around her slight shoulders for a moment, a silent gesture of support before the public ordeal ahead. They descended the stairs together.

They headed out to Annabelle's cream-colored GMC Acadia. The drive to the funeral home unfolded in a heavy silence, the earlier tensions replaced by a shared, solemn anticipation. Annabelle kept her eyes fixed on the road, hands steady on the wheel. Devin watched the familiar Victorian houses of Jim Thorpe slide past, the streets feeling alien, imbued with a somber new significance. Rachel and Manny were quiet in the back seat.

As Annabelle made the turn onto the street where the funeral home stood, the building came into view, its brick facade imposing, a stark punctuation mark. The immediate, tangible weight of loss eclipsed the swirling questions about toxins and threats, at least for this moment.

Devin saw faces he recognized gathering near the entrance, their expressions uniformly sad, bringing the abstract news into sharp, painful focus.

Annabelle pulled into the parking lot. Devin took a deep, steadying breath, glancing back at Manny and Rachel, finding a quiet reinforcement in their presence before opening his door.

The funeral home was stately, quiet. Inside, the air hung thick with the cloying sweetness of lilies and the low murmur of hushed conversations. Soft music drifted from unseen speakers. They followed Annabelle towards the front of the main viewing room.

There, beneath soft lights, lay his father. His face looked strangely peaceful, smoothed out, unfamiliar. Devin felt his throat tighten, a physical constriction making it hard to breathe. They arranged themselves near the casket—Devin and Manny flanking Annabelle, shoulders squared, a silent guard, while Rachel stood close beside Devin, her presence a quiet source of strength.

A line began to form, a slow stream of familiar faces etched with varying degrees of sympathy and loss. Whispered condolences, gentle hands on Annabelle's arm—small touches across the immense space grief had carved.

"Annabelle, dear," a woman with kind, sorrowful eyes murmured, clasping Annabelle's hand. "So sorry. John was wonderful. Always made everyone feel seen".

Annabelle managed a weak, tear-blurred smile. "Thank you, Martha," she whispered. "He... he did love this town". Tears slipped down her cheeks freely now. Devin gently squeezed her hand, murmuring something low and reassuring, quickly brushing away a betraying sting in his own eye before meeting the gazes of the approaching mourners, forcing his expression into one of steadfastness. Be the pillar.

A young man stepped forward awkwardly. "Mr. Jones? Your dad... that scholarship... he believed in me." Devin nodded, vaguely recognizing the face—one of the many local kids his father had quietly mentored. "He was proud of you, Jake. Said you'd do great things".

An elderly gentleman, leaning heavily on a cane, patted Devin's arm. "True gentleman, your father, Devin. Always time for a word. Saved the old train depot, you know? Classic John, looking out for Jim Thorpe". Pride flickered through Devin's grief, a sudden glimpse into depths of his father's community ties he hadn't fully grasped.

Another woman tearfully recounted the Founder's Day picnic where faulty fireworks and blueberry pie filling had combined disastrously. Annabelle actually chuckled through her tears. "Oh, he could be mischievous," she agreed, a hint of warmth returning to her voice. "He brought joy".

The line moved slowly, each person adding a fragment, a memory, painting a collective portrait of John Jones—dedicated, complex, flawed perhaps, but undeniably woven into the very fabric of the town. As the last condolences were murmured and the doors to the viewing room were quietly closed, Devin felt a profound, anchoring connection to that complicated legacy. A certainty settled in his chest, solidifying amidst the grief: honoring that memory meant more than just mourning.

A different kind of silence fell then, heavy and absolute, broken only by the hushed reverence as the pallbearers entered. Devin stood beside Annabelle, his hand a steadying presence on her arm, as they followed the polished wood casket out of the funeral home and into the unexpectedly crisp autumn air. The waiting black hearse gleamed dully under the overcast sky. They climbed into the lead car behind it, the doors closing with a soft, final thud, sealing the immediate family in a capsule of shared loss.

The procession began, a slow crawl through the familiar streets of Jim Thorpe, past shops and houses where neighbors stood silently on porches or sidewalks, heads bowed in respect. The line of cars following stretched long behind them, a visible measure of the town's mourning. As they made the final turn onto the road leading up the gentle slope towards Immaculate Conception Cemetery, the sheer number of people already gathered became apparent.

The crisp autumn air over the cemetery held a stillness broken only by the low murmur of the crowd and the distant, mournful skirl of a lone bagpipe. A vast number of mourners flowed up the gentle hill, a silent testament to John Jones's reach within the community. People from every corner of Jim Thorpe gathered beneath the grey, overcast sky.

Ancient oaks shed crimson and gold leaves onto the weathered headstones standing like silent sentinels among the plots. The air was heavy with the scent of pine needles and damp earth.

Devin, Manny, and Rachel formed a tight knot beside Annabelle near the freshly dug grave. Devin's jaw ached from clenching it, his gaze fixed on the polished wood of the casket, a hollow space where his breath should be. He glanced at his mother beside him, her face pale, lines of strain visible around her mouth, and gently squeezed her hand. Manny stood tall on her other side, his usual restless energy subdued into a quiet, watchful vigilance, his eyes scanning the periphery. Rachel stood near Devin, her expression reflecting a mix of sorrow for the family and the sharp awareness of a reporter taking in the scene – this wasn't just a burial; it was a town grappling with a loss.

The priest's voice resonated, reciting familiar scripture, but the words felt distant to Devin, muffled. He kept his focus on the casket, the smooth dark wood, time seeming to warp, stretching and slowing. The pressure behind his eyes intensified, the urge to simply let go immense, but he held it in check, consciously squaring his shoulders. Be strong. For Mom.

Then the ritual changed. One by one, people stepped forward, dropping flowers onto the casket lid—roses, carnations, mums—a cascade of color against the dark wood. The simple, poignant act broke through Devin's carefully maintained control. A single hot tear escaped, tracing a slow path down his cheek. He didn't wipe it away, just let it fall, acknowledging the weight of the loss in the presence of his community.

As the final mourners offered quiet words and began to drift away down the leaf-scattered paths, the cemetery quieted. Devin kept an arm around Annabelle's shoulders, which trembled slightly beneath his touch. He murmured something low, comforting.

"He's really gone," she whispered, leaning against him.

"I know, Mom," Devin replied, his own voice thick. "But we carry him with us".

Rachel stepped back slightly, giving them space. Her gaze wandered towards the wrought iron gates near the parking area. She saw her father, Chief Miller, standing near the entrance. He wasn't alone. He was talking to a broad-shouldered man in a brown leather jacket—the man's build solid, impassive, like hired muscle. Something about him tickled the edge of Rachel's memory, but she couldn't place it. Her father looked agitated, gesturing sharply, while the other man just stood there, radiating a quiet intimidation. Rachel frowned, a knot of unease tightening in her stomach. What are they arguing about? Before she could contemplate approaching, the conversation broke off. Her father gave the man a curt nod, turned abruptly, and walked quickly to where her mother waited in their car. They drove off, leaving Rachel watching the man in the leather jacket turn and blend back into the thinning crowd, the sense of vague familiarity nagging at her.

A few rows away, Manny felt the familiar pull of his own mother's grave. The shared sadness of the day unearthed his own buried grief. Excusing himself quietly from Devin and Annabelle, he walked the short distance, his steps heavy on the damp grass. Kneeling beside the simple, weathered headstone, the past rushed back—his mother's smile, the echoing shouts of his father's drunken rages, the clench of fear in his own small chest, the acrid taste of their last argument before he'd left for the Marines.

"Mama," he whispered, tracing the faded letters carved into the stone, the wall he'd built around that pain finally crumbling, tears blurring the worn inscription. "Miss you".

A shadow fell across the grave marker. Manny looked up, startled. His father stood there. Older, thinner, hardship etched into the lines around his eyes, but the eyes themselves were unchanged. Manny froze, caught in a maelstrom of old anger, shock, and the phantom chill of childhood fear.

"Manuel?" his father asked, his voice hesitant. After a moment of taut silence, he took a tentative step closer, hands held slightly out. "I know... I don't deserve your forgiveness. But I read about Mayor Jones. Knew you'd be here. I came to pay respects... and hoping I'd see you". He looked down at the grass, then met Manny's wary gaze again. "Five years sober now, son. Trying to... make things right".

*Sober?* The word echoed in the quiet cemetery air. Manny stared, a part of him wanting desperately to believe, warring with years of bitterness. Forgiveness felt like an impossible distance. He glanced from his father's face to the name on his mother's headstone, the weight of everything pressing down. He took a shaky breath. "I'll try," he whispered, the words barely audible even to himself. "For Mom. For me".

A flicker of something – hope? relief? – softened his father's eyes. He reached out, placing a hand gently on Manny's shoulder. "Thank you, Manuel. I know... I know it's not easy. I'm here. If you ever... need anything".

Manny could only nod, unable to speak past the knot in his throat, tears now blurring his father's face as well. He didn't know if this was forgiveness, but it felt like... something. A beginning, maybe. After another charged moment, Manny pushed himself to his feet and walked back towards Devin and Annabelle, leaving his father standing alone by the grave, watching him go, his expression a mixture of fragile hope and deep regret.

Manny rejoined the others by John's graveside, placing a hand on Devin's shoulder. "Time to go," he said gently.

Devin nodded, the emotional and physical exhaustion settling deep in his bones. "Yeah. Let's head back".

Annabelle took a deep breath, her posture seeming a little less fragile. "Let's go," she agreed softly.

They walked together down the winding cemetery path, autumn leaves crunching underfoot. Devin kept an arm around his mother, a fierce resolve solidifying beneath the grief—a determination to protect his family, to understand and honor his father's complex legacy. Manny walked slightly ahead, the earlier vulnerability masked now by his usual quiet alertness. Rachel walked beside Devin, her thoughtful expression suggesting a mind wrestling with empathy for the Joneses and troubling questions about her own father's tense exchange at the gate.

As they passed through the wrought iron gates and into the fading afternoon light, the unspoken connection between the three friends felt reinforced, tested by the shared ordeal but holding firm against the shadows gathering around them. The path ahead remained uncertain, the journey far from finished.

The drive back to the house was silent, the air inside the Acadia thick with the residue of the funeral, unspoken grief, and the sharp edges of suspicion. Pulling into the driveway at 218 Center Street, the familiar gables and porch railings of the Victorian seemed different, muted, offering no comfort. The house felt empty, mirroring the hollow space Devin felt expanding in his own chest.

As they got out, Annabelle swayed, leaning heavily on Devin's arm as they walked up the path. Her exhaustion was a palpable thing. Inside, the familiar scent of polish and potpourri couldn't mask the stillness, the chill that had settled in his father's absence. Without a word, Devin guided her gently towards the stairs. "Let's get you upstairs, Mom," he murmured.

Manny and Rachel watched them go, a shared look of concern passing between them before they moved quietly into the living room. Devin sat with Annabelle for a while, just holding her hand in the quiet dimness of her room, until the tension finally eased from her shoulders and her breathing evened out into a shallow, fragile sleep.

Downstairs, Manny had changed into jeans and a t-shirt, the constraints of the suit discarded. He was slumped on the couch, staring at the dark television screen without seeing it. Rachel emerged from the guest room, also changed into comfortable clothes, and quietly took the armchair opposite him. The silence stretched, weighted by the funeral, the unresolved questions, the sheer strangeness of being back here under these circumstances.

Rachel finally broke it, her voice soft in the stillness. "It feels weird, being back here like this," she said, her gaze sweeping the familiar living room. "Thinking about... all of it". She paused. "You know, I'm glad we're friends now, Manny. Really glad. Especially considering..."

Manny offered a faint, tired smile. "Yeah," he agreed. "Lifetime ago, right? We were such idiots".

"We were teenagers," Rachel corrected gently. "I just... I never really thought we'd manage to get past our family histories." She sighed. "Took Devin nearly getting killed on the field to finally knock some sense into us".

Manny's smile vanished. "That Lehighton game..." He shook his head, looking away, the memory clearly unwelcome. "Seeing Dev laid out like that... not moving... Jesus. My heart just stopped. Nothing else mattered". He remembered the metallic smell of the hospital hallway, the low murmur of the doctor explaining the concussion, the broken collarbone, how lucky Devin had been. "Standing outside his room,"

Manny continued quietly. "That's when we actually talked, right? Figured out Devin needed us both, not us tearing each other down".

Rachel nodded. "Devin always held us together," she murmured. "Even knocked out cold". "We knew we had to find a way. For him".

CRASH! Clatter-clang!

The sudden racket from outside, towards the back yard, made them both jump. Manny was on his feet instantly, already moving towards the kitchen, instincts overriding fatigue. Rachel followed, a knot of apprehension tightening in her stomach.

"Sounds like the trash cans," she whispered, recalling the incident from the night before. "Again".

Manny reached the back door and peered cautiously through the windowpane. Twilight painted the yard in shades of grey, but he could make out the familiar shapes of the metal cans overturned near the trees. He eased the door open, stepping onto the deck, listening intently, scanning the deepening shadows along the wood line. A moment later, he stepped back inside, quietly sliding the deadbolt home.

"Nothing," Manny reported, stepping back inside and locking the door, though a slight frown creased his brow. "Just the cans. Must be determined raccoons". The explanation didn't sit right, adding another layer of unease to the tense quiet.

They returned to the living room, the interruption somehow making the air feel heavier. The shared memory of the hospital hallway seemed tethered to the reason they'd needed that truce in the first place.

"Still burns me up, thinking about that hit," Manny muttered, sinking back onto the couch. "Brad always was a dirty player".

"Fourth quarter, down by four," Rachel recalled softly. "Devin was putting the team on his back...".

"Just hit me for that big gain, down near their twenty," Manny said, unconsciously rubbing his jaw. "We were driving. He called the fake blast...".

The image flared in Manny's mind—*the snap, Devin turning, planting his foot, and then just a blur of Lehighton blue and white exploding through a missed block, helmet connecting with Devin's jaw with sickening force...*

*The crack of the impact silenced the stadium. Devin crumpled, hitting the turf bonelessly, utterly still. A collective gasp seemed to steal the air. Players from both teams immediately knelt around Devin's unmoving form.*

"...never saw it coming," Manny finished, his voice low. "Woke up in the ambulance later," he added, the words likely mirroring Devin's own fragmented memory of that day.

They sat in silence again, the violence of that old memory stark against the house's somber quiet. That collision, that shared fear for Devin, had been the catalyst, forging their truce. Now, years later, surrounded by fresh grief and looming danger, that bond felt essential. Darkness crept into the corners of the room, mirroring the weight settling around them.

# Chapter 5

# Trials of Fire

The twilight bled the color from the meticulously kept lawn. Pathetic sentimentality oozed from the house itself, reflected in the low murmur of voices drifting from the living room window – Rivera and the Miller girl. He remained perfectly still within the dense woods bordering the property, the rough bark of an oak a familiar, grounding pressure against his back. Patience. He had learned patience in the hell where they had left him.

He adjusted the compact, dense package in his hand. Simple chemistry, elegant design. His own work. It had been a long time since he'd handled such things personally, since he'd gotten his own hands dirty. Usually, such tasks were delegated. Akimitsu or others handled the... groundwork. *But this? This required precision. A personal touch for the son of the man who started it all, for the man, Jones, who had failed so spectacularly years ago, condemning him to that endless suffering.*

The voices inside continued their oblivious reminiscing. Perfect. He slid from the treeline, a shadow detaching itself, moving across the grass towards the rear corner of the house. The sagging porch – old wood, dry, vulnerable. Ideal. He moved swiftly, silently—

Clatter-clang!

He froze. His boot had clipped one of the damned metal trash cans. The noise was jarringly loud. Amateur, the thought hissed, fury mixing with self-recrimination. A mistake. Unacceptable after surviving that place by eliminating mistakes. He melted instantly back against the trunk of the nearest tree, disappearing into the gloom just as the back door creaked open.

*Rivera. Predictable. Stepping onto the deck, peering into the darkness like a wary animal.* The man remained utterly still, a ghost in the trees, slowing his breath, observing the Sergeant. How easily they lived, these men who had abandoned him, forgotten him. Rivera scanned the yard, lingered, then retreated inside. *Fool. Locking the door meant nothing.*

The moment the lock clicked, the watcher flowed forward again. He reached the porch overhang, knelt in the shadows. The rich scent of damp earth and cut grass filled his nostrils – the smell of a life he had been denied for years. He located the crawl space access, pushed the device deep inside, wedging it firmly against a thick support beam. A faint click as he armed the chemical timer – reliable, untraceable. Designed for the deep hours of the night.

He rose, surveyed his work for a fraction of a second. Satisfactory. He turned and retreated back towards the woods, his movements swift, fluid, leaving no trace. *Let Jones return to ashes. A small measure of balance restored.* It was merely the beginning.

The moon climbed, washing the quiet street in pale, silvery light. Inside the aging Victorian, downstairs lights clicked off, followed eventually by those on the upper floors, until the house stood dark and still against the night sky. The only sounds were the gentle sigh of the wind through the pines bordering the property and the rhythmic chirping of late-autumn crickets. Within the walls, exhausted occupants surrendered to sleep, oblivious to the slow, inevitable chemical reaction unfolding in the damp earth beneath the porch, silently counting down the final minutes of their sanctuary.

Around 2 AM, the sharp, acrid tang of smoke bit into Devin's subconscious, wrenching him from sleep into a darkness that felt heavy, unnaturally warm. He coughed, eyes flying open, the smell intense now—burning wood, sharp and terrifying. Disoriented, heart pounding, his hand slapped the nightstand, fumbling for the lamp—finding only the cool, smooth face of his father's antique clock—but the switch did nothing. Power was out. An angry orange glow pulsed beneath his bedroom door, casting frantic shadows across the ceiling.
*Fire.*
The realization struck like a physical blow. He threw himself from bed, bare feet landing on hardwood that radiated an alarming heat. He

stumbled towards the door, lungs burning, eyes stinging from the thickening smoke, and yanked it open.

A wall of heat and smoke hit him, driving him back, the roar of the flames already a deafening presence in the hallway.

"Mom! Rachel! Manny!" he choked out, his voice raw, nearly lost in the inferno engulfing his childhood home. He peered frantically through the swirling, blinding smoke.

His mother stumbled from her doorway down the hall, a silhouette of terror in her billowing nightgown. He lunged, grabbing her arm.

"Devin!" she gasped, eyes wide. "What's happening?".

"Fire, Mom! Out! Now!" he yelled, pulling her towards the main staircase just as Manny burst from his own room further down, coughing violently, soot already streaking his face.

"Rachel!" Manny choked, pointing towards the guest room. "Still in there!" He shoved past Devin, making for the stairs.

Devin spun, pushing his mother firmly towards Manny. "Mom, go with Manny! Go! I'll get Rachel!".

Manny grabbed Annabelle's hand instantly. "Move, Mrs. J! Now!" he urged, half-guiding, half-pulling her down the smoke-filled staircase, the heat radiating upwards with every step. Reaching the bottom, Manny saw the living room was already a wall of flame, fire licking towards the front door, cutting off that escape. "Can't go front! Too late!" he yelled over the roar. He glanced towards the kitchen. "Back door, Mrs. J! Go! Get the extinguisher!". He gave her a gentle shove towards the kitchen, then sprinted that way himself, ripping the red cylinder from under the sink, racing back to blast foam at the flames encroaching from the living room, trying to keep the path clear. Annabelle, propelled by sheer terror and urgency, stumbled through the kitchen towards the back.

Upstairs, Devin kicked open the guest room door. Smoke poured out, thick and choking. Through the haze, he saw Rachel crumpled on the floor, partly shielded by the heavy, fallen headboard. Unconscious. He lunged, scooping her limp form into his arms—a dead weight. He staggered back into the hallway, heat searing his skin, smoke stealing his breath, vision tunneling. He reached the top of the stairs, legs trembling, strength giving out.

Crrreeeak-CRACK!

He looked up—the ceiling directly above the stairwell groaned, sagged, then gave way. Instinctively, Devin hunched over Rachel, shielding her body with his own as burning plaster and wood rained down, missing them by inches as he stumbled down the remaining steps.

Manny saw them emerge from the smoke at the bottom, still spraying the edge of the fire. "Hurry, Devin!" he shouted, his voice strained against the roar. "It's coming fast!".

Devin's legs threatened to buckle as he reached the bottom, nearly dropping Rachel. Manny tossed the extinguisher aside, grabbing Devin's arm, taking some of Rachel's weight as they half-carried, half-dragged her through the smoky kitchen, following Annabelle towards the back door.

They burst out onto the deck together, tumbling onto the cool, dew-slick grass, gasping, choking, faces and clothes blackened. Annabelle rushed towards them from the edge of the yard, her relief warring with horror.

At that instant, the first siren wailed in the distance, growing rapidly closer. Red and blue lights strobed through the trees as a fire engine screamed onto Center Street. Firefighters spilled out, bulky in their turnout gear, faces grim, voices sharp, taking in the scene, shouting questions over the roar.

"Everyone accounted for?" one yelled, his gaze sweeping over the four of them huddled on the lawn.

"Yes," Devin managed, his throat raw. "We're all out".

The firefighters moved them quickly back towards the street, where neighbors were beginning to gather, faces stark with shock in the flashing lights. They watched, numb, as flames consumed the house, blowing out windows, the roof sagging inward in a shower of sparks. The roar of the fire mingled with the hiss of water cannons. The house, his history, turning to ash before his eyes.

By 5:45 AM, the fire was out, subdued by the relentless crews. Dawn's first grey light revealed the skeletal ruin of the grand Victorian. The façade was barely recognizable, walls reduced to charred beams and crumbling brick. Windows gaped like empty sockets. The collapsed roof exposed the ravaged upper floors. Inside the shell, furniture lay in charred, broken heaps on floors slick with ash and water. Ghosts of photos lined vanished walls. The grand staircase was a dangerous twist of blackened wood. Kitchen appliances stood as melted husks; Manny's discarded extinguisher lay near the living room entrance. The air hung thick with the sickening smell of burnt wood, wet ash, and chemicals. Firefighters moved through the wreckage, dousing hotspots, their movements casting long shadows. Neighbors huddled on the sidewalk, offering blankets, murmuring condolences. Devin stared at the ruin, the weight of it all – his father's murder, Brad's threats, this deliberate destruction – pressing down. The house was gone. But Annabelle, Rachel, Manny – they were alive. He clung to that.

Paramedics checked them over – smoke inhalation, minor scrapes and burns – confirming no critical injuries among the four of them. Devin waved them off. As the emergency vehicles began to disperse, leaving only a police cruiser and the fire marshal's vehicle, Devin walked to where his mother stood staring numbly at the wreckage, Rachel and Manny flanking her.

"Mom," he said, his voice rough with smoke. "I'm sorry. I'll fix this. Promise. We'll rebuild".

Annabelle looked at him, her eyes hollowed by grief but holding a faint spark of gratitude. "Oh, Devin," she whispered, shaking her head slightly. "You don't...".

"I want to, Mom," he insisted, his voice firm, finding an anchor in the vow. "This was home. It's not gone". He looked at the ruin, his jaw set. "Crew's here tomorrow. We clear this. We rebuild".

Manny stepped closer, his face grim, voice hoarse. "First things first, Dev. Place to stay. Clothes. Everything's gone". Rachel, clothes singed, the smell of smoke sharp on her, nodded agreement.

Devin's gaze hardened, turning from the wreckage back to his friends, his family. "And first," he said, his voice low, dangerously quiet, "we find out who did this". He looked at them. "My phone's gone. Anyone get theirs?".

They all shook their heads, exhaustion and shock etched onto their faces.

"Okay," Devin said, a cold determination displacing the numbness. "Backup plan". He spotted the lone police officer talking to the fire marshal. Devin strode towards them, his bearing regaining its authority despite his soot-streaked appearance.

"Excuse me, officer," he said clearly. "Need to borrow your phone. Emergency".

The officer looked him up and down, taking in the soot, the intensity in his eyes, then glanced at the smoldering ruin. He hesitated only a second before handing over his department-issued phone. "Go ahead. Quick".

Devin nodded his thanks, dialing a number committed to memory. It rang twice. A crisp voice answered, betraying no hint of the pre-dawn hour.

"Sarah Blake".

"Sarah, it's Devin," he said, his voice steady, controlled.

"Mr. Jones!" Relief flooded her tone, instantly followed by sharp concern. "Kate mentioned a situation yesterday evening... your father, being followed... Is everything alright?".

Devin's voice hardened. "Escalated, Sarah. The house... they burned it down last night. We're safe, but it's gone". A beat of stunned silence. "Need you to wire ten thousand cash, Jim Thorpe City Financial, soon as they open. And arrange a three-man security team, plus a Tier-One analyst. Full kit, hostile engagement specs. Have them meet us, location to follow shortly".

"My God... Understood, Mr. Jones," Sarah replied instantly, her professional efficiency overriding the shock. "Team and analyst mobilized immediately. Funds wired at bank opening. Anything else?".

"Confirm team ETA," Devin said. "And Sarah... need-to-know only on the details".

"Always, sir. Stay safe," Sarah replied.

Devin ended the call, a sliver of control regained as he handed the phone back to the officer with a curt nod. He rejoined the others, his expression resolute.

"Okay," he announced, meeting their questioning looks. "Sarah's handling EAG support. Help's coming". He looked at the ruin, then back at Annabelle, Rachel, Manny. "Bank first, when it opens. Get cash, clothes, find somewhere safe. Mom's keys are likely melted slag," he glanced towards the wreckage, "so... looks like we walk".

Annabelle simply nodded, seeming to draw strength from having a concrete plan.

Manny placed a hand on Devin's shoulder. "Got your back, brother".

Rachel nodded agreement, her eyes determined despite the soot smudging her face. "We'll get through this, Devin. Together".

As the first true rays of dawn struggled through the lingering smoke, casting long, distorted shadows from the ruined house, a grim purpose settled over the small group. United by loss and the certainty of attack, they turned away from the ashes and prepared to face the uncertain light of the new day.

# Chapter 6

# From the Ashes

The sun, barely cresting the ridge, cast long, skeletal shadows down the deserted streets of Jim Thorpe. Devin, Manny, Rachel, and Annabelle walked quickly, a grim procession, faces smudged with soot, the sharp smell of smoke embedded in their singed clothes. The early morning air bit, cool and crisp, a world away from the furnace they'd escaped hours before.

Their footsteps echoed loudly in the neighborhood's quiet. The familiar Victorian homes, usually charming, seemed alien now, their peaceful facades mocking reminders of the inferno and the certainty of the attack. Devin's gaze stayed fixed ahead, jaw tight. Cash, phones, clothes, a vehicle—they needed resources, fast. Without them, they were targets. Walking was the only way forward; the keys to the Acadia, the Range Rover, the rented Sierra—all consumed by the fire on Center Street. As they neared the town square, the imposing brick facade of the Jim Thorpe City Financial rose before them, white pillars stark against the brightening sky. Devin paused instinctively at the locked glass doors, acutely aware of his soot-stained clothes, the reek of smoke, the absence of any identification. Desperation wasn't usually part of his morning routine.

"They'll help," Rachel murmured, touching his arm briefly, her own face pale but set with resolve.

Devin gave a curt nod. They settled onto the cold metal benches outside the entrance, waiting for opening time, the silence between them stretched thin with exhaustion and unspoken anxieties. The rising sun painted the clouds in hues of orange and pink that felt like a cruel joke. Finally, the distinct clink of a deadbolt turning sounded from within, followed by the soft whoosh of the heavy glass doors swinging inward. The bank's interior—cool, quiet, gleaming with polished marble and brass—felt jarringly clean, utterly disconnected from their reality. Devin pushed past the feeling, heading straight for the teller counter, the others close behind.

A young teller, name tag reading EMILY, offered a practiced smile. "Good morning, welcome to JTCF. How can I help you?".

"Need to make a withdrawal," Devin stated, keeping his voice steady despite the slight tremor in his hands. "I don't have identification".

Emily's smile faltered. "I'm sorry, sir, bank policy requires...".

"Our house burned down last night," Devin cut in, gesturing to their smoke-stained clothes, their disheveled appearance speaking for itself. "We lost everything. ID included".

Emily gasped, professional caution instantly replaced by wide-eyed sympathy. "Oh, my goodness! I... I'm so sorry... but the policy...".

"Emily, dear?" Annabelle stepped forward. Her voice was quiet, but it held an authority that immediately commanded the young teller's attention.

"Mrs. Jones!" Emily exclaimed, recognition dawning.

"This is my son, Devin," Annabelle said firmly, placing a steadying hand on Devin's arm. "He's telling the truth. The fire on Center Street... we lost it all".

Concern flooded Emily's face. "Oh, Mrs. Jones, I had no idea! Mr. Jones used to talk about Devin all the time – the football star!" She flushed slightly. "I... I was so sorry to hear about the Mayor".

Annabelle nodded, her eyes glistening. "Thank you, Emily. John always said you were his favorite teller".

Emily turned towards the glass-walled office behind the counter. "Mr. Lundinberger," she called out, her voice gaining confidence. "Could you come here a moment?".

The bank manager, a tall man with a severe expression, emerged and approached the counter. Emily quickly explained the situation in hushed tones. Mr. Lundinberger listened, his stern features softening slightly as his gaze took in their soot-streaked faces, Annabelle's quiet dignity. "I understand the circumstances," he said gravely, "but policy requires identification...".

"Mr. Lundinberger," Annabelle stated, meeting his gaze directly, her voice unwavering. "This is an emergency. My son requires these funds".

Lundinberger looked from Annabelle's steady gaze to Devin's exhausted but resolute face. He let out a sigh, heavy with reluctance. "Very well," he conceded. "Given the extraordinary circumstances... Emily, authorize a limited withdrawal. Mr. Jones," he fixed his eyes on Devin, "you will need to return with proper identification as soon as possible for full account access".

A wave of sharp relief washed through Devin. "Thank you, sir," he said sincerely. "We will".

Emily quickly processed the transaction, sliding a thick envelope across the counter. "I hope this helps, Mr. Jones. Please, take care".

"Thank you, Emily. You have no idea," Devin said, the weight of the cash in the envelope a tangible first step.

Stepping back out into the bright morning sun, the first hurdle was down. Devin turned to the others, managing a slight, tired smile. "Okay. Step one".

Manny let out a short, humorless chuckle. "Hope the rest are that easy".

"Priorities," Devin said, the smile vanishing as his focus snapped back. "Phones. Need secure comms, need to coordinate with Sarah, find out the ETA on the EAG team".

"Hillside up the street has burners," Rachel suggested.

"Perfect," Devin agreed. "Then clothes. We look like hell".

"Lucy's Thrift Box on Broadway," Manny offered. "Should have basics".

Devin nodded, taking in the determined, albeit exhausted, faces of his mother and friends. "Alright. Stay together. Phones, then clothes. Let's move".

They set off again, crossing the town square, turning onto Broadway. The morning sun was warmer now, but the familiar charm of the shops felt distant, muted by fatigue and the lingering sense of danger. They passed the Opera House, Josiah White Park—landmarks rendered strange by circumstance. Turning onto Susquehanna Street towards the Hillside near the river bridge, the contrast between the town's peaceful morning routine and their own grim reality felt stark.

"Alright, I'll grab the phones. Back in a minute," Devin said, heading into the convenience store as Manny, Rachel, and Annabelle waited near the entrance, drawing a few curious glances from patrons fueling up or grabbing coffee.

As they stood there, the mundane morning bustle a world away from their own reality, Manny's attention snagged on movement across the street, in the parking lot of the Grocery & More.

"Well, speak of the devil," he muttered, nodding subtly.

Rachel and Annabelle followed his gaze...

Brad Ewing strode towards the market entrance, instantly recognizable by his broad shoulders and confident posture, though internally he cursed the traffic jam that had made him ten minutes late. *Just what I needed.* He wasn't alone. Three other men faced him near the doors, forming a loose semi-circle, their impatience a palpable thing under the shadow of their wide-brimmed hats. Bulky frames beneath worn leather jackets, stances anything but casual—tension radiated off them. Across the street, Brad caught a flicker of movement – Annabelle Jones? And the reporter? He saw Annabelle stiffen slightly, her expression smoothing into careful neutrality. Great. An audience.

"You're late, Ewing," the lead man growled, his accent thick and grating. "Ten minutes. Not smart".

"Traffic," Brad clipped, forcing nonchalance, refusing to acknowledge the implied threat. He subtly passed the thick envelope to the lead man.

"Payment for transport".

The man snatched the envelope, his fingers quickly riffling through the bills, his face tightening beneath the hat's shadow. "This isn't right. Agreement was full value on confirmation".

"Confirmation hasn't happened," Brad countered, keeping his voice level, though he could feel the man's agitation rising like heat off pavement. "This is the deposit. Per the terms. The rest clears when the shipment does".

"Not acceptable!" the man snapped, his voice sharp enough to draw a glance from a nearby shopper. "Instructions were clear. Full payment now, or consequences".

Anger surged in Brad, quickly followed by a cold prickle of unease. These weren't Sal's usual delivery boys. "Consequences? For sticking to the terms?" He met the shadowy gazes, forcing defiance into his own. "We have a deal. I honor my deals. You get paid when the product lands. Not before".

The three men exchanged a look, a silent, tense calculation passing between them – weighing their orders against the potential fallout of pushing too hard. A moment stretched. Then, the lead man gave Brad a curt, sharp nod that conveyed barely suppressed fury. Without another word, they turned and melted back between the rows of parked cars, vanishing from sight. Brad watched them go, consciously relaxing his jaw, ignoring the sudden dryness in his mouth. He straightened his suit jacket, then turned and strode purposefully down the sidewalk towards the pawn shop. He needed to make another call.

Just as Brad vanished around the corner, Devin emerged from Hillside, holding several blister packs of prepaid phones. Manny and Rachel exchanged a quick, loaded glance.

"You are not gonna believe who we just saw," Manny said quietly as Devin rejoined them.

"Brad?" Devin asked instantly, his eyes narrowing.

"Holding court with three shady characters in hats right over there," Rachel confirmed, recounting the tense exchange and the envelope handoff. "Definitely not locals. Heavy accents on the one guy".

"Yeah, figures," Devin agreed, a knot of unease tightening in his gut as he connected this to Brad's behavior after the murder confirmation, the veiled threats. "Just throws more fuel on the fire, doesn't it?". He tore open the phone packages, passing them around. "Okay. Let's get clothes". Phones activated, they walked back towards Broadway. The familiar street felt different now, overlaid with the recent, unsettling observation.

At Lucy's Thrift Box, they made quick work of finding functional replacements – jeans, dark shirts, jackets – shedding the soot-stained remnants of the fire felt like shedding a layer of helplessness, regaining a small measure of control.

Back out on the sidewalk, the sun higher now, nearly 11:15 AM, Devin turned to his mother. "Mom, the cabin out near Lehighton – Dad kept it?".

Annabelle nodded firmly. "Yes. He'd never sell that place".

"Good. That's our base," Devin decided instantly. "Okay, listen. Mom, Rach, head back to the auto rental place," he pointed down Broadway. "Get a spare key for the Sierra. Say the originals burned, use Dad's name if needed".

Rachel nodded, determination solidifying her features. "We can do that, Devin".

Annabelle added, "It's only fifteen minutes from here. We'll hurry".

Devin watched them walk away, then turned to Manny, handing him one of the newly activated burner phones. "Okay, Manny. Call Sarah. Update her – Brad meeting with unknowns, possible payoff. Confirm the EAG team's ETA and give her the RV point: Limpony Gas station,

Interchange Road, Lehighton. Emphasize discretion. They meet Annabelle and Rachel there. Not us. Not the cabin yet".

While Manny stepped aside to make the call, Devin used another burner to arrange a cab, requesting pickup nearby in twenty to thirty minutes.

Manny finished his call. "Done. Sarah got it. Team was delayed near Allentown, ETA for the Limpony RV is about thirty minutes".

"Cab's twenty to thirty," Devin confirmed. "Good timing". They found a nearby bench to wait, the minutes stretching, feeling both too long and too short.

After what felt like an hour but was likely closer to twenty minutes on the hard bench, they saw Annabelle and Rachel approaching, walking quickly back up Broadway. Rachel held up a set of keys, a grin splitting her tired face. "Got 'em! Your mom can be very persuasive!". Annabelle allowed herself a small, satisfied smile.

Relief, sharp and genuine, washed through Devin. "Excellent work. Okay," his tone shifted back to command mode. "You two take the Sierra now". He handed the keys back to Rachel. "Head straight to the Limpony Gas station on Interchange Road in Lehighton. EAG team meets you there. Follow them to the cabin once they arrive. No stops. Stay alert".

Rachel nodded, pocketing the keys, her expression serious again. "Understood. See you there. Be careful, you two".

As the women headed towards where they'd left the Sierra, the yellow cab Devin had called earlier pulled alongside the curb. Devin and Manny exchanged a final look – resolute, focused – and climbed into the back seat.

"Where to?" the cabbie asked, adjusting his rearview mirror.

"Carbon County Sheriff's Department, back here in Jim Thorpe," Devin instructed. "And wait for us, please? Maybe fifteen, twenty minutes".

The driver shrugged. "Meter's running".

They rode in silence back through town. Manny glanced at Devin.

"Think Davis will actually tell us anything?".

"No," Devin said grimly. "But we ask. See what he avoids saying".

The cab pulled up to the Sheriff's building. "Back shortly," Devin told the driver, leaving the meter ticking. Inside, a deputy directed them to Interview Room 1. Detective Davis met them at the door, his face etched with resignation.

"Mr. Jones, Mr. Rivera," Davis acknowledged. "Fire Marshal confirms arson at your mother's house. Accelerants used. It's active".

"Leads?" Devin asked bluntly.

Davis shifted his weight, avoiding Devin's eyes. "Too early. We're reviewing several recent fires in the county".

"And my father's murder?".

Davis sighed. "Like I mentioned, Chief Miller prefers Echelon not be involved. We are pursuing leads, but that's all I can share".

"So, zero connection made between my father being murdered and my family home being torched hours later?" Devin pressed, his voice dangerously quiet.

"The Arson Unit has the case file," Davis deflected, gesturing vaguely down the hall. "They wouldn't have specifics yet".

They found the Arson Investigator's office piled high with folders and smelling faintly of stale coffee. "Look, Mr. Jones," the investigator said tiredly after brief introductions, "Active case. Can't release details". He shuffled a stack of papers on his desk, momentarily revealing the label on a manila folder beneath: Recent Arsons - Suspects/Witnesses. Clearly typed below another name was: Malone, Richard ('Ricky the Torch'). Devin's eyes locked onto it. He stood abruptly. "Thanks for nothing".

Back in the cab, Devin gave the driver Ricky Malone's address on North Street in Lehighton. "Saw a name," he told Manny quietly as they pulled away. "Ricky the Torch".

Manny nodded grimly. "Figures".

The cab headed south again, entering Lehighton and pulling up to a run-down house with peeling paint. "Wait here," Devin instructed the driver again. They climbed the rickety porch steps.

Ricky Malone opened the door, looking more gaunt and haunted than Devin remembered. His eyes widened in fear, darting past them to the street before flicking back. "Devin? Manny? What—? Get outta here!" He tried to slam the door shut.

"Not so fast, Ricky," Manny blocked the door with his foot, easily pushing it back open. Devin stepped firmly onto the porch, forcing Ricky back into the dingy entryway. The smell of stale cigarette smoke and desperation hung in the air.

"We need to talk, Ricky," Devin said, his voice low but firm.

"Talk? About what?" Ricky stammered, wringing his hands, backing away further into the cramped hallway. "I ain't done nothin'! Look, guys, you being here... asking questions... if they find out..." His voice trailed off, raw terror replacing the denial. "They'll kill me! You gotta go!"

"Who's 'they', Ricky?" Manny asked, his voice dangerously quiet, taking a step closer. "The guys who pay 'Ricky the Torch' for jobs? We saw your name on a file down at the Sheriff's."

Ricky visibly paled, sweat beading on his forehead. He shook his head frantically. "That list don't mean nothing! Look, the Jones place! Swear to God! Wasn't me! I wouldn't touch that! But the other stuff... those guys... you don't understand how dangerous they are!"

"We didn't ask about my family's house," Devin said, his voice like ice, crowding Ricky further. "We know you're scared. Who are you working for, Ricky? Who hired you last?"

Ricky flinched, cornered, the terror overwhelming him. He glanced wildly around the hallway as if looking for an escape route that didn't exist. "Alright! Okay! Jesus!" he blurted out, hands twisting together nervously. "Weeks back! Three, maybe." His voice dropped to a terrified whisper. "Sal Demarco. He came here." He visibly shuddered. "Know him from way back. Bad news. Offered cash, big cash... torch an address near Beltzville Lake. Said make it look like faulty wiring. Said it was abandoned, no one would get hurt! That's the only recent job, I swear! The only one!"

"Just Sal?" Devin pressed, keeping his voice level, watching Ricky's terrified face closely.

"No... another guy," Ricky frowned, digging into his memory, sweat dripping now. "Never saw him before. Big dude, expensive suit. Didn't say much, just... stood there, looking mean. Sal did all the talking, laid out the job." The description, vague as it was, screamed Brad Ewing.

"Okay, Ricky," Devin said, stepping back slightly, acknowledging the fear that had driven the confession. "You did right telling us, despite the risk." He met Ricky's terrified eyes. "Now, because Sal will find out you talked, you need to disappear. Tonight. Go to New York. EAG headquarters. Ask for Sarah Blake, use my name. She'll get you safe, new ID. You stay here..." The implication hung heavy.

Ricky nodded frantically, pale, seeming to shrink into himself. "Okay... Okay, Devin. Thank you." His voice was barely a whisper. "Sal... he ain't someone you cross. You gotta believe me."

"We believe you. Stay safe, Ricky." They turned and walked quickly back to the waiting cab, leaving Ricky looking utterly terrified in his doorway.

"Sal and Brad," Manny said grimly as they settled into the backseat, the cab pulling away from Ricky's dilapidated house. "Hiring Ricky weeks ago for an arson. Doesn't prove the house fire, but damn...".

"Proves they're partners," Devin finished, his jaw tight. "And that Brad farms out his wet work". He leaned forward, giving the driver the address for Ewing Automotive on Blakeslee Boulevard. "Let's pay Mr. Ewing a visit".

Manny nodded, a dark understanding in his eyes. "Time to get some wheels, and maybe rattle Brad's cage". He tapped the thick envelope Devin held. "About eighty-nine hundred left?"

"Enough," Devin agreed, gaze fixed on the passing scenery

Pulling into the sprawling Ewing Automotive lot, the dealership looked incongruously bright and busy under the afternoon sun. Devin paid the cabbie generously and waved him off. They turned towards the rows of used trucks, affecting the air of casual shoppers.

A 2012 Ford F-150 quickly caught Devin's eye – looked solid enough. A young salesman approached, radiating eagerness. "Afternoon! Looking at the F-150?".

"Price?" Devin asked.

"$8,500," the salesman replied after checking his tablet. "Good condition".

Manny drew the salesman aside slightly, letting the edge of the thick cash envelope show. "Listen," he said quietly. "Eighty-nine hundred. Eighty-five for the truck, four hundred cash for you, right now. Quick title transfer, minimal paperwork".

The salesman glanced nervously towards the main showroom windows, then back at the cash peeking from the envelope. He hesitated, licked his lips, then gave a jerky nod. "Okay. Yeah, alright. This way".

They followed him into a small back office. The deal concluded swiftly, the paperwork sparse. Minutes later, they stood beside the F-150 as the salesman hurried off to fetch the keys. Just then, Brad Ewing emerged from the showroom, shouting instructions at an employee.

Devin and Manny angled towards him. Brad stopped mid-sentence, his confident stride faltering as he saw them. He quickly pasted on a strained smile.

"Jones! Rivera! Didn't expect to see you here!". Brad attempted casualness.

"Buying a truck, Brad," Devin replied evenly, gesturing towards the F-150. "This one".

Brad's smile tightened. "Oh. Good choice. Anything else?".

Manny stepped slightly closer. "Funny you ask. EAG's always exploring... local opportunities. Maybe you and I could chat sometime? Discuss mutual interests?".

Brad shifted, visibly uncomfortable. "Uh, maybe. Bit busy now".

"By the way," Devin added nonchalantly, meeting Brad's eyes directly, "Sal Demarco mentioned you. Said you run a tight ship here".

Brad froze. His eyes widened almost imperceptibly, color draining slightly from his face before he hastily masked it with forced indifference.

"Sal? Oh... yeah. Know the name," he stammered slightly. "Good... good he sent you".

"We'll be in touch about that chat," Devin said, allowing a small, knowing smile, watching Brad's barely concealed panic with grim satisfaction. He turned back towards the truck.

The salesperson scurried out, keys and signed title in hand. "All set!". Devin took them with a curt nod. They climbed into the F-150, started the engine, and pulled out onto Blakeslee Boulevard, leaving Brad standing frozen on the asphalt, watching them go.

Brad watched the F-150 merge into traffic, his heart hammering against his ribs. Jones knew about Sal. How? How the hell? Had Sal slipped up? Seen together? Did the boss know Jones was asking? Cold panic seized him. This could destroy everything.

He spun away from the lot, storming back towards his office, ignoring the greetings from his staff. He slammed the door shut, the click loud in the sudden quiet. His hands trembled as he snatched the phone, punching in Sal's number from memory.

"Yeah? What?" Sal answered, his voice rough with irritation.

"Sal! It's Brad!" Panic made his voice tight, high-pitched. "Jones! He was just here! Him and Rivera!".

"So?".

"He mentioned you, Sal!" Brad nearly shouted. "Asked about you! Said you recommended this place! How the hell does he know?! Does the boss know they're asking?".

A beat of charged silence, then Sal swore violently. "Calm down, idiot! They're fishing! Trying to rattle your cage! Did you bite? Say anything stupid?".

"No! I... I just said I knew the name! Said I was busy!".

"Good," Sal snapped, though Brad heard the tension simmering beneath the command. "Listen. Lay low. Act normal. Talk to no one. I'll handle Jones. Just make damn sure nothing traces back. Nothing. Got it?".

Brad swallowed hard against the knot of fear tightening his throat. "Yeah. Got it".

"Don't screw this up, Brad," Sal's voice dropped, low and menacing, before the line clicked dead.

Brad stood shaking, the silence in the office deafening. Lay low. He couldn't stay here. Not with Jones knowing about Sal. Too close. He needed to vanish for a few days. Let Sal handle it. He wrenched his office door open. "Megan!".

His assistant appeared, concern on her face. "Yes, Mr. Ewing?".

"Cancel my appointments!" he snapped, grabbing his keys and phone from the desk. "Everything! I'm unreachable for a few days. Handle it! Don't tell anyone where I am!". Ignoring her startled expression, he bolted through the showroom, out to the parking lot, jumped into his Mercedes, and peeled out, heading for the illusory safety of home.

# Chapter 7

# Fractured Facade

The Ford F-150 swung onto Mahoning Street, the commercial strip shrinking in the rearview mirror. Devin's knuckles shone white against the steering wheel; Ricky Malone's confession—Sal Demarco, arson-for-hire, the partner fitting Brad's build—churned like acid in his gut. He needed confirmation. He needed leverage. Kaitlyn. She was the pressure point.

Number 510 Mahoning came into view – a sprawling ranch house presiding over a lawn so perfect it looked artificial. The image of suburban prosperity struck Devin as hollow, brittle. He killed the engine in the wide driveway, the sudden silence amplifying the weight in the cab. Manny shifted beside him, his gaze already sweeping the street, the house, the adjacent properties. "I'll hang back here. Keep eyes open."

Devin gave a curt nod. "Shouldn't be long." The solid thud of the truck door seemed overly loud as he closed it. He walked the path, the brass door knocker gleaming under the afternoon sun. He took a shallow breath, smoothing his expression into one of casual concern, a mask hiding the calculated intent beneath, and pressed the bell.

The door opened almost instantly. Kaitlyn. Framed in the doorway, her vibrant blonde hair haloed by the light. Surprise widened her brown eyes, quickly replaced by something warmer – excitement? "Devin?" Disbelief colored her tone. "What are you doing here?"

He offered a tight smile, shoving down the memory of her clinging embrace at his mother's house. "Hey, Kaitlyn," he kept his voice even, deliberately casual. "Was just driving... needed to clear my head after... everything." He made a vague gesture. "Saw I was nearby. Thought I'd see how you were holding up. You seemed... stressed, when you stopped by Mom's the other day."

A faint blush rose on her cheeks. "Oh. That's... thoughtful, Devin." Her eyes darted nervously back into the house, a flicker of uncertainty crossing her features before she seemed to make a decision. She stepped aside. "Please, come in."

He crossed the threshold. The air inside was cool, scented faintly with vanilla. The click of the closing door felt soft, final. Polished marble stretched underfoot, expensive art adorned the walls, and sunlight refracted through a crystal chandelier overhead. The sheer display of wealth felt jarring after the lived-in warmth of his parents' home.

"It's... quite the place," Devin commented, his gaze sweeping the foyer, intentionally letting the contrast hang in the air.

Kaitlyn offered a small, dismissive shrug, her hand smoothing down her expensive-looking silk blouse. "It's just a house." Her smile didn't reach her eyes. "Come on through to the living room. Coffee?"

"Coffee sounds great, thanks." He followed her through the grand foyer into an equally impressive living room, dominated by large windows and plush, unwelcoming furniture.

"Make yourself comfortable," she gestured towards a leather sofa, then disappeared towards the kitchen.

Devin remained standing, drawn to the mantelpiece. Perfectly arranged photos stared back – Kaitlyn and Brad smiling on some tropical beach, Kaitlyn and Brad polished and posed at a gala. He let his fingers trail near a small, carved wooden box on a side table, a deliberate slowness to the motion.

Kaitlyn returned with two mugs. "Careful, hot." She handed him one.

"That box? My grandmother's. Antique."

"It's beautiful," he murmured, setting it down carefully. His gaze intentionally snagged on the gala photo again. "You two looked happy then."

A shadow flickered across Kaitlyn's face. She sank onto the edge of an armchair, opposite the sofa where Devin now sat, her eyes fixed on the steam rising from her mug. "We were," she admitted softly. "A long time ago."

He leaned forward slightly, pitching his voice lower, shifting from observation to probing. "Listen, Kaitlyn... I know the timing is awful, but when Brad visited Mom, he mentioned dealing with 'difficult people'. He seemed... tense. More than usual?"

Kaitlyn stiffened almost imperceptibly, her fingers tightening on the mug handle. She looked away towards the large windows. "Brad's always under pressure, Devin. The business... it's demanding." Her tone was defensive, brittle. "Why do you ask?"

Devin held her gaze, keeping his own expression soft, concerned. "Because I saw you, Kat." He used the old nickname deliberately, softly. "At Mom's. You looked scared. It reminded me..." He let the sentence hang, implying a shared past, a shared understanding, letting her fill the blank. "Is he okay? Is he scared?"

She stood abruptly, turning her back to him, walking towards the mantelpiece, running a finger over one of the picture frames. "Brad doesn't get scared. He handles things." Her voice was tight, rejecting the premise, but her posture radiated tension.

Devin rose slowly and approached her, stopping a few feet away. He kept his voice low, intimate. "He's been different though, hasn't he? You can tell me." He risked placing a light hand on her arm. "If he's in some kind of trouble... if you're worried..."

Kaitlyn flinched slightly at his touch but didn't pull away immediately. She remained facing the photos, her shoulders slumping slightly. After a long moment, she spoke, her voice barely a whisper. "He's... different," she conceded, the resistance crumbling under the weight of her own fear and perhaps the memory his presence evoked. "Secretive. Late nights.

Whispers on the phone, steps out of the room to take calls." She finally turned, looking up, meeting his eyes, a silent plea for understanding – or maybe help – reflecting in their depths. "Sometimes... the look on his face... it's not just stress, Devin. It's... raw fear. Like he's seen a ghost."

"Fear?" Devin kept his tone gentle, but the probe was insistent. "Of what? Business trouble? Or is it someone?"

She hesitated, her thumb worrying the delicate silver chain at her neck. "I... I don't know for sure," she whispered, glancing towards the hallway as if expecting Brad to appear. She leaned closer conspiratorially. "But there's this man... Sal Demarco. He's been around more lately. Gives me the creeps." Her voice dropped further. "And whenever Brad talks to him, or even just gets a call from a blocked number... he gets that look. That terrified look."

Sal Demarco. Bingo. Devin kept his expression impassive, a mask of thoughtful concern, though his pulse hammered against his ribs. Kaitlyn confirmed the link, unprompted. "Demarco," he repeated, feigning unfamiliarity. "Doesn't ring a bell." He watched her reaction closely – the relief that he didn't know the name, quickly followed by renewed anxiety. "Look, Kaitlyn," he pressed gently, focusing the danger back on her, "if Brad's involved with people who scare him like that... people like this Demarco... that could put you in danger too."

Tears welled instantly in her eyes, his feigned concern hitting its mark. "Please, Devin," she interrupted, her voice trembling now, reaching out instinctively, grabbing his forearm. "Just... promise me you'll be careful. Whatever you're doing, whatever you're looking into... please be careful."

He covered her hand briefly with his own, the touch lingering a moment longer than necessary. "I promise, Kaitlyn. Always careful." He squeezed gently, letting the reassurance mingle with the subtle confirmation he'd gotten what he needed. "And thank you. For trusting me." He released her hand and rose from the sofa. "I should probably get going. Let you get back to your day."

She nodded, wiping hastily at her eyes. "Thanks for stopping by, Dev. It... it was good to see you."

He offered another tight smile and walked back through the foyer, letting himself out into the afternoon sun. The click of the closing door echoed behind him. He strode quickly back to the truck, his mind racing. Sal Demarco. Brad's terrified of him. The connection was solid. It wasn't proof Brad ordered the fire or killed his father, but the net tightened significantly.

He climbed back into the F-150. "Let's roll," he said curtly to Manny. Devin put the truck in gear, the engine rumbling. As he pulled away from the curb, a sleek black Mercedes E-Class turned onto Mahoning Street from the main road.

"Speak of the devil," Manny muttered, eyes fixed on the rearview mirror.

Brad didn't slow as the Mercedes passed the F-150, but Devin caught the sharp turn of his head. Instead of pulling into his own driveway, Brad continued past, stopping at the curb several houses down, waiting, watching until the truck turned the corner. Only then did he pull into his drive.

He killed the engine and sat, gripping the wheel, forcing deep breaths against the sudden tightness in his chest before heading inside, the heavy front door locking firmly behind him. He checked the street through the sidelight window, confirming it was empty before turning inward.

"Kaitlyn!" His voice, sharp with anxiety he couldn't fully mask, echoed in the foyer.

She appeared from the kitchen doorway, towel in hand, her expression unreadable. "Brad. You're back early. Something wrong?"

His eyes narrowed, sweeping the foyer before locking onto her. "Don't play games, Kaitlyn. Whose truck was that? Looked like Jones."

She met his gaze, her chin lifting slightly. "It was. Dev stopped by."

"Stopped by?" He stalked towards her, his voice rising. "Why? What did he want? What did you tell him?"

"He was checking on me," Kaitlyn stated, refusing to shrink back. "He said I looked stressed the other day at Annabelle's. He didn't ask about you. He didn't ask about anything specific."

"And I'm supposed to believe that?" Brad scoffed, invading her space. "After everything? You always had a weakness for that loser! What are you doing, trying to undermine everything I've built for us? Running back to him now that things are... difficult?"

Fire flashed in Kaitlyn's eyes, fear momentarily replaced by defiance. "Undermine you? Brad, that's ridiculous! And leave Dev out of this! Remember Moya? Remember how we started? You were charming then. You cared about me, my painting, my life!"

"And I gave you this life!" Brad gestured, not wildly, but encompassing the opulent foyer, the implied security. "This house! The travel, the parties! Don't you think that takes work? Sacrifices? Don't you think keeping all this safe requires things you wouldn't understand?"

"I loved you!" Kaitlyn cried, her voice cracking. "I thought we were building something real! Like you promised that first night, watching your business grow! But it became your business, your success! When was the last time you asked about my work? Or saw me as anything more than an accessory for your galas?" She mimicked his public tone, bitterness sharpening her words, "'Isn't she stunning?' Like I'm just another acquisition!"

"I built this for you!" Brad roared, face flushing. "So you'd be safe! So you'd have everything! And you benefited!"

"Benefited?" Kaitlyn laughed, a harsh, broken sound. "By being ignored? By watching you whisper on the phone late at night and sneak out? Refusing to tell me where you're going?" Her voice dropped, anger morphing into weary accusation. "Is that part of keeping me safe, Brad?

When you come back looking like you've seen a ghost? Is that when you see Sal Demarco? Is that who has you jumping at shadows?"

Brad froze, Sal's name striking him like ice water. Suspicion hardened his eyes. "You told Jones about Sal?" he whispered, the menace unmistakable.

"No!" Kaitlyn shot back. "He didn't ask! But I see the look on your face when that name comes up! You're terrified of him, aren't you? What have you dragged us into? What danger are you protecting me from by dealing with people like that?"

"Stay out of it, Kaitlyn!" Brad snarled, deflecting, his voice tight with a fear he couldn't hide. "My business is protecting you! Protecting this! You knowing things... it puts you in danger! Can't you see that? Everything I do... every late night, every call I have to take outside... it's to keep this whole damn thing from collapsing! To keep you safe!" He jabbed a finger towards her. "I swear, if you said anything..."

"I haven't said anything because I don't know anything!" Kaitlyn yelled, frustration finally spilling over in tears. "Because you shut me out! Always! You demand trust?" She shook her head, disillusionment washing over her features. "How? When you treat me like this?"

Brad glared, his mind racing, panic clawing at him again. She didn't understand. Couldn't understand the risks, the necessity of what he did to maintain this life, their life. He couldn't handle this, not now. He needed to think, call Sal, figure out how Dev knew. He spun away, storming towards the back hallway leading to his office. The heavy door slammed shut moments later, the sound echoing through the house.

Kaitlyn stood alone in the cavernous foyer, trembling slightly, the argument reverberating off the cold marble. The beautiful life she thought she had felt like fractured glass around her feet. She took a shaky breath and walked slowly towards the kitchen, desperate for something to numb the ache. From the wine fridge, she pulled a bottle of expensive Cabernet, pouring a generous glass, the deep red liquid swirling as her hand shook. Sinking onto a barstool at the island, she took a long, desperate gulp, closing her eyes, seeking refuge in the wine's deceptive warmth.

Behind the slammed office door, the house sounds vanished, but the frantic thrumming in Brad's chest didn't quiet. Dev knew about Sal. How? He scanned the room – the unlocked window, the files piled on the desk, the computer humming innocently. Each felt like a potential indictment. Evidence. It had to disappear. Now.

His hands shook as he wrenched open file drawers, grabbing handfuls of folders without looking – invoices, agreements, old letters. He shoved them into the heavy-duty shredder, the machine's whine a frantic counterpoint to his own ragged breathing. He kept glancing over his shoulder, imagining footsteps in the hall.

Too slow. He grabbed another stack, dumping it into the metal waste bin. A struck match flared, dropped onto the papers. Flames leaped, greedy, consuming the documents, the sharp, chemical smell stinging his nostrils.

He spun to the computer, fingers clumsy on the keyboard. Click-click-click. Delete. Delete. Empty recycle bin. Secure erase? Too slow. He ripped the tower out, tearing cables free, and flung it against the far wall. Plastic cracked, components scattered. Enough? What else? What had he missed?

He scrubbed at his temples, a dull ache pulsing behind his eyes. His breath came in short, shallow gasps. His mind replayed the confrontation – Dev's face, the mention of Sal, Kaitlyn's accusing stare. He slid down the wall, landing hard on the floor, back against the oversized bookshelf filled with pristine, unread hardbacks. He pulled his knees to his chest amidst the scattered papers and the smoldering ashes in the bin.

Why Dev? Why now? Why was he always there, a shadow, digging, questioning? Why did Kaitlyn still look at him that way? Where did this venom, this rivalry that felt etched into his bones, truly begin? He squeezed his eyes shut, the memory clawing its way forward, unbidden...

*The biting autumn air under the Friday night lights, electric, thick with the roar of the state championship crowd. A gutting loss, 24-21. And Devin Jones, a damn sophomore, bathed in the spotlight, praised despite the defeat. 2700 yards, 23 touchdowns on the season – the numbers echoing, erasing the defensive stops, the punishing hits Brad had delivered all season.*

*Weeks later, the suffocating heat of the Drexelbrook ballroom. The polite applause, a physical blow as they announced Devin Jones, winner of the Jim Henry Award. Brad watched from the crowd – Devin, impossibly young in* a cheap suit, accepting the trophy. Beside him, Mayor John Jones, the town's golden boy, the man who seemed to control everything, even, Brad was sure, the award committee, beamed with pride. First-team all-defense, Mini Max winner – accolades turned to ash. Dev got the one that mattered. The injustice burned, a hot coal in his gut.

Back home, it was inescapable. Jones this, Jones that. Whispers over coffee cups, praise bleeding from the local radio. The resentment simmered, festered, grew toxic. Social media became his weapon. Stat-padding. Weak schedule. System QB. Daddy's boy. He typed the accusations, fingers hammering the keys, pouring bitterness into pixels that spread like wildfire. "Wouldn't make varsity if his daddy wasn't coach."

The poison took root. Other resentful players, bored locals, faceless trolls – they amplified it. Dev's name became tangled with controversy. Even ESPN debated the award, casting a shadow not just on Devin, but on the Mayor's reputation. Brad saw the weariness creep into the Mayor's eyes, heard the frustrated whispers. "Tarnished because of some jealous teenager," John Jones had supposedly grumbled. The feedback loop fueled Brad's righteous anger. He saw Dev too – saw the confidence flicker behind the forced smiles, saw the joy drain from his game. Good.

The next year, Dev played like a man possessed. Every pass seemed perfect, every run relentless. He shattered state records, leading Jim Thorpe through an undefeated season. Brad, meanwhile, captained Lehighton, putting up monstrous defensive numbers, carrying his own team with grit and fury, determined to finally eclipse his rival. The hype built all season towards *their inevitable clash. But in the championship game, under the cold November lights, Dev was untouchable. Jim Thorpe dominated, 35-14. Brad could only watch helplessly from the field as Dev carved up his defense, the cheers for his rival echoing like mocking laughter in his helmet. The second Jim Henry Award ceremony felt like a cruel repeat. Brad, despite another stellar All-State season, sat in the audience again as Dev accepted the trophy, the applause deafening this time, his rival's redemption arc complete in everyone's eyes but Brad's. The rivalry wasn't just about football anymore; it was embedded deep, a bitter constant.*

Brad opened his eyes, the bitter taste of the memory coating his tongue. Huddled on the office floor, surrounded by the chaotic evidence of his panic, the old resentment felt thin against a new, sharper fear. He'd let that bitterness steer him for years, down paths he couldn't retrace, into deals... deals with consequences. A fleeting thought of amends, of fixing things, flickered and died. Too late. Far too late. Too many players involved now wouldn't tolerate loose ends. There was no going back. Survival was the only move left.

The sudden, shrill ring of the desk phone tore through Brad's chaotic thoughts, making him jump. The caller ID flashed: Sal. Brad snatched the receiver, his voice unsteady. "Sal?"

"Brad, listen," Sal's voice was urgent, clipped. "Boss wants a meet. Tonight. Nine."

Brad's stomach lurched. "Tonight? Where?"

"R & C Knitting Mill." Sal spat the name out. "Don't be late."

The mill. A rotting monument on the edge of Lehighton, bricks crumbling, windows like vacant eyes choked with weeds. Brad had never met the boss face-to-face, only dealt through Sal or the unnervingly composed Akimitsu. This desolate location, this abrupt summons... a knot of dread tightened in his gut. "Why there, Sal?" He tried to keep the tremor from his voice.

"Don't know, don't care," Sal snapped. "Just be there. Ready." The line clicked dead. Brad stood frozen, the receiver still pressed to his ear. The shadows in his ravaged office seemed to deepen, whispering warnings. Tonight, the architect of this whole mess would finally reveal himself. He poured a heavy measure of whiskey, downing it in one burning gulp that did little to steady his shaking hands. Ignoring Kaitlyn's tentative knock on the office door, he grabbed his keys and fled, climbing into the Mercedes, the impending meeting a physical weight pressing down. The familiar downtown streets blurred past, alien now under the grim significance of his destination. The hulking brick structure of the mill rose before him, a silhouette against the fading light.

He parked, heart pounding against his ribs, and waited. Moments later, Sal's car pulled up. Sal emerged, his usual swagger replaced by a visible tension. "Ready?" he asked, his eyes scanning the decaying facade. Brad forced a smirk. "Always," he lied, tilting his head back to take in the dilapidated structure. "Charming."

"Thinks it'll spook us," Sal muttered, jaw tight. "We show him we handle business. Regardless."

"Together," Brad echoed, trying to borrow some of Sal's strained resolve.

They approached the entrance. The heavy doors groaned open, releasing a thick stench of rot and decay. Inside, the vast space swallowed sound, their footsteps echoing unnervingly.

Three men materialized from the gloom, apparitions in tailored suits that seemed violently out of place amidst the decay. Their faces were hard, impassive. The lead man, tall with chillingly empty eyes, simply said, "Follow us."

Brad exchanged a nervous glance with Sal, then they followed, navigating decaying halls, the silence broken only by the creak of warped floorboards and the distant scuttling of unseen vermin. "Definitely knows how to set a mood," Sal whispered, the bravado thin.

"Just get this over with," Brad hissed back.

The lead man glanced back, his expression unchanging. "The boss expects punctuality. Keep up."

They reached a large, open space. A single industrial bulb, high overhead, flickered weakly, casting more shadows than light. At the far end, a figure sat behind a makeshift table, obscured by the gloom.

One of the suited men stepped forward, gesturing. "Right this way..."

Crack!

The gunshot was deafening, ripping through the cavernous space, echoing off the high ceiling. The gesturing man crumpled instantly, a crimson mist blooming where his head had been, spattering Brad and Sal. Brad recoiled, reflexively wiping gore from his face, his mind screaming. "He moved without instruction," the voice from the shadows stated, cold and measured. The figure remained seated. The other two guards stood impassive, seemingly unfazed by their colleague's execution. "Precision is paramount. Sloppiness," the voice indicated the body with a subtle gesture, "will not be tolerated."

Sal swallowed hard, finding his voice, though it trembled. "Understood. No... imprecision."

The figure leaned forward slightly. The weak light caught piercing blue eyes and a pale, scarred cheek – Viktor Mikhailov. "Good," he said, his faint accent coating the word with ice. "Now... let's discuss complications."

His gaze locked onto Brad. "And you, Brad. Your... personal distractions? Your continued, reckless fixation on Jones?" Viktor's voice was dangerously soft. "It complicates matters. Draws attention we cannot afford. It forces me," steel entered his tone, "to adjust timelines. To accelerate... contingencies. Your feud jeopardizes far more than you comprehend."

He let the veiled threat settle before shifting focus, his voice regaining its cold edge. "Then there is the Russian shipment. You paid. It has not arrived. Explain."

Brad's heart hammered. "I... I don't know, Sir. The deal was clear. They confirmed..."

Sal stepped forward slightly. "It wasn't just him, Sir. We handled it together. The Russians..."

Crack!

Sal screamed, collapsing as the bullet tore through his leg, blood instantly darkening the grimy concrete. Brad stared, frozen in horror.

Viktor watched Sal writhe for a moment, his expression unreadable, before turning his cold gaze back to Brad. "Do you understand failure, Brad? Do you grasp the consequences?" He paused, letting the terror saturate the air. "I built this organization," his voice dropped, almost conversational, yet charged with menace, "from the ashes of betrayal. I forged alliances across continents – the Vultures in Africa, the Sakura Syndicate in Asia, the Iron Syndicate, the Vero Alliance. Each piece meticulously placed. Each demands absolute loyalty, flawless execution." His eyes bored into Brad. "Your failure with this shipment, compounded by your juvenile games with Jones, threatens that structure. It invites weakness. And weakness," he gestured towards Sal, "is purged."

"Consider this your final warning," Viktor's voice turned to ice. "Recover that shipment. Seventy-two hours. Succeed, or the next bullet finds a more permanent home."

Brad nodded frantically, terror stripping away any semblance of composure. "Yes, Sir. We'll fix it. Seventy-two hours. We'll get it."

Viktor leaned back, melting into the shadows. "Good. Go."

The two remaining guards stepped forward, hauling the bleeding, groaning Sal upright. Brad scrambled to help, his own legs unsteady, as they were guided back through the decaying mill. The weight of the encounter, the casual brutality, Viktor's chilling words – it crushed Brad. Failure wasn't survivable.

He helped Sal into the passenger seat of the Mercedes, the sharp smell of blood filling the enclosed space. Starting the engine, he peeled away from the mill, the image of the executed guard and Sal's agony seared into his mind. Their lives dangled by Viktor's whim.

The tension in the car was a physical presence. Sal clutched his leg, face pale, teeth gritted. Brad gripped the steering wheel, knuckles white.

"Fix it... how?" Brad finally choked out. "How do we make the Russians deliver?"

Sal inhaled sharply. "Find out what went wrong," he gasped. "Contact Cape Town. Pressure. No more games."

"Years we dealt with them!" Brad spat, frustration briefly overriding fear. "Now this? We're dead if we don't deliver!"

His mind raced. "You're right. But... why focus on Jones? Why bring him up instead of the guns?"

Sal frowned, shifting painfully. "Good question. He knows something. Testing our loyalty? Seeing if we'd use Jones against him? Or maybe," his eyes darkened, "Jones is part of his endgame, and our feud is just... static he wants gone."

"Doesn't feel right," Brad muttered. He glanced at Sal. "The fire at the Jones house... sure that wasn't you? Sending a message?"

Sal glared, anger flaring through the pain. "I thought it was you! Trying to impress the boss?!"

Brad slammed a hand on the wheel. "Me? Are you crazy?!"

Sal let out a harsh, pained laugh. "Great. So who the hell torched the place?"

"Rivals? Cops? Someone else?" Brad listed frantically. "We gotta find out. Fast. No more surprises."

"Agreed," Sal gritted out. "First, this leg. Get me somewhere safe. Need to patch this up. Can't think straight."

Brad nodded, shoving down his own panic, focusing on the immediate crisis. "Hang on, Sal. We get through this." He pressed the accelerator, the car swallowing the dark miles, the weight of Viktor's threats and the unanswered questions pressing down, heavy and suffocating.

# Chapter 8

# The Storm Breaks

Devin's eyes snapped open. *Fall back! Fall back!* The command echoed not in the quiet Pennsylvania woods but in the dust-choked memory of an Afghan gorge. The phantom smell of cordite, sharp and acrid, clung for a moment before dissolving into the scent of pine and distant coffee. He pushed himself up, shaking his head, trying to dislodge the nightmare's residue. Another night, another replay of failure.

Downstairs, morning sun streamed through the large windows of the log cabin. Annabelle and Rach had arrived the previous night, the EAG team dispatched by Sarah close behind. The place felt like a refuge, sturdy logs holding back the tranquil Pocono dawn, yet the tension inside was a palpable thing. Manny was already up, nursing coffee by the large wooden table in the main living area. Annabelle and Rach sat on the sofa, worry drawn tight on their faces.

The security team—Kate, Thomas, and Frank—stood near the fireplace, alert, posture stiff. Frank shifted his weight almost imperceptibly, a flicker of something other than the current tension in his eyes.

"He almost had that touchdown, Tom," Frank rumbled, his voice a low counterpoint to the crackling fire. "Third quarter, red zone. Kid's got an arm, just needs to trust his line more."

Thomas permitted himself a slight smirk, not looking away from the main door. "Good thing he doesn't throw like his old man then, Franky. We'd be five-and-oh in the loss column."

Kate's lips twitched, but her gaze remained fixed on the window, sweeping the tree line. Even a moment of levity didn't dull their readiness.

Earl Jenkins, the analyst Sarah sent, perched anxiously in an armchair, laptop already open. Dev leaned against the table, the solid wood a grounding anchor. He scanned the room: his mother's lingering grief, Rach's concern overlaid with a reporter's intensity, Manny's weary readiness, the sharp focus of the EAG team. Kate Richards, their Head of Security, stood slightly apart, her efficient posture and keen green eyes radiating competence. No one here knows the storm she represents, Dev thought. Not yet.

"Alright, listen up," Dev began, his voice cutting through the stillness, overriding his own fatigue. "Manny and I have some intel from yesterday. It clarifies some things, muddies others."

Manny nodded, stepping forward. "Our source confirmed he was hired for an arson near Beltzville Lake about three weeks back. Swore he didn't touch Mom's house, though." He paused. "The contractor? Sal Demarco."

A ripple went through the EAG team. Familiar name.

"Demarco wasn't alone," Manny continued. "Source described a partner – big guy, expensive clothes, kept quiet. Fits Brad Ewing."

Rach added, "We saw Brad yesterday, meeting three men—looked like hired muscle, not locals. An envelope changed hands."

Dev picked up the thread. "And Kaitlyn confirmed Brad's been seeing Demarco frequently. Said Brad seems scared of him." He looked back at the group. "We also confronted Brad at his dealership. Mentioned Sal's name."

Manny smirked grimly. "He nearly swallowed his tongue. Definitely hit a nerve."

Kate stepped forward, crisp, professional. "So, Demarco and Ewing are linked. A potential arson connection, but not definitively to Mrs. Jones' house. We need more." Her gaze was sharp. "Next move?"

Dev nodded. "Agreed. Intel is priority. Earl," he turned to the analyst, "start with recent fires. Carbon and surrounding counties, last month. Residential, commercial. Cross-reference ownership, insurance payouts."

Rach leaned forward. "Let me work with Earl. I can pull public records, business licenses, LLCs tied to Brad or known Demarco fronts. See if anything connects."

"Good," Dev approved. "Coordinate. Earl, also run deep digital background – comms, financials, link analysis—Brad, Sal, any known associates."

He looked at Thomas and Frank. "Chief Miller wants EAG out of the Sheriff's investigation," Dev stated, the frustration evident in his tight voice. "So, no direct contact. Focus on background. Use EAG resources: pull everything on Davis, the investigating officers on Dad's case and the arson. Procedures, past cases, associates – learn how they operate, find blind spots. Monitor local channels, scanners, any public chatter on their progress with Brad and Sal. We need their intel, even if they won't share."

Thomas nodded. "Understood. Indirect approach. We'll work their flank."

Dev then turned to Kate, meeting her steady gaze. "Kate, contact HQ. See if Sarah can arrange discreet surveillance on Ewing Automotive and any properties linked to Brad or Sal. Need eyes on them."

Kate nodded once, already reaching for her secure phone. "Consider it done. Additional personnel request?"

"Yes," Dev confirmed as she moved away. "Three more three-man teams, fully kitted, ASAP."

Annabelle stood, managing a faint smile that didn't mask her weariness. "While you all strategize, I'll make breakfast. You need fuel."

"I can help!" Rach volunteered quickly, rising. "Let me give Mrs. J a hand, then Earl, let me know when you have that fire list, and we can dive into the records."

Dev watched them head to the kitchen, then turned back to Manny. "Alright. Perimeter check. Let's make sure this refuge is actually secure."

He clapped Manny on the shoulder. "Stay sharp. Feels like this is escalating."

As the others dispersed to their tasks, the cabin humming with low, urgent activity, Dev and Manny grabbed jackets and stepped onto the wraparound deck. The crisp morning air felt clean, almost mocking the complexity of their situation. They walked down the steps into the clearing, stopping near the treeline. The dense woods offered cover, but also concealment for threats.

"Debrief went smoother than I expected," Manny said, hands shoved deep in his pockets, eyes scanning the trees opposite, towards the unseen lake. "Thought Rach might balk at us running parallel intel."

Dev leaned against a thick pine, body seemingly relaxed but eyes sharp. "She gets it," he replied, voice low. "Davis is dragging his feet. We need answers now. Total coverage." He glanced back at the cabin, warm light spilling faintly into the dawn. "And Mom... she's holding strong. Helps everyone's pulling together."

Manny nodded, gaze sweeping the clearing again. "Yeah. Solid." A faint smile touched his lips. "Like when she busted us sneaking off to the creek? Grounded us for a week, never told your dad."

A brief grin flickered across Dev's face. "Best OpSec failure ever." The smile evaporated. His gaze drifted back to the cabin windows, his hand instinctively hovering near the sidearm beneath his jacket. "Still... need to confirm this place is secure. Perimeter check. Now."

"Roger that." Manny clapped him briefly on the shoulder, his own gaze returning to the woods. "Let's move."

They started parallel to the treeline, heading towards the rear of the property. Nearing the edge of the wide clearing behind the house, a sudden, sharp rustling deep within the woods across the open space snapped their heads around. Dark shapes exploded from the tree cover, moving fast against the forest backdrop near the lake path.

"Contact!" Dev yelled, shoving Manny hard towards the nearest thick oak as the first flat crack of unsuppressed rifle fire split the air. Leaves shredded overhead; rounds thudded solidly into tree trunks beside them. They scrambled behind cover, hearts hammering. Dev risked a look.

"Seven, maybe eight!" he hissed, tracking figures advancing across the open ground, firing as they moved. "Damn it! Exposed! Move!"

They broke cover, sprinting low, weaving between scattered trees and thick rhododendron. Gunfire chewed the ground where they'd been. Bark splintered nearby.

"Pros!" Manny yelled, dropping behind a boulder, swapping magazines with lightning speed. "Timed ambush! Need to flank!"

Dev nodded, adrenaline a sharp sting. "Split! Right flank, follow me!"

Dev cut right, plunging into denser woods. Manny veered left, using the initial treeline for cover, aiming to get behind the attackers. The woods swallowed them. Dev moved fast, weaving through ferns, breath misting. He spotted an attacker who had pushed forward, scanning the cabin.

Closing silently, Dev brought his pistol butt down hard against the man's temple. The attacker crumpled without a sound.

Across the clearing, Manny neutralized another with swift, practiced brutality. They were momentarily behind the main advance. They opened fire, dropping one more, but the remaining five pressed relentlessly towards the cabin deck, undeterred.

Dev met Manny's eyes across the contested ground. The message was clear: House. They needed hard cover. Laying down bursts to keep heads down, they began a fighting withdrawal towards the rear deck.

"Go! Go! Go!" Dev shouted, laying down sustained fire as Manny bolted across the last open stretch towards the back door. Manny reached it, spun, and returned fire, covering Dev's sprint. Dev zigzagged, dirt kicking up at his heels. One last burst towards the attackers—one stumbled—then Dev launched himself through the door Manny held.

"Inside! Now!" Dev slammed the door shut just as bullets hammered into the heavy wood.

The first sharp cracks of gunfire from outside plunged the cabin's tense quiet into chaos. Kate reacted instantly, weapon materializing in her hand. "Contact rear! Everyone down, cover!" she commanded, her voice a sharp anchor in the sudden panic.

Annabelle and Rach dove behind the heavy oak dining table. Earl scrambled behind the massive stone fireplace, laptop case clutched tight. Thomas and Frank, nearer the back, moved tactically—Frank reinforcing the door, Thomas kneeling near the master suite windows overlooking the deck, sidearm tracking movement.

"Stay low! Report!" Kate ordered, positioning herself to cover the dining area and living room entrance, her focus absolute. Bullets impacted the rear logs with terrifying force, splintering wood, shattering upper windows.

The back door flew open. Dev and Manny tumbled inside, weapons up, chests heaving. "Door!" Dev yelled.

"Took out three, maybe four!" Manny reported, moving cautiously towards the windows beside the door. "Rest are pushing!"

As he spoke, a sustained burst ripped through the back door. Frank cried out, stumbling back, clutching his abdomen, collapsing behind the table, shirt instantly blooming red. Simultaneously, a round shattered the window near Thomas, ricocheting. Thomas grunted, grabbing his shoulder, but kept his weapon aimed out.

"Man down!" Kate yelled, eyes flicking from Frank to Thomas. "Frank's hit bad! Thomas?"

"Hit! Shoulder! Still in it!" Thomas gritted, firing twice at movement outside.

Manny was already beside Frank. "Hang on, Frank! Stay with me!" he urged, pressing hard on the wound.

Gunfire outside intensified. Figures moved onto the deck. "They're at the door!" Kate yelled. "Barricade! Annabelle! Rach! Help me with the table!"

Adrenaline propelled them. Annabelle and Rach shoved the heavy oak table against the bullet-riddled door as Kate, Dev, and the injured Thomas laid covering fire. The table shuddered as attackers slammed against it from outside.

"Hold them!" Dev shouted, reloading.

An attacker smashed a large dining room window near the barricaded door. Kate spun, a controlled burst dropping him before he could enter. Another slammed the back door again; Manny kicked it open outwards into the charging attacker, tackling him onto the deck. A brief, brutal struggle—an elbow connected sharply—the attacker went limp.

A third tried a bedroom window further down. Dev sprinted, intercepting the figure climbing through, slamming him hard against the interior wall. Silenced.

Thomas, pain radiating from his shoulder, saw movement at the master suite's sliding glass door. He swiveled, fired twice. The figure outside stumbled, hit, then dropped as Thomas fired again.

The last attacker, seeing the breach fail, turned, fleeing towards the woods. Earl, peering from behind the fireplace, took a steadying breath, raised the pistol Kate likely armed him with, and fired. The shot hit the fleeing figure in the back. He collapsed at the edge of the clearing.

Silence crashed down, abrupt and deafening, broken only by Frank's shallow gasps, Manny's low reassurances, and the frantic pounding of their own hearts against their ribs.

The sudden silence was thick with the smell of spent cordite, splintered wood, and the metallic tang of blood. Adrenaline hummed, leaving hands shaking, ears ringing.

Kate moved first, weapon sweeping, expression unreadable. "Status?" she clipped out, eyes assessing the wounded.

Manny knelt beside Frank, pressing makeshift bandages against the bleed. "Bad," he grunted, glancing up, face streaked with grime. "Needs a surgeon. Now."

Thomas leaned heavily against the master suite doorframe, face pale, hand clamped over his bleeding shoulder. "Good to move," he stated through clenched teeth, "but need this packed."

Annabelle, chalk-white but steady, scrambled out from behind the table with Rach. "We have to get them help!" she urged, looking straight at Dev.

Dev surveyed the aftermath – Frank critical, Thomas wounded, bullet holes scarring the log walls, bodies sprawled outside. His jaw tightened. Calling 911 wasn't an option. Miller's suspicion, the inevitable questions... an official report would detonate their already precarious situation.

"No," Dev stated, his voice cutting through the ringing silence. "No official channels. Too exposed. We handle this." He looked at Manny kneeling beside Frank. "Can you stabilize him for transport?"

Manny nodded grimly, focus locked on Frank. "Bleeding's slowed. But he needs a surgeon, Dev. Now."

"Right." Dev turned to his mother. "Mom, I need you to drive the Sierra. You and Rach. Get Frank and Thomas to St. Luke's Carbon Campus ER. Closest trauma center."

Annabelle absorbed the command, shock yielding to resolve. "What do I tell them?" she asked, her voice low.

"Hunting accident," Dev supplied instantly. "Near Beltzville Lake, way off trail. Separated, heard shots, found them. That's it. No details, just get them medical help." He met Rach's eyes. "Can you handle the story, help Mom?"

Rach nodded immediately, reporter instincts shelved for loyalty. "Yes. Hunting accident. We'll get them there." She moved to help Annabelle, the two women carefully assisting the grievously injured Frank and the pain-wracked Thomas towards the front door.

Dev turned to Kate. "Priority call to Sarah at HQ. Activate Black Site Cleanup Crew. Full sanitation, immediate dispatch. Confirm ETA on reinforcements. Need this perimeter locked down before anyone stumbles onto this."

"Understood." Kate's reply was crisp. She pulled her secure phone, moved towards the living room, dialing, her back to them as she relayed the coded request.

Dev then addressed Manny and Earl. "Okay. Maybe an hour before cleanup arrives. Manny, Earl. Check the attackers outside. Confirm kills, secure any survivors. Get the living upstairs, bound, gagged, out of sight. Search the dead – phones, IDs, patches, tattoos – anything identifying. Bag everything."

Manny nodded, carefully rising as Annabelle and Rach took over supporting Frank. "Got it." Earl gave a jerky nod, pale but resolved.

The groups moved with grim efficiency. Annabelle and Rach guided the wounded out. Manny and Earl slipped out the rear door onto the bullet-strewn deck, weapons ready. Kate's low, professional voice drifted from the living room. Dev took a final sweep of the dining room, gaze lingering on the scarred log walls, then followed Manny and Earl outside.

Dev rejoined Manny and Earl as they finished their work on the deck and lawn. Six attackers confirmed dead; two breathing but unconscious were bound and moved upstairs. Evidence bags accumulated near the back door.

"Anything stand out?" Dev asked Manny quietly.

Manny shook his head, wiping grime from his cheek. "Standard gear, mixed weapons. Nothing unique. Except two had this." He showed Dev the sketch Earl made in his notebook: a snake coiled around a dagger. "Same marking."

They headed back inside. The thick smell of cordite and splintered wood hung heavy. Kate was ending her call near the living room entrance, turning as they entered. Earl immediately set up his laptop at the scarred dining table.

"Alright, Earl," Dev said, emptying an evidence bag onto the table – a cracked burner phone, a damp notebook. "Notebook's yours. Crack those symbols. Run the tattoo."

"On it." Earl connected cables.

"Kate," Dev turned as she approached. "That phone."

Kate picked up the bagged phone, examining the cracked screen. "HQ forensics will be faster, but I can try pulling immediate data – logs, texts, maybe GPS." She attached a device from her kit.

"Do it." Dev nodded towards the stairs. "Manny, let's check on our guests."

They ascended quietly. Reaching the back bedroom, Manny eased the door open. Devin entered first, weapon ready. The two attackers slumped in the chairs, unnaturally still. Dev strode forward, checked the first pulse, then the second. Nothing. He tilted one man's head back, checked his mouth, swore under his breath.

"Cyanide," Manny confirmed grimly from behind, recognizing the faint almond scent, the slack jaws. "Tooth capsules. Professionals."

"Or working for pros who don't leave loose ends," Dev countered, fury tightening his jaw. He kicked the leg of one chair hard. "Silenced before they could talk." They searched the bodies again, finding nothing, then headed back downstairs, frustration a palpable weight.

Kate and Earl looked up as they descended. "Well?" Kate asked.

"Not talking," Dev said flatly. "Cyanide."

Earl flinched. Kate's expression tightened almost imperceptibly. "Suicide pills. Disciplined. Organized." She frowned down at the burner phone connected to her device. "Managed to pull some fragmented texts before it wiped remotely. Initials 'V' mentioned payment, confirming arrival times at the cabin." She set the phone back in its evidence bag. "Likely coordinating the hired guns."

Dev's eyes narrowed slightly at her quick assessment, but he focused on the intel. "Maybe. Bag it for HQ analysis. Tattoo, Earl?"

Earl adjusted his glasses, keyboard clicking rapidly. "Multiple cross-references. Snake and dagger... consistently linked to a group called the 'Shadow Serpents'." He read from the screen, "'Highly compartmentalized, suspected involvement in international arms dealing, political destabilization, corporate espionage. MO involves infiltration, leveraging betrayal. Minimal leadership intel, operates globally...'"

Shadow Serpents. Cyanide pills. This escalated far beyond Sal or Brad.

"Keep digging, Earl," Dev ordered. "Anything on that group – structure, names, locations."

Just then, tires crunched on the gravel drive. Kate glanced out a front window. "Reinforcements." Three black Suburbans rolled to a stop. Dev nodded. "Integrate them into the perimeter. Tighten the cordon. No unscheduled arrivals or departures." Kate moved to meet the teams.

Minutes later, the Sierra's low rumble returned. Annabelle and Rach hurried inside, faces pale, strained.

"How are they?" Dev asked immediately, going to his mother.

"ER took them right back," Annabelle reported, voice trembling slightly. "Frank's critical, rushed to surgery. Thomas is stable, treating the shoulder."

"Good work, Mom." Dev gently put an arm around her. "You did great."

"Cover story held," Rach added quietly, meeting Dev's eyes. "Hunting accident. They asked questions, but seemed to buy it." She looked utterly drained.

"Okay," Dev addressed the remaining group – Manny, Earl, Rach, Kate, who had returned. "New teams securing the site. Cleanup crew en route, ETA forty-five." He glanced at the bullet holes, the overturned furniture, the bloodstains Earl was processing. "We stay until cleanup scrubs this place. Earl, keep working the notebook, the Serpent connection. Kate, coordinate with HQ, see if forensics can pull anything useful remotely." He looked at Manny and Rach. "We need our next move. This Shadow Serpent lead... this just went global."

The air in the cabin was thick with exhaustion, grief, the chilling implications. They had survived, but the battle had shifted to a larger, more dangerous arena. Annabelle quietly excused herself upstairs, overwhelmed. The rest gathered around the dining table, laptops open, the grim work continuing under the shadow of loss and betrayal.

# Chapter 9

# Uneasy Alliances

The sharp, sterile scent of disinfectant couldn't completely erase the stale air clinging to Sal Demarco's private room at St. Luke's Carbon Campus. A dull, constant throb emanated from beneath the crisp white bandage on his leg—a reminder of Viktor Mikhailov's bullet, fired 36 hours prior. Thirty-six hours trapped in this antiseptic box, the garbage flickering across the wall-mounted TV a poor distraction from Viktor's 72-hour deadline ticking relentlessly closer. Sal scowled, shifting against the stiff sheets, impatience a physical itch.

A nurse bustled in, her smile practiced, failing to mask the weariness in her eyes. "Looking much better today, Mr. Demarco," she chirped, checking his vitals. "But the doctor feels another 24 hours for observation—"

"Heard him yesterday," Sal grunted, waving her off. "Got places to be, sweetheart. Business calls. Get me the discharge papers. AMA."

The nurse sighed, the professional smile dissolving. "As you wish." She exited, leaving Sal alone with the low hum of machines and his own simmering frustration. Moments later, the door opened again. Brad

Ewing slipped inside, his expensive suit rumpled, anxiety tightening the skin around his eyes.

"The leg?" Brad asked, pulling a chair close, his voice hushed.

Sal glared at the bandaged limb. "Like fire. The Russians? Did you connect?" Less than 36 hours remained. Tick-tock.

Brad nodded, running a hand through his meticulously styled hair. "Yeah. Noon. Ivan and Mikal." He glanced nervously towards the door. "You sure you can manage getting out?"

A humorless smirk twisted Sal's lips. "Watch me."

"Where?"

"Fish Head Diner," Brad replied, nose wrinkling slightly. "Allentown. Their pick. Said they needed somewhere... public."

"Public," Sal scoffed, the word foul on his tongue. "Their public means a greasy spoon crawling with their own thugs. Figures." He swung his legs carefully over the side of the bed just as the doctor entered, discharge papers held loosely, expression resigned.

"Mr. Demarco," the doctor began, "leaving against medical advice involves significant risks—infection, complications..."

"Noted, Doc." Sal snatched the papers. "Urgent business." He scrawled his signature, then pushed himself upright, leaning heavily on Brad as white-hot pain shot up his leg, momentarily stealing his breath. "Let's move."

Ignoring the doctor's final protests, Sal limped determinedly out of the room, leaning on Brad more than he liked, the need to escape warring with the relentless throb in his leg.

The drive out of the hospital parking lot in Brad's Mercedes was silent, thick with unspoken tension. Sal stared out the window, fingers drumming an impatient rhythm on the door panel, jaw clenched. Brad kept glancing over, knuckles white on the steering wheel.

"Don't trust 'em," Sal finally grumbled, shifting in the plush leather seat. "Not an inch."

"Me neither," Brad agreed quickly. "They short us, Viktor shoots you, gives us three days, and now they pick the meet? In their backyard? Smells like another setup."

"Exactly." A predatory light flickered in Sal's eyes. "So we play along, but we're ready." He jerked his head towards an upcoming exit. "My place first. Clean up. Grab some insurance."

They pulled up to Sal's house—a modest, neglected two-story tucked away in Lehighton. Inside, the living room air was stale with old beer and takeout remnants. "Relax," Sal said sarcastically, gesturing towards a worn couch as he limped towards the stairs. "Fifteen minutes."

Brad sank uneasily onto the couch, the silence amplifying his anxiety. The minutes stretched. Twenty-five passed before Sal reappeared—showered, changed, the limp still present but less pronounced. A fresh bulge beneath his jacket confirmed he was armed.

"Let's roll," Sal said, eyes hard.

They drove towards Allentown, the familiar green hills offering no comfort. As urban sprawl replaced the countryside, the retro neon sign of the Fish Head Diner glowed ahead, an odd beacon.

"Alright," Sal said as Brad parked down the street, voice low. "No screw-ups. We walk out with confirmation that shipment moves tonight. By midnight. Or it gets messy. Understand?"

"Understood." Brad's hand hovered near his own jacket.

Inside, the diner was jarring—classic American booths and chrome trim clashed with Cyrillic lettering on menus behind the counter. The low murmur of Russian drifted from several tables. Sal spotted Mikal instantly—back corner booth, alone, nursing coffee. No sign of Ivan. Sal scanned the other patrons—families, truckers, but too many solitary men nursing drinks, eyes sweeping the room with practiced nonchalance. Wrong.

He nudged Brad subtly. "Eyes open," he muttered. "Too crowded."

Brad nodded almost imperceptibly, following Sal towards the booth. Mikal looked up, a faint, unreadable smile touching his lips as he gestured to the opposite bench.

"Sal. Brad. Please," Mikal said, his voice smooth as worn silk. "Join me. Ivan is... delayed."

Sal slid in, ignoring the jolt of pain from his leg. Brad sat beside him, rigid. "Enough games, Mikal," Sal leaned forward slightly. "The shipment?"

Mikal raised an eyebrow, affecting mild surprise. "So direct? No time for civilities?"

"Ask the hole in my leg about civilities," Sal snarled, his hand dropping beneath the table.

Brad put a restraining hand on Sal's arm. "Easy, Sal."

Mikal sighed dramatically. "Such hostility. Unwarranted." He took a slow sip of coffee. "Friends. There was... a directive. From superiors. A temporary hold was required."

"Hold?" Brad echoed, incredulous. "We paid! The deadline—"

"We do not question directives." Ivan's flat voice cut him off. He'd materialized beside Mikal, seemingly from nowhere, his eyes cold and empty. "We obey."

"You work for us on this!" Sal practically spat the words. "This shipment is vital!"

"Was vital," Mikal corrected smoothly. "Circumstances evolve. New directives supersede old ones." He leaned forward again. "However... the situation is now... clarified. The hold is lifted." Another small smile flickered. "Delivery can proceed at your convenience."

Brad narrowed his eyes, unconvinced. "Our convenience was three days ago. When Viktor—"

"Yes, yes, regrettable timing," Mikal waved a dismissive hand. "Easily resolved. Your preferred time and location?"

"Midnight," Sal snapped. "Conner's Lumber Yard. You know it."

Mikal nodded slowly. "Midnight it is." He raised his coffee cup slightly. "Consider it done."

Sal didn't buy the easy capitulation. He pushed himself up, the movement jarring his injured leg. He jerked his head at Brad. "We're done." He turned, limping towards the diner entrance, Brad scrambling to follow.

Back in the Mercedes, suspicion hung heavy in the air. "Interesting," Brad finally ventured as he pulled away from the curb.

"Yeah," Sal agreed, staring out the window, eyes hard. "Too damn easy. They caved too fast." He turned to Brad. "I don't buy it. Get back, round up your guys. The reliable ones. Tonight, we go heavy. No chances."

The drive back to Lehighton began, the miles ticking past, each man consumed by grim calculations for the midnight rendezvous, the certainty that the Russians' easy compliance masked another, deadlier move thickening the air between them.

Sunlight streamed through the expansive windows of the grand log home, illuminating the spacious living room. Dev paced restlessly across the worn floorboards, their familiar creak a counterpoint to the tension remaining from the ambush, mingling with the smell of pine and faint coffee.

Earl, perched on the sofa, laptop balanced, looked up, his eyes bright behind his glasses. "Mr. Jones," he announced, gesturing to the screen. "You need to see this."

Dev strode over, boots sharp on the wood. "What is it, Jenkins?"

"The fire reports?" Earl pointed. "Four residential incidents flagged, last three weeks. This one," he highlighted a line, "the 14th. Listed 'possible arson'." He scrolled. "If our source's timeline holds, this matches when he claims Sal hired him for that Beltzville job." Devin's face hardened.

"So, our source wasn't lying about Mom's house—he didn't know. He was hired for a different fire." A thoughtful frown touched Dev's forehead. "Okay, Earl. Keep digging. Cross-reference the victim of that Beltzville fire with any known associates of Brad or Sal. Check insurance claims—that property, and Mom's house."

The smell of sizzling bacon drifted from the kitchen —Annabelle, creating an island of normalcy. Dev turned towards the front door, needing air, respite.

Just as his hand reached the knob, Kate's sharp voice stopped him.

"Devin, look." She held out the burner phone from one of the dead attackers.

Dev took it, eyes narrowing at the cracked screen:

* Hey man, it's Sal.

* Boss doesn't have you tied up, could use backup.

* Shipment coming in. Might get rough.

A flicker of something—anticipation? grim excitement?—crossed Dev's face. "Finally. Actionable," he muttered. "We need the meet location."

"Jenkins!" he barked over his shoulder.

Earl scrambled over. "Yes, boss?"

"Connections. Sal, Brad, Shadow Serpents. Anything solid?"

"Y-yes," Earl stammered, adjusting his glasses. "A little."

Dev's voice dropped, quiet, intense. "Spit it out."

"Right." Earl gathered himself. "Sal Demarco. Intel confirms early links to the Serpents. Rose fast —assault, extortion, suspected trafficking..."

"And?" Dev urged.

"And then," Earl pointed at his screen, "around 2015? Charges vanish. Sealed, dismissed. Can't trace the pull yet, but it smells like high-level influence. Financials suggest he's still a key Serpent operative—regional enforcement, logistics maybe."

"Fits the cyanide pills," Manny commented grimly, having entered silently.

"Brad?" Kate inquired.

"Ewing's tougher," Earl admitted. "Surface financials inflated but laundered clean, skillfully done. Few direct links... except this." He hesitated.

"What is it?" Kate pressed.

"A photo." Earl pulled it up. "Deep archive, mislabeled. Brad Ewing... having lunch with Mayor Jones. Your father, Dev."

Dev's breath caught. The image jarred —his father, a faint smile, across a diner table from Brad Ewing. He forced the shock down. "Focus on the meet," he ordered Earl, voice tight. "Digital chatter, known Serpent hangouts, anything local."

He turned to Kate, gaze intense. "Kate, need that location. Now. Coordinate with Sarah at HQ. All available analysts dig —feeds, intercepts, ping known associates of Demarco or Serpent fronts in northeastern PA. Need it yesterday."

"Understood." Kate moved towards the living room's quiet end, secure phone already to her ear, relaying the urgent request.

Dev stepped onto the wraparound deck, the cold morning air biting. He needed a moment. Dad and Brad. He pushed the image aside. Compartmentalize. Focus. The meet.

He keyed his radio. "Manny. Byron, Jackson, team leaders. Deck. Now. Over."

Static crackled. "Roger."

"Remaining teams, lock down the perimeter tight," Dev added.

Moments later, Manny, Byron, and Jackson emerged onto the deck, faces set, alert. Dev briefed them quickly—Earl's intel on Sal and the Serpents, the burner text about the shipment, the jarring photo, the urgent push for the meet location.

"HQ will get it soon," Dev concluded, scanning their faces. "Intel points local, Lehighton area likely. Need to be ready to roll when the call comes. We stage close, react instantly. Byron, Jackson – need three of your best, volunteers, roll with us. Tight team. Eight total: myself, Manny, Kate, plus the five of you. Thirty minutes to move out."

The leaders nodded, understanding.

"Makes sense," Manny conceded, a slight smirk touching his lips despite the tension. "Boss's orders."

The group dispersed, urgency in their movements. Dev found Annabelle and Rach in the kitchen, outlining the mobilization.

"Stay inside," he instructed firmly. "Perimeter's secure. You're safe here."

"Be careful, Devin," Annabelle pleaded softly. Rach simply met his eyes, a silent acknowledgment of the danger, a promise of strength held between them.

Dev headed upstairs, the need for action a physical force. Tactical vest over base layer, ceramic plates checked, boots laced tight. Glock holstered, spare mags secured. Suppressed AR-15 checked, slung across his chest.

Downstairs, the team assembled: Manny, Kate, Byron, Jackson, the three chosen operators —lean professionals, their eyes steady with experience. Geared up, weapons checked. Ready.

"Okay." Dev scanned the eight faces. "Two vehicles. Lead Suburban: myself, Manny, Kate, Byron. Second: Jackson leads the operators. Move out now. Stage near Lehighton, await confirmation."

They moved, the heavy cabin door closing behind them. Two black Suburbans rumbled to life, pulling out onto Poho Poco Drive, heading into the unknown.

The journey down was tense, silent except for the engine hum and comms checks. They passed Beltzville Lake's shimmer, turned onto PA-209 South, Blakeslee Boulevard, the road widening near Lehighton.

Dev drove lead, eyes constantly scanning; Manny mirrored him. Kate and Byron sat quietly in back, focused, hands near weapons.

Kate's secure phone chirped, sharp in the quiet. "Richards." She listened, expression tightening. "Confirmed. Conner's Lumber Yard. 1500 Blakeslee Boulevard Drive East. Midnight." Pause. "Understood. Thank you." She disconnected, turning immediately to Devin. "HQ confirms via SIGINT and Serpent chatter. Conner's Lumber Yard, Lehighton. Midnight."

Dev glanced at the dash clock. Mid-afternoon. "Midnight. Gives us roughly seven hours."

Manny grabbed the radio. "Jackson, Team 2, copy location: Conner's Lumber Yard, 1500 Blakeslee East. RV Kanibomb Park, 2100 hours, recon brief. We have time. Proceed independently, maintain comms silence unless critical. Over."

"Roger, Lead. See you 2100," Jackson's voice crackled back.

The Suburbans continued into Lehighton. Past Carbon Plaza Mall, the everyday scenery felt dissonant.

"Okay, seven hours," Manny broke the silence. "Plan until recon?"

"Need to stop by the house," Dev replied, voice tight, gaze fixed ahead.

"See the damage. Talk to Sarah's foreman."

"Could call, boss," Byron suggested quietly from the back.

"Need to see it," Dev repeated curtly.

They drove on, leaving Lehighton, heading back towards Jim Thorpe. Steep slopes rose around them, the Lehigh River a silver thread below.

Pulling onto Center Street felt wrong, like visiting a grave. The charred skeleton of 218 stood starkly against the afternoon sky.

They climbed out. The smell of wet ash and burnt wood clung heavily. Devastation. Porch gone, windows empty sockets, roof collapsed. A construction crew, Sarah's dispatch, secured the site for the night. Dev spotted the foreman, a burly man wiping dust from his face, and walked over.

"Mr. Jones?" the foreman asked, extending a calloused hand, sympathy in his eyes. "Saw the news... awful. Ms. Blake called, said you might stop by. Shored up the unstable sections, cleared some debris. Waiting on the structural report tomorrow before demo and rebuild."

"Timeline?" Dev asked flatly.

The foreman sighed, scratching his head. "Honestly? Depends on the engineer. Best case? Six weeks once we get the green light, full crews. Longer if the foundation's shot."

Weary frustration washed over Dev. "Just... get it done," the words felt inadequate. "Double crews if needed. Bill EAG. Sarah Blake."

"Yes, sir." The foreman nodded.

Dev turned back to the Suburban, the image of the ruined house burning behind his eyes. The sun dipped towards the ridgeline, casting long, distorted shadows across the wreckage. They climbed back in, the silence profound. The drive back towards Lehighton began, each lost in thought, the hours relentlessly ticking down towards midnight at

Conner's Lumber Yard, towards the confrontation waiting in the darkness.

# Chapter 10

# Rendezvous Under Doubtful Skies

*October 28th, 2018, 2100 Hours EST*

The waning gibbous moon cast long, distorted shadows across the deserted asphalt of Kanibomb Park. A lone sodium vapor light at the lot's edge flickered, its weak orange glow failing to penetrate the darkness swallowing the baseball fields and playground beyond. The autumn air hung still and heavy, amplifying the chirping crickets and the distant rumble of trucks on the highway.

Dev sat parked in the lead Suburban, engine off, scanning the empty lot. Manny sat beside him, equally focused. In the back, Kate and Byron were quiet, watchful presences. The fatigue, anticipation, and apprehension were visible on the faces of the operators in both vehicles. Moments later, the second Suburban, carrying Jackson and three operators, pulled up silently, headlights briefly slicing the gloom before extinguishing.

Eight figures emerged, gathering in a tight circle between the SUVs, breath misting in the cool air. Weapons remained low, but readiness emanated from their tense postures. "Sit-rep?" Dev asked, his voice a low rumble.

Jackson stepped forward slightly. "Conner's Lumber Yard," he began, voice concise. "Ten acres, possibly more. Main warehouse dominates; multiple loading docks face south. Dense woods border rear and east—best approach for stealth. Perimeter's active.".

One of Jackson's operators added, "Counted twenty-five, maybe thirty hostiles on exterior patrol during the drive-by. Mixed long guns, sidearms. Look alert, not just clocking hours.".

"Could be an advantage," Manny suggested quietly. "If it goes loud inside, they might focus there, give us extraction room.".

"Good point," Dev replied curtly. "Plan holds. Recon primary. Eyes on Sal, Brad, the shipment—gather intel. If, only if, a clean opportunity arises to grab Brad or Sal without compromising the team or alerting unknowns, we take it. Otherwise, observe and report. No unnecessary contact.".

The team re-entered the Suburbans, engines starting with a low growl. They pulled out, heading towards the lumber yard, bypassing the main entrance. Dev turned onto Country Club Road, then a barely visible dirt track vanishing into the woods behind the target, Jackson's vehicle close behind. Branches scraped the SUVs as they navigated the rutted surface, moonlight filtering down in fragmented patches.

The track ended in a small, secluded clearing surrounded by towering pines. Silvery moonlight bathed the space, dappled with deep shadows.

They killed the engines; the sudden silence felt absolute. Exiting the vehicles, Jackson pointed towards the thicker darkness. "Lumber yard, quarter click that way," he confirmed. "Straight through.".

"Perfect." Dev's voice was tight. "Gear up. Final checks.".

They gathered silently at the rear of the vehicles, movements swift, practiced in the dim light. Kate and Jackson moved among the operators, distributing mags, checking comms, passing out NVGs. Suppressed weapons were checked, safeties toggled. Tailgates closed gently. They melted into the woods, eight figures in staggered formation, Dev on point. They moved like ghosts through the undergrowth, boots barely disturbing the thick layer of fallen leaves.

After a tense, silent trek, navigating by compass and fragmented moonlight, they reached the woods bordering the rear of the lumber yard. The vast industrial site spread before them, bathed in the cold, sterile glow of security lamps. The main warehouse loomed, dark and imposing. Under brighter lights, the loading dock area showed low, purposeful activity. Figures moved between lumber stacks and parked flatbeds.

"Okay," Dev ordered, voice a near-whisper over comms. "Splitting here. Manny, Kate, with me—center position, eyes on the docks. Jackson," he glanced at the other team leader, "take your two operators right, secure flank observation. Byron," he nodded to the remaining leader, "you and your operator take left flank. Find elevation if possible. Approximately forty minutes to midnight. Comms silence unless critical contact or movement. Stay sharp.".

The teams acknowledged silently, fanning out, vanishing into shadows and deeper undergrowth along the wood line. Dev, Kate, and Manny crept forward, using the uneven terrain and scattered debris for cover, moving towards a clearer view of the loading dock. The air felt thick, the silence punctuated only by the facility's distant hum and occasional muffled sounds from the dock area.

Dev settled behind a large, discarded pile of concrete forms, raising his compact NVG monocular. Through the green-tinged view, figures milled around the loading dock bays, indistinct under the harsh lights. He adjusted the focus, trying to isolate faces.

Suddenly, a heavy metal door at the rear of the warehouse slammed open, the sound echoing faintly across the yard. Two figures emerged, walking briskly towards the docks. Even at this distance, the swagger of one, the slight limp of the other, were unmistakable. Sal Demarco. Brad Ewing.

Devin's breath caught, his grip tightening on his weapon.

"Hold," he whispered into comms, voice tight. "Targets acquired. Sal and Brad, entering dock area from warehouse rear. All teams maintain observation. Let's see how this unfolds."

On the concrete expanse, Sal and Brad emerged into the brighter light. Behind them, the warehouse interior was vast and dim, sporadic lights casting long shadows across stacked lumber and drywall. The smell of sawdust and pine drifted out, sharp against the metallic tension radiating from Devin's hidden team.

Faintly, they heard Sal bark orders at thugs huddled near the open door before the figures retreated inside. "Get back to work! ...Can't trust these damn Russians, stay alert! ...Unless you don't want paid, do as I say!"

"They should be rolling any minute," Brad's voice was lower, harder to catch, but his anxious glance towards the truck entrance was clear through the NVGs. "Move closer to the bays."

They walked towards the massive, roll-up metal doors. As they neared, the rumble of heavy engines intensified. Headlights cut through the darkness as multiple large box trucks maneuvered, backing into the loading bays. Sal exchanged a wary look with Brad, visible even from Devin's vantage point.

"Bad feeling," Sal muttered, audible now on a nearby feed. "Eyes open."

"Yeah," Brad replied, hand hovering near his waistband. "Eighty percent odds these guys pull something."

"Higher," Sal agreed grimly, hitting the button to raise the middle bay door.

The heavy door groaned upward, chains clattering, revealing the bay's darkness. Two figures stepped out beside the first truck as it settled—Mikal and Ivan, faces stark under the dock lights.

"Good evening, gentlemen," Mikal began, his voice smooth, deceptively casual. "Your items, as requested. Shall we put this... misunderstanding... behind us?"

"Misunderstanding?" Brad scoffed audibly.

"Call it what you like," Ivan barked, impatient.

"Now, now," Mikal interjected, playing peacemaker. "Let us inspect the merchandise."

The four—Sal, Brad, Mikal, Ivan—walked towards the middle truck. Ivan moved to the rear, reaching down as if to unlatch the doors. A glint of metal from inside the darkened truck caught the light. Sal saw it. His reaction was pure instinct, born of paranoia. "GUN!" he roared, shoving Brad violently aside as he dove for the scant cover of a nearby lumber stack.

Brad stumbled back, shoved hard, eyes wide with confusion. He fumbled for the weapon at his waist, his movements sluggish, betraying years spent behind a desk, not dodging fire.

The back doors of the box truck burst open. Eight Russians spilled out, AK-47s already spitting fire. Muzzle flashes strobed in the loading bay. A deafening wall of automatic gunfire erupted, rounds stitching across concrete, whining off steel supports. The loading dock instantly became a kill zone. Sal's men near the warehouse entrance crumpled in the onslaught.

Return fire erupted from within the warehouse as the hidden thugs reacted. Bullets ricocheted wildly, turning the vast space into an echo chamber of lethal metal. Sparks showered down as rounds hit beams. Overhead lights shattered, plunging sections into disorienting darkness.

Sal, miraculously untouched, was already returning fire from behind the lumber, handgun barking rapidly. He moved with a predator's economy, using the chaos.

Brad, the betrayal finally registering, managed to draw his pistol, firing one wild shot before scrambling behind a stack of drywall near the warehouse wall. Plasterboard exploded inches from his head. He could hear Sal yelling, cursing, firing, the sounds nearly lost in the cacophony. Cordite and the smell of hot blood thickened the air. A slaughterhouse. Sal and the few remaining thugs inside were pinned, returning fire bravely but futilely. Brad, seeing no escape back through the warehouse, scrambled along the wall towards the rear exterior door, seeking any way out of the inferno.

From the wood line, Dev, Kate, and Manny watched the ambush explode. The sheer volume of fire, the brutal Russian efficiency—it was overwhelming.

"Jesus," Kate breathed, pressing lower behind their cover. "It's a massacre."

"Gotta move," Manny hissed, eyes scanning the chaos, calculating. "Crossfire here, we're dead."

Dev nodded, mind racing, assessing the lethal calculus. Recon only. But Brad held the link to his father's murder. Sal held keys to the Serpents. Leaving felt wrong. Intervening was suicide. *The team. Make the call.*

Just then, Brad burst through the rear warehouse door, stumbling into the relative quiet, gasping, eyes wide with panic.

Dev saw the opening. Risk assessed in a heartbeat.

"Now!" he hissed to Kate and Manny. "On me! Objective Brad! Byron, Jackson – suppress rear exit! Move!"

They broke cover, low and fast through shadows and debris towards the warehouse wall. The firefight still raged near the loading docks, a hellish soundtrack.

Brad leaned heavily against the rough brick, disoriented, fighting for breath. Dev closed the distance in seconds, tackling Brad low, driving the air from his lungs. Before Brad could react, Dev brought his rifle butt down sharply against Brad's temple. Brad went limp, collapsing unconscious.

"Grab him! Move!" Dev barked, adrenaline singing.

Manny and Kate surged forward, grabbing Brad's arms, dragging his considerable weight towards the concealing woods. As they reached the treeline, two Russians rounded the corner, AKs leveled, likely sent to secure the rear.

Two sharp, near-simultaneous cracks from deeper in the woods – Jackson and Byron reacting instantly. The Russians dropped onto the concrete without firing.

"Clear!" Jackson confirmed over comms.

"Thanks!" Manny grunted, hauling Brad deeper into the undergrowth.

"Exfil! Now!" Dev pushed through branches, thorns snagging his gear. The main firefight felt slightly more distant, but the sounds were still terrifyingly close. They scrambled through the woods, darkness enveloping them.

Dev, Kate, and Manny half-carried, half-dragged Brad. Byron, Jackson, and the three operators moved fluidly around them, a protective perimeter, weapons scanning the dark woods.

"Status?" Dev panted into comms.

"Clear," Byron responded immediately.

"Good," Dev gasped, glancing down at Brad's slack, unconscious face in the filtered moonlight. "He's alive. For now."

They pressed on, the weight heavy, adrenaline slowly ebbing, replaced by the cold reality of extraction. Trees thinned ahead. The moonlit clearing, the waiting Suburbans – a promise of temporary safety from the slaughterhouse behind them.

Back inside Conner's Lumber Yard, the firefight continued, a maelstrom of automatic fire, ricocheting rounds, and screams.

Sal, pinned behind a heavy forklift near the center, yelled orders into the din, voice raw. "Push 'em back! Suppressing fire! They flank those shelves, we're done!" He popped up, pistol barking twice – muzzle flashes briefly illuminating his grim face – before ducking as rounds chewed concrete near his head. Where the hell was Brad? "Anyone seen Ewing?" Sal shouted during a lull.

"Headed back!" one of his few remaining men yelled, firing from behind plywood near the rear access door.

The back. Maybe Brad found a way out. "Move! Rear door!" Sal ordered, adrenaline overriding the throb in his leg. "Cover!" His men laid down a desperate barrage. Sal scrambled low across the floor, diving behind pallets, using the gruesome cover of fallen bodies. He reached the relative safety near the back wall, the main firefight still concentrated near the loading docks. "Brad!" he yelled towards the rear door. "Back here?!" Silence, punctuated by the rattle of AKs.

"Brad!" Sal roared again, desperation sharpening his voice. "Answer me, dammit!"

Still nothing. Heart pounding, Sal risked exposure, shoving the heavy steel door open, peering out. The back lot was deserted except for Brad's gleaming Mercedes, unnervingly abandoned under the security lights. Then Sal saw them – two dead Russians near the corner, killed cleanly. Not Brad's work. Hope died. Someone else had been here. Someone else took Brad.

Gunfire inside intensified, closer. The Russians were advancing. A loud crash from within, panicked shouts from his men. Time was up. "Out! Now!" Sal yelled back into the warehouse. Three of his men burst through the door, firing wildly as they retreated.

Sal joined them, scrambling towards the beat-up vehicles parked further down the lot. "My truck!" one man shouted, pointing at a dented pickup.

They piled in, bullets pinging off the tailgate as they peeled out, leaving the lumber yard a chaotic scene of flashing gunfire, smoke, and screams. As the sounds faded, Sal slumped back against the seat, ragged breaths mixing relief with adrenaline, quickly curdling into cold dread about Brad. He pulled out his burner, fingers fumbling, dialing Brad's number. Ring... ring... ring... Voicemail.

Sal swore, hung up, dialed again. Same result. He slammed his fist against the truck's dusty dashboard. "Dammit!" he bellowed, anger raw. "Setup! And where the hell is Brad?!"

"Maybe he ran?" the driver offered uncertainly.

"Ran? After popping two Russians with headshots?" Sal retorted, sarcasm dripping, certainty dawning. "Not likely. Someone else grabbed him." He stared at the dark road. Captured. Probably by Jones.

Taking another deep breath, he scrolled through contacts, selecting the rarely used encrypted number. It connected after several rings.

"Report," Viktor Mikhailov's voice, cold and clipped.

"Sir," Sal began, forcing composure. "Meet went south. Russians ambushed us. Heavy losses."

"Losses are replaceable, Demarco. The shipment?" Viktor's tone was flat, devoid of concern.

"Didn't deliver. Opened fire soon as the trucks opened. Planned setup," Sal explained quickly.

"And Ewing?" Viktor asked, voice unchanged.

Sal hesitated. "Gone, Sir. Vanished mid-fight. Two dead Russians near the back, clean kills. Someone else was there. Think... think Jones might have him."

A beat of silence. Then, a dry, humorless chuckle from Viktor. "Ewing? Captured? Perhaps a few days of... inconvenience... will adjust his priorities." Sal could almost hear the dismissive gesture. "I endured six months in a mud hut, Demarco, surviving on ditch water, while Jones and his ilk 'failed' to retrieve me. Ewing can manage rough handling. Might improve his focus."

Viktor's tone shifted back to ice. "Your failure with the shipment, however, is significant. Handle it. The seventy-two-hour clock continues. Do not disappoint me again." The line went dead.

Sal stared at the phone, Viktor's chilling indifference echoing. Brad's capture, Jones's involvement, the ambush – secondary to the delayed guns. Sal gripped the phone tighter, cold dread solidifying. Expendable. They all were. The truck sped through the darkness, under a sky heavy with unshed storms, carrying Sal away from one disaster, deeper into another.

# Chapter 11

# Dark Clouds

The mountain air tasted electric as lightning split the darkening sky, the immediate thunder vibrating through the floorboards of the approaching Suburbans. Rain lashed down, turning the gravel drive into a muddy slurry. A heavy sense of foreboding, thick as the storm clouds boiling overhead, settled over the returning team.

The two SUVs, headlights struggling against the driving rain, lurched to a halt before the weathered log cabin. Inside the lead vehicle, Kate leaned forward, rapping Brad Ewing's head sharply with her knuckle.

"Wake up!" she hissed, her voice sharp against the storm's drumming on the roof.

"Ugh!" Brad groaned, head lolling, eyes fluttering. "What the—?"

Byron yanked open the rear door, the metal echoing. He hauled Brad out by the arm, shoving him onto the rain-slicked gravel. Wind tore at them, whipping wet pine needles.

"Get off me," Brad snarled, stumbling against the mud-splattered SUV, trying to find his footing.

Byron simply drove an elbow hard into Brad's gut. Brad doubled over with a gasp. "Shut up. Move," Byron growled, grabbing Brad's arm again, marching him forcefully towards the cabin's dimly lit porch.

"Take him downstairs," Dev ordered, climbing out, pulling his jacket tighter against the sudden chill. The single porch light threw long, distorted shadows. "Everyone else inside is likely asleep."

Manny, already at the rear of the second SUV checking gear, turned to Jackson as the operators disembarked. Rain plastered Manny's hair to his forehead. "Four hours rest for your team, Jackson, then relieve perimeter patrol. Heavy rotation tonight."

"Understood," Jackson replied, already issuing quiet orders to his operators, voices swallowed by the wind.

Manny joined Dev and Kate on the porch, the wind rattling the hanging lantern. "Okay," Manny said, wiping rain from his face. "What now?"

"Now?" Dev stared out at the churning clouds obscuring the peaks. "Now we're careful. After that firefight, we don't know who else is involved, who knows we grabbed Brad, or who else he's pissed off besides the Russians. This is volatile. We can't afford mistakes."

"He's just Brad," Manny scoffed, glancing as Byron shoved their prisoner through the front door.

"Maybe," Dev countered, voice low, intense. "But he's Brad tangled with ambush-happy Russians and potentially the Shadow Serpents. We handle this with extreme care." The cabin, usually a sanctuary, felt suddenly exposed, isolated against the storm.

Kate and Manny nodded grimly, the flickering porch light catching the grim set of their faces.

Inside, the main living area was dim, lit only by the faint red glow from embers in the massive stone fireplace. Dev found his mother and Rach huddled on the sofa, blankets wrapped around them, clearly awake despite the hour. Rach sprang up as he entered, rushing forward, arms tight around him.

"Heard the vehicles... so worried," she said, voice trembling slightly against his chest. "Thank God you're back." She pulled back, hazel-green eyes searching his face, taking in the grime, the sheer exhaustion.

"Yeah," Dev said, voice rough, gently disengaging. His gaze shifted instinctively towards the closed basement door. "We're back. But it's not over." Outside, the wind howled, rattling windows, rain drumming hard on the roof.

"Mom, Rach," Dev said, tone firm but gentle. "You need sleep. Seriously. We'll deal with Brad."

"Just... be careful, Devin," Annabelle murmured, pulling her blanket tighter, fear plain in her eyes. Rach nodded, her gaze lingering on Dev, unspoken questions swirling, before they both slowly headed up the creaking stairs.

Once their footsteps faded, Dev nodded to Manny and Kate. They moved to the basement door. Dev pulled it open, revealing the dark, narrow staircase. He went first, Manny and Kate following, the air growing colder, damper, smelling of concrete and earth.

At the bottom, the scene was stark. Byron stood near the stairs, weapon ready. Brad Ewing was secured tightly to a heavy wooden chair bolted mid-floor – likely left from an old workshop. A single bare bulb hanging from the low ceiling cast harsh shadows, highlighting stacked boxes and a rusted utility sink against the far wall.

"Brad," Dev began, stopping a few feet away, his voice quiet, devoid of emotion. "Personal history aside... I'm disappointed you're mixed up in this level of crap."

Brad lifted his head, a sneer twisting his bruised lips, though fear flickered in his eyes. "Mixed up? You storm in, drag me from a legitimate... lumber purchase. Why don't you and your hired thugs crawl back under whatever rock you came from?"

Manny let out a low, humorless chuckle. "Same arrogant Brad. Playing tough even strapped to a chair."

"Cornered?" Brad scoffed, trying to project confidence, but his voice trembled slightly. "Think this kidnapping gives you leverage? Please. You have no idea what you walked into." His eyes darted nervously around the bare room. "If you knew half of it, Jones, you'd be running."

"Running scared? Like you were?" Dev interrupted, stepping closer, voice like ice. "When we pulled you out from under that Russian double-cross tonight?"

Brad's face paled, the sneer faltering. "Saved me? You delusional—" He tried to bluster, but the tremor was obvious.

"Enough games," Dev demanded, voice dropping, leaning in until they were inches apart. "Why did you burn down my parents' house?"

Brad flinched but held Dev's gaze, defiance flickering. "Told you," he smirked, though his eyes remained shifty, "Nothing to do with it. But," the smirk widened, ugly now, "can't say I lost sleep over your family's bad luck."

The air vibrated. Dev's fist lashed out, the sharp crack echoing as knuckles met jaw. Brad's head snapped sideways. "Try again," Dev hissed. Brad spat blood onto the concrete, breathing hard, glaring. After a long moment, through clenched teeth: "Fine. Want the truth? Believe it or not... I didn't torch the house. Wasn't my job."

Manny leaned in, crowding Brad from the other side, radiating menace. "Okay. Let's say we believe that. What the hell were you doing at a lumberyard at midnight with guys carrying AKs?"

Brad stammered, eyes darting between them. "Told you... looking at lumber! For the deck! Late pickup!"

Manny raised a skeptical eyebrow. "Midnight lumber run? Didn't know Conner's kept those hours. Or just for preferred customers, Brad? Special discount?"

Brad forced a weak chuckle. "Yeah... something like that. Owners... old family friends..."

"Right," Dev said, sarcasm heavy. He straightened abruptly, disgust plain on his face. He nodded curtly to Manny and Kate. "Let's go. Let him think about his 'old friends'."

They turned towards the stairs. As they reached the top, Byron, still posted there, reached down, flicked off the bare bulb, plunging Brad into absolute darkness. The heavy door slammed shut, the sound final, echoing from the basement.

Upstairs, Dev sank onto the sofa near the dying embers, burying his face in his hands, letting out a long, shuddering sigh. "If he's telling the truth about the house fire..." he looked up wearily at Manny and Kate, who remained standing, watchful, "then we're back to square one on who ordered it."

"Could still be lying, Dev," Manny pointed out, leaning against the stone mantel. "Or outsourced it."

"Or maybe it wasn't him," Kate added, voice sharp, analytical. "His denial felt marginally more real than the lumber excuse. Doesn't clear him on your father's death, or his ties to Demarco and the Serpents. Just suggests the arson might be separate."

"She's right," Manny nodded slowly. "Let him sit in the dark. Might get more cooperative after contemplating." He looked at Dev's exhausted face. "We all need sleep, brother. Can't think straight on empty."

Dev rubbed his temples, the ache relentless. "Yeah," he conceded reluctantly. "Okay." He gestured vaguely upstairs. "You two head up. Get some rest."

Manny and Kate exchanged a brief glance – concern, understanding – then nodded, ascending the creaking stairs, footsteps fading.

Dev remained alone, staring into the dying embers, the fading storm outside mirroring the one inside him. Exhaustion finally claimed him, pulling him into a restless sleep right there on the sofa.

The first grey light seeped through the cabin windows as the house began to stir. The storm had passed, leaving the air washed clean, the woods dripping silently. Manny came down the stairs quietly, pausing at the bottom, seeing Dev still crashed awkwardly on the sofa.

"Dev," Manny called softly, walking over. "Rough night?"

Dev startled awake, muscles seizing as he sat up, momentarily disoriented. "Damn... Guess so," he mumbled, scrubbing sleep and tension from his face.

Manny offered a tired grin. "Yeah, well, rise and shine. Prisoner in the basement, world of crap to solve."

"Up, I'm up," Dev groaned, pushing stiffly to his feet. The adrenaline was long gone, leaving bone-deep exhaustion and simmering anger. "Need a shower. Can you get Kate, Byron, Jackson, plus Rach and Earl together? Briefing. Brad's capture, the firefight. Emphasize perimeter rotation. Need everyone sharp."

"On it, boss." Manny headed for the kitchen, towards coffee.

"Give me twenty," Dev said, heading upstairs. "Then we talk to Brad again."

Twenty minutes later, showered, changed into fresh tactical gear, Dev descended. The core team – Manny, Kate, Byron, Jackson, Rach, and Earl – were gathered in the living area. Manny stood by the fireplace, relaying the previous night's events. The air was thick with tension and coffee steam. Kate conferred quietly with Byron and Jackson about integrating the reinforcements into the perimeter. Earl was hunched over his laptop. Rach watched Dev come down, handing him a steaming mug, her eyes full of concern.

Dev bypassed the discussions, nodding curtly to Manny. "Ready?" They exchanged a look, then headed towards the basement door. Dev pulled it open and flipped the light switch. Below, the single bare bulb flickered harshly to life. They descended, boots echoing on the concrete. Brad was slumped in the chair, head lolling, his bruised face swollen in the stark light.

Dev didn't hesitate. He approached and kicked the chair leg sharply. Brad jolted awake, straining against the restraints. "Didn't do it! I didn't!"

"We'll see," Dev responded coldly, circling slowly. "Even if you're clean on the house fire – if – you're still swimming in this shit. Time to talk."

"Start with who pulls your strings," Manny said, pacing deliberately across the concrete, his quiet movement radiating menace.

Brad tried to muster some bravado, forcing a shaky smile. "Strings? What makes you think anyone pulls my strings? I run my own operation."

"Don't insult us," Manny scoffed. "The dealership washes cash, and you take orders from whoever has Sal Demarco on a leash."

"You really have no idea, do you?" Brad shook his head, a flicker of genuine fear cutting through the arrogance. He tried shifting tactics. "Look... I'll make you a deal."

"We're listening," Dev said flatly, his patience visibly thinning.

"I'll tell you... a story," Brad began, a nervous grin attempting to regain control. "Fill in some blanks. Might not answer everything, but it'll get you up to speed."

"The price?" Dev stepped closer again.

"Let me walk," Brad said, the arrogant smile widening, completely misreading the room.

In a blur, Devin drew his Ka-Bar, the blade flashing under the bulb. He pressed the cold steel against Brad's throat, leaning in, face inches away. The air vibrated. "How about this deal?" Dev hissed, voice a low, deadly rasp. "I open your throat right here, dump you where no one finds the body, and we figure out the rest ourselves?"

Color drained from Brad's face. He froze, rigid, eyes wide with raw terror, breath caught against the blade.

Manny placed a heavy hand on Devin's shoulder. A beat passed. Devin held Brad's terrified gaze, then slowly, deliberately, retracted the knife. The scrape of steel against the sheath sounded loud in the sudden quiet. "I don't trust you, Brad," Dev said, his voice tight, unwavering. "Not an inch. But you're telling us your story. And if it proves useful... maybe you see tomorrow. Understand?"

Brad swallowed hard, nodding jerkily, bravado gone. "Whatever you say, Jones," he whispered nervously. "But... Jesus, after you hear it... you'll probably kill me anyway."

Dev's jaw clenched. The air felt thick, charged.

"Start talking," Manny instructed calmly, easing the immediate tension slightly.

Brad leaned back as much as the restraints allowed, taking a shaky breath. The smirk returned, brittle now, a fragile defense. "Alright. Fine. You want the truth?" He paused, gathering himself. "It goes deep, Jones. Started years back. April 2014. Sal and me, just getting traction. We get summoned. Nakamura Akimitsu – yeah, the boss's number one, the quiet scary bastard – says we got a meeting."

"Meeting? With who?" Manny pressed.

Brad shifted uncomfortably. "That's the kicker. The damn Borough Office. In Jim Thorpe. I thought he was joking. Asked him, 'The Mayor?' He just gives me that dead-eye stare. 'Yes. And the Chief of Police. You keep quiet while there.' Sal muttered something about me being an idiot."

"My father and Chief Miller?" Dev's voice was dangerously low. "What kind of meeting?"

"The kind where they're losing," Brad said, narrative confidence returning. "Place was dead quiet. Back conference room. And there they are. Your dad. And Miller. Your old man tries to be polite, but Miller just blows up, yelling about how our 'business' is wrecking the town."

"So they threatened you?" Manny interjected.

Brad laughed, a harsh sound. "Threatened? No. Sal snaps back, asks if they think they can stop us. Akimitsu shuts him down quick." He looked directly at Devin. "Then your dad... he admits it. Says they can't stop us. Says that's why they called the meet. To lay down terms."

"Terms?" Devin demanded, leaning forward again.

"Yeah. Rules of engagement," Brad sneered. "We operate quiet, stay out of downtown, no more street-level noise. We clean up our own messes, keep the local blues out of it. In return?" He paused for effect. "The boss pays them thirty-six grand a month. Cash. For the 'community'," he added sarcastically. "Akimitsu agreed to relay the terms. Deal done."

Brad shifted again, the arrogant smirk cementing itself. "After that? Smooth sailing. For years. We ran our business, paid the town tax, cops looked the other way. Perfect." He took a long breath, meeting Devin's burning gaze. "Until about six months ago. That's when your old man decided to renegotiate. Pulled some dirt he must've sat on for years, had Miller arrest Akimitsu."

Devin's eyes widened, the pieces slamming together—his father's distraction, the tension with Miller, the sudden investigation. A dark fury rose. "Are you saying," Dev's voice trembled slightly, dangerously low, "you had something to do with my father's death because he arrested Nakamura?"

Brad threw his head back, laughter grating off the concrete walls. "Me? Kill him?" He leaned forward, the smirk turning venomous. "No, Jones. Didn't have to lift a finger." He savored the look washing over Devin's face. "The Boss... doesn't tolerate betrayal. Your father signed his own death warrant crossing him like that. The Boss just... collected."

Brad's voice dripped malice. "Your father was a fool. Played a game way over his head, paid the price. Thought he was pulling the strings, but he was just a pawn." He sneered, meeting Devin's furious gaze. "Just like you. Running around playing hero? You're just like him. Weak."

That broke him. With a roar, Devin lunged, grabbing Brad's shirt, yanking him violently against the restraints, the heavy chair skidding. Brad's head snapped forward. Devin unleashed a savage flurry of punches, fists connecting brutally with Brad's face, torso. Brad, bound, helpless, twisted, grunting, unable to defend as Devin rained blows down.

"Devin, stop! Enough!" Manny yelled, grabbing Devin's arms from behind, struggling to pull him off the bloodied, gasping figure. Devin fought the restraint, chest heaving, blind rage consuming him. Manny dragged him bodily towards the stairs, but not before Devin lashed out with a final, vicious kick to Brad's ribs. The sharp crack of bone echoed, followed instantly by Brad's agonized yell as he slumped forward, trembling uncontrollably.

Manuel shoved Devin towards the stairs. "Cool off, bro!" he commanded, voice strained but firm. "Now! We kill him like this, we're no better than them!"

Devin stood at the top of the stairs, face flushed dark, knuckles split and bleeding, breath ragged. He didn't respond, just spun and stormed out the main cabin door into the gray morning, slamming the heavy door behind him. The sound reverberated, a punctuation mark of violence and devastating betrayal.

# Chapter 12

# Hidden Histories

Dev slammed back into the cabin, the heavy front door shuddering in its frame. Fury radiated off him, jaw tight, eyes blazing. He stalked past Manny near the kitchen entrance, ignoring his friend's questioning look, and headed straight for the makeshift bar on the living room side table. He poured a heavy measure of whiskey, downed it, poured another.

Moments later, Rach stumbled in through the back door, distress and frustration warring on her face. She stopped short at the sight of Manny. "What—?" She ran a shaky hand through her hair.

"What happened?" Manny asked quietly, nodding towards Dev, who stood rigidly by the fireplace, swirling whiskey, staring into the cold hearth. "He came in like a category five."

Rach sighed, leaning against the doorframe, the shock about her father layering onto the new conflict. "My editor called," she explained, voice strained. "Gary. Down by the lake." She recounted the conversation—the leak about potential corruption tied to Mayor Jones, Gary's aggressive demands for a story, the threat of assigning it elsewhere if she didn't comply.

"He knows, Manny. Or part of it. Says if I don't file, someone else will, and they won't care about accuracy, or the fallout. But Devin..." Her gaze drifted towards the living room. "He just... shut down. Walked off. He thinks I'm choosing the story over him, but I... what else can I do?"

Manny listened, his expression grim. He understood Dev's raw reaction, but Rach's dilemma presented a tactical nightmare. An uncontrolled media leak could be disastrous. He nodded slowly. "Okay. Let me try." He walked into the living room, approaching Dev cautiously. "Dev," he started calmly. "About Rachel."

Dev didn't turn. "Nothing to talk about," he growled into his glass.

"Yeah, there is," Manny pushed gently. "Look, I get you're pissed. But she's jammed up. Editor's on her ass, someone leaked the corruption angle. If she doesn't write something, some hack looking for clicks will, and they won't care about the truth, or protecting anyone. It could splash back on your mom, us, everything."

Dev finally turned, the storm still in his eyes, but a flicker of pragmatism surfaced through the rage.

Manny pressed on. "Maybe talking to Miller is the move anyway? Get his side of Brad's story? See if there's an angle Rach can use? Control the damage, satisfy her editor without burning us? Plus," he added, "we need to know what he knows about your dad. Good or bad."

Dev was silent, swirling the amber liquid. The muscle in his jaw pulsed. Finally, a curt, reluctant nod. "Fine," he conceded, voice tight. "We talk to Miller. But we control what Rach writes. She follows our lead. Period."

"Fair enough." Relief eased some of the tension in Manny's shoulders. He turned back towards the dining area where Rach waited, twisting her hands. "Rach, can you make the call? See where your dad is? Keep it casual—just want to stop by."

Rach nodded, taking a deep breath, though her fingers trembled slightly as she pulled out her phone. Her heart hammered as she dialed the familiar number. Dev came over, standing beside her, a silent, steadying presence. Manny watched from the doorway. The phone rang, each tone stretching the tension.

"Hello?" Chief Miller's voice, thick with weariness.

"Hey, Daddy," Rach managed, keeping her tone light, though it wavered slightly.

"Rachel, honey? That you?" His voice shifted, a hint of warmth cutting through the fatigue.

"Yeah, Daddy, me." She forced casualness. "Haven't seen you guys since the funeral, just wanted to stop by. Are you home?"

"Leaving the office now," he replied, pleased surprise in his voice. "Home in a few. Where are you?"

"Visiting friends nearby," Rach answered carefully. "Could be there in about an hour?"

"Okay, honey. See you then. Your mother will be thrilled."

"Okay, love you. Bye, Daddy," Rach said, her voice catching slightly. She hung up, letting out a long, shaky breath.

"Good job, Rach," Manny gave an approving nod.

"That was... hard," Rach admitted, eyes wide. "Wanted to just ask him everything right then."

"Soon," Dev responded, voice calm but firm, meeting her gaze. "Tactfully. He's your father. We only have Brad's version."

"I agree, but straightforward is better. I know him," Rach pleaded, determination mixing with fear in her eyes. "Trust me?"

"Okay," Dev conceded after a moment, giving a slight nod. "Your lead on the approach."

"Just the three of us," she replied, gaze locking with Dev's, emphasizing the need for sensitivity.

Just as Dev opened his mouth to agree, the sharp chime of the doorbell echoed through the cabin. All three jumped, exchanging wary glances. Who else knew they were here?

Manny moved cautiously towards the door, hand instinctively checking the pistol at his back. Peering through the peephole, his posture relaxed slightly, replaced by surprise. He opened the door.

A courier stood there, holding two large, flat garment bags and a smaller, heavy box. "Delivery for Devin Jones and Manuel Rivera," the courier stated blandly, holding out a signature pad.

Manny signed, took the items. "Thanks," he muttered, closing the door, intrigued. He carried the delivery into the living room, laying the garment bags on the sofa, placing the box on the coffee table. Dev and Rach watched, frowning.

"Sarah?" Dev guessed.

"Has to be." Manny unzipped one bag. Inside: a perfectly pressed, charcoal Polo Ralph Lauren suit. He unzipped the second—Dev's high blue Emporio Armani. Manny opened the box. Inside: two pairs of dress shoes—elegant black Jimmy Choos for Devin, classic Allen Edmonds oxfords for Manny—plus two new wallets with pristine driver's licenses, credit cards, and EAG credentials. Two sleek burner phones and two expensive watches completed the set.

"Damn," Manny whistled softly, picking up a wallet. "Sarah. Thinks of everything. Fast." He tossed Dev's wallet over.

Dev caught it, examining the flawless ID. A flicker of the man he used to be—the polished CEO—crossed his face as he looked from the ID to the Armani suit. He needed to project control when facing Miller. This was armor.

"Alright," Dev said, decision made, a measure of command returning. He picked up the Armani garment bag. "Fifteen minutes. Shower, change. Then we see the Chief."

Manny nodded, examining the burner phone. "Sounds good. We'll be ready."

Dev headed upstairs, the luxurious feel of the suit bag a jarring contrast to the violence and uncertainty swirling around them. Time to face another front.

Dev returned downstairs shortly after, the impeccably tailored Armani suit settling on his frame like a familiar second skin, the subtle sheen of the Super 130s wool catching the lamplight. He moved with a renewed, albeit cold, purpose, the feel of quality tailoring restoring a fraction of his usual confidence.

"Well, well," Manny said, looking up from the burner phone, a low whistle escaping as he took in the transformation. "CEO's back in the building."

Rach, who had been talking quietly with Manny near the fireplace, turned. Her eyes took in the suit, surprised admiration warring briefly with the worry still etched deep in her expression. "Where did that come from?"

"No idea," Dev replied, adjusting his tie, the ghost of a smile touching his lips. "Magic. Or Sarah."

"Definitely Sarah," Manny remarked with a knowing grin. "Always one step ahead."

"Alright," Dev said, the brief moment passing, his tone shifting back to business. He looked at Manny and Rach. "Let's go see the Chief."

They moved out, piling into one of the black Suburbans parked near the cabin. The drive down the mountain, towards Jim Thorpe, then onward to Lehighton and Miller's neighborhood, felt endless, each passing minute stretching the tension taut. The quiet luxury of the SUV felt alien against the grim reality they faced.

They finally pulled up before Rachel's childhood home at 107 Pinoak Drive. The traditional brick facade stood solid, nestled in the wooded embrace of the Poconos, projecting an image of normalcy they knew was fractured. Towering trees offered seclusion on the large lot; a deck wrapped around the back promised peaceful evenings the Chief likely hadn't enjoyed recently.

They exited into the cool, still air. Rach led the way, taking a deep, visible breath before pressing the doorbell. Moments later, the door swung open. Rachel's mother stood there, her face lighting up with genuine warmth at the sight of her daughter, then widening further as she saw Dev and Manny behind her.

"Rachel, honey! And Devin! Manny! What a wonderful surprise!" she exclaimed, enveloping each in a warm hug, apparently oblivious to the tension radiating from them. "Come in, come in! Your father just got home; he's in his office."

"Thanks, Ma," Rach replied, her smile strained as they stepped inside. They followed the familiar path to her father's office off the main living room. Rach paused at the doorway, exchanged a quick, nervous glance with Dev and Manny, then entered.

Chief Miller sat behind his large oak desk, looking up from his laptop. His weary face softened instantly at the sight of Rach. "Rachel, honey, good to see you."

"Hey, Daddy," Rach replied, her voice steady, though apprehension shadowed her eyes. As she spoke, Dev and Manny stepped into the doorway behind her. The atmosphere in the room shifted palpably. The warmth vanished from Miller's face, replaced by deep concern and tired resignation. He sighed, leaning back in his leather chair. "So," he said heavily, gaze shifting past Rach to meet Dev's directly. "Guessing this isn't purely social, sweetheart. Honestly... given your father's death being ruled homicide, and knowing your resources, Dev," he gestured vaguely towards Echelon Axiom, "I knew it was only a matter of time before you came asking questions I probably can't answer." He motioned to the chairs opposite his desk. "Sit. Tell me what you think you know. I'll fill in what I can."

They sat, the leather cool beneath them. Dev took his time, carefully recounting Brad Ewing's story—the 2014 meeting, the deal between town leadership and Akimitsu representing "The Boss," the monthly payments, the quiet agreement, and finally, Brad's claim that John Jones broke the deal by arresting Akimitsu, sealing his fate.

When Dev finished, the office was heavy with silence. Miller stared down at his desk, then sighed, the sound weighted with years of compromise. "He told you that much?" He shook his head slowly. "Less than I feared, maybe. More than enough."

He looked up, meeting Dev's hard gaze. "Yes, Devin. It's true. Your father and I... made that deal. Back in 2014. We thought we were doing the right thing." He seemed to search for justification. "You have to understand the context."

"Enlighten us," Manny said dryly, arms crossed.

Miller leaned forward, eyes pleading. "You were gone, Dev. Deployed. This town... it was spiraling. Drugs, violence, turf wars turning Main Street into a battlefield. We were losing officers, making zero headway against the organization pulling the strings—running Demarco, running Ewing, apparently."

He spread his hands wide. "They were ghosts. Arrests fell apart. Witnesses vanished. Evidence... gone. We were losing. That protection racket crew from the old warehouses? Disappeared a month after the deal. The money they paid? Funded the new youth center, resurfaced park courts, bought cruisers without council fights. We saw results, even if the methods felt... compromised." He hesitated. "When the offer came—operate discreetly, contain your business, pay substantially, police your own violence—John and I debated it for weeks. It felt dirty. The alternative? Watching Jim Thorpe implode? We traded visible chaos for contained corruption."

"A deal with the devil," Dev stated flatly.

"Maybe." Miller looked down again. "Your father wrestled with it more than I did. Especially later. About a year ago, he started questioning it. 'Are we doing right, Colin?' We argued. I said we'd chosen the best bad option. Didn't realize how deep it went for him until he walked in here, six, maybe seven months back."

He shifted uneasily. "Drops a file on my desk—intel he'd gathered somehow, solid evidence linking Akimitsu directly to international trafficking, bypassing Sal and Brad. Told me, 'Arrest him.' Just like that. I thought he was nuts, told him it would detonate everything, break the truce. But he had that look... the coaching look, the one that said the play was called, risk be damned. He wouldn't yield."

The Chief flinched, the memory obviously sharp. "So, we did it. Quietly, with federal contacts. Nabbed Akimitsu outside Philly. Almost immediately... it started." His gaze grew distant. "Anonymous threats first. Vague, menacing. Voicemails, unsigned letters here at the house. Then... the fires."

"Fires?" Rach repeated, leaning forward, voice sharp. "Plural? How many?"

"Last four months?" Miller dragged a weary hand over his face. "Twelve confirmed arsons—homes, businesses. Another fifteen suspicious incidents we couldn't prove. Including," his gaze met Dev's, heavy with shared loss, "your parents' home."

"Leads? Patterns?" Dev pressed, grief momentarily sidelined by the need for intel.

"Scattered," Miller admitted with a sigh. "Different methods, targets. Doesn't feel like one source. Some similarities, but we close in, they vanish. We suspect outside pros for specific jobs."

"Ricky Malone," Manny interjected, his tone flat. "Recognize the name?"

Miller's eyes widened slightly. "Malone? 'Ricky the Torch'? Yes, absolutely. We suspected him for at least three fires, including one out near Beltzville about three weeks ago. Lost track of him since. Why? You found him?"

"Let's just say Malone provided some... context," Dev stated firmly, cutting off further questions. "He confirmed Sal Demarco hired him for the Beltzville fire, along with another man matching Brad's description. But Ricky swore he didn't touch my family's house."

Fresh concern flooded Miller's face. "If you've talked to Malone... Devin, this is incredibly dangerous. This whole mess... it was supposed to end when John died!"

"Wait," Dev's voice cracked slightly. "What do you mean, 'supposed to end'? What aren't you telling us?"

Miller hesitated, then reached into his desk drawer, pulling out a folded sheet. He slid it across the desk. Devin unfolded it. Crude, mismatched letters cut from magazines screamed silently: Chief, It ends now. ...or else.

Dev looked up, eyes boring into Miller's. "When?"

"Morning after... they found John," Miller confessed, shame heavy in his voice. "On my porch. No signature, no demands. Just... that." He slumped back. "I knew. They killed John for breaking the deal. They wanted me back in line. Ensure Akimitsu stayed quiet, ensure I stayed quiet. Keep operations running smoothly."

"Daddy," Rach whispered, voice trembling, "what did you do?"

Miller couldn't meet her eyes. "I agreed," he admitted, barely audible. "Made contact. Agreed to... the status quo. Silence. Non-interference, within limits. In exchange for safety. For your mother. For you, Rachel." He looked up, desperation raw in his eyes. "I couldn't risk it. Couldn't lose you too."

"So you let them murder John? Let them keep operating?" Dev demanded, disbelief warring with disgust.

"What choice did I have?!" Miller shot back, anger flashing desperately. "Think I haven't tried finding the one pulling the strings? We've known for years Akimitsu was number two—enforcer, negotiator. But The Boss? A ghost. Always."

"Ghost?" Manny pressed. "How?"

Miller sighed, anger deflating into weary resignation. "Untraceable calls. Encrypted, self-destructing messages. Voice distorted sometimes, normal others, never consistent. No face, no meetings, never a slip in all these years. Runs everything through cutouts like Akimitsu, like Demarco. It's like he doesn't exist outside the network."

"Where's Akimitsu now?" Dev asked sharply.

"Extradited to New York," Miller replied, gaze dropping. "Federal case. Denied bail, trial next month. Assume Rikers, but no confirmation."

Rikers. Devin stored the name. He stood abruptly, the movement sharp. Done here. Miller had made his choice. "Let's go," he directed curtly at Rach and Manny. "Back to the cabin." A grim mask settled over his features as he turned, leaving Miller looking small and defeated behind the large oak desk.

"Rachel, honey, wait," Miller pleaded as she followed the others out, his voice desperate. "Please understand... I did it for you. For Mom."

Rachel didn't turn, couldn't. Betrayal, confusion, fear—a sickening vortex. She kept walking, exiting into the cool evening air.

They piled back into the Suburban, the silence thick. As Dev pulled away, leaving the picture-perfect house behind, Manny finally spoke.

"Alright," he said quietly, glancing at Rach staring blankly out the back window, then meeting Dev's eyes in the mirror. "Pack up. Time to head back to New York. Figure this out on our turf."

"Yeah," Dev replied, gaze fixed on the road, hands tight on the wheel. "But something's still not right. Feels like we're missing a key piece."

"We'll figure it out, Dev," Rach said softly from the back, conviction absent but support present. "We have to."

The drive back was silent, each lost in thought. By the time they arrived at the cabin, night had fallen completely. The moon bathed the logs and woods in cool, silver light. Crickets and the rustle of unseen animals filled the air, a deceptive peace.

"Alright," Dev directed as they climbed out, voice firm, pushing aside the turmoil. "Wheels up 0630 tomorrow. Pass the word. Pack essential gear. Whatever comes next, we meet it head-on."

"On it," Manny replied, his tone reflecting the gravity.

They entered the cabin. The night unfolded quietly – soft sounds of bags being packed, gear checked, whispered conversations, all underscored by the heavy weight of anticipation for the journey ahead.

# Chapter 13

# Road to Ruin

*Dust swirled around retreating marines, their faces grim masks of exhaustion as they carried the wounded. Manny, covering the rear, laid down bursts of suppressive fire, each crack echoing futility against the indifferent hills.*

*They reached a cluster of rocks, collapsing behind the inadequate cover. Dev, chest heaving, scanned the faces of the remaining men. Good men down. Ammo dwindling. The target compound, silent, mocking.*

*Manny knelt beside him, face tight. "What now, Lieutenant?"*

*Dev met his friend's gaze, the raw need to succeed warring with the grim reality. Retreat wasn't an option. Neither was another frontal assault.*

*"Alternate approach," Dev said, voice firm despite the tremor he felt inside. "Small team infiltrates. Rest create a diversion."*

*Manny nodded instantly. "With you."*

*"No, Manny." Dev clapped his shoulder. "You command the diversion. Keep their eyes off us."*

*A flicker of protest in Manny's eyes, then acceptance. "Alright, Lieutenant. Watch your back."*

*Dev handpicked his team. They moved like shadows under the thin cover of darkness as Manny's force erupted in controlled chaos, gunfire drawing attention away. Reaching the compound, they found a breach, slipping inside the maze of mud-brick alleys.*

*Room by room. Methodical, silent. Empty.*

*The high-value target—the chemist—gone.*

*Defeat settled, thick and choking like the dust. As they fell back towards the breach point, shadows detached from doorways. Ambush. Taliban fighters materialized, AKs barking in the narrow confines. Outnumbered, outgunned. Dev ordered the retreat, fighting back through the alleys, losing more men with each desperate yard.*

*They slipped back through the breach, regrouping with Manny's bloodied diversion team under the relative safety of the night. Dev looked back at the dark compound, the weight of the failure a physical blow.*

*Manny approached, concern etched onto his face. "Did our best, Lieutenant."*

*Dev nodded, throat tight. "I know, Manny. Wasn't enough."*

*The long walk back to Kandahar began, failure a heavier burden than their packs, leaving a scar deeper than any bullet wound...*

Dev's breath hitched, the phantom weight settling onto his chest as his eyes snapped open. He jolted awake, the smell of cordite and dust momentarily thick in the pre-dawn darkness of the cabin before dissolving into the familiar scents of pine and brewing coffee. Shaking off the dream's residue, he swung his legs out of bed.

Downstairs, the cabin hummed with controlled urgency. People moved with efficiency born of crisis. Weapons were cleaned, checked—quiet clicks in the tense air. Gear stowed in go-bags. Vests adjusted. Even Brad Ewing, nursing cracked ribs and a swollen jaw under an operator's watchful eye in the corner, was being prepped for transport, zip-ties cinched, his sullen presence a grating reminder of the dangers still circling.

Outside, the sky paled. Four black Suburbans waited, engines idling softly, solid shapes against the misty dawn. Jackson took the lead vehicle with two operators. Dev slid behind the wheel of the second SUV, Manny settling beside him. Kate and Byron took the back, Brad bundled onto the floor between them. The third Suburban held another driver, Earl clutching his laptop case, while Rach and Annabelle occupied the back. The remaining four operators filled the last vehicle, forming the rear guard.

The convoy rolled out just as the first sun rays pierced the mountain peaks, tires crunching gravel. Down Poho Poco Drive, heading east towards New York, the weight of their uncertain mission— expose the boss, survive—pressed heavily in the confined space. Dense woods lined the road, overhanging branches creating a tunnel effect, casting long, dancing shadows.

Up ahead, maybe a mile down the winding road, an old, beat-up pickup truck sat diagonally, blocking the lane entirely. Thick black smoke billowed convincingly from under its raised hood.

Jackson's voice crackled over the radio, calm, alert. "Lead has visual, disabled vehicle blocking roadway. Looks legit, but diverting onto Jamestown as precaution. All vehicles follow. Over."

"Copy, Lead," Manny replied instantly, voice tight with suspicion. He leaned forward slightly, scanning the dense woods flanking the road. "Eyes open, everyone. Feels staged." Acknowledgments clicked back—clipped, professional, alert.

The convoy slowed, turning onto the narrower, tree-lined Jamestown Road. Navigating the first sharp curve, maybe fifty yards in, the lead Suburban suddenly lurched, engine sputtering violently before cutting out completely. Dead silence from the lead vehicle over the comms.

"EMP?" Manny hissed, hand already moving to his sidearm.

Before Dev could react, Jackson's brake lights flared red. Dev slammed his own brakes, wrenching the wheel hard left, tires screaming on damp pavement as the heavy Suburban fishtailed, the right rear quarter panel smashing into Jackson's disabled SUV with a sickening crunch of metal and glass.

In that instant, the woods erupted. Gunfire exploded from both sides—a perfectly executed L-shaped ambush. The air cracked, ripped by supersonic rounds. Muzzle flashes flickered like predatory eyes among the trees. Sal Demarco and at least a dozen Shadow Serpent operatives unleashed a hailstorm of lead.

Bullets hammered the Suburbans' armored bodies and glass, a relentless, deafening drumbeat. Windows starred but held; paint vaporized.

Jackson's crippled lead SUV, caught dead center, absorbed the worst of the initial assault. Inside, Jackson and his operators returned fire through lowered windows, suppressed weapons spitting controlled bursts into the trees.

Dev fought the wheel, the collision having thrown them partially off the road, ears ringing. Manny was already leaning across the console, firing his Glock through the passenger window, laying down cover. In back, Kate and Byron had weapons out, firing measured shots towards muzzle flashes.

Vehicle three, carrying Rach, Annabelle, and Earl, skidded to a halt behind Dev's. Rounds immediately stitched across its sides. Inside, Annabelle cried out, clutching her injured shoulder as a bullet punched through metal nearby, spraying shrapnel. Rach reacted instantly, pulling Annabelle down, pressing against the new wound while simultaneously drawing the pistol Dev had insisted she carry, firing back towards the woods, her face set in grim determination. Earl frantically tried to shield them both.

The rear security vehicle engaged immediately, laying down heavy suppressing fire, attempting to draw the attackers' focus.

The ambush was brutal, chaotic, lethally precise. Surprise belonged entirely to the attackers. But Dev's team reacted with disciplined fury. The armored Suburbans provided critical cover. Return fire intensified—accurate, deadly. EAG operators, using tactics honed in harsher environments, began to gain fire superiority on the flanks.

Slowly, painstakingly, the momentum shifted. Caught between fire from the vehicles and the rear security team's flanking pressure, the attackers' volleys slackened. Figures began withdrawing, fading back into the deeper woods. The firefight's rhythm slowed, replaced by the ringing in Dev's ears and the groaning protest of damaged metal.

The immediate aftermath was brutal. Jackson emerged from the lead vehicle, reporting grimly, "Two operators down. KIA."

The rear guard reported one KIA, two wounded but mobile. Dev's vehicle and the third SUV were scarred, bullet-pocked, but operational. Annabelle leaned heavily against Rach, pale but conscious, breathing shallowly through the pain.

And Brad Ewing? Gone. Sometime during the collision, the chaos—vanished from the floor of Dev's vehicle.

Manny, face dark with fury, moved immediately towards the treeline, towards the sprawled bodies of attackers. He spotted Sal Demarco near the edge of the woods, slumped against a tree, eyes glassy, blood pooling beneath him from multiple wounds.

"Where is he? Brad?" Manny's voice was rough, grabbing Sal's vest. Sal stared blankly, a gurgle escaping his lips. Manny shook him slightly. Sal's eyes rolled back. Dead.

The fight was over. The cost, devastating. Three EAG operators dead, Annabelle wounded, their prisoner gone. The silence that fell felt oppressive, broken only by the crackle of radios confirming casualties and the ragged breathing of survivors amidst the wreckage.

"How the hell do they keep finding us?!" Dev slammed his fist against the steering wheel, the sound jarring. He surveyed the carnage—the disabled lead SUV, the bullet-riddled vehicles, bodies near the trees, smoke hanging in the cool morning air.

"Don't know, brother, but we can't stay," Manny said grimly, returning from Sal's body, weapon still scanning the woods. "Could be more coming."

"I know." Dev pushed down the rage, forcing tactical thought. Jackson's SUV was finished. The other three drivable, though battered. He went to check on his mother. Annabelle was pale, biting her lip, but met his concerned gaze with resolve. "Mom, New York? Or nearest ER?"

She nodded weakly. "I... I can make it. Let's go. Get out of here."

Working quickly, they consolidated personnel and essential gear into the three functional SUVs. The bodies of their fallen comrades were treated with grim respect, secured for extraction arranged via secure comms. Maneuvering carefully around the wreckage and the staged pickup still blocking the main road, the battered convoy continued down Jamestown Road, turning east, pushing towards New York. The rising sun cast long shadows, the Pennsylvania landscape's beauty feeling like a bitter joke. The drive was tense, fast, punctuated only by curt radio checks. They crossed into New Jersey, the landscape flattening, then finally, the familiar jagged silhouette of Manhattan emerged through the morning haze. Dev navigated the city's arteries, the urgency of their arrival cutting through the dense morning traffic.

Finally, he pulled the lead SUV—his own scarred vehicle now—up to the controlled chaos of the NYU Langone Health emergency entrance. "Alright, let's get Mom inside," he ordered, voice tight.

Manny was already out, opening the rear door of the third vehicle, carefully helping Annabelle, who leaned heavily on Rach. Other EAG team members formed a subtle cordon, easing their path through the automatic doors. Inside the bright, antiseptic bustle of the ER, Manny's command cut through the noise. "Gunshot wound, shoulder. Immediate attention needed." Staff reacted instantly, whisking Annabelle towards a treatment bay. Dev watched her disappear, the worry tightening in his chest, before turning back to the task at hand.

He pulled out his secure phone, dialing Sarah Blake. "Sarah, it's me." Low, urgent. "Another ambush. Heavy casualties. Mom's wounded—stable, we're at NYU Langone. Where did you relocate the informant?"

Sarah's voice, sharp with concern but focused. "Safe House Three, Astoria. Fully secured."

"Okay," Dev replied. "Rach stays with Mom. The rest—Kate, Byron, Jackson, the operators—need to get to HQ. Now. Tell Alex Thompson I need a full debrief, threat assessment, resource inventory waiting. Manny and I hit the apartment first, then head to see the source."

"Understood, Devin. Teams en route to Riverdale. Be careful."

Dev disconnected, rejoining Manny near the ER entrance. They quickly briefed the team leaders. Kate acknowledged with a grim nod, organizing transport to EAG HQ. Rach confirmed she'd stay with Annabelle, relaying updates via burner.

Dev turned to Manny. "Our place first. Shower, re-arm, clean gear. Then find out what our source really knows."

Manny nodded grimly. "Agreed. Better have answers this time."

They separated, Dev and Manny heading for their waiting apartment, leaving the others, the weight of the mission—the missing prisoner, the fallen comrades, the escalating threat—pressing down.

The sterile quiet of the ER faded as Dev and Manny walked out into the city morning, leaving Rach and the others behind. They climbed into one of the waiting Suburbans—battered but functional. Necessary. Dev navigated the city's veins towards Brooklyn Heights, the usual vibrant pulse of New York feeling muted, heavy. Crossing boroughs, the East River a somber ribbon between Manhattan's towers and Queens' sprawling landscape, the stark silhouette of Rikers Island loomed against the pale sky.

Rikers. A concrete island holding countless secrets.

As Dev drove towards the Queensboro Bridge, the sun cast long shadows from its skeletal frame. Traffic thickened on the lower level, a sluggish crawl towards Manhattan. Unseen by them, caught in that same crawl, events were unfolding that would change everything.

An armored transport van, flanked by two standard escort SUVs—high-risk inmate protocol—navigated the congestion. Inside, Akimitsu Nakamura sat restrained, composed, gaze fixed impassively on the cityscape. Loyalty was a commodity. Armed C.O.s maintained a tense watch, comms linked to NYPD. Akimitsu's trial threatened empires. His allies, Shadow Serpent operatives, moved with silent precision for a daring extraction. The Queensboro Bridge—a chokepoint—was the stage.

Before the van even left Rikers, Serpent teams were in position. Blockades ready, neutralization teams set, escape routes secured. Suppressed weapons, smoke grenades, tactical gear—lethal efficiency. Near the bridge's midpoint, a rusted sedan feigned breakdown, steam curling from the open hood. Two disguised operatives watched traffic. Others melted into the bridge's steel shadows. Near the Manhattan exit, another team waited with smoke grenades.

The armored van entered the lower level. Traffic crawled. Perfect conditions. As the convoy neared the staged sedan, it blocked the lane. The lead escort slowed. "Obstruction ahead," the driver radioed. "Disabled vehicle..."

The trap snapped. Spike strips unfurled. An EMP pulsed from the sedan, scrambling the escorts' electronics, killing engines. The armored van screeched to a halt. Officers yelled into dead radios.

Figures erupted from shadows. Smoke grenades hissed, engulfing the convoy in thick gray fog. Gunfire cracked—controlled bursts disabling tires, neutralizing officers before defenses could form. Chaos. Operatives breached the van's reinforced doors. Akimitsu was freed, bundled into a waiting black SUV. More smoke deployed. The escape vehicle accelerated, weaving through stalled traffic towards Manhattan. Motorcycles materialized, blocking ramps, delaying pursuit. Audacious, meticulous, flawless. By the time NYPD reacted, Akimitsu and his rescuers were gone, swallowed by the city, leaving disabled vehicles, incapacitated guards, and the chilling message of their reach. The news would soon ignite—this was no ordinary jailbreak.

Dev maneuvered the Suburban through the final blocks towards Brooklyn Heights, pulling into the secure underground garage beneath Quay Tower. The elevator's luxurious ascent felt jarringly disconnected from the grit and violence outside.

Manny stepped out first into the expansive penthouse living room. The panoramic Manhattan skyline formed a stunning backdrop through the floor-to-ceiling windows. He headed for the bar, needing a drink, but stopped short. The large flat-screen, on low volume, flashed a breaking news alert. He grabbed the remote, increasing the sound.

Dev entered moments later, tossing his keys onto the marble kitchen island. He saw Manny staring intently at the screen—chaotic aerial footage of the Queensboro Bridge aftermath. Disabled vehicles, flashing lights, lingering smoke. Akimitsu Nakamura's face appeared as a reporter detailed the audacious extraction.

"You seeing this?" Manny asked grimly, turning as Dev approached.

Dev watched, his expression hardening. "Akimitsu's out. Right after we confirm he's number two."

"Not a coincidence," Manny said, clicking off the TV. "The timing... They knew we were close, or this is the start of something bigger."

"Or both," Dev muttered, running a hand through his hair. "Forget the shower. Need to talk to Ricky. Now." He grabbed his pre-packed go-bag from the entryway closet.

Manny nodded, grabbing his own bag. "Let's roll."

They headed back down, into the same battered Suburban. Dev started the engine, maneuvering back into the city flow, pointing towards Astoria, Queens. The drive was tense, Akimitsu's escape adding another layer of dangerous urgency.

"He lied, Devin," Manny said finally, voice low as they crossed the East River again via the Williamsburg Bridge. "Ricky. About how much he knew. Had to."

Dev gripped the steering wheel, knuckles white. "If he did, Sarah putting him in that safe house just put a bullseye on his back."

They exited into Queens, Manhattan receding, replaced by the industrial landscape of Astoria. Warehouses lined the streets. Dev turned onto a smaller side street, the air heavy with neglect. He parked before a nondescript two-story brick warehouse – Safe House Three. Aged brick, graffiti splashes, dark upper windows – it blended anonymously.

They approached the heavy steel door. Devin knocked firmly, a specific pattern. The door creaked open. Ricky Malone stood there, looking more gaunt than before, eyes wide with raw terror.

"Devin! Manny! What—?" he stammered, glancing nervously past them down the empty street.

Dev stepped forward, crowding him, voice dangerously low. "Enough bullshit, Ricky. We know you held back. You're under my protection because you gave us Sal. Who else? Who were you working with? Who knew about the arson jobs? Who connects to Akimitsu's crew?"

"No! Told you everything!" Ricky pleaded, voice trembling, trying to back into the warehouse loft. "Just Sal, the other guy! Swear!"

Manny moved past Dev, blocking Ricky's retreat. "Liar," Manny stated flatly. "You know more. Who paid Sal? Who connects to Akimitsu? Start talking before—"

Crack!

The sharp report of a high-velocity rifle shattered the confrontation. The round punched through a large industrial window high on the opposite wall, crossing the loft in an instant. Ricky gasped, a neat hole appearing high on his chest, blood blooming suddenly on his thin shirt. His eyes widened in shock, rolled back. He crumpled silently to the floor.

Dev and Manny reacted instantly, dropping low, weapons snapping up, scanning windows, the street. "Sniper! Roof across!" Manny yelled, pinpointing the source.

They bolted out the steel door, adrenaline surging. They needed the shooter. Racing across the street, scanning rooftops, searching for access—fire escape, open hatch. A clatter of metal from an alley beside the target building snapped their attention. They rounded the corner just as a figure in dark clothing stumbled, clutching a bleeding leg, scrambling away towards the back.

"There!" Dev shouted. They chased, boots pounding on cracked pavement. The shooter glanced back, saw them gaining, made a desperate attempt to scale a chain-link fence at the alley's dead end. Halfway up, Devin, aiming while running, fired his sidearm. The bullet tore through the shooter's injured leg. He cried out, lost his grip, tumbled onto the garbage-strewn ground.

Manny was on him instantly, kicking the sniper rifle away, pinning him. Dev arrived a second later, roughly zip-tying the shooter's hands. The man groaned, face contorted, blood spreading quickly.

"Hospital... gotta get... hospital..." the shooter gasped, panic in his voice.

"Not happening," Manny growled, hauling him roughly up. "Who sent you? Who ordered the hit on Ricky?"

The shooter clamped his mouth shut, eyes wide with pain and fear. Manny shoved him towards the street. "Done talking."

They dragged the groaning shooter back across the street, bundling him into the Suburban's back seat. Devin and Manny exchanged a grim look, climbing back into the front. Dev started the engine, pulling away, turning south, heading back towards Manhattan, the East River, the Henry Hudson Parkway, north to the Bronx.

The journey to EAG HQ began, the SUV's atmosphere thick with tension and the metallic smell of the prisoner's blood. Crossing the Queensboro Bridge back into Manhattan, the interrogation started.

"Who do you work for?" Dev asked, voice cold, eyes on the road, attention fixed on the man in the back.

Silence. The shooter stared out the window, jaw clenched.

"Answer him," Manny bit out, glancing back.

The shooter swallowed hard. "Ain't... sayin' nothin'."

Dev's grip tightened on the wheel. "Wrong answer. We know you were involved in the Akimitsu extraction. You just killed our witness. Start talking. Now. Who gives the orders?" They continued south on 2nd Avenue, turned onto the FDR Drive northbound, traffic flowing obliviously around them.

"Why kill Ricky?" Manny pressed. "What did he know?"

The shooter coughed, blood flecking his lips. "Don't know... what you're talkin' about."

They merged onto the Harlem River Drive, then the Henry Hudson Parkway, the city yielding to the greener Bronx. The shooter stayed silent, sweating, occasionally whimpering.

"You're protecting someone," Manny stated flatly. "Powerful enough to order hits and break Akimitsu out." The shooter's eyes flickered—just a fraction of a second's confirmation—before he locked down again.

Dev glanced in the mirror. Time and options were dwindling. Exiting onto Riverdale Avenue, approaching the familiar sleek building, Dev tried once more. "Last chance. A name. Anything. Cooperate, maybe you get medical help. Stay silent..." The threat hung.

The shooter looked between them, pale, drawn. Fear warred with ingrained loyalty. "I... I can't," he finally whispered, voice ragged. "He'd... they'd kill me anyway."

Manny scoffed. "Might save them the trouble."

Dev pulled the Suburban up to 5450 Riverdale Avenue, EAG HQ looming before them. The interrogation yielded nothing. They had a prisoner, but no closer to understanding the threat, or the identity of the ghost pulling the strings.

# Chapter 14

# Vanishing Point

Late afternoon sun cast long shadows across Riverdale Avenue as Dev and Manny, escorting the subdued, bleeding shooter, approached the entrance of Echelon Axiom Global HQ. The seven-story building, sleek glass and steel gleaming under the waning light, projected quiet power—a fortress known for its resources and high-value clientele. Inside, the lobby was a world away from the city's grit—a spacious, meticulously designed area radiating quiet authority. Polished marble floors reflected the shifting light from the digital wall display behind reception, where live feeds of global maps showcased EAG's extensive reach, hinting at the international scope beyond its New York, Brooklyn, and DC offices.

Dev guided Manny and their captive towards the elevators, giving the stationed security guard a curt nod. "Take this one to interrogation." Turning to the receptionist, he added, "Have Earl and Kate meet me in meeting room 3, ASAP."

Without waiting for acknowledgment, Dev and Manny headed towards the designated meeting room on the fifth floor—the operations hub.

Dev settled at the head of the polished conference table, his expression grim. Moments later, Kate entered, her athletic frame radiating focused intensity. Earl followed closely, his usual fidgety energy a stark contrast to Kate's composure.

"Guessing you saw the news," Kate stated grimly, taking a seat, dispensing with pleasantries. The tension from Akimitsu's extraction felt thick even within these walls.

"Yeah," Dev responded, voice tight. "Akimitsu's out. This just went exponential. Whoever's behind this has reach we didn't anticipate."

Earl nodded nervously, clutching a tablet. "The extraction's precision, the simultaneous attack on the witness... suggests deep planning, likely inside knowledge—maybe not of EAG, but definitely law enforcement protocols."

Manny leaned forward onto the table. "Forget inside knowledge. The shooter we brought in? Anything?"

"Interrogation team's starting," Kate replied. "No standard ID. Running facial recognition now against mercenary and criminal databases."

"Good." Dev's gaze hardened. "Earl, prioritize identifying him, any known associates. Cross-reference Akimitsu's network, Serpent affiliations. I want to know who he is and who he answers to."

"On it, boss." Earl's fingers flew across his tablet.

Dev turned back to Kate. "Need every available NY operator mobilized. Full tactical readiness, within the hour. We took heavy losses in PA, ambushed again securing the witness. Akimitsu wouldn't be sprung unless something bigger is imminent. We can't be caught unprepared again."

"Already coordinating dispatch," Kate confirmed. "Teams are mustering."

As the brief, tense meeting concluded, Earl hurrying off to liaise with analysts, Dev and Manny headed back to the elevator. Destination: sixth floor, executive offices.

The elevator ascended smoothly. As the doors opened onto the plush executive floor carpeting, Sarah Blake stood waiting, her expression a mixture of relief and barely suppressed anxiety. She rushed forward, wrapping both Dev and Manny in a brief, fierce hug. "Why must you two constantly court disaster?"

Sarah, young at 24 but undeniably poised, had a presence that belied her 5'4" height. Her fit build, warm complexion, and striking blue eyes conveyed competence and approachability.

"Magnet for chaos, Sarah," Manny responded, managing a tired chuckle as she stepped back.

Dev offered only a tight nod, his mind clearly elsewhere, moving past them towards his office door. He left Manny and Sarah exchanging brief updates, his long strides carrying him quickly into his private sanctuary. Inside the spacious office, Dev went straight to the floor-to-ceiling window, gaze lost in the sprawling cityscape below. He pulled out his personal cell, dialing Rach's number automatically. As it rang, his mind replayed the chaos—the ambush, Sal's death, Brad's disappearance, Akimitsu free, the informant silenced...

"Hello?" Rach's voice came through the line, thin and distant.

"Hey," Dev replied, the weight of his worry heavy in that single word. "Checking in."

"She's sleeping," Rach reported, a profound fatigue dragging at her words. "Patched up, pain meds kicked in. Surgery went well, they said, still sedated."

"Good." Dev felt a knot in his chest loosen fractionally. "And you?" he asked, his tone gentling.

A long sigh feathered across the line. "Don't know. Stepped outside for air." Her voice cracked. "Just... haven't processed... Dad..."

She stopped. A sharp crash reverberated through the phone, followed by Rach's hitched gasp, then a raw, terrified scream abruptly silenced. The line clicked dead.

"Rachel?!" Dev gripped the phone, ice flooding his veins. "RACHEL!" He shot to his feet, a surge of raw energy hitting him. He bolted from his office, slamming Manny's door open across the hall without breaking stride. Manny looked up, startled from his chair.

"Hospital. Now!" Dev's voice was tight, barely controlled.

"What's wrong, Dev?" Manny was instantly on his feet, alarm sharpening his features. "Your mom?"

"Yeah—No! Rach!" Dev fought for coherence. "On the phone—crash—scream—line dead! Attack, kidnap—don't know! We need to go!"

They sprinted for the elevator, boots hammering the quiet corridor. The wait felt agonizing. Inside, the silent descent amplified the frantic beat against Dev's ribs. Bursting through the lobby doors, they raced to the waiting Suburban, tires screaming out of the garage, Dev accelerating hard towards NYU Langone, a desperate hope warring with the certainty they were moving too slowly.

In the hospital parking lot, the setting sun painted long, menacing shadows between the cars. Rach fought against rough hands, her cries swallowed by the evening sounds. Her attackers were strong, practiced, dragging her towards a dark van parked in a poorly lit corner.

Akimitsu, his face a blank mask, spoke, his calm voice chilling against the violence. "The more you fight, the worse this will be."

Seeing the overwhelming force, the impossibility of escape, Rach ceased her struggles. Her fear remained, a cold weight, but a spark of defiance hardened her eyes. They pushed her into the van; she focused, absorbing details—the smell of stale cigarettes, the feel of ripped upholstery.

The van pulled out quickly, swallowed by the Brooklyn night. A second man beside Akimitsu forced a rough burlap sack over her head; the world dissolved into scratchy darkness and the smell of dust. Blinded, heart pounding, she focused outward—sounds, smells, the van's vibrations. The journey was a confusion of city noise—distant sirens, the rumble of traffic, indistinct shouts. After maybe fifteen, twenty minutes, the soundscape shifted. The city hum faded, replaced by heavy diesel drones, the rhythmic beeping of reversing trucks, the clang of heavy metal. The hiss of air brakes nearby. The low vibration of forklifts. The air changed too—salt tang from the water, acrid diesel fumes, a faint chemical sharpness underneath. Not just a warehouse—a working port. Red Hook, she guessed, judging by the sounds and smells.

The van stopped. Rough hands pulled her out onto uneven ground, then through heavy doors into an echoing space. The port sounds continued, slightly muffled now but still present.

Dev slammed the Suburban into park near the ER entrance, the engine protesting. He and Manny bailed out, their eyes sweeping the darkening parking lot. Evening shift change added to the confusion—staff arriving, visitors leaving, headlights cutting through the gloom. They moved systematically through the rows, checking the spaces where Rach might have stepped out for air.

Asphalt blurred beneath their boots. They scanned under cars, checked behind dumpsters, searched for any disturbed gravel, any sign of a struggle. Nearly an hour bled away, each empty pass tightening the knot in Dev's stomach. Then, near the poorly lit far corner, a glint caught his eye—shattered plastic and metal reflecting the distant security lights. Rach's phone. Cracked, crushed, lying abandoned on the pavement. Dev picked up the broken pieces, the sharp edges pressing into his palm.

"This isn't good, Manny." His voice was low, grim. "What the hell happened?"

"We find her," Manny stated, his tone unwavering, though a flicker of Dev's own tension reflected in his eyes. "We've handled worse."

"Yeah, but this feels different." Dev clenched his fist around the phone fragments. "Precise. Planned." He pulled out his secure phone, dialing Kate at HQ with quick, decisive taps. He paced as the call connected.

"Kate, it's Dev," he said, keeping his voice low despite the urgency churning inside him. "Problem."

"What's going on, boss?" Kate's immediate reply was sharp, alert.

"Rachael's gone. Taken from the hospital parking lot. Found her phone—smashed. Need eyes on all surveillance around NYU Langone, starting an hour ago. Anything out of place, suspicious vehicles, dark vans."

"God... Okay, Dev. Right on it. Analysts pulling feeds now," Kate responded, her focus immediate. Dev hung up, the silence amplifying the thrum beneath his ribs.

"Inside," Manny urged, gesturing towards the ER. "Hospital security cams might have caught something."

They headed back in. Manny quickly found a uniformed supervisor, explaining the situation with terse urgency. The guard, after verifying their credentials, nodded, his expression creasing with concern, and led them through coded doors into a small, monitor-lined security office.

"Okay," the guard said, turning to them. "Timeframe?"

Dev checked his phone, relaying the time Rach's call had abruptly ended. "Alright..." the guard acknowledged, fingers moving rapidly across a keyboard, cycling through camera angles, rewinding feeds. He scanned the monitors. Suddenly, he leaned closer to one screen. "Here. Maybe."

Dev and Manny crowded behind him. Grainy, monochrome footage showed Rach pacing near the edge of the lot, phone pressed to her ear. A figure emerged from the deep shadows between parked cars, moving fast, grabbing her from behind. She struggled briefly before being dragged backward, out of the camera's frame. Just before vanishing, a second figure stepped into view, raised a boot, and brought it down hard on the spot where Rach had dropped her phone. Then, both were gone. Seconds later, a dark van—color obscured by the night-vision feed—drove past that corner, turned south onto 1st Avenue, and disappeared from view.

Dev drew a sharp breath, the grainy image making the abduction sickeningly concrete. "Other angles? The van? Plates?" he pressed, knowing the likely answer.

"Checked adjacent feeds," the guard confirmed, shaking his head. "Bad angles, too dark, too far for a plate. Turned south on 1st, then nothing."

Manny thanked the guard curtly as they were escorted out. They walked back towards their Suburban, the certainty of Rach's abduction a heavy weight. Dev immediately dialed Kate again.

"Kate, update," he said when she answered. "Hospital cams confirm abduction. Two suspects, maybe more in the van. Dark van, older model maybe, no make or plate confirmed. Headed south on 1st Ave around 18:10. Need DOT cams, traffic feeds—anything tracking south from Langone around that time."

"Working it," Kate replied instantly. "Pulling feeds now. Ping you the second we get a hit."

Dev hung up. He met Manny's gaze, the question silent between them.

"South," Manny answered, already climbing into the passenger seat. "Head south on 1st. Start looking. Beats sitting here."

"Alright." Dev slid behind the wheel. "Let's go." He put the Suburban in gear, easing out onto 1st Avenue, merging into the river of headlights, hunting for a shadow in the city's vastness.

"Eyes open," Dev directed as they navigated the heavy southbound traffic. City lights smeared across the wet pavement. They scanned the urban tangle—dark alleys, loading zones, parked vans—searching for Rach, for the van from the grainy footage. At each red light, their gazes swept the cross streets, hope a fragile thing against the rising dread.

Rolling to a stop at 1st and 23rd, the encrypted chime from Dev's secure phone cut through the tense quiet.

"Report," Dev answered immediately, hitting the speaker function.

"Got DOT camera access," Kate's voice came through, crisp, efficient. "Tracked a dark van matching the hospital description south on 1st. Took the Hamilton Avenue exit—Red Hook, Brooklyn. Lost visual after that. Cameras are spotty near the port terminals."

"Thanks, Kate." Dev's mind seized the new vector. "Keep digging. Private security feeds nearby, port authority cams—call in markers if you have to."

"Understood," Kate acknowledged.

"Kate," Manny leaned towards the speaker, "Red Hook... isn't that close to the Brooklyn Field Office? Get boots on the ground there. Teams canvassing, now."

"Way ahead of you, Manny," Kate confirmed. "Brooklyn office is right off Beard Street. Ideal staging. Alerted Director Thompson. He's deploying teams to canvass immediately."

"Perfect." Dev executed a U-turn as soon as traffic cleared. "Tell Thompson we're heading his way. ETA fifteen. Send any intel he has—known fronts, recent activity—to my device."

Dev ended the call, accelerating towards the Brooklyn-Battery Tunnel. The new lead pulsed between them as they drove towards the field office. As they approached 155 Beard Street, the contrast sharpened. The sturdy brick warehouse conversion stood solid amidst Red Hook's working waterfront grit. They were buzzed through the secure gate, parking the Suburban.

Inside, the lobby presented sleek modernity against the industrial backdrop. Biometric scanners guarded access; a receptionist monitored arrivals. Dev and Manny badged through, entering the Central Hub. The energy instantly shifted. Over fifty personnel moved with quiet focus, bathed in the cool blue glow of monitors. A massive video wall displayed real-time city feeds, data streams, personnel locations. The air hummed with the controlled energy of an operation in progress. The usual background noise subsided momentarily as Dev and Manny strode towards the large glass-walled conference room overlooking the Hub. Inside, the room felt primed for crisis. A long, polished table reflected the tense faces of Field Office Director Alex Thompson, Hub Supervisor Emily Chen, and Team Leader Mike Davis, among others. They rose as Dev entered, their expressions set. The glass wall offered a constant, wide view of the bustling Ops Hub below. Dev went straight to the head of the table, facing the massive 100-inch monitor, and sank into a chair.

"Report," Dev commanded, his voice cutting the tension.

Thompson stepped forward, gesturing towards the main screen where various feeds flickered – details lost in the motion. "Canvassing teams deployed on Kate's alert. Ten-block radius from the Hamilton Ave exit point – warehouses, access roads, potential holding sites. Nothing solid yet, sir. Awaiting direction."

"Increase the radius," Dev ordered instantly, leaning forward, fatigue momentarily burned away by urgency. "Double the teams. Four more out, now. Link operations directly with Kate at HQ – sync data, share intel immediately. Work this from both sides."

As Dev spoke, the massive screen abruptly flared, overriding the tactical displays. A new video feed snapped into view. A man sat behind a substantial desk in a bright, minimalist office – stark white walls, spare decor. Standing calmly beside and slightly behind him was Akimitsu Nakamura, instantly recognizable, his stillness radiating danger. Dev focused on the seated man. Older, late 50s maybe, short dark hair graying sharply at the temples. His pale, weathered complexion made the cold calculation in his blue eyes seem more intense. A faded white scar marked his left cheekbone. He leaned forward slightly, his smooth, measured words colored by a faint, unfamiliar accent.

"I imagine," the seated man began, his voice calm, conversational, yet underscored with menace, "you wonder who I am. That," a faint, unreadable smile touched his lips, "can wait." Manny, beside Dev, stiffened slightly, clearly registering the accent. "What is important," the man continued, his tone chilling, his blue eyes seeming to fix on them through the screen, "is that I have Ms. Miller. Her continued survival... depends entirely on you."

Dev fought the immediate urge to react, the image of Rach flashing sharp and painful in his mind. He kept his voice level, the quiet amplifying the threat. "What do you want?"

The man chuckled, a dry, cold sound. "Want? An interesting question." He leaned back slightly, steepling his fingers. Akimitsu, standing calmly beside and slightly behind him, remained a study in dangerous stillness.

"Perhaps I want you to understand consequence, Jones. You, and your faithful associate Rivera." His eyes flickered briefly towards Manny. "You understand being hunted, cornered. But do you understand being... forgotten? Left for months in conditions unfit for an animal?" As Viktor's voice dropped, taking on a distinct bitterness, the only perceptible change in Akimitsu was the slightest shift in his weight from one foot to the other, a micro-adjustment almost lost in the stillness that surrounded him. "Abandoned by those sworn to retrieve you? Forced to rely on your own... resources," Viktor's eyes glinted with hidden meaning, "chemistry, even... to negotiate survival?" He leaned forward again, intensity replacing the faint amusement. "No, I suspect not. But you will. My objective is simple: your suffering."

The screen went black. The sudden void reflected the tense, stunned expressions around the conference table.

For a beat, silence held. Then the room erupted – shouts, questions, demands for traces, analysts talking rapidly into comms. Dev slammed his hand flat on the polished table, the sharp crack silencing the room instantly. "Enough!" His voice, tight with a fury born of chilling understanding, cut through the rising panic.

Silence fell again, thick and absolute.

# Chapter 15

# Tracing Shadows

Silence settled again in the conference room after Devin's sharp command cut through the noise. Blank screens stared back where Viktor's face had been moments before. The polished mahogany table reflected the strained, shocked expressions of the assembled personnel. Manny entered then, his rugged features tight with resolve. Behind him were Alex Thompson, the Field Office Director, Emily Chen, the Hub Supervisor, and Mike Davis, Team Leader 1. The air in the room felt electric, shifting with new purpose.

"Dev," Manny began, his voice low and urgent, "HQ patch is live. They think they've got something on our caller."

Thompson nodded to Davis, who brought the large monitor back to life. The screen split. On one side, the EAG HQ conference room appeared—Kate stood near their main display, flanked by Rebecca Moore and other analysts, the tension radiating even through the feed. The other side mirrored an analyst's laptop, data streams blurring across it.

Davis addressed the Brooklyn room first, his tone crisp, professional. "Facial recognition run on the recorded call. Subject one confirmed as Akimitsu Nakamura, verified against federal databases and bridge extraction reports." He paused, inhaling sharply. "The primary subject, seated... required deeper archive protocols. Flagged a potential match against a 2010 file photo." The screen shifted, displaying the call image beside an older photograph. "Subject ID'd as Viktor Mikhailov, Russian national, expert chemist. Listed kidnapped by Taliban affiliates circa late 2010, presumed KIA after a failed extraction, April 2011."

Dev stared at the screen. Mikhailov. The name, the face—it landed like a physical blow, memory flooding back with sudden, unwelcome intensity. April 23rd, 2011. KAF TOC. The briefing room hum. Drone feed flickering. His own voice, younger: "Objective: extract Viktor Mikhailov, Russian chemist..." Manny beside him, insertion points, mud walls... The hit on the Chinook... The firefight... Breaching... Empty compound... Failure.

Dev snapped back to the present, the ghosts settling cold in his gut. He met Manny's eyes across the table—the same shock, the same understanding reflected there. "Hey," Dev said, his voice tight, almost lost.

"Yeah," Manny breathed, the connection forged. "KAF. The HVT..."

"The chemist," Dev finished, his jaw tightening. "The mission... the one we barely walked away from, empty-handed. Viktor Mikhailov. Alive."

"And carrying the receipts," Manny added grimly. "What else do we have? How does he go from dead in Afghanistan to... this?"

Kate's image leaned forward on the screen, taking over the HQ brief, her voice sharp. "Mikhailov vanished from intel grids after that April 2011 mission failure. Nakamura is the thread. His movements post-2011 are traceable, though difficult." Maps and timelines populated the screen. "He surfaced in Japan soon after, documented association with the Sakura Syndicate Yakuza under Hiroshi Takeda, late 2011 to mid-2013. Nakamura's recent US activity," Kate continued, "including meetings tied to shell corporations, points directly to Mercury International as a primary operational front."

Kate paused, her gaze direct through the camera. "And Dev, regarding Mercury International – yes, the client who booked the Halloween detail. My review approved it; credentials and financials passed all standard EAG vetting." Her expression tightened almost imperceptibly. "Given the connection to Nakamura and potentially Mikhailov, I've been attempting backchannel contact with our deployed team there for the past hour. No response."

Rebecca Moore stepped beside Kate. "Lack of contact is concerning. Intel suggests Mikhailov likely negotiated his release or escaped captivity late 2011. Unconfirmed reports indicate he leveraged his chemical expertise – possibly developing a potent, unknown chemical agent," she emphasized the phrase, "as a bargaining chip. First with captors, then securing protection and backing from Takeda's Yakuza once Nakamura located him."

Rebecca continued, "Nakamura became Mikhailov's right hand. His timeline shows extensive travel—Japan, Russia, Europe, Africa—from 2013 onwards, coinciding with major disruptions in the global underworld. Financial forensics show massive capital consolidation, systematic absorption or elimination of rivals."

Kate added, "Analysts assess with high confidence Mikhailov, operating from the shadows via Nakamura, forged alliances, then integrated powerful independent syndicates—Iron Syndicate, Vero Alliance, Red Vultures, starting with the Sakura Syndicate—uniting them under one entity: The Shadow Serpents. Viktor Mikhailov, presumed dead, is the ghost leading this network."

"And Mercury International is a key node," Rebecca concluded. "Still mapping its structure. Outwardly clean—logistics, import/export, manufacturing. Untangling legitimate business from Serpent operations is complex. Earl is working encrypted financials now, searching for anomalies linking Mikhailov directly."

"Strong work," Dev responded, struggling to process the confirmation of Viktor's survival, the sheer scale of his reach. He forced his focus back to the immediate. "Kate – keep trying to raise that Mercury team. Non-stop. Assume compromised until confirmed otherwise. Need their status ASAP."

Manny spoke up, his tone firm. "Get surveillance on Mercury International facilities—HQ, major logistics hubs. Discreet eyes on access points. Need to know who's coming and going."

"Understood," Kate confirmed from the screen. "Teams mobilizing."

The monitor clicked off, plunging the Brooklyn conference room back into its own tense quiet. The remaining team members shifted, the weight of the revelations settling in the air. Dev gestured for Manny to stay as the others – Thompson, Chen, Davis – filed out to relay orders and manage the escalating crisis.

The heavy door to the conference room clicked shut, leaving Dev and Manny alone in the sudden, charged quiet. The large monitor was dark now, but the image of Viktor Mikhailov – alive, pulling the strings – remained fixed in Dev's vision. The low hum of the Central Operations Hub outside felt distant.

Manny remained standing near the table, watching Dev, who had sunk back into the chair at the head, running a hand wearily over his face. The adrenaline from the briefing was fading, leaving behind a profound exhaustion mixed with a vibrating unease.

"Manny..." Dev started, his voice low, rough. He looked up, meeting his friend's unwavering gaze across the polished table. "Those dreams I mentioned? The ones I've had since Dad... since this started?"

Manny nodded slowly, leaning back against the edge of the table, crossing his arms. He knew Dev rarely discussed the nightmares that haunted many veterans, himself included. "Yeah? What about 'em?"

Dev pushed his chair back slightly, looking towards the glass wall overlooking the Ops Hub, but his focus was internal. "It's that mission, man. Kandahar. April 2011." His voice was tight. "Every night. The Chinook going down, the firefight, breaching that compound... empty." He turned back to Manny, his eyes intense. "The target we failed to extract. All this time, reliving that failure."

He let out a short, harsh breath, shaking his head slightly. "And now... knowing he's alive? That he's the ghost behind all this – Dad's death, Rach's abduction, ... It's like the nightmare just walked out of my head into the real world." He leaned forward, elbows on the table, covering his face for a brief moment. "It's messing with me, Manny. The sheer irony..."

Manny was silent for a moment, absorbing the chilling connection between their past failure and their present nightmare. He pushed off the table and walked around to stand beside Dev's chair, clapping a heavy, grounding hand on his shoulder.

"Yeah," Manny said quietly, his voice filled with shared understanding. "Yeah, I get it. It's... twisted. Like the universe enjoys a cruel joke." He squeezed Dev's shoulder briefly. "That mission was cursed. Bad intel, bad timing. We did everything we could. We didn't leave him behind by choice."

His tone firmed slightly, pulling Dev's focus back. "But listen, Dev. Him being alive? Him being this... architect of misery? Doesn't change the objective. Just raises the stakes. Makes it personal, yeah, maybe more than anything we've faced." He met Dev's shadowed gaze. "We failed to get him out once. We won't fail to put him down now. And we will get Rach back."

Dev looked up, seeing the resolve in Manny's eyes mirror the purpose reigniting within himself. He took a deep breath, the exhaustion still profound, but the frantic edge smoothed slightly by the shared burden, replaced by a colder, harder determination. He gave a curt nod.

"Yeah," he agreed, his voice steadier. "You're right." He pushed himself to his feet, the need for action overriding the body's protest. "Let's get moving. HQ has teams mobilizing on Mercury International, but I want our eyes there too. We need to join the search, find Rach."

They turned and walked towards the door, leaving the loaded silence of the conference room behind them, the ghost of Viktor Mikhailov now a tangible enemy with a face, a history, and a reckoning long overdue. Their next move was clear: head towards Mercury International and find Rach.

They exited the Brooklyn Field Office, the sleek building feeling dissonant after the information revealed inside. Climbing back into the waiting black Suburban, their objective felt immense. Dev took the wheel, navigating the industrial streets of Red Hook under the descending night sky, heading towards the address linked to Mercury

International where Kate's team had tracked the van. Manny rode shotgun, scanning the landscape – warehouses cloaked in darkness, chain-link fences topped with razor wire reflecting sparse streetlights, the distant, isolated sounds of the port drifting on the cool night air.

Dev's secure phone buzzed, the sound sharp in the quiet cab. He answered via the hands-free system. "Kate, report."

"Dev, confirmation," Kate's voice came through, efficient and urgent. "Analysts cross-referenced DOT cams with vehicle registrations tied to Mercury shells and port authority logs. The dark van from the hospital footage entered the main gate for the Mercury International warehouse facility at 683 Court Street about forty minutes after leaving Langone. It hasn't exited. That's the target."

"Confirmed," Dev replied, his knuckles tight on the steering wheel. "Send coordinates for a nearby RV point. Need eyes on before teams move."

"Sourced a likely spot," Kate responded. "Abandoned multi-story warehouse, north perimeter, offers rooftop view. Coordinates incoming. Jackson, Byron, and I are mobilizing assault teams, ETA to RV approx twenty minutes."

"Copy. See you there." Dev disconnected.

They found the location easily – a decaying brick warehouse looming dark among the slightly less derelict structures near the target Mercury facility. Parking the Suburban several blocks away in deep shadow, they approached on foot, moving through the urban decay. A rusted fire escape offered shaky access to the roof.

Thin moonlight offered scant illumination, cut by the insistent wind whipping across the exposed rooftop. Below, the floodlit Mercury International warehouse complex at 683 Court Street sprawled wide. Armed figures moved methodically around the perimeter fence and near the southern loading docks, their shapes stark under the security lights. The wind carried the faint smell of diesel and salt air over the low industrial hum.

"Definitely prepared for visitors," Manny's voice was low, rough against the wind's whine, his NVG monocular steady. "Counting thirty, maybe thirty-five plus, just outside."

Dev, jaw tight, scanned through his own NVG. "Heavy gear, too. Not just handguns. They're expecting us, or guarding something critical."

"Yeah, more than just standard warehouse guards," Manny lowered the monocular, his mouth set in a grim line.

They remained still for several more minutes, observing the guards' patterns—pacing, communication, routes—noting details, searching for exploitable gaps. Finally, as darkened vehicles began moving into position on the streets below—the first EAG teams arriving—they turned, descending the rusted, protesting steel staircase.

They reached the cracked concrete floor of the main hall, moving quietly toward the center of the vast, empty space. Beneath a shattered light fixture that threw distorted shadows, the rest of their core team waited: Kate, Jackson, Byron, and Lisa Monroe, the surveillance expert, her face intent in the dimness filtering through grimy windows. Weapons, vests, and blueprints lay scattered around a central workbench.

Lisa immediately unrolled a large blueprint across the workbench's scarred surface, the paper rustling. "City archives. Mercury Warehouse, 683 Court Street. Main structure, admin offices here, docks south."

Dev leaned over the blueprint, tracing the lines under the stark white beam of a portable LED lamp clamped to the table. "Okay, initial recon confirms heavy exterior presence. Thirty-five plus outside." He pointed. "Staggered patrols here, potential blind spots near the rear bays... expect internal patrols too." He quickly summarized their rooftop observations.

"Stealth is critical," Dev's voice was a low growl, his gaze sweeping Kate, Manny, Byron, Jackson, and Lisa. "Move like ghosts. They don't know we're here until we're breathing down their necks."

He turned to Byron, standing with the operators designated Delta Squad. Dev picked up a dusty pencil. "Byron, adjacent structures," he indicated neighboring warehouses, "and the container stacks west—good elevation. Take Delta, set overwatch. Synchronized takedown of exterior sentries is crucial for silence."

Byron gave a curt nod.

Dev's focus shifted. "Kate, Charlie Squad. Employee entrance, east wall. That's your breach." He met Manny's eyes. "Manny, Beta Squad hits the docks. Fast. Neutralize internals before they react." Finally, Dev's finger tapped the main entrance to the admin section. "Alpha Squad, with me. Main entrance. Hard and fast once the perimeter's clear."

Manny nodded grimly. "Keep it clean, Dev. We all know the stakes here. Stick to the plan, execute clean."

Kate laid three photos on the workbench—Mikhailov, Nakamura, and Rach, her face tight with fear but her eyes defiant. "Primary objective: locate and rescue Rachel," Kate stated firmly. "Secondary: capture or neutralize Mikhailov and Nakamura."

Dev's eyes flickered over Rach's photo for only a moment before his focus hardened back onto the blueprint. "Alright. Squads are ten to fifteen operators. Final gear check. Move out in ten."

His order settled into the warehouse air, the silence charged with the impending violence and the hope of rescue.

# Chapter 16

# Calculated Chaos

The silence in the abandoned warehouse felt charged, broken only by the soft click-clack of weapons checks and the whisper of tactical gear. The complex infiltration plan Devin had detailed settled over the team, a shared map for the dangerous path ahead.

"Comms check," Dev's voice was a low murmur, barely carrying as he and Alpha Squad hugged the shadows along the western fence line. The hulking shapes of rusted shipping containers offered cover from the thin moonlight.

"Check," Manny's reply was immediate from his position near the southern fence.

"Check," came Kate's level tone near the eastern boundary.

"Solid," Byron's voice confirmed from his overwatch staging point.

"Charlie, go for breach and hold," Dev's order was precise.

Kate and Charlie Squad moved with smooth coordination. Crouching behind overgrown shrubs near the eastern fence, Kate signaled an operative forward. He moved towards the chain-link barrier, heavy bolt cutters held low, shielded from the moonlight. The sharp snip of steel seemed loud in the stillness but was quickly muffled as he pulled the cut wire aside, creating a dark opening in the perimeter.

"Delta, keep them covered," Dev's voice, low through the comms, held an edge that demanded compliance.

"East perimeter breached," Kate's acknowledgment was quick, all business.

"Beta, you're up," Dev instructed, his attention already shifting.

From their cover behind a stack of shipping containers near the southern fence, Manny and Beta Squad replicated Charlie's movements. The crunch of the bolt cutters was brief; silence quickly returned.

Simultaneously, closer to the main entrance, Dev and Alpha Squad finished their own breach. The cut section of fence sagged before being pulled open, their entry point secured.

"Delta," Dev's voice suddenly sharpened, tight with contained anger. "Take out elevated targets. Now."

The night held its breath for a moment—then, from the rooftops of Mercury International, a series of muffled phuts broke the quiet. One... two... three... four... Figures in tactical gear slumped against concrete and steel, their watch abruptly finished.

"Done," Byron's voice was flat, revealing nothing of his team's lethal efficiency.

"All teams, enter perimeter, secure designated entry points," Dev commanded, the words unleashing the coiled readiness of the waiting squads.

Moving like shadows through the newly created openings, each squad flowed through the fence line. The previously quiet night now held the soft thwack of suppressed gunfire. One by one, armed figures patrolling the Mercury grounds crumpled, oblivious to the disciplined enemy moving among them. The force guarding Rach was being taken apart with calculated efficiency.

"Loading docks clear," Manny's voice reported over Dev's comms from near the west side truck lot. Darkness dominated the area, broken only by faint beams from motion-activated floodlights above "Bay 3" and "Bay 4."

"Side entrance clear," Kate reported from her position near the eastern staff access door.

Dev crouched against the wall beside Alpha Squad at the main entrance, just outside the sleek glass double doors framed in brushed aluminum. His gloved hand rested lightly on his Heckler & Koch MP7 as he scanned their surroundings under harsh artificial light that cast long shadows across the manicured landscaping flanking the walkway.

"Main entrance secure," Dev confirmed quietly into his comms. "Looks clear—breach on my..."

A deafening crack ripped through the night, obliterating the tense quiet. The operative beside Dev spasmed, red blossoming on his chest before he collapsed onto the concrete walkway, his weapon skittering away.

Pure reaction fired through Dev. With a raw sound torn from his throat, he spun toward the shot's origin, MP7 snapping up. A short burst hammered the air—controlled, precise. The Shadow Serpent operative, previously hidden near a landscaped planter, staggered backward as rounds struck his chest. His eyes widened before he fell onto the manicured shrubs.

"There goes stealth," Dev spat into his comms, his voice tight with fury.

"Breach now! Everyone move!"

The ordered silence dissolved.

From their breach point near "Bay 3," Beta Squad pushed into the Mercury loading dock area, weapons up, alert. The truck lot was unnervingly still—no idling engines, no movement—but Beta Squad moved with practiced coordination, clearing corners, securing entry points to the warehouse storage beyond.

At their breach near the side entrance, Charlie Squad advanced toward an unguarded steel door marked "Authorized Personnel Only." Inside, dimly lit utility corridors lined with pipes and panels offered a jarring difference from Mercury's polished exterior.

As Alpha team moved on the main doors, gunfire erupted from within, shattering the remaining glass, sending sharp fragments flying. Several operators fell immediately, crumpling against the building's sleek wall. The team pulled back, seeking cover behind the inadequate protection of the facade.

Dev, his expression set, pressed tight against the wall near the shattered opening. He pulled the pin on a flashbang, tossed it through the broken doorway into the reception area, and flattened himself against the wall again.

The grenade detonated—a blinding white flash, a concussive bang that shook the building. Disoriented shouts and panicked cries echoed from inside. Dev and his team surged forward, weapons firing into the confusion. The remaining Serpent operatives near the entrance, stunned and blinded, were taken down quickly. Alpha Squad cleared the immediate area, their movements efficient, lethal.

Before they could advance further, heavy gunfire hammered from deeper within the administrative offices. Bullets tore through the broken doorway, chewing concrete, shredding overturned furniture.

"Take cover!" Dev roared, diving behind the wreckage of the reception desk. The remnants of Alpha squad—maybe eight or nine left—scrambled for any available protection, weapons raised, but the intensity of the incoming fire pinned them. More operators went down, their cries swallowed by the roar of automatic weapons. Alpha fought back, desperately returning fire, trying to stop the Serpent thugs positioned down the office corridors from overrunning the reception area.

Meanwhile, Charlie Squad, led by Kate, having secured the employee hallway, moved on the heavy security doors marked "Authorized Personnel Only" separating the utility corridors from the main offices. Using ballistic shields, they breached the doors—the thump echoing—and entered the office corridor, flanking the enemy position.

They took the Shadow Serpent operatives by surprise, their focus still locked on the pinned Alpha Squad.

Kate signaled half her team towards the reception firefight; their sudden crossfire immediately shifted the balance. The other half of Charlie Squad simultaneously cleared the adjacent breakroom, neutralizing two Serpents caught inside.

Gunfire echoed relentlessly down the main administrative corridor. A Serpent operative rose from behind a cubicle wall, rifle finding a bead on a pinned Alpha operator near the shattered reception desk. Kate, moving fast along the opposite wall, registered the threat. Her weapon came up, sights aligning instantly. For a bare fraction of a second, her eyes held an unreadable stillness—a pause almost too brief to notice—then her rifle fired. The shot struck the Serpent operative true, but the infinitesimal delay proved critical. The Serpent fired his own weapon simultaneously with Kate's impact. A pained cry sounded from Alpha's position; the operator Kate targeted spun, clutching his side, managing to drag himself deeper behind cover, clearly hit.

Dev, seeing Kate's flanking team fully engaged, vaulted over the ruined desk, his MP7 adding to the cacophony. "Engage!" he roared, the command raw against the gunfire.

The converging fire from Charlie Squad and the depleted Alpha team overwhelmed the Serpent defenders. Caught in the crossfire, they were eliminated with brutal efficiency. Bullets tore through overturned desks and shredded partitions. The air thickened with the acrid bite of gunpowder and the scent of blood. One thug, scrambling behind a filing cabinet, took multiple rounds across the chest from Kate's weapon. Another, attempting a flanking move, dropped from a clean headshot delivered by one of Dev's remaining operators. The once-pristine administrative wing of Mercury International was now a ruin of overturned furniture, shattered glass, and sprawled bodies.

"On me," Dev commanded, his voice tight with urgency, motioning towards the heavy steel warehouse access door at the corridor's end. The air itself seemed to hum with anticipation.

Meanwhile, on the far side of the vast warehouse, Manny's Beta Squad faced their own inferno. Having placed charges along the loading dock doors, they triggered the synchronized detonations. The ground bucked violently as the explosions ripped through metal, disintegrating the doors into twisted shrapnel.

"Move!" Manny ordered, his voice nearly swallowed by the echoing roar. Beta Squad poured through the mangled openings, immediately met by a wall of gunfire from dozens—seventy-five plus—Shadow Serpent operatives positioned deeper inside the warehouse. The air filled with the sharp crack-snap of incoming rounds and the high whine of ricochets. Beta Squad was cut apart in the initial volley. Men fell, their shouts lost in the overwhelming noise. Manny, with only six operators still functional, scrambled backward, diving behind the loading bay structures and parked trucks, seeking any viable cover.

"Taking heavy fire!" Manny yelled into his comms, his voice strained over the din. "Pinned down!"

Beta Squad, heavily outnumbered, returned fire when they could—short bursts aimed at muzzle flashes glimpsed in the warehouse gloom—desperately trying to hold their position, buying time for Alpha to break through from the admin side.

Back in the cleared corridor, the remaining members of Alpha Squad gathered near the steel warehouse access door. The tension was a physical pressure. Manny's strained voice over their comms painted the grim situation near the docks.

"Sounds like they've pulled focus to the loading bay," Dev said, his voice low, exchanging a look with Kate. "Our window. Move."

He slapped a breaching charge onto the steel door, waved the team back. The charge detonated with a sharp crack, buckling the door inward, tearing a jagged opening into the cavernous warehouse beyond.

Alpha Squad flowed through the breach, weapons up. Dimly lit aisles stretched before them, flanked by towering shelves piled high with crates and pallets. Through the gaps, figures moved—Serpent operatives turning from the dock fight, alerted by the new breach.

The warehouse immediately dissolved into a fresh storm of gunfire as bullets tore through the air from this new angle. Crates exploded into splinters, debris showered down from impacted shelving. Alpha Squad reacted fast, Dev directing them hard left into the first aisle. They used the stacked crates and towering shelves as immediate cover, returning fire, engaging Serpent operatives caught moving between aisles.

An Alpha operator yelled, collapsing against a crate. Another took a round to the shoulder, his jaw tightening against the pain, but he kept his weapon up, firing back. Dev, his MP7 barking, eliminated two Serpent members attempting to flank them down an adjacent aisle. By the time they cleared the initial aisle, Alpha Squad was down three more operators, but they'd bloodied the enemy near their breach point, securing a precarious foothold.

Dev's remaining squad advanced cautiously, moving deeper into the warehouse toward the central staging area, angling towards the loading docks where Manny was still pinned. They swept each aisle, using crates and pallets for cover, engaging knots of Serpent resistance, advancing under covering fire, leapfrogging from one position to the next. Meanwhile, hearing the altered pattern of gunfire from the admin breach, Beta Squad recognized Alpha's push. Manny ordered his remaining six operators to increase their volume of fire. Seeing Alpha draw the enemy's focus, Manny yelled, "Now! Move out!" His operators surged from behind the loading bay structures and parked trucks. They re-entered the fight from the loading dock end, adding their fire to Dev's squad, catching the last few Shadow Serpent operatives in a pincer. The final takedowns were brutally efficient. The warehouse finally fell silent, the sudden quiet broken only by the electric crackle of damaged overhead lights and the harsh, gasping breaths of the survivors.

# Chapter 17

# Fractured Skies

Faint dawn light filtered through the warehouse's grimy, shattered windows, barely touching the gloom inside. The air was a thick brew of gunpowder, spilled blood, and the sharp ozone smell from damaged electronics. Flickering emergency lights threw distorted shadows across splintered pallets, overturned crates, and the still forms of the fallen scattered through the wreckage.

In the relative openness of the central staging area, Dev gathered the remaining EAG operators. Their faces were smudged with grime, streaked with sweat and blood, their eyes holding the hollowed look of men who had just walked through hell. Beneath the exhaustion, a coiled tension remained; their gazes constantly swept the dangerous surroundings.

"If they're still in here, only a couple places left," Dev stated, his voice low but clear in the near-silence. He stood straight, fatigue pulling at his frame, but his posture resolute. He surveyed his team, seeing his own grim focus reflected back.

He pointed towards the loading docks on the blueprint spread across a crate. "Jackson, take seven – secure dock entrances. Containment. Now."

Jackson gave a sharp nod, his team already moving, checking gear.

Before Dev could continue, Kate stepped forward slightly, her voice crisp, professional. "Dev, while you and Manny focus on the rec room," she indicated the area on the blueprint, "my team can sweep the east corridor – equipment room, storage access. Secure the flank, prevent surprises."

Dev paused for a fraction of a second, processing the tactical logic amidst the storm in his head. It covered a blind spot. "Okay, Kate. Do it," he confirmed, attention snapping back to the main objective. "Rest of you," Dev continued, his gaze moving over the remaining operators, "split between Manny and me."

A moment of charged silence stretched. "We hit the rec room. Both doors. Simultaneously." Dev's eyes hardened. "Intel suggests Rach might be there. Stay sharp."

The name hung in the air, a raw nerve exposed amidst the tactical planning.

Without another word, the teams separated, moving into the shadowed aisles thick with debris. Dev led his group down the first aisle, boots crunching on glass and shell casings, weaving around dark stains spreading on the concrete. Manny's squad mirrored their advance, heading for the rec room door off the second aisle.

Every shadow seemed to shift; every distant drip of water echoed like a footstep in the vast, echoing space.

"In position," Manny's voice crackled over the comms, tight.

Dev raised a hand, glanced at his chrono. "Breaching on mark. Ten seconds." He took a slow, deliberate breath.

Five... four... three... two... one...

With coordinated force, Dev and Manny slammed through their respective doors, teams pouring in behind them, weapons raised, anticipating resistance—but not this.

The Recreation Area, likely once a simple break room, was now arranged for maximum horror. Thirteen EAG security personnel—the team assigned to Mercury International—knelt in a tight, terrified group under the flat glare of fluorescent lights. Behind each knelt man stood a Shadow Serpent operative, pistol pressed firmly to his skull. Their faces were blank, eyes cold; the snake-and-dagger tattoo was visible on some near collars or rolled sleeves.

And against the back wall, near an open doorway leading to the administrative section, stood Viktor Mikhailov and Akimitsu Nakamura. Viktor, tall, his pale face marked by weariness but his blue eyes alight with cold amusement, the scar stark on his cheek. Beside him, Nakamura stood poised, radiating a calm deadliness almost more chilling than Viktor's presence.

"Hold your fire!" Dev's command ripped through the sudden silence, shock warring with the tactical nightmare presented. His eyes scanned the kneeling men—bruised, bloodied, emanating raw terror. Rach wasn't among them. Relief warred with dread. He forced his voice level, clamping down on the panic trying to claw its way up his throat. "Where is she?"

Viktor offered a thin, cruel smirk. "Not here," he stated, his voice echoing slightly. He surveyed Dev and his team with assessing eyes. "Predictable, Jones. Your arrival was anticipated. Naturally, I prepared... insurance." His gaze flickered towards the hostages. "I die, she dies. A simple transaction."

He let the threat hang, pacing a step, looking over the kneeling men with open contempt. "Such a shame," Viktor mused, mock sympathy dripping from his tone. "Your carelessness with assets. Still... considering our long... complicated history," his eyes met Dev's, "a small gesture of goodwill seems appropriate."

Nakamura offered a faint, chilling snicker. Without another word, he and Viktor turned, stepping back through the open doorway, vanishing into the administrative break room beyond.

For a frozen second, absolute stillness gripped the rec room. Dev's team, the Serpents, the hostages—locked in stunned uncertainty.

Then, as one, without command, the Shadow Serpent members acted. Coordinated, brutal. Muzzles flashed. The deafening roar of thirteen simultaneous shots hammered the small room. Casings spun onto the concrete as the hostages crumpled, extinguished in a final, horrific spasm. The sharp odor of hot metal overwhelmed the stale air, turning the rec room into a charnel house.

The scene held for less than a heartbeat before combat reflex took over. Dev reacted without thought, his weapon firing, dropping three executioners before they fully registered their task was done. The remaining EAG operators erupted in disciplined fire, cutting down the other Serpent members amidst the overturned furniture and widening pools of blood. The sharp smell of fresh cordite filled the room, layering onto the warehouse's foul air.

"Jackson, Kate!" Dev roared into his comms the instant the last Serpent fell, his voice tight with fury. "Lock down the perimeter! Seal all exits! Nobody gets out!"

Not waiting for confirmation, Dev moved immediately, heading for the open doorway on the east wall where Viktor and Nakamura had disappeared. "Manny, with me! Alpha remnants, secure this room!" he commanded over his shoulder. He entered the administrative break room—a clean, sterile space jarringly different from the carnage behind—then pushed into the main office corridor beyond. Fluorescent lights hummed overhead, bathing standard office cubicles and closed doors in flat, revealing light. He swept every opening, MP7 ready, Manny and the remaining Alpha operators moving tight behind him, boots soft on the industrial carpet, covering angles, checking blind spots.

Dev hit a side exit door, shoving it open, the cool dawn air a sudden shock against his skin. He scanned the loading area outside—concrete, parked trucks, distant chain-link glistening with razor wire. Empty. "Dammit!" Dev swore, his fist hitting the metal doorframe, the sound sharp in the quiet.

"Gone clean," Manny acknowledged, frustration evident in his soot-stained features as he surveyed the empty loading zone.

Just then, Kate's voice came over the comms, calm despite the chaos. "Charlie Squad secure, east corridor clear. No sign of egress." Seconds later, she appeared at the end of the office corridor they'd just cleared, rifle ready, her sharp gaze taking in the empty loading area where Dev and Manny stood.

Dev spun towards her, his face tight, exhaustion warring with disbelief. "Kate! Report!" he snapped, voice sharper than intended. "They didn't exit east? You were supposed to have that corridor locked! How did they vanish? Did you see anything?"

Kate met his glare, her own expression unreadable, controlled. "Negative, Dev. East corridor clear, secured per orders. No sign." She gestured back the way she'd come. "Must have used another exit we didn't anticipate—doubled back, lower level access maybe—before the perimeter was fully sealed."

"Another exit? Unanticipated?" Dev repeated, disbelief making his voice raw. He stepped closer, lowering his voice but increasing the intensity. "After everything, Kate? Dammit!" He shook his head, turning away abruptly, frustration rolling off him in waves. "I expect better! Secure this entire admin area. Sweep it again, top to bottom. Find something!"

The sun was just beginning its climb, sending weak, watery rays across the Brooklyn sky, doing little to pierce the gloom hanging over the team. Inside the Suburban, the drive back to EAG HQ in the Bronx was oppressively quiet. The images wouldn't stop—the thirteen executed men, their own fallen operators, Viktor's cold smirk—a relentless mental replay.

As the familiar glass and steel facade of 5450 Riverdale Avenue slid into view, Dev finally broke the silence. "Manny, when we get inside, find Kate. Lean on that shooter again. See if the Akimitsu news rattled him."

They pulled into the secure parking area, the heavy gate closing behind them.

They walked through the pristine lobby, the building's usual professional calm feeling like a different universe from the warehouse, and took the elevator up. The soft chime announced their arrival on the fifth floor, the Operations Hub. Manny stepped out into the low thrum of activity, nodding once to Dev as the doors slid shut.

The elevator continued its smooth ascent. When the doors opened on the sixth floor, Sarah Blake was waiting, her expression shifting from eager anticipation to open concern as she took in Dev's appearance—the grime, the bone-deep weariness, the invisible weight he carried.

"How did it—" Sarah began, her voice bright with anticipation, but the words died as she registered Dev's appearance—the grime coating his clothes, the profound weariness pulling at his features, the aura of defeat clinging to him.

"Not good," Dev said, the words heavy, shaking his head as he stepped out of the elevator.

"I'm sorry," Sarah whispered, stepping forward, wrapping him in a brief, firm embrace.

Dev allowed the contact for a moment, the simple gesture a small anchor, before gently easing away. He walked towards his office without another word, the weight of the warehouse pressing down on him. Entering the spacious, quiet room, he crossed to the deep sofa against one wall and stretched out, closing his eyes, seeking refuge from the internal storm, even for a few minutes.

Back down on the fifth floor, Manny found Kate in Meeting Room 2, debriefing Jackson and other team leaders from the Mercury operation. He pushed the door open without knocking. "Change of plans. Dev wants us back on the shooter. Now."

"Copy," Kate responded instantly, turning command over to Jackson with a quick nod. "Let's go."

They moved through the secure corridors to the designated interrogation room—a bare, windowless space containing only a metal table and three chairs. The shooter sat slumped in one, pale and gaunt under the single overhead bulb, his leg roughly bandaged.

For the next several hours, Manny and Kate worked him relentlessly. Manny leaned across the table, voice low, dangerous; Kate kept her tone deceptively calm, probing for inconsistencies.

"Where's Rachel Miller?" Manny demanded.

The shooter flinched but shook his head. "Don't know any Rachel."

"Viktor Mikhailov. His base when not at Mercury?" Kate asked smoothly.

Silence. The shooter stared at the table's scratched surface.

"Why kill Ricky Malone?" Manny pressed. "What did he know?"

"Never heard of him," the shooter mumbled, though his eyes darted nervously.

"Who else is involved? Who are you protecting?" Kate's voice gained an edge. "Were you at the cabin? The Jamestown ambush?"

The shooter licked his dry lips, sweat glistening on his forehead. He shifted in the hard chair. "I... I can't..." He began to tremble, his composure fraying under the sustained pressure.

Suddenly, the wall intercom buzzed, loud in the small room, making them both jump. Manny's assistant's voice crackled through. "Boss, sorry to interrupt. Call on line 3, urgent, insists on speaking with you, won't give a name."

Manny frowned. "One moment," he replied into the intercom. He turned to Kate. "Take over, back shortly. Keep on him." As Manny turned for the door, Kate gave a curt nod, her gaze flicking momentarily towards the sterile observation mirror before locking back onto the shaking suspect.

The heavy door clicked shut behind Manny, leaving Kate alone with the shooter. The harsh light reflected off the sweat on his pale forehead. He trembled, eyes darting from the mirror to Kate.

Kate leaned forward, her voice dropping, unnervingly intimate. "Was it worth it?" she asked softly. "Protecting him? After what he's done? What he'll do to you anyway?"

The shooter stared back, terror warring with a last flicker of defiance. He licked his lips again. A strange, broken smirk twisted his mouth.

"Enough... enough games... Katerina."

Kate's expression remained unchanged, but her eyes turned glacial. In one fluid, impossibly fast motion, she produced a small, disposable syringe from an inner pocket of her vest. Before the shooter could fully process the name—the name she didn't deny—she lunged.

The needle sank into the side of his neck, near the carotid artery. He gasped, eyes flying wide in shock, pain, a choked sound rattling in his throat. Kate depressed the plunger fully, her movements economical, precise.

"My father said you were an idiot," she whispered, her voice utterly flat, withdrawing the needle.

The shooter slumped forward onto the table, a thin line of saliva trailing from his slack lips, his eyes fixed, wide and unseeing.

Kate straightened, wiping the syringe clean with an alcohol pad produced just as quickly. She pocketed the used syringe, gave the body a final, indifferent glance, then turned. Without looking back, showing no haste, no flicker of emotion, she walked calmly to the interrogation room door, opened it, and stepped out, pulling it shut behind her, gone seconds before Manny would return.

# Chapter 18

# The Enemy Within

Manny ducked into the small, soundproofed conference room off the secure corridor, irritation tightening his expression. Urgent call, anonymous? Probably McDaniels again. He picked up the secure desk phone, hitting the flashing button for line 3. "Yeah, Arthur, what now?" he sighed, leaning back against the door, bracing for the usual.

"Manuel! Thank God!" McDaniels's voice came through, strained and fast, confirming Manny's expectation. "She's doing it again! I swear! The soup! Smells wrong—like almonds!"

Manny rubbed the bridge of his nose, closing his eyes for a moment. Hours spent interrogating a trained killer linked to a global threat, and McDaniels was panicking about soup. Again. "Arthur," Manny said, injecting calm into his tone, "we talked about this last month. Your wife isn't poisoning you. Did you buy new cleaning supplies? Ammonia can sometimes—"

"No! It's her! She knows I know! The way she looks at me! Send someone! Now!"

"Arthur, listen," Manny cut in, keeping his voice low, even, despite the critical interrogation waiting down the hall. "I understand the concern. But I'm handling a high-priority situation right now. I promise, I'll have Sarah dispatch a junior associate this afternoon to check in, okay? Just... maybe skip the soup if you're worried. Order pizza. We'll follow up later."

"But—"

"Later, Arthur. Gotta go." Manny disconnected before McDaniels could argue further, shaking his head slightly. Clients. Perfect timing. He put the interruption out of his mind, refocusing on the interrogation room, on getting the shooter to break with Kate.

He turned, heading quickly back down the corridor, and pushed open the heavy door. He froze.

The shooter was slumped forward onto the table, eyes fixed and vacant, saliva trailing from the corner of his mouth. Kate wasn't there. The room was empty except for the body.

Manny moved fast to the shooter's side. A quick check confirmed his suspicion—a tiny puncture mark on the side of the neck, near the carotid artery. A needle. Clean, professional, silent.

Shock solidified into cold dread, instantly replaced by fierce urgency. Manny slammed the red emergency alarm button on the wall. The klaxon erupted, its piercing shriek echoing through the secure facility. He grabbed the intercom, his voice sharp, ringing with command.

"Lockdown! Floor Five compromised! Agent Richards is missing, repeat,

Agent Richards missing! Suspect neutralized, Interrogation Room Two! Seal all exits, now!"

The low hum of the Echelon Axiom Ops Hub instantly pitched higher, shifting into the coordinated response of high alert.

The building-wide alarm shrieked, a high, insistent wail cutting through the background hum, jarring Dev from the exhausted slump on his office sofa. The brief quiet shattered. Adrenaline hit him, cold and sharp, burning away the fatigue. He launched himself upright, the sofa leather groaning, his focus instantly narrowed, senses heightened. The luxurious calm of his sixth-floor suite—the skyline view, the abstract art—felt suddenly absurd against the blare of the klaxon.

He moved with the ingrained economy of combat zones, bypassing conscious thought, simply reacting. Out of his office, his boots hammered the polished floor of the executive corridor, drawing startled looks from the few personnel emerging cautiously from their own offices. He reached the elevator bank, slammed the call button, the wait stretching intolerably. Finally, the doors slid open. He lunged inside, jabbing the button for five—the Ops Hub.

The descent felt compressed, tense. The doors opened onto a scene of managed pandemonium. The Ops Hub's usual focused energy had fractured into urgent shouts, the staccato clatter of keyboards, and the now slightly muffled, but still overwhelming, blare of the alarm. Red emergency lights pulsed, casting frantic, rhythmic flashes across workstations and the faces of scrambling personnel. Manny stood near the entrance to the secure corridor leading to interrogation, his face thunderous, the usual easygoing lines hardened into grim intensity. Dev strode towards him. Their eyes met—a silent confirmation of the crisis unfolding.

"Want a forensic team in that interrogation room, now. Dust everything. Vents, panels—tear it apart if needed," Manny commanded, his voice tight, barely controlled, gesturing sharply towards the corridor. "Also need tac teams sweeping all floors, room by room, starting immediately. Richards was in there with the suspect," he emphasized, jabbing a finger towards interrogation, "then gone. Vanished. Could be another kidnapping, Dev, or worse."

Nearby team leaders acknowledged curtly, relaying orders into their comms. Personnel moved with new, sharp urgency, fanning out, initiating methodical sweeps. The immediate area around Dev and Manny cleared slightly as teams dispersed according to search protocols.

"What are we really looking at, Manny?" Dev asked, voice low, hearing something beneath the surface of Manny's briefing. More than just a missing agent, a dead suspect.

Manny dragged a hand down his face, the gesture revealing deep exhaustion and frustration. "Something's off," he confirmed, his voice dropping further, leaning in. "Right before the alarm, moments before I found the shooter dead, Kate gone—I got pulled out. Call on line three. McDaniels, paranoid about his wife's soup. Again. Wasted time talking him down. By the time I got back..." He trailed off, shaking his head, the implication settling heavy between them.

Dev nodded slowly, a cold suspicion forming in his gut. "Don't like coincidences," he agreed grimly. An inside job? Or timing so perfect it felt orchestrated? Either way, it reeked.

The sleek EAG headquarters became a hive of urgent, methodical activity. Teams moved through the building, Kevlar vests rustling, boots quiet on marble, muffled on executive floor carpets. Radios crackled with terse status reports as personnel swept every office, lab, and meeting room from the lower levels up to the seventh-floor residences.

Down in Interrogation Room Two, a forensic team worked with focused care. The metal table reflected the harsh lights dully; chairs sat askew. They dusted surfaces meticulously, bagged fibers, analyzed the dead shooter's position, hunting for any clue, any trace of Kate's attacker, or Kate herself. Outside the room, another team examined the corridor, lights probing every inch. Near the doorway, tucked inside a standard office waste bin among crumpled paper towels, a technician spotted it—the small gleam of plastic and metal. Using specialized tongs, they carefully retrieved a small, disposable syringe. Empty. Used.

The syringe was bagged, tagged, and expedited to the fourth-floor labs. Inside the humming, sterile environment of the Crime Lab Section, analysts received the evidence. Under sterile conditions, they began the analysis. Swabs searched for residual substances; magnification hoped for a latent print. The partial print they managed to lift was faint, smudged, but possibly usable. It was photographed, scanned, cross-referenced against EAG's internal databases and linked law enforcement records. The wait for results commenced.

Simultaneously, a security team, faces set, used override codes on Kate Richards' seventh-floor apartment. The spacious one-bedroom, usually reflecting Kate's disciplined order in its neutral tones and functional layout, felt unnaturally still. They moved through the open-plan living room, the kitchenette, checked the bedroom, the walk-in closet, the en-suite bath. No forced entry. No struggle. Nothing out of place. It was as if she had simply dissolved, leaving only absence and the cold fear she hadn't left willingly.

Back in the Ops Hub, cybersecurity specialists worked furiously to recover surveillance footage. Their expressions tightened with each blocked attempt. The feeds covering the interrogation room, the secure corridor outside, the nearby elevator banks—wiped clean. Not deleted, scrubbed. Blank screens and error logs mocked them, a void in their digital security confirming Dev's fear: this wasn't just an attack, it was infiltration. Someone knew their systems intimately.

Deep within the fourth-floor lab, a monitor pinged an alert. The partial print from the syringe matched an internal profile. An analyst leaned closer, eyes widening as the profile loaded.

Amidst the lab's sterile hum and the focused quiet of analysts, Priya Singh motioned urgently to Earl Jenkins, her usual calm fractured by disbelief. "Earl, look. Now."

Earl, his usual fidgeting stopped cold, leaned over Priya's shoulder, staring at the monitor. The partial fingerprint analysis from the syringe returned a positive ID against EAG personnel. His eyes widened behind his glasses. The vibrant colors of the data display seemed to leech away, the hum of the server racks beside them swelling to a disorienting thrum in his ears. Kate? The name echoed, a silent detonation in the core of his professional world. Head of Security. He felt a tremor start in his hands, the warmth draining from his skin, leaving it clammy. This wasn't just a rogue agent; this was the keystone of their security apparatus. A dry, metallic taste filled his mouth. "No. It... it can't be," he breathed, the words catching in his throat. "Kate? Run it again! Now!"

Priya reran the comparison; the result flashed identically. The confirmation struck Earl with the force of a physical blow; he swayed, his hand instinctively reaching out to grip the edge of Priya's console, the cool laminate a necessary anchor. Kate Richards. Every classified briefing she'd attended, every security protocol she'd designed, every operator she'd vetted—all of it now suspect, potentially compromised. The intricate network of trust and procedure that formed EAG's backbone felt like it was unraveling before his eyes. The very integrity of their operations, their reputation... he could almost see it fracturing. "Okay... okay," he stammered, his mind struggling to process the sheer, cascading implications. The deception was a viper coiled at the heart of everything they'd built. He straightened, a new, harsher resolve hardening his features despite the tremor still running through him. "Initiate emergency deep background on Richards. Everything – financials, comms, vitals, cross-reference international databases. Flag any anomaly, however small. Lock this finding down until we report directly to Jones and Rivera."

Priya nodded grimly, fingers already flying across the keyboard, initiating the request, the weight of what they'd found settling like lead in the sterile air.

Hours later, the atmosphere in the main fifth-floor conference room was heavy with exhaustion and apprehension. Emergency lighting cast long shadows, supplementing the standard overheads. Dev sat at the head of the long table, his face controlled, taut. Manny sat to his right, expression grim. Key personnel – department heads, team leaders Jackson Reed and Byron Jackson – filled the remaining chairs, postures stiff, eyes alert.

The room quieted as Dev surveyed the faces, then nodded curtly to Jackson Reed.

Reed began the briefing, his voice crisp, professional, slicing the silence. "Building sweeps complete. Floor by floor, room by room. No sign of Kate Richards. No unauthorized personnel found."

Byron Jackson added, "Surveillance in and around Interrogation Two is gone for the relevant timeframe, wiped. Seventh floor executive residence feeds show no movement in or out of any apartment, including Kate's, during the hours surrounding the incident."

A lab technician stepped forward, his tone clinical. "Initial panels and screens on the deceased point to cyanide poisoning. Confirmed by trace residue analysis from the recovered syringe."

Earl Jenkins, looking even more pale and agitated than usual, stood near the large monitor. "The lab lifted a partial print off that syringe," he began, his voice tight, strained. He clicked the remote; the screen stayed blank for a charged moment. "Ran it against all databases – EAG internal, federal, international partners... we got a confirmed match."

The room held its breath, every eye fixed on Earl.

He took a shallow breath, clicked the remote again. Kate Richards' EAG security badge photo filled the massive screen – the familiar fiery hair, the intent green eyes, the official FSO designation clear beneath her name.

A collective inhale sounded through the room. Disbelieving murmurs started, growing quickly into a confused, angry buzz. Kate? Our FSO? How?

"Yes," Earl confirmed, his voice barely audible over the rising noise. "The partial print belongs to Kate Richards. Given her disappearance immediately after the suspect's neutralization via cyanide, we initiated emergency deep background verification." He took another unsteady breath. "Her service record, financials, associates... everything here looked clean. Standard checks found nothing. Until we accessed restricted vital records archives, cross-referencing international databases."

He clicked the remote again. The screen split. Kate's photo remained; beside it appeared two scanned documents: a U.S. birth certificate, 1987, for Katerina Mikhailova, mother Dr. Eleanor Vance, father Viktor Mikhailov; and a legal name change document from her adolescence, officially making Katerina Mikhailova into Kate Richards.

The murmurs died instantly. A heavy, suffocating silence descended, filled with unspoken questions, curses caught in throats, as the implication slammed into them.

"Order!" Devin's voice, though not loud, cut through the shocked stillness like a blade. Every eye snapped from the screen to Dev and Manny, whose own faces were tight, unreadable masks trying to contain shock and horror.

Earl, visibly sweating but pushing onward, spoke quickly, laying out the findings before the room could fully fracture. "Records show Katerina Mikhailova, born 1987, daughter of Viktor Mikhailov, the Russian chemist—our primary adversary. The name change to Kate Richards appears legitimate, likely done early, given Mikhailov's sensitive work then. Her military service is confirmed genuine."

He paused, letting the facts land before delivering the final, crushing blow. "However, Viktor Mikhailov was captured in 2010. April 2011," Earl's eyes flickered towards Dev and Manny, "the rescue attempt you led... failed. Intel suggests Mikhailov blamed you both directly, fueling a vendetta. Between late 2011 and 2013, while building his network, he tasked Nakamura with locating his daughter, Kate Richards. Contact was re-established around 2012-2013. He fed Kate a twisted narrative—himself the victim, blaming you," he looked directly at Dev and Manny, "for his capture, his suffering. When Echelon was founded in 2014, Viktor saw his opening. He activated Kate, directing her to use her background to infiltrate this company."

Earl clicked the remote. The screen went black, plunging the room back into the tense, dim emergency lighting. "She's been his deep cover agent from the beginning."

The silence that followed was absolute, broken only by the low electronic hum of the building and the ragged sound of people breathing. The betrayal, audacious, complete, settled over the room like a physical weight. Kate Richards, Head of Security, colleague, friend... the enemy inside their walls.

# Chapter 19

# Shattered Fortress

The air in the fifth-floor conference room felt static, charged with the aftershock of betrayal. Kate—their FSO, their colleague—an operative embedded within Echelon Axiom since its founding. The revelation resonated in the silence, underscored by the frantic energy humming from the Operations Hub outside. Polished mahogany reflected the strained expressions around the table, each person grappling with the scale of the deception.

Dev shot to his feet, the scrape of his chair loud in the stunned quiet. "Containment protocols, now!" His voice was a low growl, thick with fury held barely in check. "Revoke Richards' access. All levels. Network, physical, financial – lock it down." He fixed Marcus Chen, the IT Head, with a hard stare. "Go!"

Chen scrambled from his seat, stumbling in his haste, his face pale as he rushed out to execute the order.

Dev slammed a fist onto the table, the impact echoing the tremor in his own body. "Four years!" The words were torn from him, raw disbelief, the sting of violation. He inhaled sharply, visibly forcing the rage down, hands clenching at his sides until his knuckles were white. When he spoke again, his voice was dangerously quiet, stripped of the earlier outburst but vibrating with cold intensity. "Kate knows this company. Every protocol, safe house, weakness. Assume total compromise. Factor that into every decision."

Manny leaned forward, his usual relaxed posture gone, replaced by sharp focus. "If we find Kate," he stated, hazel eyes narrowed, "it's a line to Viktor. And probably to Rach."

"Definitely," Dev agreed, though the thought of Kate leading them anywhere felt like another turn of the knife. "But contain the breach first. Initiate deep background checks—every employee. HQ, field offices, contractors." His gaze swept the room, leaving no room for doubt. "Pull every available analyst off non-critical tasks. Triple verification—three independent analysts per file, cross-referencing. Trust no one."

As if triggered by the word betrayal, the large monitor dominating the far wall illuminated. The image that appeared sent a fresh wave of ice through Dev's veins. Rachel. Chained. Arms stretched high, wrists locked to a rusted ceiling beam. She was in a dim, bare concrete room, dust motes swirling in the single harsh beam of light. Her face was bruised, her eyes wide with a terror that threatened Dev's control, yet beneath it, defiance still sparked. In the upper corner, a smaller window showed Viktor Mikhailov's face – pale, weathered, the scar livid against his cheek, cold amusement glinting in his blue eyes.

"I see you finally deduced the truth about my daughter," Viktor's voice, smooth, faintly accented, filled the room, mocking them. He chuckled, a dry, grating sound. "Took longer than I expected, Jones. Disappointing." Dev's hand tightened into a fist again, the image of Rach chained burning behind his eyes. "What's the game, Viktor?" he bit out, each word sharp, controlled.

"Game?" Viktor echoed, feigning surprise. "No game. My objectives were clear. Your suffering." His gaze drifted to the image of Rach. "Perhaps a demonstration of consequences is needed? A bullet for the reporter? Or," his voice dropped, turning silkier, menacing, "perhaps I dispatch an acquaintance to visit your mother."

The threat landed like a blow. Dev felt the blood recede from his face but forced himself to sink slowly back into his chair, gripping the armrests, knuckles showing white. He held Viktor's gaze on the screen, fighting the urge to destroy the monitor, to rip through the building to reach him.

"Better," Viktor remarked, seeing the shift. "Compliance is... preferable. Katerina's recent... improvisation," he indicated the situation subtly, "was not my design, Jones. Your pressure forced her hand, it seems. No matter. It merely required this adjustment—a change of location, and of the stakes."

The large monitor split vertically, fracturing Viktor's image. On the right, Rach remained chained, her terrified eyes fixed on the camera feed, meeting Dev's. On the left, a new, live feed appeared: a high-angle view capturing the constant motion of commuters through the vast Main

Concourse of Grand Central Terminal, the unaware crowd a stark contrast to Rach's isolated fear.

Viktor's voice resumed, the earlier mockery gone, replaced by a colder, expansive tone. "For years, my focus was singular. You. Rivera. The instruments of my suffering. But isolation clarifies perspective. I built a global network on revenge, yes, but the true disease runs deeper than two failed soldiers. It is your nation, your government—its empty promises, its indifference to those it abandons, those it deems expendable. They, too, must learn the price of forgetting."

He paused, letting the broadened threat hang in the room. "You pride yourselves on Echelon Axiom's capabilities. This private army, this shield against the chaos you helped sow. So," Viktor's voice took on a sharp, challenging quality, "let us test your resources, your expertise, your resolve."

His gaze, visible in the corner feed, flickered towards the Grand Central stream. "Your first trial. Somewhere within that magnificent terminal," he gestured implicitly towards the busy station, "a device containing my signature VX-13 compound awaits discovery. A subtle message, but potent."

"You have eighteen hours precisely from... now," a digital timer materialized over the Grand Central feed, stark red numbers beginning their descent from 18:00:00, "to locate and neutralize this device."

He leaned closer again, his tone hardening into sharp command. "One rule must be obeyed without deviation. Any sign of evacuation, any action that causes public panic within that terminal, and I will trigger the device remotely. Instantly. Beyond that restriction... consider all other tactics valid. Use your technology, your operators. Just do not startle the flock before the shearing."

Viktor allowed a thin smile, devoid of warmth. "Your clock ticks, Jones, Rivera. Rachel's fate... remains in the balance. Let's see how you perform when faced with impossible choices and fractured resources." His final chuckle was abrupt, sharp. "Begin."

The monitor went black, plunging the conference room back into the dim emergency lighting and the sudden, heavy silence filled only by the weight of Viktor's challenge.

His final, sharp chuckle hadn't faded when the building seemed to lurch. A low whump resonated from below, followed instantly by a violent upward shockwave. The polished mahogany table bucked, sending laptops and mugs crashing. Ceiling tiles shattered downwards; dust and debris filled the air as the suspended framework twisted. Cracks spiderwebbed across the reinforced walls. The floor beneath them groaned, shifting ominously. Emergency lights strobed red, painting the sudden chaos.

Shouts erupted. Chairs scraped violently as personnel lunged for the door, their cries lost in the immediate roar of groaning metal, shattering glass, and the sudden, piercing shriek of the building's alarms.

"Move! Everyone out!" Dev roared, already shoving people towards the exit, his reaction overriding the shock. He grabbed Manny's arm, pulling him through the panicked throng.

They burst from the conference room into the fifth-floor Operations Hub. It was chaos. Monitors dangled from buckled mounts, screens dark or filled with static. Desks lay overturned, buried under fallen ceiling tiles, tangled wires, broken light fixtures. Thick dust filled the air, stinging eyes, coating throats, the smell acrid. Sections of the floor had buckled or collapsed entirely, offering horrifying glimpses of fire blooming on the floor below. Injured personnel lay amidst the wreckage, moaning.

"Get these people out!" Dev yelled, coughing against the dust, his eyes assessing the immediate dangers—unstable structures, potential secondary blasts, panicked survivors.

Manny nodded grimly, already moving towards a young analyst partially trapped beneath a heavy bank of monitors. "Stairs only! Elevators are dead!"

"Agreed! Top-down! Clear five, then four!" Dev directed, his voice cutting through the noise. He spotted Jacob Turner, an analyst, pinned by collapsed shelving near the Ops Center's main display wall. "Manny! Hand here!"

Together, straining against the heavy shelving, they lifted it just enough for Jacob to scramble free, blood flowing from a deep gash on his leg. "Thanks, boss," Jacob gasped, wincing. Dev gave a curt nod. "Walk?" Jacob tested the leg. "Yeah... think so." "Good. Help clear this floor. West stairwell! Anyone mobile, help the injured!" Dev shouted, his command slicing through the din. They began moving survivors towards the designated stairs, a frantic improvisation of rescue and retreat.

Reaching the stairwell, Dev paused, keying his comms, the signal cutting in and out. "All teams, report! Fifth floor compromised, heavy damage! Evacuate west stairwell! Repeat, evacuate west!" Only static answered. He exchanged a grim look with Manny. "On our own for now. Move!" They started down, the concrete stairs already slick with dust and sprinkler water.

The fourth floor—R&D—was a smoke-choked inferno. Flames licked up through buckled flooring from the blast zone below, casting wild, flickering shadows. The air burned with the fumes of chemicals and melting plastic.

Near the entrance to an Innovation Lab, they found Priya Singh and another R&D specialist trapped by heavy, collapsed ventilation ducting. Smoke swirled thickly around them. "Help!" Priya cried out, coughing racking her body. Dev spotted a discarded metal support beam. He and Manny jammed it under the ducting, using it as a crude lever. Straining together, muscles protesting against the weight, they managed to shift the wreckage just enough for the two women to crawl free, choking, gasping for clean air.

"Stairs! West side! Go!" Manny urged, pointing through the haze towards the evacuation route.

Descending further, the destruction intensified as they reached the third floor – the blast's origin. It was annihilated. The Cybersecurity Command Center was a mangled cavern of twisted steel and shattered servers. Walls had vanished, exposing the building's structural bones. Fires burned freely in several areas, the heat radiating intensely. Amidst the wreckage near the obliterated server room, they found Marcus Chen, Head of IT, alive but impaled by a jagged piece of shrapnel, barely clinging to consciousness. His breathing was a shallow flutter. "Hold on, Marcus!" Manny yelled, dropping beside him instantly. Ripping open a salvaged med kit, Manny pressed gauze hard against the wound, his movements quick, drawing on ingrained field training. "Dev, gotta carry him! He won't make it otherwise!" Dev nodded grimly. 'Okay. Let's do it.' Gritting their teeth against the strain, they carefully positioned themselves, taking Marcus's full weight. His low groans echoed in the fiery chaos as they began the slow, difficult descent, navigating buckled stairs littered with falling debris, the burden testing their combined strength.

The second floor (Administrative) was heavily damaged but relatively intact compared to the devastation above. Dust hung thick in the air, sprinklers drizzling water onto the chaos, and the administrative staff milled in a state of shock and rising panic.

Dev spotted Elena Martinez, Manny's assistant, trying to calm an older finance worker who was gasping for air, hyperventilating. "Elena! Get him moving!" Dev commanded, his voice calm but firm, cutting through the man's fear. "Stay low, keep moving towards the west stairs. We're right behind you." His certainty seemed to reach them; Elena managed to guide the trembling man forward just as Dev and Manny arrived on the landing, carefully negotiating the stairs with the barely conscious Marcus Chen.

The stairwell below became choked with people. Smoke rolled down, reducing visibility with each step. Panicked employees crowded the landings further down, some frozen, others shoving blindly. Manny, bracing Marcus's weight against the wall, raised his voice, taking command from the landing, his tone slicing through the escalating hysteria. "Stay low! Cover your mouths! Form a line against the wall! Move!" he bellowed, directing the flow below. He spotted a young HR staffer nearby who had tripped, clutching an injured ankle, unable to stand. Thinking fast, Manny yelled, "You!" He pointed to an IT tech he'd just cleared space for on the stairs below. "Help her! Get her down! Now!" The tech nodded and moved to assist the woman as Manny refocused, urging Dev and the others forward with Marcus. "Keep moving! Almost there!"

Finally, gasping, choked with smoke, the first survivors stumbled out of the ground floor lobby. The polished marble floor was cracked, coated in soot; the large digital wall display was a spiderweb of shattered glass. They burst out onto Riverdale Avenue into the cool dawn air, joining a growing huddle of soot-covered, coughing, injured Echelon employees. The wail of approaching sirens grew louder, closer, red and blue lights flashing against the building's damaged facade. They were out, but the toll of the attack was starkly visible on every survivor's face, the devastation inside a brutal contrast to the emerging daylight.

## Chapter 20

## Race Against Time

The late afternoon sun struggled through the thick smoke and dust hovering over Riverdale Avenue. Emergency lights strobed red and blue against the deepening twilight. Firefighters aimed hoses at the ravaged Echelon Axiom Global Headquarters, water arcing onto the still-smoldering middle floors. The building's glass and steel facade was a ruin of jagged edges, reflecting the frantic emergency lights.

Dev and Manny stood near the police tape amidst the crowd of dazed survivors and focused emergency personnel. Soot streaked their faces; their clothes were torn, smelling sharply of smoke. Their eyes scanned the faces, a silent, painful tally—Jacob Turner loaded into an ambulance, Elena Martinez wrapped in a shock blanket, others wandering numbly. Each recognized face was a small relief against the unknown number still missing, or being carried out under sheets.

The weight of Viktor's ultimatum—Rach chained, the Grand Central clock counting down—pressed harder than the physical exhaustion. Kate's betrayal felt like an open wound.

Manny's voice beside him was quiet, roughened by smoke. "First things first, Dev. Need to bring in the locals. Official."

Dev nodded, the haze of shock clearing, replaced by a cold determination. He pulled out his satellite phone—assuming standard comms were down or monitored—and dialed a secure number from memory. After a moment, a familiar, direct voice answered. "Riley." Deputy Commissioner John Riley.

"John, it's Devin Jones." Dev kept his voice low, turning slightly from the surrounding activity. "EAG HQ, Riverdale Avenue. Major explosive attack. Third floor. Multiple casualties, situation ongoing."

A pause, then Riley's voice, sharp. "Jesus, Dev. Understood. On my way. Need?"

"Full disaster response, yes, but it's bigger. Believe it's linked to an imminent threat downtown—potential target Grand Central. Have actionable intel, but internal comms are compromised." Dev stated the facts plainly. "Need operational interface, now."

"Right." Riley didn't hesitate. "Head to the 50th Precinct, Kingsbridge. Captain Eva Rostova is expecting you. Sharp, ex-CT. She's your NYPD point. Go. I'll manage this end."

"Thanks, John." Dev disconnected, meeting Manny's eyes. One step. He immediately dialed again, the secure line for the Brooklyn field office.

"Thompson," Director Alex Thompson answered, his voice professional but tight.

"Alex," Dev responded, his own voice strained but level. "Devin. Manny's here. HQ took a major hit. Bomb, third floor."

A beat of stunned silence. "God... Everyone okay?" Alex asked, the concern immediate.

"No," Dev said grimly. "Heavy losses. Targeted. Your status?"

"Secure here, but..." Alex paused, the hesitation confirming Dev's unease. "Lost access—all systems—about an hour ago, Dev. Network, comms, surveillance—dark. Ethan's team can't penetrate. Looks like a sophisticated cyberattack."

"Coordinated, Alex. HQ is wiped too." The pieces slammed into place—Kate's access, the bomb masking the digital assault. "Conference Director Bellwether. Now."

The line beeped. Seconds later, Cass Bellwether's sharp voice cut in. "Alex? Devin? What the hell is going on? My entire DC network just went dark!"

"Cass, listen carefully," Dev cut in, voice tight, urgent. "Bombing here, cyberattacks hitting us, Brooklyn, DC – all connected. The man behind it is Viktor Mikhailov." He let the name settle.

"Mikhailov?" Cass repeated, confusion in her tone. "Vaguely familiar... old file? Connection?"

"He is the connection," Manny interjected grimly.

"He turned Kate Richards, Cass," Dev stated flatly, dropping the revelation like a grenade. "She's Katerina Mikhailova. His daughter. His deep cover agent since EAG's founding."

A sharp inhale on Cass's end. "Kate... Mikhailov's daughter? Inside EAG? All this time?" The shock was palpable, darkening into horror.

"Yes," Dev confirmed, pushing past the disbelief. "Viktor has Rachel Miller hostage. Right before the bomb hit, he contacted us. Planted a VX-13 device somewhere inside Grand Central Terminal. Less than eighteen hours to find and neutralize it. His rule: any attempt at evacuation, any public panic, he detonates it remotely."

"Jesus Christ," Cass breathed. "Mikhailov... Kate... Grand Central... VX-13?" The flood of information was clearly staggering.

"Process the betrayal later," Dev said, his tone regaining command. "Right now, a clock is ticking on thousands of lives. Alex – Prep NY teams to support NYPD at Grand Central. Full discretion. Coordinate directly with Captain Rostova, 50th—I'm heading there. Maintain lockdown in Brooklyn."

"Understood," Alex replied, his voice tight.

"Cass," Dev continued, "Need federal resources mobilized yesterday. FBI, DHS – leverage every contact for intel on Mikhailov, known associates, potential locations for Rachel. Get assets moving towards Grand Central, support NYPD covertly. Feed everything to Rostova. You're our comms hub. We're operating blind here. Run point from DC."

"Right. Okay." Cass took a noticeable breath over the line, shock hardening into resolve. "Mikhailov. Kate. Grand Central. 18 hours. Done, Devin. On it. Keep me posted."

"Will do. Moving now." Dev ended the call, the weight of the next eighteen hours pressing down, immense and immediate.

He and Manny pushed through the throng of dazed EAG employees and the organized chaos of first responders. The air was thick with the smell of burnt electronics, concrete dust, and something sickeningly chemical. Dev scanned the faces, his own a mask of soot and grim determination, until he spotted her near a mobile command unit set up by the FDNY. Sarah Blake stood talking to a fire captain, her usual impeccable composure frayed, her smart business attire smudged with soot, a streak of grime across one cheek. Her blue eyes, usually bright with efficiency, were wide, reflecting the flashing emergency lights and the deeper shock of the building's ravaged state. When she saw Dev and Manny approaching, relief warred with a fresh wave of horror on her face.

"Devin! Manny!" Her voice was huskier than usual. She took a step towards them, then stopped, her gaze flicking over their torn, smoke-stained clothing, the exhaustion etched into their features. A small, involuntary tremor went through her. "The... the reports coming out... I couldn't... it's even worse than I imagined." Her hand gestured vaguely towards the shattered facade of the EAG building, a gesture encompassing the sheer scale of the catastrophe.

"It was a direct hit, Sarah," Dev said, his voice low, rough. "Third floor. Cybersecurity was likely the primary target, meant to cripple us."

"Viktor," Manny added, his own voice gravelly. "He's making his move. This, Grand Central... he's not holding back."

Sarah's eyes, already wide, seemed to absorb the impact of their words. Her shoulders, which had been squared with a professional's attempt at control, sagged almost imperceptibly. For a moment, she just looked at the ruined building, the lifeblood of their organization, now a smoldering casualty. Her lower lip trembled slightly before she visibly firmed her jaw, pushing the shock down, her training and innate capability kicking in.

"I've started a preliminary headcount with the floor wardens who made it out," she reported, her voice gaining a measure of its familiar steadiness, though the underlying tremor remained. "Casualties are... significant. We're still trying to account for everyone." She looked from Dev to Manny, a silent question in her eyes.

"We need to move," Dev stated, answering the unspoken. "NYPD liaison is waiting. Grand Central is the priority." He met her gaze directly.

"Sarah, I need you here. You know how this company runs inside and out better than anyone left standing. With Kate... gone," the name was a flat, hard stone in his mouth, "you're the one I trust to take point on this. Coordinate with the fire department, with EMS, with Riley's people on the ground. Oversee the casualty lists, ensure our people are getting what they need. Secure any EAG assets that are salvageable, especially sensitive data, if possible. But prioritize our people."

Sarah straightened, a flicker of her usual competence returning, though her eyes still held the shadow of the day's horror. The responsibility was immense, dropped on her amidst chaos, but she didn't hesitate.

"Understood, Devin. I'll manage this end. Keep me updated. And... be careful. Both of you."

Dev gave a curt nod. "You too, Sarah."

Moving through the emergency vehicles, they flagged down an unmarked police cruiser, flashing credentials the first responders recognized. The drive to the 50th Precinct on Kingsbridge Road was fast, weaving through the early evening traffic, leaving Sarah to face the daunting task of managing the immediate aftermath of EAG HQ's destruction. Captain Eva Rostova met them in a small conference room already buzzing with low, urgent activity. Maps of Midtown and GCT schematics glowed on wall-mounted monitors. "Commissioner Riley sends regards, pledges full cooperation," she said, her directness bypassing formalities. "He agrees—absolute discretion is paramount. Tell me about the device."

"That's the issue—no description," Dev stated, his voice level despite the fatigue. "The perpetrator, Viktor Mikhailov, just said it contains 'VX-13 compound,' somewhere in Grand Central. No specific location beyond the Main Concourse shown on his feed. Gave us 18 hours. Swore detonation if we trigger panic or attempt evacuation."

Rostova absorbed the information, her expression tightening. "No description multiplies the difficulty. VX-13... lethal. Dispersal method? Could be aerosolized, hidden in ventilation, luggage, anywhere." She turned to a GCT map on a screen. "Okay, phase one must be covert. Plainclothes transit units, precinct officers reassigned. Focus on anomalies—unattended bags, odd activity near vents, secure zones, track entrances. Anything that feels wrong."

Just then, Dev's sat phone vibrated. Cass. "Quick update, Dev. Confirmation—FBI HRT and WMD Directorate moving. Estimate boots on ground, staging near GCT around 0500-0600."

Dev relayed the ETA. Dawn was hours off. "Which brings up the terminal closure," Rostova noted, glancing at the clock on the wall.

"GCT closes 0200 to 0500. That's our window for a harder search without violating the 'no panic' condition. We can deploy ESU, maybe K9s if available, sweep public areas thoroughly during shutdown."

"Good. Maximize it," Dev agreed. "But they have to be clear before 5 AM. Can't risk Viktor seeing an overt presence when doors reopen."

"Agreed." Rostova picked up her desk phone. "Need that TOC set up." She started dialing.

The hours leading to 2 AM crawled by, managed from the cramped, temporary Tactical Operations Center Rostova secured in a nearby federal building basement. Plainclothes officers and EAG agents moved through the evening commuters in Grand Central, searching for anything, finding nothing solid.

Then, at 2 AM sharp, the last stragglers cleared, main doors locked, the operation intensified. NYPD ESU teams moved quickly, quietly, alongside EAG agents. Methodical sweeps commenced—Main Concourse, dining levels, track platforms, accessible service corridors. K9 units worked assigned zones, noses twitching, searching for chemical signatures. Every locker was checked, every darkened corner investigated, every reachable ventilation grate examined. Reports flowed into the TOC; hope flickered briefly with each cleared sector, but by 4:30 AM, the reality was undeniable: nothing found.

The intensified search during the shutdown yielded zero. The teams began their meticulous withdrawal, erasing any sign of their presence, leaving only the usual overnight cleaning crews and transit security visible as 5 AM approached. Dawn was beginning to paint the eastern sky. Federal assets were arriving at staging points nearby. The clock showed less than eight hours remaining.

The massive doors of Grand Central Terminal swung open precisely at 5:00 AM, letting in the first trickles of early commuters and the cool pre-dawn air. The immense Main Concourse began to awaken, silence yielding to the echo of solitary footsteps, the distant rumble of arriving trains. Plainclothes officers from NYPD and EAG melted back into the slowly growing crowd, their faces taut with fatigue after the long, unsuccessful night, their professional calm a thin shield over frayed nerves. Newly arrived FBI agents, also blending in, subtly moved into observation positions, coordinating via encrypted channels with the TOC, where Dev, Manny, and Rostova watched the feeds, the sense of dread thickening with each passing minute.

Officer Daniel Henderson, NYPD, running on caffeine after the long overnight shift, patrolled near the northwest mezzanine. The weight of the failed search pressed on him, amplifying now as the station filled and the FBI arrived. He scanned the still-sparse crowd, automatically noting faces, bags, movements. That's when he saw him—a man in a slightly grimy maintenance uniform near the wall, partly hidden by a large potted plant. The man worked quickly, almost furtively, using a power screwdriver on a ventilation grate low on the marble wall. He kept glancing around, his movements jerky, unlike the deliberate pace of the regular GCT crews Henderson knew by sight.

Henderson frowned. That specific grate had been inspected just hours ago during the lockdown sweep. Why fiddle with it now, just as commuters started arriving? As Henderson watched, the man finished securing the grate, stood, then deliberately nudged the heavy planter slightly, further concealing the vent. He tugged a knit cap lower and walked quickly away, dissolving into the growing stream of people heading for the subway lines.

Wrong. Every nerve ending in Henderson screamed. Not maintenance. Staged. Suspicious. The timing, the concealed grate, the man's nervous haste—it clicked with the threat briefing, the city-wide tension. He fumbled for his radio, heart hammering his ribs. Suspicious individual, possible device placement, northwest mezz vent...

He thumbed the transmit button. "Control, Officer Henderson, possible suspect—" Loud static erupted from the speaker. He tried again. Only static. Jammed?

He looked frantically towards the subway entrance, but the maintenance man was gone, swallowed by the crowd. The man was gone, but what was behind that grate? Panic seized Henderson. The device. He knew it was there. The clock was running out. FBI was here, ESU nearby, but he saw it. He had to do something.

Abandoning protocol, abandoning training, Henderson lunged forward, eyes locked on the grate, and did the one thing guaranteed to trigger disaster.

He screamed.

"EVERYBODY OUT! BOMB! GET OUT NOW!"

His shout ripped through the vast hall. Heads snapped up. Commuter conversations died. Confusion flashed across faces, instantly replaced by raw terror. The scene fractured into chaos—screams echoed off the marble, people surged blindly for exits, a distant alarm began its frantic clang.

From his remote location, Viktor Mikhailov watched the predictable pandemonium unfold on his monitors. The officer's shout, the stampede—humanity's inevitable response to fear. The condition was violated. A faint, cold smile touched Viktor's lips. Predictable. He calmly lifted his secure satellite phone, entered the activation sequence for the dispersal mechanism, and spoke a single, quiet word into the receiver.

"Сейчас." (Now.)

Inside the cramped TOC, Dev, Manny, and Captain Rostova watched the chaos erupt on their screens. They heard Henderson's panicked yell split the audio feed moments before the visual turned into a stampede. "Dammit!" Rostova slammed her hand on the console, already grabbing her radio. "He broke protocol! Lock down the perimeter, notify HAZMAT! Go, go, go!"

Dev and Manny watched, immobilized by horror, as the crowds surged. They braced instinctively for a blast, a shockwave that never arrived. Instead, after moments of pure, screaming chaos, the scene began to change in a way that chilled them to the bone.

Near the ventilation grate Henderson had focused on, a figure stumbled, collapsing silently to the marble floor. Then another. A running woman simply crumpled. No smoke. No explosion. Just people dropping without a sound amidst the panicked throng. The screaming lessened, replaced by choked, gasping sounds.

"What's happening?" an analyst breathed, eyes wide, fixed on the monitor.

"VX-13," Manny said, his voice a low, strangled whisper. "Airborne. He triggered it."

Dev felt a coldness spread through him, colder than the fear of any bomb. He watched the horrifyingly efficient, silent death cascade across the monitors. People collapsing in mid-stride. The stampede slowing, faltering, as its runners succumbed. Within minutes, the screens showed an unnervingly still tableau: the vast Main Concourse littered with hundreds, perhaps thousands, of motionless forms beneath the glittering, indifferent constellations of the celestial ceiling.

Silence fell in the TOC, thick, suffocating, broken only by the unheard, frantic orders Rostova still relayed over the radio and the low electronic hum of the monitors displaying the unspeakable carnage. Viktor had made his point. The consequence was absolute.

# Chapter 21

# Impossible Choices

Dawn broke cold and gray over Manhattan, stretching long shadows down the streets surrounding Grand Central Terminal. The usual morning energy was absent, replaced by the stark silence of a major HAZMAT zone. Emergency lights pulsed rhythmically, reflecting off wet pavement and the impassive marble facade of the terminal, now sealed like a tomb. Teams in bulky hazmat suits moved with quiet purpose around the cordoned-off entrances, managing decon tents, coordinating the removal of bodies. Ambulances waited in silent rows. The air felt heavy, thick with the unimaginable weight of the silent tragedy that had occurred inside.

Dev and Manny stood near the outer police tape, having moved back after reporting to the federal liaisons coordinating with Captain Rostova. They watched the methodical, horrifying process, the number of victims staggering. The silence from the terminal itself was the most disturbing element.

Dev's satellite phone vibrated, a harsh sound against the quiet. Unknown caller, secure relay. Viktor. He answered, putting it on speaker.

"Predictable, Jones." Mikhailov's voice was clinical, stripped of warmth. "Panic always overcomes protocol. Unfortunate for those commuters, but rules exist to be enforced. A valuable lesson in consequence, wouldn't you agree?"

Dev's knuckles tightened, but he held his silence, letting Viktor reveal his purpose.

"That, however, was merely prelude," Viktor continued. "A public display. Now... for your personal test. One designed for you, leveraging that powerful motivator: revenge."

A chill colder than the morning air traced its way down Dev's spine. "What do you want, Viktor?"

"Efficiency. I approve. Your former associate, Brad Ewing. He has proven... unreliable. He is currently at his dealership, Ewing Automotive, in Lehighton, Pennsylvania."

Lehighton. Near the cabin. The coordinates clicked into place with dreadful familiarity.

"Your task is simple, Jones," Viktor's voice was flat, issuing a command. "Kill him. Yourself. No proxies. This requires a personal demonstration."

"And if I refuse?" Dev asked, his voice taut.

"Refusal is unwise." Viktor's tone held a faint trace of amusement now. "The consequences would be... severe. For Ms. Miller... and for your mother, Annabelle." He paused. "Poor Kaitlyn Ewing would be tragically widowed regardless, no?"

Dev felt Manny stiffen beside him. "You leave my mother out of this!"

"Too late, I fear," Viktor replied smoothly. "While your attention was occupied by Grand Central's unpleasantness, my associates retrieved her from the hospital. She rests comfortably... under my care. Along with Ms. Miller. A matched pair."

The world seemed to tilt. Annabelle. Taken. Nausea churned in Dev's gut. He reached out, gripping the side of the nearby command vehicle to steady himself.

"You have 24 hours, starting now," Viktor stated, voice crisp, all business again. "Go to Lehighton. Eliminate Brad Ewing. Make no attempt—I repeat, no attempt—to locate or rescue the women. Follow instructions, or they both suffer greatly before death finds them. Consider it streamlining, Jones. You solve my Ewing problem, and perhaps... perhaps... my generosity will extend further." Viktor disconnected, leaving only silence and the weight of the new ultimatum.

Dev lowered the phone slowly. Annabelle and Rach hostages. Brad marked for death. A 24-hour deadline.

"He played us," Manny breathed, his face grim. "GCT was a diversion... to grab your mom."

"Need help, Manny," Dev said, his voice raspy. "Real help. Someone trustworthy. Absolutely." After Kate, the circle felt dangerously small.

"Cass," Manny said without hesitation.

Dev nodded, already dialing her secure number.

"Bellwether," Cass answered, her voice sharp, clearly still dealing with the DC and GCT fallout.

"Cass. It's worse." Dev relayed Viktor's call—the order to kill Brad, Annabelle joining Rach as a hostage, the deadline, Lehighton. "He's forcing my hand. Trying to break me."

A string of sharp, fluent curses came through the line. "He has Annabelle now? That calculating son of a bitch! Okay, Devin. Okay. What's the play?"

"Have to go to Lehighton," Dev said, the words feeling like poison. "Need you there. Eyes and ears I trust. The cabin, near Lehighton. Can you be there in twelve hours?"

"Already wheels up—first priority flight to Allentown. I'll be there," Cass stated firmly. "Backup?"

"No rescue attempts allowed for Annabelle and Rach. Means EAG teams are out—too high profile, risk is too great. Need off-book assets if possible, but mostly... need you."

"Understood. Bringing everything I can. Stay safe, Dev."

"You too, Cass." Dev ended the call. He looked at Manny. The path forward felt impossible, but it was the only one they had. "Need gear."

Manny nodded. "Penthouse first, then Brooklyn."

Stepping from the arranged SUV back into the Quay Tower lobby felt like crossing into a different dimension. The grim atmosphere of the GCT disaster zone dissolved into the polished, quiet luxury of the penthouse entrance. They rode the private elevator up in heavy silence. Inside the apartment, they moved with focused efficiency, the stunning skyline views through the panoramic windows feeling like a cruel counterpoint. Quick showers washed away the grime, though not the internal residue of the last eighteen hours. They changed into fresh tactical clothing stored there, gathering encrypted laptops, backup weapons, comms gear, and essential go-bags.

"Heavy gear's at the field office," Manny said, slinging a duffel bag over his shoulder.

Dev nodded, checking the tactical watch on his wrist. Less than twenty-three hours remaining on Viktor's clock. "Let's move." They left the apartment, the elevator descending rapidly, returning them to the ground floor and the waiting black SUV.

By the time they reached the Brooklyn Field Office on Beard Street, the sun was higher, muted by overcast skies. They were buzzed through the secure gate. Inside, the office maintained a strained operational readiness under Director Thompson's command, staff grappling with the cyberattack aftermath while prepping teams for NYPD support. Dev and Manny bypassed the busy main areas, heading directly for the armory. Inside the secure vault, they selected additional weapons with methodical care – suppressed pistols, specific rifle loadouts, breaching charges, advanced surveillance tools – packing them into unmarked duffels.

From the armory, they moved to the motor pool, selecting a black Chevy Suburban. They loaded the gear. As they climbed into the front seats, the solid thud of the heavy doors closing sealed them into a capsule of grim focus.

Pulling out of the Brooklyn Field Office gates and merging onto the expressway heading west, the gray morning sky mirrored the oppressive weight inside the Suburban. Manny drove, handling the early city traffic with ingrained skill, while Dev stared out the window, Viktor's ultimatum—Kill Brad Ewing—a repeating echo in his mind.

Twenty-two hours and change left. Kill Brad, or lose Rach and his mother.

Silence stretched for miles, thick with fury and unspoken grief. Finally, Dev broke it. "Need one more piece, Manny."

Manny glanced over, recognition already dawning in his eyes before Dev spoke the name. "Someone off-grid. Outside EAG."

"Deuce," Dev confirmed. Marcus "Deuce" Johnson. A name, a presence from their shared history in the service. Loyalty unquestioned, skills forged in situations Dev wouldn't entrust to anyone else right now.

"Jersey. Toms River. Mostly on the way to PA."

"Good call," Manny agreed immediately, already inputting new coordinates into the GPS. "If anyone can watch our six through... this," he gestured vaguely, encompassing the impossible scenario, "it's Deuce."

The drive south through New Jersey blurred past, fueled by caffeine and tense planning. They established new comms channels through burner phones, trying to create secure lines independent of EAG's compromised network. Around mid-morning, they exited the Garden State Parkway, navigating the quiet suburban streets of Toms River, pulling up to a tidy but unremarkable house set back from the road. Reinforced doors and strategically placed cameras were the only hints of the occupant's paranoia, visible only to a trained eye.

Deuce opened the door before they knocked, alerted by perimeter sensors. Marcus Johnson stood tall, the same contained energy radiating from his solid frame that Dev remembered from countless ops. Close-cropped brown hair, sharp blue eyes that scanned them both, taking in their tense expressions, the exhaustion clinging to them. His weathered face spoke of shared deployments. No extended greetings needed; a curt nod acknowledged the severity that brought them here unannounced. "Trouble still follows you two, huh?" he said, his voice low as he stepped aside. "Get in."

The interior was neat, ordered, reflecting Deuce's disciplined nature. Once the door was secured, Dev didn't waste words. He laid it all out—Viktor Mikhailov alive, Kate's betrayal, EAG compromised, the GCT attack, Rach and Annabelle hostage, the 24-hour ultimatum: kill Brad Ewing in Lehighton or the women die.

Deuce listened intently, his calm shifting to a cold stillness, particularly when Dev mentioned Annabelle being taken. He'd known Devin's mother, respected her deeply. When Dev finished, Deuce simply nodded once, his blue eyes like ice chips. "Viktor Mikhailov. Son of a bitch is still breathing?" He ran a hand over his short hair. "And Annabelle... damn it. Okay. What's the plan? Point me." No questions, no hesitation. Just readiness.

Relief hit Dev, sharp and immediate. "Heading to the cabin near Lehighton. Setting up there. Viktor gave me 24 hours for Ewing. Explicitly forbade rescue attempts for the women."

As Deuce went to grab his go-bag and lock down the house, Dev's sat phone buzzed. A text from Cass.

*ETA ABE approx 1600. Have POTUS brief + prelim intel package. Need secure meet.*

Dev showed the message to Manny. "Cass lands at ABE around 1600." He glanced at his watch. Nearly noon. "Slight change. Pick her up first, then the cabin. All three of us."

Manny nodded. "Makes sense. Consolidate."

Deuce emerged moments later, heavy tactical pack slung over one shoulder, his expression set. "Ready."

"New plan," Dev told him. "Detour first. Picking up our DC Director at Lehigh Valley Airport, 1600 hours. Head to the cabin together after."

Deuce just nodded again. "Lead the way."

The three men exited the house, climbing back into the waiting Suburban. The team felt stronger with Deuce added, the trust between them implicit, unspoken. But Viktor's clock kept ticking down, and the road ahead led towards a choice Dev dreaded making. Dev pulled away from the curb, turning the SUV northwest towards Pennsylvania, towards an airport meeting and whatever confrontation lay beyond.

The drive northwest into Pennsylvania was quiet, charged with grim purpose. Deuce, alert in the back seat, familiarized himself with the encrypted comms unit Manny passed back. Dev navigated, mind calculating angles, risks, the sickening possibility of Kate's continued influence. Manny rode shotgun, scanning traffic, his usual relaxed posture replaced by sharp vigilance. They spoke little; the stakes—Annabelle and Rach's lives balanced against Viktor's demand—needed no lengthy discussion. The hours bled away.

By late afternoon, around 3:45 PM, they approached Lehigh Valley International Airport near Allentown. Dev noted the time against Cass's ETA, as he guided the Suburban towards Arrivals, easing into the constantly shifting pickup lane. The distorted PA voice echoed, repeating the familiar warning about immediate loading only. Cars edged for position, travelers hurried with luggage—the ordinary airport rhythm a dissonant counterpoint to the tension coiled tight inside their vehicle.

Dev scanned the figures emerging from the sliding glass doors. A few minutes later, precisely at 1600, Cassandra Bellwether appeared. Even amidst the bustle, she moved with purpose. Roughly 5'9", lean, athletic, her shoulder-length blonde hair was pulled back efficiently. She carried a single, unremarkable carry-on, her intense blue eyes sweeping the pickup lane until they found their Suburban.

Manny had already stepped out as she approached. Cass offered Dev, leaning across from the driver's seat, a firm, professional handshake through the open passenger door window. "Devin." Her gaze flickered to Deuce in the back, a brief nod of recognition. She turned to Manny. A subtle warmth touched her expression despite the circumstances. A brief, familiar hug, ending with a quick kiss to his cheek. "Manny."

"Cass," Manny acknowledged quietly, taking her bag, tossing it into the back with their own gear.

"Good flight?" Deuce asked from the back seat, his tone even, as Cass slid in beside him.

"Productive," Cass replied, already retrieving a tablet from her briefcase. "Started the intel package. We'll brief fully at the cabin."

Dev nodded, putting the Suburban in gear. Manny settled back into the passenger seat. With Cass added to their small circle, their operational strength felt bolstered, but the weight of Viktor's deadline, the impossible choice, still rested heavily on Dev's shoulders. He pulled away from the curb, leaving the airport behind, steering towards the winding back roads that led to Lehighton, and the remote cabin—their necessary base for the fight to come. The team was assembled. The next stage began now.

# Chapter 22

# Reaction

Inside the familiar cabin near Lehighton, the four quickly set up a temporary command post around the sturdy oak table. Laptop screens glowed, encrypted devices emitted soft beeps, and tactical gear lay open nearby. Outside, the Pennsylvania woods were fully dark; the time pushed past 1800 hours. Less than thirteen hours remained on Viktor's clock.

Cass efficiently summarized the intel gathered during the flight—grim updates on the stalled GCT investigation, no new leads on Annabelle or Rach.

Deuce, cycling the action on his preferred SIG Sauer, shook his head. "Just like old times. Dumped in the shit with half the intel and a timer counting down." He looked at the others, a wry smile touching his lips despite the situation's gravity. "Seriously though, when was the last time the four of us ran an op together?"

A thick silence filled the cabin, heavy with shared, difficult history. Then, almost as one, voices low, Dev, Manny, and Cass replied:

"Kabul."

The single word brought back the taste of dust, the echo of gunfire, the ghosts of desperate missions. Dev and Manny exchanged a look—brothers forged in fire. Deuce nodded slowly, remembering the unique brand of chaos that place delivered. Manny's gaze flickered towards Cass, the former CIA operative—their lifeline, handler, sometimes confidante in that tangled war, and once, briefly, more than that to him. She met his look for a heartbeat, a fleeting acknowledgment of their shared past, before her expression returned to professional focus.

"Well, this isn't Kabul, and war stories won't help," Cass stated, her voice pulling them back to the present. "We have a task assigned by Mikhailov." She looked directly at Dev.

Dev rubbed his eyes, fatigue momentarily winning. "Less than 13 hours. Take out Brad Ewing at his dealership. Me. Personally. Or he kills Mom and Rach. No rescue attempts."

"Straightforward, then," Deuce stated, racking the slide on his pistol with decisive finality. "Infiltrate, neutralize Ewing, confirm kill for Viktor. Dirty work, but it buys the hostages time."

"No." Dev's voice was quiet but firm. "I won't kill him, Deuce. Not like this. Not on Viktor's command."

"Dev," Manny started, worry etching lines around his eyes, "your mother..."

"I know what's at stake, Manny!" Dev cut him off, his voice fraying. "But becoming Viktor's puppet? That doesn't save them, it costs us everything. He wants to break me, force me into his darkness. I won't give him that win."

"Your principles over their lives?" Deuce countered, his pragmatism blunt. "This isn't about right or wrong, Devin, it's about bad choices and worse ones. Taking out Ewing is the tactical play to keep Annabelle and Rach breathing right now."

"Or," Cass interjected smoothly, stepping into the charged silence, "Viktor doesn't need Ewing dead. He needs proof Dev followed the order. He needs Dev compromised—by the act, or by the belief he committed the act."

The distinction resonated. "Think we can fake it?" Manny asked, a spark returning to his eyes.

"High-risk," Cass admitted. "Viktor might have eyes or ears. Surveillance?"

"He didn't specify proof," Dev recalled, grasping the potential opening.

"That ambiguity is our only edge," Cass continued. "But Deuce is right—direct surveillance is the primary threat to a deception." She paused. "Which suggests countermeasures. A localized EMP burst, timed precisely? Could blind cameras, mics..."

"Risky," Manny noted. "But maybe required."

"It's an option," Dev agreed. "But we don't use it without eyes on." He looked decisively at the others. "Plan B: Deception. We make Viktor believe I killed Brad. How depends on the situation on the ground." He stood up. "No time for separate recon. We move now. All of us, towards

Lehighton. Cass, work dealership intel en route—layout, security, any accessible feeds. Manny, Deuce, let's plan the drive-by approach."

The team nodded, the debate resolved, the risky deception plan locked in. They began packing the last items, the efficient, familiar movements of preparing gear a stark contrast to the precarious moral ground they were about to tread. They loaded into the Suburban, leaving the cabin's temporary security behind, heading back into the night towards Lehighton, Ewing Automotive, and a deadly performance where failure was not an option.

The drive towards the outskirts of Lehighton was taut, the team reviewing satellite images and schematics displayed on Cass's tablet. Ewing Automotive occupied a lot on a relatively busy commercial strip, flanked by other businesses, though most were dark, closed for the night by the time they arrived after 2000 hours. Finding a hidden observation point was critical. They identified a vacant office building directly across the four-lane road, its darkened upper floor offering an unobstructed view of the dealership lot and showroom.

Inside the chilly, dust-filled room, Deuce positioned himself near a grimy window, deploying a high-powered scope with thermal imaging. Cass connected her tablet to a portable signal scanner, beginning to probe the dealership's network frequencies. Dev and Manny used binoculars, scanning the grounds below.

Ewing Automotive blazed under bright floodlights, casting harsh light onto the rows of new and used cars. The main showroom windows revealed polished floors and spotlighted vehicles. More importantly, movement.

"Movement," Deuce reported quietly, adjusting his scope's focus.

"Perimeter patrols. Not dealership security. Four visible on the lot, maybe two more near service bays. Armed. Rifles."

"Confirmed," Cass murmured, looking up from her tablet. "Picking up multiple encrypted comm signals—dealership grounds, patrols. Military-grade. Matches Shadow Serpent signatures."

Dev focused his binoculars on the showroom. After a moment, he found him. Brad Ewing, looking pale, agitated, pacing near a desk, talking emphatically to two large, impassive men in dark suits. Three other suited figures stood near the showroom entrances. "Brad's inside. With company. Five suits visible, plus the six Deuce tagged outside."

"Minimum eleven," Manny calculated grimly, sweeping the lot again with his own binos. "Likely more. Service bays, maybe roof access..."

"Cass, any sign of interior surveillance Viktor could be accessing?" Dev asked.

"Standard security cams are up. Trying to access their feed, but the network is locked down tight. No indication of a dedicated feed out to Viktor, but can't rule out hidden devices," Cass reported. "The number of guards suggests Viktor wants Ewing contained, not necessarily under constant watch."

"Twenty, maybe twenty-five total if they're properly garrisoned," Deuce estimated aloud, applying standard protocols for securing a high-value, potentially hostile asset. "Figured Viktor wouldn't leave his pawn loose," he added, his jaw tight.

Dev considered the situation. Less than eleven hours left. Plan A—a direct approach to 'kill' Brad—was impossible. Faking it surrounded by this many guards, under potential unknown surveillance, was equally suicidal. The objective had to change.

"Alright," Dev said, his voice decisive. "Plan A—dealing with Brad, fake or real—is scrubbed. Too many guards, too many unknowns. Plan B: Extraction. We get Brad out. If I can't fulfill Viktor's order because Brad's gone, it buys us time. Maybe leverage, if we can make him talk."

"Extract him through that?" Manny questioned, gesturing towards the heavily guarded dealership, though his eyes were already calculating approach vectors. "Stealth is the only play. We get made, it turns hot fast, firefight we can't win. And Viktor kills the hostages."

"Stealth it is," Dev confirmed. "Need to thin the outside patrols first, create an entry. Deuce, maintain overwatch here. Sniper support, comms relay only if mission critical—can't risk exposing your position unless it goes sideways."

Deuce gave a curt nod, settling behind his rifle.

"Cass, Manny, with me," Dev continued. "Move across the street, find a blind spot, breach the perimeter behind the service bays. Standard infiltration. Suppressed weapons, silent takedowns. Eliminate exterior patrols—west and rear—then assess entry into the service area, away from the showroom."

The three did a final gear check—suppressed pistols, knives, comms, NVGs. Cass tucked a compact EMP generator into her vest—a contingency. They moved out, down from the abandoned building, using the alley's shadows, then darting between parked cars and darkened storefronts to cross the main road further down, outside the dealership's immediate sightlines.

They located a section of chain-link fence behind the service bays, partly hidden by overgrown bushes. Manny made quick, nearly silent work of it with bolt cutters. They slipped through the opening onto the dealership lot, the gravel crunching loudly under their boots in the relative quiet.

Moving low and fast between rows of parked cars, they headed towards the rear corner patrol route Deuce had identified.

The first Serpent guard rounded the corner of the service bay, rifle held ready, scanning the darkness. Manny, pressed into the shadows of a large SUV, let him pass, then moved with blinding speed, clamping a hand over the guard's mouth, dragging him backward as Dev drove his combat knife into the man's side. The takedown was silent, brutally quick. They pulled the body deeper into the shadows between vehicles. One down.

They continued along the rear perimeter. Cass, using a handheld thermal scanner, picked up another heat signature near the dumpsters. They split, approaching from opposite sides. Cass tossed a small stone against a metal container—a brief sound drawing the guard's attention just as Dev and Manny closed the distance. Two seconds later, two more bodies were hidden. Three down.

Moving along the western side, towards the front but staying deep in the car rows, they spotted a pair of Serpents talking quietly near the edge of the building's light. More complex. Dev signaled Manny and Cass: simultaneous takedown. Counting down silently with hand signals, they moved together. Dev took the left, Manny the right. Cass moved close behind, pistol ready. The takedowns were fast, efficient, but one guard managed a brief, choked gasp before Manny fully silenced him. Four. Five down.

They froze, listening intently. Did anyone hear the gasp? Seconds stretched. No alarms. No shouts. Clear. Dev signaled forward, towards the service bay doors. Cass moved to the nearest door, scanning the lock, checking for electronic bypasses.

Suddenly, floodlights ignited, bathing the side lot in harsh brilliance, pinning them between rows of sedans. An amplified, abrasive voice boomed from unseen loudspeakers.

"Drop weapons! Hands visible! Now!"

Figures emerged from all directions—stepping from behind cars, appearing on the service bay roofline, spilling from the employee entrance. At least fifteen Shadow Serpent operatives materialized, weapons leveled, forming an inescapable ring around them. A trap, or their infiltration compromised far earlier than suspected.

Dev exchanged a look with Manny and Cass. No way out. Raising a hand slowly, palm out, he lowered his weapon. Manny and Cass mirrored him. Fighting now was suicide, sealing Annabelle and Rach's fates.

"Don't shoot!" Dev called out, his voice steady despite the adrenaline pounding in his chest. "We surrender."

The Serpents advanced cautiously, rifles still trained, surrounding them, their expressions grim, professional. The faint hope of a stealth extraction evaporated into the cold certainty of capture.

Rough hands shoved Dev, Manny, and Cass through the main glass doors of the Ewing Automotive showroom. The bright interior lights felt blinding after the darkness. They were forced to their knees on the polished floor, heavy zip ties cinching their wrists hard behind their backs. The air smelled of new car plastic and cleaning fluid, a strange counterpoint to the electric tension. About ten Serpents fanned out, securing entrances, watching the captives with impassive vigilance.

Brad Ewing emerged from a back hallway, swaggering, his face flushed, a volatile mix of fear and triumphant arrogance in his eyes. He circled the kneeling group, pausing before Dev.

"Well, well," Brad sneered. "Look what crawled in. The great Devin Jones, on his knees. Didn't expect to see you groveling on my showroom floor."

Dev met his gaze, silent, mind calculating, assessing the guards, searching for an opening.

Just then, two more Serpents emerged from the hall, roughly dragging Kaitlyn, bound and gagged. Her eyes were wide with terror as they forced her down nearby.

"Ah, darling," Brad said, looking down at her, feigned concern quickly twisting into possessiveness. "Sorry about this. But," his gaze slid meaningfully to Dev, "maybe it's fitting. Always had a soft spot for her, didn't you, Jones? Even when she was mine?" He chuckled, clearly enjoying the moment. "Don't worry, Kat. Once Dev fulfills his little task for our friend, maybe I'll let him watch while I... console you."

Kaitlyn struggled, muffled sounds escaping the gag, tears tracking through the dust on her face. Cass shot Brad a look of pure disgust. "Piece of slime," Manny spat.

Brad ignored them, focus locked on Dev, relishing his perceived upper hand. "This is your fault, Jones. Yours and your sainted father's." He paced again, fueled by their presence. "Mayor John Jones. Pillar of the community." Brad's voice dripped sarcasm. "Thought he could control everything. Thought he could make deals with dangerous men, then just walk away clean."

He leaned down towards Dev, voice dropping to a conspiratorial whisper. "Want to know about dear old Dad? Forget the official story. 'Sudden heart attack'?" Brad's eyes glittered. "Viktor needed leverage. Loyalty tests. Knew about us. Killing your father bound me to him, sent a message. He gave me the job."

Brad straightened, puffing his chest. "Pathetic, really. Coffee, Sunrise Diner, usual spot. Predictable." He flicked his fingers dismissively. "Little something extra wiped on the cup rim while the waitress turned her back. Contact poison. Fast, untraceable, absorbs through the skin." He smirked. "Paid my check, walked out. Saw the ambulance later. 'Tragic cardiac event'. Clean. Simple. Job done." He laughed, a high, brittle sound. "Got what he deserved! Thinking he was better than everyone!" Brad stepped closer, looming over Dev, spittle flying. "And now look at you! On your knees! You're next!"

That shattered something inside Dev. Hearing the callous confession, seeing the man who murdered his father gloating—the control snapped. With a guttural roar of grief and rage, Dev launched himself upwards from his knees, driving the crown of his head into Brad's lower jaw with savage force.

A sickening crunch echoed in the showroom. Brad's eyes rolled back; he crumpled instantly, hitting the polished floor like dead weight, motionless.

The showroom froze for a split second. Then, chaos. Two Serpents lunged for Dev. Reacting instantly, Dev twisted, slamming his shoulder into the nearest guard, knocking him off balance. Dev grabbed the man's dropped rifle—not to fire, but swinging the heavy butt in a tight arc, connecting solidly with the Serpent's temple. The guard dropped, stunned.

Other Serpents raised weapons, shouting commands. The scarred leader barked, "Hold fire! Check Ewing!"

One guard knelt beside Brad, felt for a pulse, checked his airway. His eyes widened slightly. He looked up at the leader, shaking his head. "Gone, sir. Neck's broken. Dead."

The leader stared at Brad's body, then at Dev, now being restrained by two other guards. Surprise, then calculation, flickered across the leader's face. He pulled out his phone, dialed quickly. "Sir, condition met, but... unexpectedly. Jones neutralized Ewing personally. Subject deceased. Request instructions regarding Jones, Rivera, and Bellwether."

## Chapter 23

## Aftermath in Lehighton

Watching through his scope from the darkened office across the street, Deuce saw the Serpent leader lower his comm unit after reporting Brad Ewing's death. He didn't need to hear Viktor Mikhailov's reply to know the likely order: Terminate the witnesses. Time had evaporated for Dev, Manny, and Cass. Waiting wasn't an option.

"Moving," Deuce muttered into his own encrypted comms—a self-command, knowing the others wouldn't hear, but needing the process. He slid back from the window, grabbed his pack, and moved out the door, taking the emergency stairs down to the ground floor alley in silent, double-time strides.

He emerged into the shadows, eyes automatically sweeping the dealership perimeter. Thermal picked up two guards still patrolling the rear lot near the service bays—complacent, sloppy. Deuce moved fluidly along the darkened street, using parked cars for cover, closing the distance soundlessly. The first guard dropped from a single, silenced pistol round before registering Deuce's presence. The second began to turn at the soft thump of the body hitting asphalt, but Deuce was already there, his combat knife ending the threat cleanly.

Rear clear. Deuce moved fast along the side lot, keeping deep within the vehicle rows until he had a line of sight to the front display area. He pulled out the multi-frequency activator Cass had given him. Taking a steadying breath, he selected the sequence for maximum sensory overload and pressed the trigger.

WEE-OOO! HONK! AROOOOGA! WEE-OOO-WEE-OOO!

The night fractured as a dozen car alarms erupted simultaneously, horns blaring, lights flashing—a wave of disorienting chaos washing over the lot.

Concealed behind a large pickup, Deuce watched the main showroom doors fly open. Seven armed Serpents spilled out, rifles up, fanning out to find the source of the automotive bedlam, their attention ripped from the prisoners inside.

Now.

Deuce broke cover, sprinting low and fast straight for the main entrance, left slightly ajar. He slipped through the opening, weapon raised, instantly taking in the scene. Three Serpents remained inside. Two stood over Dev, Manny, and Cass—whose hands were bound securely behind their backs—weapons aimed but clearly diverted by the noise outside. The third, the scarred leader, yelled into his comms, trying to regain control of the external situation.

Deuce didn't hesitate. Targeting the Serpent nearest the door, whose back was partially turned, he took two silent steps, his knife finding the gap below the man's vest. Deuce eased the body down behind a sales kiosk without a sound.

The slight movement, the sudden vacancy, alerted the second guard just as Manny, seeing Deuce, drove upwards from his knees, his hands still tied behind him, slamming his bound weight into the Serpent's legs. Simultaneously, Cass, her own hands bound behind her back, twisted sharply, driving her head backward into the leader's face as he turned from his comms. He gagged, stumbling back, dropping the unit. Deuce moved past them, knife flashing, slicing through the zip ties binding Manny's hands, then Cass's. Freed, Manny wrenched the sidearm from the Serpent he grappled with, shoving the man hard off balance. Cass scrambled for her own dropped pistol nearby, bringing it up smoothly.

The leader, recovering quickly from Cass's headbutt, lunged for his fallen weapon. Cass fired twice, precise shots striking his center mass. The last guard, still wrestling with Manny, looked up directly into the muzzle of Deuce's pistol. Deuce ended the fight. In less than ten seconds, the showroom was theirs.

Cass snatched Devin's discarded weapon from the floor, tossing it to him as Deuce moved to cover the entrance, listening for the anticipated return of the seven guards. Manny hauled Devin to his feet, steadying him. "You good?"

Devin shook his head, the lingering fog from the headbutt receding. His gaze, despite the impact, was sharp. "Yeah," he confirmed, gripping his pistol. He glanced at Brad's body, then towards Kaitlyn, whom Cass was now cutting free. "Status?"

"Three down inside," Deuce reported, his voice clipped as he performed a quick magazine check. "Seven went to check the noise outside." He nodded towards the flashing lights and blaring horns still echoing from the lot. "They'll realize it's a diversion soon enough."

The words had barely left Deuce's mouth when the blaring car alarms outside abruptly ceased. A tense silence descended, swiftly broken by the crunch of boots on gravel as multiple figures moved rapidly towards the showroom.

"Contact!" Deuce called, dropping into a firing stance near the main entrance, a sturdy sales kiosk his shield.

"Cass, Kaitlyn, get back!" Devin ordered. He guided a still-dazed Kaitlyn towards the back office hallway where Cass was retreating. Manny kicked over a heavy glass coffee table, its bulk providing makeshift cover in the showroom's center.

The main glass doors imploded as the first two Serpents charged through, rifles raised. Deuce met them with controlled bursts from his suppressed pistol, felling both before they could zero in on a target. Almost simultaneously, two more Serpents shattered a side window near the service bay access, angling for a crossfire. Manny reacted, his weapon spitting fire from behind the overturned table, forcing them to recoil momentarily.

"West side window!" Manny yelled.

Cass, positioned deeper in the showroom near the hallway, leaned out and fired with precision, hitting one Serpent in the window frame. The other scrambled back outside.

Devin moved to Deuce's side, his own fire adding to the barrage aimed at the main entrance where three more Serpents were attempting a coordinated breach. Suppressed rounds zipped through the air, striking displays and pulverizing the remaining glass panels. One Serpent crumpled in the doorway. The other two dove behind vehicles just outside, returning fire. Bullets thudded into the kiosk shielding Deuce and Devin.

"They're pinned at the front!" Devin shouted over the din. "Manny, flanking window!"

Manny acknowledged with a nod, rolling away from the table an instant before bullets stitched the floor where he'd been. He sprinted for the service bay access corridor, seeking an angle on the Serpent still pinned by Cass near the shattered side window.

Deuce maintained controlled fire on the two Serpents trapped outside the main entrance, halting their advance. Devin seized the momentary pause to check their rear. Clear.

A sudden burst of automatic fire erupted from the west side window – the Serpent there making a frantic play. Cass ducked back just as Manny appeared at the end of the service bay corridor inside. He had a clear line of sight. His pistol barked twice; the firing from the window stopped.

"West window clear!" Manny confirmed.

The odds had shifted: four against two. The remaining Serpents at the main entrance clearly saw their position deteriorating. One bolted, attempting to retreat across the lot. Deuce tracked him smoothly, firing three rounds. The man stumbled, then collapsed onto the asphalt. The last Serpent hesitated, his weapon clattering to the ground as he slowly raised his hands.

"Hold fire!" Devin commanded. Deuce kept his weapon trained on the surrendering Serpent while Manny cautiously approached to secure him. A heavy quiet settled over the showroom, punctuated only by the distant hum of traffic on the main road and the ragged breaths of the team. Seven down outside, three inside, plus their leader. Ten Serpents dealt with, and Brad Ewing lifeless on the floor.

"Clear?" Devin asked, his eyes scanning the dark lot through the shattered doors.

"For now," Deuce confirmed, checking his ammunition.

Cass emerged from the hallway with Kaitlyn. Kaitlyn was pale but unbound and alert. "She's okay. Scared, but okay."

Devin nodded, his gaze settling on the dead Serpent leader near Cass's feet. He knelt, retrieving the man's satellite phone from his vest pocket. It felt substantial in his hand. Drawing a breath, he found the last dialed number – probably Viktor. He pressed call.

It connected almost immediately. Viktor's voice, cold and impatient, crackled from the small speaker. "Is it done? Report status."

Devin held the phone slightly away, his own voice flat, controlled. "Your welcoming committee had a change in management, Viktor. This is Jones."

A heartbeat of stunned silence, then Viktor's voice returned, laced with sharp annoyance and an underlying chill. "Jones... So, the rat escapes the trap, killing the bait. Predictable, in its own fashion. You continue to disappoint... and surprise."

"Where are they, Viktor? My mother and Rachel."

A dry chuckle echoed from the phone. "Patience, Jones. You fulfilled your task, though with your customary level of destruction. Your defiance alters nothing. You've merely postponed what's coming and made their situation more dire." The line went quiet for a beat, then Viktor's voice, devoid of any inflection, stated, "This ends now."

The call disconnected with an abrupt click.

Devin stared at the phone, a hollowness expanding in his chest. "He hung up."

The quiet in the showroom after Viktor's call disconnected was profound, disturbed only by Kaitlyn's muffled sobs and the distant swish of traffic on Blakeslee Boulevard. Devin's gaze remained fixed on the satellite phone, its screen displaying the stark coordinates: 39.9061° N, 75.13671° W.

"He gave us the location," Manny breathed, his eyes shifting from the glowing screen to Devin.

"Coordinates," Cass confirmed, already looking up from her tablet where she'd entered them. "Looks like... the industrial outskirts of Philadelphia. Near the port area."

"He wants a final meeting," Devin said, his voice low as he pocketed the dead leader's phone. "On his ground. At a place he controls." He surveyed his team, Kaitlyn huddled nearby, Brad's body a stark reminder on the floor. The success here offered no relief, only a shift to the next, perhaps final, confrontation. "Alright. Let's get Kaitlyn somewhere secure, manage this scene, and prepare to finish this."

Deuce nodded. "First, her." He gently helped Kaitlyn to her feet. "We'll drop you at the local PD. Tell them Brad was killed by intruders, you were held hostage, we rescued you. Keep it straightforward."

Kaitlyn, pale but regaining her composure, nodded once, wordlessly. After ensuring Kaitlyn was on her way to safety and altering the scene to suggest a robbery gone awry, Devin, Manny, Deuce, and Cass returned to the Suburban. The drive to reach Annabelle and Rachel, to dismantle Viktor's network, fueled them with a raw, pressing energy.

They drove south out of Lehighton, the small town and the evidence of Brad's death receding behind them. Highway miles dissolved under the dark sky. Inside the vehicle, the quiet stretched, heavy with fatigue and the unspoken understanding of Devin's actions—and Viktor's manipulation.

Manny finally broke the silence, his voice subdued. "Dev... about Brad..."
Devin stared straight ahead, his grip tightening on the steering wheel until his knuckles showed white. "Don't, Manny."
"We need to," Manny insisted gently. "Viktor manipulated you. Used your past, pushed until you reacted." He paused. "Yeah, Brad confessed, even boasted about killing your dad. You responded. Anyone would have."
"It wasn't just a response," Devin's voice was rough, strained. "That rage... it was cold, Manny. I wanted him dead. Not for Viktor, but for everything. And Viktor knew that." He swallowed. "He didn't just want Brad eliminated; he wanted me to be the one to do it, to see me fracture." His voice dropped. "And I gave him that."
"You defended yourself after he admitted to murdering your father and then came at you," Cass interjected from the back, her tone firm yet understanding. "It was a direct confrontation, not some calculated hit for Viktor. Don't let him warp your perception of it."
"Call it what you want," Deuce added quietly from the passenger seat. "The result's the same. Brad's dealt with. Viktor got an outcome he desired, even if the execution wasn't precisely his plan." He turned slightly. "Concentrate on what's next. Saving Rachel and Annabelle."
The remainder of the drive was consumed by intense planning. They reviewed the intelligence Cass pulled on the Philadelphia port area, discussed potential entry points, and tried to anticipate Viktor's defensive

measures. Logistics, fallback positions, and the critical need for precision dominated their conversation.

As the first subtle streaks of dawn painted the eastern sky, the dense urban spread of Philadelphia materialized from the receding darkness. They navigated the final miles, the scenery transforming from open highway to industrial zones—rows of warehouses, sprawling container yards, and the distant, skeletal silhouettes of cranes against the lightening horizon.

Following the GPS coordinates Cass had plotted, they turned onto a service road paralleling the Delaware River waterfront. The air grew thick with the smells of diesel and brackish water. Ahead, under the sparse glow of industrial lighting, lay their objective: a vast container terminal, a complex grid of stacked metal boxes, towering cranes, and loading equipment—the exact destination indicated by the coordinates.

Devin pulled the Suburban to a stop in the deep shadows of a seldom-used access road and killed the engine. The ensuing silence felt vast, broken only by the low, persistent hum of the port and the sharp cries of gulls overhead.

They had arrived. Their ultimate confrontation with Viktor waited within the cold, metallic maze of the container yard.

# Chapter 24

# Strong Winds

The heavy silence in Viktor's makeshift office was a coiled thing, thick and venomous. He slammed the satellite phone onto the scarred metal desk, the crack echoing the tremor in his own hand. Outside the thin walls, the low hum of the Mercury International Container Terminal's operations continued, oblivious to the storm raging within this small room.

Kate watched him, her expression carefully neutral, a mask honed by years of navigating his volatile tempers. Akimitsu, a shadow near the door, remained impassive, his stillness a counterpoint to Viktor's barely contained fury.

Viktor's chest heaved, the expensive fabric of his shirt straining over his shoulders. "Gone," he bit out, the word a shard of glass. "Ewing. Gone. And those imbeciles I sent with him... neutralized." He spat the last word as if it were poison. His piercing blue eyes, usually so cold and calculating, now burned with a raw, almost feral frustration. He paced the confines of the small office, a caged predator. "Jones. Always Jones. How does he continue to... interfere?"

Kate stepped forward slightly, her voice calm, a carefully modulated counterpoint to his rising agitation. "Father, perhaps this is a momentary setback. Jones is resourceful, but—"

"Resourceful?" Viktor spun, his glare pinning her. "He dismantled an entire operation! My operatives, Brad's supposed network... all for nothing!" He struck the desk again, the force rattling the cheap lamp. "The plan was precise. Ewing was to deal with Jones. Simple. Now..." He trailed off, his breath coming in ragged bursts, the mask of control fracturing.

Akimitsu shifted, his movement almost imperceptible, but it drew Viktor's eye. "What is it?" Viktor snapped, his gaze fixing on Akimitsu. "You have something to say? Some ancient wisdom to impart?"

Akimitsu's gaze was steady, his voice low, carrying weight despite its quietness. "Viktor-sama," he began, the honorific a stark contrast to the tension in the room, "the path of vengeance is a hungry ghost. It devours clarity. It consumes reason."

Viktor's lip curled. "Are you suggesting I abandon this? After everything?" The raw pain in his voice was a visceral thing, momentarily eclipsing the anger.

"Your drive is understood, Viktor-sama," Akimitsu acknowledged, his voice softening almost imperceptibly. "But this vendetta against Jones... it has led to compromised operations, escalating risks, significant losses. First the GCT incident, which drew unforeseen levels of federal attention, and now this failure with Ewing." He paused. "Perhaps... there is a point where the pursuit of retribution yields diminishing returns, where the cost becomes too great for the desired satisfaction."

Kate watched them, silent, her own thoughts unreadable. She had seen her father's single-mindedness before, but the layers of this particular obsession with Devin Jones were complex, deeply personal.

Viktor turned sharply towards Akimitsu, his face contorted. "Cost? You speak to me of cost? Jones and Rivera, they cost me everything years ago. They left me to rot." His voice was a low growl. "They embody the indifference, the betrayal that has defined my existence since. This isn't mere revenge, Akimitsu. It is... rebalancing. It is a lesson they, and the system that created them, must learn."

"And what if the lesson consumes the teacher?" Akimitsu countered, his tone still respectful but unyielding. "The Shadow Serpents were built on meticulous planning, on global reach and influence, not on personal vendettas that expose the entire network to such direct, chaotic confrontations." He gestured vaguely, encompassing the recent string of violent encounters. "This current path... it feels... reckless."

Viktor stared, a muscle twitching in his scarred cheek, his eyes burning with barely suppressed rage. For a moment, Kate thought he might physically lash out. But then, a chilling smile touched his lips, one that didn't reach his eyes. "Reckless? Perhaps. Or perhaps, Akimitsu, it is simply the only path left that holds any meaning." He turned away, his back to them, staring out the grimy window at the indifferent stacks of containers. "Brad Ewing's failure to handle Jones changes little. Devin

Jones will be brought to heel. And he will understand the price of what he took from me."

Kate spoke then, her voice still measured, but with an edge of urgency. "The ambush in Lehighton, Father... if Jones and Rivera are as capable as you say, they won't stop. They'll trace this back. This facility..."

"Is a fortress," Viktor cut her off, turning back, his composure partially restored, the cold mask slipping back into place. "Let them come. Akimitsu, ensure our guests are... secure. And double the perimeter patrols. Jones wants a confrontation? He will find one he cannot possibly win."

Akimitsu bowed slightly. "As you command, Viktor-sama." He then looked pointedly at Kate. "And you, Katerina? Your counsel to your father in this... it carries weight. Ensure it is... wise."

Kate met Akimitsu's gaze, a flicker of something unreadable in her eyes, before she nodded curtly. The air in the small office remained heavy, the cracks in Viktor's control, and perhaps in his carefully constructed empire, more visible than ever. The storm that was Devin Jones was coming, and the ground beneath them felt increasingly unstable.

The dim, oppressive silence of the concrete cell was broken only by the rhythmic drip of water from a rusted pipe and the occasional muffled clang from the warehouse operations far above. Rachel shifted, the cold metal of the chains biting into her already raw wrists. Her arms ached from being stretched above her head, locked to the heavy ceiling beam.

"He'll come, Mrs. J," Rachel whispered, her voice hoarse, the words a fragile offering against the despair that threatened to engulf them. "Devin... he won't stop. Manny won't either."

Annabelle, huddled on the cold floor a few feet away, her hands bound simply but securely with zip ties, looked up. Her face, though pale and etched with worry, held a spark of fierce maternal certainty. "I know, dear. I know my son." She drew a shuddering breath. "It's what terrifies me. What Viktor will do to him... to them... because he won't stop." The unspoken fear of what Viktor might do to them to get to Devin hung heavy between them.

"We have to believe," Rachel insisted, more for herself than for Annabelle. She closed her eyes, picturing Devin's face, clinging to the image. "He found us before..."

The heavy steel door at the far end of the cell creaked open, the sound loud and jarring, making both women jump. Akimitsu entered, his presence filling the small space with a quiet, unnerving authority. Two more of Viktor's guards, armed and impassive, flanked him.

He surveyed them for a moment, his gaze unreadable. Annabelle met his look with a surprising firmness, while Rachel's fear was overlaid with a defiant glare.

"It is time to move," Akimitsu stated, his voice calm, devoid of inflection. He gestured to one of the guards. "Unchain the reporter. Secure her properly for transport upstairs. Mrs. Jones, you will come as well."

The guard approached Rachel with a key, the metallic click of the manacles unlocking echoing in the small room. Freedom from the beam was a momentary, agonizing relief for Rachel's shoulders, quickly replaced by the rough cinching of zip ties around her wrists behind her back. The other guard helped Annabelle to her feet.

"Where are you taking us?" Rachel demanded, her voice trembling slightly despite her effort to keep it steady.

Akimitsu merely gestured towards the open door. "Viktor-sama requires your presence."

There was no room for argument. Flanked by the guards, with Akimitsu leading the way, they were escorted out of the grim cell and into the narrow utility corridor. The air here was slightly fresher, but the sense of dread only intensified as they were led towards the sound of distant, muted activity and, presumably, closer to Viktor.

The ascent in a small, clanking service elevator was tense and silent, the single floor they passed heightening their apprehension about what awaited them in Viktor's office above. The doors slid open with a groan, revealing the short, utilitarian hallway that led to the office they had glimpsed from the warehouse floor. Akimitsu gestured them forward.

The heavy wooden doors to Viktor's office were ajar. Akimitsu pushed one open wider, and the guards nudged Rachel and Annabelle inside. The scene that greeted them stole the air from their lungs.

Viktor stood behind his large desk, his earlier agitation now a veneer of icy control, though the storm still flickered deep in his eyes. But it wasn't just him. Standing near the window, looking out as if contemplating the distant city, was Kate.

"Kate!" Rachel gasped, the name a raw wound. Annabelle simply stared, her hand flying to her mouth, a silent testament to the profound shock. "You!" Rachel's voice, when it came, was laced with a fury born of disbelief and pain. "How could you? After everything? Devin... Manny... they trusted you! We trusted you!"

Annabelle found her voice, trembling but strong. "Kate... after all these years... this is who you are? Part of this... this nightmare?"

Kate turned slowly, her face composed, an unreadable mask. There was no surprise in her eyes, only a kind of weary resignation. "Mrs. Jones. Rachel." Her voice was calm, eerily so. "It's not as simple as you think."

"Not simple?" Rachel's laugh was harsh, devoid of humor. "You betrayed them! You watched them suffer, you helped him," she gestured wildly towards Viktor, "plot against them! What part of that isn't simple?"

"He is my father," Kate stated, her voice still level, her gaze unwavering as she looked at Annabelle. "You, of all people, Mrs. Jones, should understand what one does to protect their family, to uphold their name. Devin has spent his life doing just that, has he not? Taking risks, making hard choices, all for the Jones legacy, for his family. Is my loyalty to my own blood so different?"

Rachel shook her head, tears of anger and betrayal spilling down her cheeks. "Loyalty? You call this loyalty? Condemning two men who took you into their company, who showed you nothing but an abundance of trust? Who considered you family? How could you watch them go through hell, knowing you were part of the reason?"

Viktor chuckled then, a dry, grating sound that cut through the charged air. He leaned forward, steepling his fingers on the desk. "Perhaps your Devin shouldn't be so quick to offer his trust, Ms. Miller. It seems to be a recurring vulnerability in the Jones lineage. A rather exploitable flaw, wouldn't you agree?"

His eyes glinted with malice, settling on Annabelle, then Rachel, before dismissing them with a wave of his hand towards Akimitsu. "Ensure they are comfortable. The final act is approaching, and I want them to have a clear view when the curtain falls on Devin Jones."

Akimitsu gave a subtle nod, his unblinking gaze shifting to Annabelle and Rachel, who remained bound and watched by the other guards. He moved with quiet purpose to position himself where he could observe both the prisoners and the room's entrance, a silent, formidable sentinel. The heavy silence descended again, thick with unspoken threats and the raw edges of the earlier confrontation.

Kate remained by the window, her back to her father and the tense tableau. The skyline outside, usually a vista of detached power, seemed to press in on her, the distant city lights blurring at the edges. Her fingers, unseen, tightened into fists, nails biting into her palms until the skin threatened to break. The smooth, cool fabric of her tactical gear felt abrasive, a constraint she hadn't registered before. She heard the soft clink of glass as Viktor presumably refreshed his drink, the sound unnaturally loud in the strained silence. The words Rachel had hurled – condemning two men who took you into their company, who showed you nothing but an abundance of trust – replayed, a discordant echo against the chilling certainty of her father's final pronouncement and the terrified, accusing eyes of the women still in the room.

# Chapter 25

# Collision Course

From their observation post across the Delaware River—likely the elevated terrain of Red Bank Battlefield Park in New Jersey—the Mercury International Container Terminal stretched out below Devin's team. The distance, roughly a mile across the choppy water, demanded high-powered optics. Shipping containers formed massive, colored blocks; cranes, stark against the hazy skyline, punctuated the view; and trucks navigated the access roads within the 160-acre facility with a steady, ant-like purpose.

Devin focused his optics on the target building: a secluded warehouse in the farthest corner, its weathered brick barely distinguishable from the surrounding industrial decay. Armed patrols traced the perimeter fence, their routes predictable yet thorough. More guards were visible near the loading docks that jutted out towards the harbor. Nearby, Cass, bent over her ruggedized tablet, typed rapidly, her brow furrowed in concentration. "Network security is tight," she muttered. "Trying to find an access point into their camera feeds, but it's heavily layered."

"Sixty, maybe seventy tangos outside, matching our estimate," Deuce murmured, fine-tuning the focus on his spotting scope. "Movement patterns are regular. Shift changes probably every four to six hours. They're alert, but not agitated. I'd say they don't know we're looking at this location yet."

Manny, using his own binoculars, scanned the approaches. "Vehicles appear standard for port operations. No obvious heavy reinforcements staged close by, but it's hard to be certain from this distance."

Devin nodded, his gaze unwavering from the target building. Fine. He would operate within the obscurity Viktor favored, but not alone.

He zoomed in on the warehouse again. A single, reinforced side door near the rear appeared to have less traffic than the main loading bays. Chain-link fencing, crowned with barbed wire, encircled the immediate area, but Devin spotted a section partially hidden by overgrown weeds and discarded pallets—a clear blind spot between two surveillance cameras.

"There," Devin said, transmitting his optic feed to the others. "That's our way in. Breach the fence there, use the container stacks as cover to approach that rear side door."

Deuce studied the image. "It'll be tight, but manageable. Exterior patrols circle back on that section every ten minutes. The window is small."

"If you can give us a five-minute heads-up on that patrol loop, Cass, it'll be crucial," Manny added.

"Working on their exact pathing from this angle now," Cass replied, her eyes still glued to her screen.

Devin checked his chrono again. Time was slipping away. Waiting for an ideal moment wasn't feasible. They had to move, confirm if the hostages were present, and then devise an extraction—assuming they hadn't been relocated again.

"Alright," Devin stated, his voice low but firm. He met the eyes of his team. "Gear up. We move as one. Cass, keep attempting network access as we advance. Stay close." He paused. "We move now."

They packed their optics swiftly, checking that their suppressed M4A1s and sidearms were secure. The four departed the observation post, returning to the nondescript Suburban. The drive across the bridge and into the outskirts of the industrial zone was taut, each occupant lost in their thoughts. They parked several blocks from their target, the ambient noise and activity of legitimate port operations offering a fragile screen for their presence.

Moving on foot, the four kept to the darker margins, using parked trucks and dilapidated structures for concealment as they neared the Mercury International perimeter. Upon reaching the targeted section of fence, Devin produced compact bolt cutters. The snip of metal was sharp but brief. Manny pulled the cut section aside as Cass and Deuce slipped through, Devin and Manny following immediately. The barbed wire caught for a second on Devin's tactical pants.

"We're inside," Devin reported quietly into his comms.

"Copy that. Patrol passed your breach point seventy seconds ago. Next pass expected in approximately eight minutes," Cass relayed, already moving smoothly behind Deuce, her tablet held securely.

Inside the sprawling shipping yard, the sheer size of the operation was apparent. Towering stacks of containers formed deep canyons of corrugated steel. They advanced as a cohesive unit—Devin at point, Manny and Deuce covering the flanks, Cass providing rear security while intermittently consulting her tablet. Their boots made soft sounds on gravel and debris as they scanned, checked corners, and listened. Twice, they froze, pressing themselves into the deep shadows cast by the container stacks as patrols passed nearby, holding their breath until the sound of footsteps receded. They neutralized two exterior sentries who crossed their path with swift, coordinated—and suppressed—shots, the sounds lost in the port's constant hum. The bodies were quickly dragged from view behind a dumpster overflowing with industrial waste.

Finally, they reached the target building—the secluded warehouse. The air here felt colder, stagnant, carrying a faint, unsettling chemical odor that Devin recalled from earlier intelligence on Viktor's dealings. They pressed themselves flat against the weathered brick wall near the reinforced side door. Deuce examined the simple lock—easily defeated. He gave Devin a nod. Cass performed a final sweep with her scanner.

"No immediate electronic signals from inside this door."

"Going dark on comms for a moment," Devin whispered.

Drawing a steadying breath, Devin eased the door inward just enough to slip through, his M4A1 preceding him. Manny followed, then Cass, and finally Deuce, who secured the door gently behind them. They were inside. The atmosphere was heavy with the scent of dust and a faint metallic odor. Dim emergency lights threw long, wavering shadows down a narrow utility corridor lined with pipes. The silence here felt distinct—charged, almost watchful. They advanced, deeper into Viktor's operational core, the need to find Rachel and Annabelle a singular, driving purpose.

The narrow utility corridor stretched before them, illuminated by the sporadic flicker of emergency lights that cast distorted shadows from the overhead pipes and conduit. The air was stale, thick with the smell of dust, dampness, and the faint, unsettling chemical trace Devin recalled. They moved as a tight formation: Devin on point with his M4A1, Manny and Deuce covering the flanks with practiced economy of motion, while Cass brought up the rear, her tablet stowed for now, her own weapon ready, her gaze sweeping behind them.

The quiet was profound, disturbed only by the soft grit of their boots on the concrete and the distant, muted thrum of the port's machinery. They methodically cleared several small, empty storage rooms and what appeared to be deserted supervisor offices, discovering only layers of dust and signs of disuse. With each cleared space, a silent tension coiled tighter among them.

"Anything, Cass?" Devin whispered into his comms.

"Still trying to penetrate their internal comms or camera network," Cass whispered back. "It's a fortress. Whoever designed this was thorough."

They rounded another corner where the corridor widened slightly near a bank of service elevators—likely descending to deeper levels, perhaps the hidden vault hinted at in earlier intelligence. Devin bypassed them.

Further on, a heavy steel door, unlabeled but clearly reinforced, stood slightly ajar.

Devin signaled a halt, gesturing for Manny and Deuce to cover the corridor's approaches. He made eye contact with Cass; she nodded, weapon raised to cover his advance. Devin moved toward the door with caution, using the barrel of his M4A1 to slowly push it further open.

The room beyond was small, little more than a reinforced concrete cell. The dim light from a single caged bulb overhead illuminated bare walls and a foul-smelling drain in the center of the floor. And something else that sent a chill through Devin.

Chains. Two sets dangled from thick steel beams bolted into the ceiling, ending in heavy manacles that swayed almost imperceptibly in the still air. The floor beneath them was scuffed and gouged, testament to a recent, frantic struggle. Devin stepped fully inside, his weapon's light playing over the compact space. Discarded zip ties lay near one wall. A small, dark stain on the concrete had the disturbing appearance of dried blood. And near the wall, almost lost in shadow, lay a single silver hoop earring—one Rachel favored. Beside it, tangled with some debris, was a thin, patterned scarf—Annabelle's.

Devin's breath caught in his throat. He knelt, his gloved fingers closing around the earring and scarf. The metal was cold, the fabric unexpectedly soft. They had been here. Together. But the cell was now empty. A wave of relief that they weren't currently in those chains was instantly overwhelmed by the stark fear of where Viktor had moved them.

"They were here," Devin said, his voice raspy as he held up the items for the others, who now cautiously entered the grim space.

Manny swore under his breath. "Moved them again. But where?"

"Upstairs? Deeper down?" Deuce mused, his gaze methodically sweeping every detail of the small room.

"Or already gone from the facility," Cass added, her tone flat. "This could be a temporary holding spot, not the final one."

Devin pocketed the earring and scarf. The small objects felt like anchors against the dread threatening to pull him under. He forced back the images trying to flood his mind—Rachel chained, his mother filled with terror. Panic was a luxury he couldn't afford. Only action mattered. "We keep moving," he ordered, his voice regaining its edge. "Clear this level. Find access to the main warehouse floor. That's where the bulk of his force will be. That's where we'll find Viktor."

They continued their sweep, the discovery in the cell lending a grim momentum to their movements. They cleared the remaining rooms and corridors of the lower level with precision, silently eliminating two more guards. At last, they reached a heavy fire door stenciled "WAREHOUSE

ACCESS." Faint sounds—movement, indistinct voices—seeped from beyond it.

Devin signaled the team to stack. Manny tested the handle—unlocked. On Devin's signal, Manny threw the door open. Devin plunged through, M4A1 raised, the others following instantly, spreading out into the cavernous main warehouse floor.

It was immense. Shipping containers and crates rose in towering formations, creating alleys of steel and wood. Forklifts stood silent. High-bay lights cast stark yellow illumination across sections of the concrete floor, leaving other areas in deep shadow. And they were not the only occupants.

At least a dozen operatives in tactical gear, some bearing the snake-and-dagger tattoo of the Shadow Serpents, were positioned near a central staging area, appearing to coordinate or await instructions. They reacted instantly to the breach, weapons swinging up, shouts erupting and echoing in the vast space. High above, from a large office window overlooking the floor, Devin saw a pale face—Viktor—watching.

"Contact!" Devin yelled, firing as he dove behind a stack of wooden pallets. Manny, Deuce, and Cass scattered, each finding cover behind crates and machinery, their weapons joining the fray.

The warehouse became a maelstrom of gunfire. Rounds sparked off metal, chipped concrete, and tore through wooden crates. Devin and Manny worked in tandem, advancing by bounds, using suppressive fire to cover each other, felling Serpents caught exposed. Deuce, having gained a slightly elevated position atop a stack of pallets, delivered accurate covering fire, his suppressed rifle cracking with methodical rhythm. Cass moved along a flank, using the aisles for concealment, engaging targets as they appeared.

They were gaining ground, pushing the Serpents back towards the loading docks, the cacophony of the firefight reverberating from the high ceilings. As Deuce paused behind his pallet cover to reload, a figure darted from the shadows of a side office doorway they hadn't cleared—Kate. She moved with a shocking speed and quietness amidst the chaos, scrambling onto the pallets behind Deuce.

Before Deuce could react to the unexpected presence, Kate lunged. A long, thin combat knife glinted under the harsh lights as she plunged it deep into a gap near his side, below his vest.

"Aagh!" Deuce's cry was a raw sound of agony and disbelief. His rifle clattered away as he twisted, falling from the pallets to crash heavily onto the concrete below.

"Kate! No!" Devin roared, witnessing the attack. A burning rage swept through him, and he broke from his cover, charging directly towards Kate, who had landed nimbly on the floor, her expression cold, unreadable. "You traitorous bitch!"

"Cass! Deuce is down!" Manny yelled at the same moment, unleashing suppressive fire towards the remaining Serpents near the docks to cover Devin, his mind reeling from Kate's sudden reappearance and vicious assault.

"On him!" Cass shouted back. She abandoned her cover and sprinted across the warehouse floor towards Deuce, bullets striking the concrete near her feet.

She skidded to his side, immediately pressing her hands to the bleeding stab wound, her movements swift and practiced despite the shock.

Just as Manny refocused after covering Devin, another figure dropped from the catwalks high above. Akimitsu landed with quiet agility near the forklift Manny used for cover, his katana already drawn.

"Manny!" Devin shouted a warning, even as he bore down on Kate.

Manny spun, his rifle coming up barely in time to meet the initial, incredibly fast slash from Akimitsu's blade. Sparks flew as the weapons collided. Manny stumbled backward, trying to create distance as Akimitsu pressed the attack, the katana a silver blur.

The warehouse floor had fractured into desperate, isolated conflicts: Devin lunging at Kate, his movements driven by fury; Manny parrying and dodging Akimitsu's lethal blade; Cass working frantically to save Deuce, all under the distant, impassive gaze of Viktor.

## Chapter 26

## Fight for Survival

Devin collided with Kate, the impact a harsh crack in the echoing warehouse. His charge was fueled by a desperate fury, but Kate, anticipating the move, shifted with a fluid, deadly grace. She absorbed his forward momentum, twisted, and drove a sharp elbow toward his temple. He grunted, a burst of pain searing through his skull, but he pushed through it, arms snaking around her in a brutal grapple, driving them both backward into a stack of industrial shelving. Metal shrieked and buckled.

Simultaneously, across the chaotic expanse near a hulking yellow forklift, Manny contorted his body, Akimitsu's katana a streak of silver that sliced the air where his head had been an instant before. Metal shrieked again as Manny thrust his rifle up in a desperate, high block, deflecting a follow-up slash aimed at his neck. The force of the impact jarred his arms, the weight and alien balance of the ancient sword a palpable threat. He scrambled backward, using the forklift's massive tires for fleeting cover, the slick concrete an unreliable surface beneath his boots. Akimitsu flowed around the obstacle, his traditional weapon a stark, lethal anachronism in the industrial setting, wielded with chilling precision. Fifty feet away, amidst scattered debris and the rapidly spreading stain of Deuce's blood, Cass worked with focused intensity. "Stay with me, Deuce! Damn it, stay with me!" she muttered, her jaw clenched as she stuffed QuikClot gauze deep into the ragged stab wound near his kidney. Deuce's face was pale, his breathing shallow and erratic, his eyelids fluttering. The signs of shock were undeniable. She had to stop the bleeding—now. The sudden crack of unsuppressed gunfire snapped her attention away for a microsecond. Two Serpent guards, seeing Devin and Manny occupied, were advancing from the loading docks, directing fire towards Manny's position by the forklift. "Not today!" Cass growled, snatching her pistol and firing three quick, aimed shots over Deuce's still form. One Serpent cried out, clutching his shoulder as he stumbled back; the other dove behind a stack of oil drums. A sustained exchange was impossible while Deuce was critical, but she had to keep them suppressed.

Pinned against the groaning shelves, Kate fought with vicious speed. She slammed her knee into Devin's thigh, striking the same spot she'd injured earlier, drawing a sharp, involuntary gasp from him. As his grip faltered, she twisted violently, creating just enough space to drive her forehead into the bridge of his nose. Devin heard a distinct crunch, and pain exploded behind his eyes in a wave of white light. He recoiled, the taste of blood filling his mouth, as Kate shoved free. Loose crates cascaded from the damaged shelves above. Devin rolled, narrowly avoiding the falling debris. Kate sprang to her feet, retrieving the combat knife she'd dropped, her eyes narrowed, fixed on him. They circled each other amidst the debris, Devin trying to breathe through the throbbing pain that now dominated his face.

Manny, using the brief lull Cass's covering fire provided, shoved hard against the forklift. It rolled a few feet towards Akimitsu, the unexpected movement forcing the assassin to adjust his stance, his katana momentarily lowered. Manny seized the opening, lunging forward, not with his knife, but snatching a heavy chain that lay discarded on the floor. He swung it in a wide, whistling arc. Akimitsu sidestepped the crude weapon with an almost contemptuous flick of his body, the chain clanging uselessly against a steel container. The move, however, disrupted Akimitsu's rhythm. Before Akimitsu could counter, Manny dropped the chain and dove low, tackling the assassin around the knees. They crashed to the concrete in a thrashing heap, Manny attempting to use his greater mass to overpower his opponent, Akimitsu struggling to create space to bring his blade or a shorter tanto into play.

The dynamics of the fight shifted again, the chaos ratcheting higher. Devin, deflecting another knife thrust from Kate, managed to pin her wrist against a stack of pallets. As they grappled, Akimitsu, having thrown Manny off with surprising strength, spotted an opening. Ignoring Manny, who was scrambling back to his feet, Akimitsu launched himself towards Devin, katana raised high, clearly intending to eliminate one opponent swiftly.

"Devin, look out!" Manny roared.

Devin registered a streak of motion, the deadly arc of the descending sword. He couldn't break free from Kate in time to evade. In a flash of desperate calculation, he shoved Kate hard into Akimitsu's path, using her as an impromptu shield while throwing himself backward.

Kate cried out, a mixture of surprise and fury, as she stumbled directly before Akimitsu. The assassin, forced to arrest his downward stroke against Devin, reacted without pause. Abandoning the katana strike, he delivered a sharp palm heel to Kate's chest. The blow sent her reeling back into Manny, who was just pushing himself to his feet.

The chaotic fight momentarily reconfigured. Devin now faced Akimitsu, who retrieved his katana with a swift, economical movement. Manny found himself opposite Kate, who snarled, knife at the ready, her expression unreadable despite being violently maneuvered by both men.

"Impressive, Jones," Akimitsu breathed, his katana held loosely, poised. "But futile." He attacked, his speed startling Devin, the blade weaving a disorienting pattern. Devin, lacking Manny's recent, brutal education in facing the sword, relied on instinct, dodging and parrying with his heavier combat knife. He felt the disparity in skill immediately. He gave ground quickly, the katana leaving searing lines where it skated off his vest or lightly scored his exposed arms.

Meanwhile, Manny charged Kate, choosing to meet her precise skill with raw power. "You picked the wrong side, Kate!" he bellowed, throwing a wide, looping punch. Kate ducked under it with ease, countering with a quick jab to his already bruised ribs, followed by a low kick aimed at his knee. Manny grunted, absorbing the impacts, and relentlessly pressed forward. He aimed to corner her against a stack of containers, intending to negate her agility with his strength in the tight confines. Kate moved like quicksilver, her knife a flickering threat that kept him at bay, slashing defensively whenever he closed the distance.

Cass risked another quick glance away from Deuce. Devin was clearly in trouble against Akimitsu's blade. Manny was engaged with Kate, a difficult, mobile target. The Serpent she'd wounded was no longer a factor, but the other was still firing sporadically from behind the oil drums. That threat needed to be eliminated. Taking careful aim during a pause in the Serpent's fire, she squeezed off two rounds. The shots echoed, then silence descended from the loading dock area. One less distraction. Deuce groaned again, his skin clammy. "Pressure's dropping," she muttered, acutely aware of the passing seconds.

Devin backpedaled, Akimitsu's katana a continuous, flashing danger, forcing him toward the warehouse center. He risked a look towards Manny and Kate—they were still enmeshed in their own difficult fight. He had to disrupt Akimitsu's rhythm. As the assassin lunged again, Devin didn't dodge sideways. He dropped, rolling forward under the thrust, surfacing almost inside Akimitsu's guard. He drove his combat knife upward, targeting the thigh. Akimitsu twisted with incredible reflexes, the blade cutting only fabric, but the evasive move momentarily unbalanced him. Devin scrambled up, gaining a few vital feet of separation.

Seeing Devin create this space, Kate recognized an opportunity to disengage from Manny's unyielding advance. She feinted a slash towards Manny's face, forcing him to recoil, then spun, sprinting towards the confrontation between Devin and Akimitsu, her intentions unclear—perhaps to flank Devin or assist Akimitsu.

Manny roared in frustration as Kate disengaged, turning just in time to see Akimitsu recover his balance and prepare to renew his assault on Devin. But Akimitsu, perhaps sensing Kate's approach or reassessing Manny as the more immediate threat, suddenly pivoted. With startling speed, he redirected his attack back towards Manny.

The brief, chaotic exchange of opponents was over; the original pairings violently resumed, but the texture of the fight had changed. Manny, his movements fueled by Kate's escape and Akimitsu's chilling skill, met the assassin's renewed assault with a desperate surge. He sidestepped the first slash, the katana biting deep into the concrete floor where he'd stood an instant before. As Akimitsu strained for a heartbeat to wrench the blade free, Manny saw an opening. Discarding his own knife, he snatched the heavy metal pry bar he'd dropped earlier near the forklift. With a raw bellow that tore from his throat, he swung the heavy bar with all the force he could muster.

Akimitsu, however, seemed to anticipate the desperate counter. He pulled the katana free with surprising speed and pivoted smoothly. The pry bar whistled through empty air, clanging against the forklift tines. Before Manny could recover his balance, Akimitsu reversed his grip on the katana and brought the heavy pommel down in a vicious arc, striking Manny hard across the side of the head. Manny staggered, vision fracturing, and collapsed to his knees, the pry bar falling from his loosened grasp. Akimitsu didn't pause, delivering a swift, brutal kick to Manny's chest that sent him sprawling onto his back, gasping for air. Akimitsu stood over him, katana poised, then his head turned slightly, his attention momentarily diverted.

Devin, in that instant Akimitsu turned, had renewed his attack on Kate. He tackled her again, harder this time, driving her back down onto the concrete amidst the scattered debris. The impact jarred the knife from her grasp; it skittered under a nearby forklift. He pinned her, straddling her chest, striking with focused, rapid blows. Kate fought back, clawing, spitting, but her strength was fading against his relentless assault. He felt her resistance weaken. Through her swollen eyes, she registered Akimitsu glancing their way, saw Manny down but trying to rise. A flicker of something—calculation, perhaps—crossed her face. With a final, explosive effort, she jammed her thumb into Devin's already injured eye. He roared, recoiling from the sharp, intrusive pain. But this time, the agony only intensified his resolve. He didn't pull back. Instead, his fist descended with brutal, conclusive force.

"How could you?" he rasped. "Traitor."

The sound of the impact was sickening. Kate's body went limp beneath him; her struggles ceased.

Devin remained there for a moment, chest heaving, the receding adrenaline leaving behind the searing throb in his eye and the profound emptiness of betrayal dealt with.

Akimitsu witnessed it all: Kate's fall, Devin's brutal efficiency. He glanced back at Manny, who was still struggling to push himself up. He saw Devin, injured, enraged, yet dangerously focused. Akimitsu's posture subtly shifted. Viktor was upstairs, his position potentially compromised. With a final, swift assessment of the scene, Akimitsu turned. He moved into the maze of crates and containers with remarkable speed, heading for the administrative access door and vanishing through it before Devin could effectively react.

Devin blinked furiously, his vision still spotted, the sharp pain in his eye a radiating pulse through his skull. He forced himself to focus, pushing past the agony. The adrenaline surge was fading, leaving a deep ache and bone-weariness in its place. He looked down at Kate's still form, then across the floor to Manny, who was slowly, painfully pushing himself upright, one hand pressed to his head.

"Akimitsu... he's heading upstairs!" Manny yelled, grabbing his rifle, his gaze fixed on the administrative access door the assassin had disappeared through.

Devin scrambled to his feet and retrieved his M4A1, the familiar weight a small comfort despite his injuries. He glanced at Cass, kneeling beside Deuce. Deuce was pale, clutching the pressure bandage Cass held tight against his side, but his eyes were open, his face set in a grimace of pain.

"Cass!" Devin shouted, his voice hoarse. "Get him out of here! Find an exit, get comms working, call for backup, extract! Go!"

Cass met his gaze, nodding sharply. "On it! Come on, Deuce, lean on me." She shifted, putting her shoulder under Deuce's arm, straining to help him. With a visible effort of will, supported by Cass, Deuce managed to stagger upright, his face a mask of agony, yet his jaw was set with determination. Cass began guiding him slowly but steadily towards the main warehouse doors, away from the administrative section, her eyes constantly scanning for any remaining threats.

Devin turned back to Manny, who stood by the admin access door Akimitsu had used. "He went up," Manny confirmed, his voice rough as he touched the side of his head where Akimitsu had struck him. "Viktor's got to be up there. And Rachel. Annabelle."

"And whatever personal guard he kept close," Devin added, checking the magazine on his rifle. His body protested with every movement—the broken nose, the throbbing eye, a map of bruises and cuts—but the thought of his mother and Rachel in Viktor's clutches overrode everything else. "Let's finish this."

"Stairs," Manny grunted, nodding towards a heavy fire door marked with an upward arrow just inside the administrative access corridor. They breached it cautiously. The stairwell was concrete, starkly lit by emergency fixtures. The air felt colder here, stale. They ascended quickly, their boots making soft sounds on the metal steps, checking each landing, moving with a synchronized readiness born of experience, despite their exhaustion and injuries.

The upper level opened into the administrative core of what had likely been Mercury International's polished public face before Viktor repurposed it. Cool fluorescent light gleamed on polished floors. Corridors branched off, lined with doors bearing titles like "Logistics Planning," "Customs Brokerage," and "Regional Manager." The orderliness here was jarring after the chaos and destruction downstairs. The silence, too, felt different—oppressive, as if holding its breath.

Resistance met them almost at once. Guards in sleeker body armor than the Serpents, carrying more advanced weaponry, rounded a corner near a bank of elevators, their rifles snapping up. Manny dropped the first with a controlled burst to the chest before the man could fully aim. Devin neutralized the second as he tried to gain cover, rounds thudding into his torso. They didn't pause, stepping over the fallen men, continuing their advance down the main corridor.

The layout matched the schematics Cass had procured: a central corridor with office wings extending to either side. They cleared systematically, room by room, leapfrogging, covering angles. They found empty offices, locked filing cabinets, computers displaying routine shipping manifests. A break room showed signs of a hasty departure—stale coffee grounds scattered near a machine, overturned chairs. A larger conference room held only a long table and more chairs pushed askew. There was no sign of Rachel or Annabelle.

They eliminated two more guards near the entrance to the main executive office wing, the exchange a brief, violent flurry in the tight space, suppressed shots flat and percussive. The pattern suggested a consolidation of forces. Viktor was likely waiting, prepared for their arrival. Akimitsu would have reached him by now.

They reached the final corridor. Plush carpeting now absorbed the sound of their steps. Polished wood doors lined the walls, bearing brass nameplates of executives Devin didn't recognize. At the far end, framed by ornate sconces, stood a set of imposing double doors—dark, solid wood, marked only with the stylized Mercury International logo. Viktor's main office. The low hum of the HVAC system seemed to intensify in the quiet, each breath loud in their own ears.

Devin glanced at Manny. He saw a mirror of his own stark focus in Manny's eyes, the deep lines of exhaustion momentarily erased by sheer resolve. They had pushed through so much to get here. This was the precipice. Devin moved to the left side of the doors, Manny taking the right. They stacked, weapons ready, their breathing deliberately controlled. Devin held up three fingers, saw Manny's confirming nod, and began the silent count with his fingers. Three... Two... One....

# Chapter 27

# Point of No Return

Devin slammed his shoulder into the heavy wood as Manny's boot struck near the handle. The lock splintered; the double doors flew inward with a crash that shattered the office's charged quiet. They moved into the room, M4A1s up, senses heightened, each sweeping their assigned sector even as the scene unfolded before them.

The office was opulent, a stark remove from the industrial harshness below. Plush carpet muffled their cautious advance. Expensive, abstract art hung on the walls, flanking a massive, polished mahogany desk positioned before a floor-to-ceiling panoramic window. Through it, the warehouse floor, with its lingering signs of conflict, looked distant, almost peaceful under the scattered security lights.

Viktor sat behind the desk, though not with composure. His knuckles were white where he gripped the polished wood, his face pale and taut, a volatile fury simmering just beneath the surface. A half-empty glass of amber liquid sat forgotten near his hand. Standing rigidly near the corner of the desk, katana held at the ready, was Akimitsu, his focus absolute. Six heavily armed men—Viktor's personal guard, their black tactical gear distinct from the Serpents—were positioned strategically. Their weapons were not trained on the door, but inward.

Their targets were Annabelle and Rachel. They knelt side-by-side in the open space between the desk and the door, hands bound tightly behind them, mouths sealed with gray duct tape. Two guards stood directly behind them, pistols aimed steadily at their heads. The other four guards flanked the hostages, their weapons covering Devin and Manny. Rachel's eyes, wide and frantic, locked onto Devin's the instant he entered, a torrent of fear held captive. Annabelle looked smaller, almost fragile, her gaze darting between her son and the seething Viktor.

"Jones..." Viktor spat the name, his voice trembling with a rage that vibrated through the room. He pushed himself slowly to his feet, leaning heavily on the desk. "You dare... You dare come here... after what you did?" His piercing blue eyes fixed on Devin, raw grief and venom swirling within them. "You killed her. My Katerina. My daughter."

Akimitsu shifted almost imperceptibly, his grip tightening on his sword hilt, attuned to the tremors in his master's voice.

"Ah, Manny," Viktor continued, his voice cracking before hardening again as his gaze flicked towards him. "Still breathing. While my daughter lies dead downstairs because of him." He gestured sharply towards Devin. "I received word he fulfilled his... task regarding Mr. Ewing in Lehighton." He gave a choked, bitter laugh. "He takes lives so easily, doesn't he? Just the wrong ones." He slammed a fist onto the desk, the sound sharp and sudden. "You arrive, battered and bleeding, believing you've won? You stand there, having stolen the only thing... the only thing... that ever mattered?"

"Let them go, Viktor," Devin's voice was low, tight, his weapon steady despite the turmoil Viktor's raw anguish ignited within him. Manny mirrored his stance, covering the guards near the hostages. "This ends now."

"ENDS?" Viktor roared, shoving his chair back so violently it nearly toppled. "It ends when I say it ends! It ends when you have paid! You think killing Ewing bought you something? You think that replaces Katerina?" He laughed again, the sound fractured, unhinged. "That task was trivial! An amusement! Leverage! This," he swept a trembling hand towards Annabelle and Rachel, "this is consequence! This is pain! The only language your kind truly understands! You took my daughter! Now you will watch them suffer!"

That final, broken roar, the sheer agony twisting Viktor's features, the explicit, brutal threat—it was enough. Devin didn't shout, didn't telegraph his intent. He moved, an explosive surge of motion, not directly at the grieving, volatile Viktor, but angling towards Akimitsu, recognizing the assassin as the immediate, lethal extension of Viktor's pain.

Simultaneously, Manny opened fire, not at Viktor, but at the two guards closest to his own position, knowing they had the clearest lines of sight to Devin. The room detonated with sound and motion.

The two guards Manny targeted returned fire instantly, scrambling for cover behind ornate armchairs. Rounds snapped through the air, shredding upholstery and smacking into the far wall. The guards behind the hostages hesitated for a crucial instant, torn between engaging the attackers or maintaining their aim on the women. That momentary indecision was fatal. Manny pivoted smoothly, his weapon stitching a three-round burst across the chest of the guard behind Annabelle. The man crumpled. Devin, even as he closed distance with Akimitsu, snapped off two shots from his M4, hitting the guard behind Rachel high in the torso, sending him staggering back.

Akimitsu met Devin's charge with swift precision, the katana a blur. He didn't retreat; he moved into Devin's attack, redirecting Devin's momentum. The M4A1 felt unwieldy against the assassin's speed. Akimitsu parried Devin's initial weapon thrust aside with the flat of his blade and, in the same fluid motion, delivered a kick to Devin's knee that nearly buckled his leg. Devin grunted, stumbling but staying on his feet, swinging the rifle to create space. Akimitsu flowed backward, the katana a shimmering arc of steel, forcing Devin onto the defensive.

The remaining four guards unleashed a barrage of automatic fire towards Manny, who had taken cover behind a sturdy credenza. Wood splintered, and plaster dust filled the air. Manny returned fire methodically, using the credenza, popping up for brief, aimed shots before ducking again, making each round count. He dropped one guard near the window with a shot to the head.

Viktor, witnessing his carefully arranged tableau shatter into violent chaos, slammed his glass down on the desk. His face contorted, he surged to his feet and moved rapidly around the desk towards the hostages. Ignoring Annabelle, he grabbed Rachel roughly by the arm, yanking her upright and pressing his pistol hard against her temple. "Enough!" he roared, dragging a terrified, stumbling Rachel towards a concealed side door behind a large painting.

Devin saw Viktor making his escape, saw Rachel's desperate eyes pleading with him, but Akimitsu gave him no opening. The assassin pressed his attack, the katana a continuous threat, forcing Devin back, step by relentless step. A shallow cut opened on Devin's forearm as he parried. He felt the sting, the burn, and knew he couldn't sustain this defense.

Manny took down another guard with a controlled pair to the chest as the man attempted to flank his position. Two left. They concentrated their fire on Manny's cover, the credenza disintegrating under the impacts. Manny stayed low, calculating his next move. He tossed an empty magazine one way, drawing their fire, then emerged on the other side, eliminating both guards with quick, precise bursts before they could reacquire him. An abrupt, ringing silence fell over Manny's side of the room, broken only by the sharp clang of Devin's weapon meeting Akimitsu's blade and Annabelle's muffled sobbing.

"Manny!" Devin grunted, narrowly evading a thrust from Akimitsu. He saw the guards were down, saw Viktor disappearing with Rachel through the side door. "Get Mom! Get them clear! Go!"

Manny didn't hesitate. He confirmed the order with a sharp nod, pushing past his own exhaustion and pain. He rushed to Annabelle, swiftly cutting her bonds with his knife and pulling the gag from her mouth. "Come on, Mrs. J, we gotta move!" he urged, helping her to her unsteady feet, guiding her towards the main office doors and the stairwell beyond.

Now it was Devin and Akimitsu, alone. The assassin pressed his advantage, his movements precise and economical, forcing Devin back towards the large panoramic window. Devin knew he was outmatched, bleeding, his energy flagging. Akimitsu lunged, katana aimed for a decisive strike. Devin, reacting on pure adrenaline and desperation, hurled his M4A1 directly at Akimitsu's face, sacrificing the weapon for a heartbeat of distraction.

Akimitsu batted the rifle aside with a flick of his wrist, but the momentary obstruction was enough. Devin dove low, tackling Akimitsu around the waist, driving him backward with every ounce of remaining strength. They crashed hard into the reinforced panoramic window. The reinforced glass spiderwebbed instantly, groaned under their combined weight and momentum, held for a taut second, then shattered outward with an explosive crack. A disorienting moment of freefall followed, the morning air a sudden rush against their faces, the sounds of the office vanishing, replaced by the shriek of wind and the rapidly approaching floor of the warehouse.

They struck the concrete below amidst the debris and bodies from the earlier firefight, the impact jarring them to their core, though the fight was far from concluded.

The landing drove the air from Devin's lungs; pain flared from multiple points as he hit the concrete amidst the warehouse wreckage. Dust, thick with the smell of cordite and something else, acrid and old, filled his nostrils. His vision pulsed, the harsh emergency lights overhead blurring into distorted streaks. He pushed himself up onto unsteady arms, coughing, dragging air back into his lungs.

Nearby, Akimitsu landed with a sickening thud but rolled, his training mitigating some of the impact. He came up favoring his left leg, his face a mask of pain for a brief moment, but his eyes, when they found Devin, were cold, sharp, and utterly focused. His katana lay gleaming on the concrete a few feet away, having tumbled with them. Ignoring his injured leg, he moved immediately towards the sword.

Devin shoved himself backward, a fresh surge of adrenaline momentarily numbing the chorus of pain signals from his body. He couldn't let Akimitsu reach the katana. His hand closed around a sturdy wooden plank, splintered from a shattered pallet. He hauled himself to his feet just as Akimitsu reached the sword, scooping it up with a smooth, practiced motion. They circled each other once more, this time amidst the carnage of the warehouse floor. The quiet was broken only by their harsh, ragged breathing and the distant drip of water. Emergency lights cast long, mobile shadows, transforming the familiar space into a grotesque arena.

Akimitsu attacked, his injured leg hampering him only slightly; his speed was still remarkable. The katana sliced through the air, aimed at Devin's head. Devin brought the plank up, blocking the blow with a heavy thud that sent vibrations jarring up his already aching arms. The wood fractured under the impact but didn't break. Devin countered at once, swinging the plank low, forcing Akimitsu to leap back awkwardly on his good leg.

Akimitsu pressed his assault, the blade a continuous, lethal threat, forcing Devin to give ground. He used the plank defensively, parrying slashes that sought to maim or kill. Devin knew this purely defensive posture was unsustainable against the swordsman, injured or not. He had to close the distance, to negate the blade's reach.

Feinting another block with the plank, Devin suddenly dropped it and lunged, tackling Akimitsu low around the waist again, driving him hard into a stack of metal drums. The drums clattered, one tipping over with a loud, booming clang. They crashed to the floor again, rolling amidst the debris, the katana flying from Akimitsu's grasp.

It became a raw, desperate struggle for survival. Fists connected with bruising impact. They clawed, kicked, bit – any opening sought, any weakness exploited. Akimitsu, though smaller, fought with sharp precision and leverage, landing quick, debilitating strikes to Devin's ribs and face. Devin tasted blood again, felt the cartilage of his broken nose grate. The pain, however, only hardened his resolve. He fought back with a grim focus, using his size and weight, absorbing Akimitsu's blows while delivering heavier ones in return.

He finally overpowered Akimitsu, trapping his wrists, pinning him. He struck with measured, heavy blows, each one fueled by a cold, hard fury, until Akimitsu's struggles weakened, his body finally going limp beneath the assault, consciousness lost.

Devin pushed himself off Akimitsu, gasping for breath, adrenaline the sole prop keeping him on his feet, every muscle in his body protesting. His eyes scanned the ruined warehouse floor. Bodies of Serpents, Akimitsu finally still... but Viktor?

Just then, Viktor emerged from a different corridor near the loading docks, dragging a terrified Rachel with him. Viktor must have taken an alternate stairwell down from the offices, aiming to escape through the loading bays. Rachel stumbled, her eyes wide and frantic, finding Devin across the debris-littered expanse. Viktor shoved her roughly towards a stack of crates near Loading Bay 3, clearly intending to use her as a shield for his escape.

Seeing Rachel, seeing Viktor still standing, a fresh, potent charge of adrenaline surged through Devin. He launched himself forward, ignoring the fire in his ribs, ignoring the exhaustion that threatened to drag him down. He hit Viktor with immense force, driving him hard away from Rachel, sending them both sprawling onto the concrete. Devin was on top instantly, his fists striking Viktor's face repeatedly, years of grief for his father, cold fury over the betrayals, and raw fear for Rachel and his mother fueling the assault. He felt bone shift beneath his knuckles, heard Viktor's choked groan, saw surprise and pain flare in those calculating blue eyes. Viktor struggled weakly, then his body went slack, still.

"Rachel!" Devin gasped, scrambling towards her, pushing himself up, his own body trembling violently. He reached her side, pulled out his tactical knife, and quickly sawed through the bindings on her wrists. "Are you okay? Hurt?"

Rachel ripped the duct tape from her mouth, gulping air, tears carving paths down her bruised face, but her eyes held a fierce, shaky relief.

"Devin... I... I'm okay. Just..."

Behind them, near the administrative doorway, Akimitsu stirred. Devin hadn't knocked him completely unconscious, merely stunned him. Unseen by Devin, whose entire focus was now on Rachel, Akimitsu's eyes fluttered open. He took in the scene—Devin alive, Viktor downed but perhaps not out. His gaze flickered towards his fallen katana lying several feet away. With a supreme effort that sent waves of agony through his body, he began to push himself silently up.

Devin finished cutting Rachel's bonds. "Rach..." he started, his voice rough, reaching for her, needing the tactile reassurance that she was truly safe.

But in that micro-pause, that shared moment of believing the most immediate threat was finally neutralized, Viktor moved. He hadn't been unconscious, merely stunned, feigning, waiting for an opportunity. His eyes snapped open, cold and sharp, alight with a venomous triumph. He fumbled beneath his torn and bloodstained jacket, producing a concealed backup pistol—a small but deadly Walther PPK.

Rachel saw the movement from the corner of her eye, the metallic gleam catching the emergency lights. "DEVIN, LOOK OUT!" she screamed again, her voice raw with renewed terror.

Devin turned, reacting to her scream, but it was a fraction of a second too slow. Viktor fired.

Bang.

The shot was a sharp, deafening crack in the cavernous warehouse. An intense, burning pain exploded low in Devin's back, stealing his breath, his legs giving way instantly. The world tilted, colors smearing, sounds dissolving into a roaring rush as he collapsed forward onto the cold, hard concrete, darkness encroaching on his vision.

Rachel stared, frozen for a horrifying beat, at Devin's crumpled form, then at Viktor struggling to push himself upright, the backup pistol clutched in his trembling hand, a faint, malevolent smile touching his bloodied lips.

Something within Rachel fractured. The terror, the helplessness she had endured—it vanished, replaced by an icy, consuming rage. Her eyes darted across the floor, spotting Devin's discarded 9mm Beretta lying on the concrete a few feet away. She didn't hesitate. She dove for it.

Her fingers closed around the familiar checkered grip—countless hours at the range with Devin and Manny, the weight, the balance, returning in a surge of muscle memory and fierce adrenaline. She brought the weapon up smoothly, rising to one knee, her hands surprisingly steady, her gaze locked onto Viktor.

Viktor raised his own pistol, his smile faltering, surprise flickering in his eyes at her sudden transformation from captive to combatant. He opened his mouth, perhaps for a final taunt, perhaps a curse—

But before either could fire, another figure intervened. Akimitsu, now on his feet, staggered slightly. "Mou ii, Viktor-sama," he said, his voice strained but carrying an undeniable note of finality. "It is enough."

Viktor, his gaze locked on Rachel, didn't even glance at him, dismissing the interruption with a contemptuous flick of his free hand. Akimitsu, seeing his plea ignored, moved then with deadly intent. He scooped up his fallen katana. He ignored Rachel, his attention fixed solely on Viktor.

"Viktor-sama," Akimitsu said, his voice low, strained but clear above the warehouse hum.

Viktor turned, startled by Akimitsu's recovery and the use of his name. Akimitsu took another step closer, katana held ready.

"I admired your ambition," he stated, his eyes holding a mixture of weariness and stark finality, "but revenge has consumed you."

He gestured vaguely around the ruined warehouse, at the bodies, the destruction.

"I suspected that choosing Lehighton was tied to the Jones family, a long-held grievance... but this current obsession has destroyed everything."

Viktor stared, momentarily bewildered, his pistol lowering slightly.

"Akimitsu? What is this? Kill them!"

Akimitsu shook his head slowly.

"Loyalty has boundaries. Honor requires an end to this."

Before Viktor could fully process the betrayal, Akimitsu surged forward, the katana flashing in a single, swift, upward arc. The blade plunged deep into Viktor's chest. Viktor gasped, eyes wide with shocked disbelief, the Walther tumbling from his grasp. Akimitsu twisted the blade with a precise, dispassionate movement, then withdrew it sharply.

Viktor collapsed onto the blood-soaked concrete, his body finally still, the architect of so much pain and suffering silenced not by his enemies, but by his most trusted retainer.

A heavy quiet filled the warehouse. Rachel remained frozen for only an instant, gun still aimed at Akimitsu, her mind struggling to comprehend Viktor's sudden death. Akimitsu looked down at Viktor's body, then turned slowly towards Rachel. He met her gaze...

But as Rachel saw his face clearly, the calm, detached expression, a vivid memory seared through her mind: this man, standing beside the one who forced the hood over her head in the van, his quiet voice cutting through her terror: "The more you fight, the worse this will be for you." The helplessness, the violation, the fear—it surged back, overwhelming the numbness, replaced by a scalding eruption of rage and pain. He wasn't just Viktor's servant; he was one of them. One of her captors.

Her hands, steady only moments before, now trembled with fury. Rachel squeezed the trigger.

BANG! BANG!

Two shots roared in the enclosed space. Akimitsu cried out, a choked gasp, as the bullets slammed into his torso, throwing him backward onto the bloodstained floor. He lay there, twitching, grievously wounded but still breathing.

Just then, Manny burst back onto the warehouse floor, weapon raised, having secured Annabelle near the stairwell. He took in the drastically changed scene in an instant—Devin down, Viktor dead, Rachel standing over the now wounded Akimitsu, gun still smoking in her hand.

"What the hell happened?!" Manny yelled, his mind racing to process the new situation as he quickly moved to cover the downed assassin.

"He... he killed Viktor," Rachel stammered, the gun lowering slightly as the adrenaline surge began to desert her, leaving her shaking. "Then... he was there... in the van..."

Manny needed no more. He cautiously approached the wounded Akimitsu, kicking the fallen katana further away before efficiently securing the gasping, bleeding assassin's hands behind his back with zip ties, assessing the wounds even as he worked.

Rachel dropped the Beretta as if it were scalding hot, the adrenaline finally crashing, leaving her trembling uncontrollably. She scrambled to

Devin's side, tears streaming down her face, mixing with the grime and blood.

"Devin? Devin, stay with me!" She fumbled frantically in Devin's pockets for his phone—miraculously intact—dialing 911 with shaking fingers, babbling their location, the situation—gunshots, officer down, multiple casualties, send ambulance, Mercury International, Court Street...

Dropping the phone, she ripped off another piece of her already torn shirt, pressing it desperately against the bleeding wound in his back, trying to slow the frighteningly rapid flow of blood.

"Thank you... you saved me..." she sobbed, her voice choked, nearly incoherent with grief and shock. "Please, Devin, don't die... Don't leave me..."

The minutes felt like hours, measured only by the shallow, labored rise and fall of Devin's chest and the frantic thumping of Rachel's heart. Then, faintly at first, steadily growing louder, came the distant wail of sirens. The sound grew, converging, echoing off the surrounding industrial buildings—a promise of aid in the desolate aftermath. Paramedics burst through one of the destroyed loading dock entrances, their lights cutting through the gloom, followed closely by uniformed police officers, weapons drawn, moving with caution. They rushed towards Devin, quickly assessing the scene—Viktor's body, the widespread destruction, Akimitsu secured by Manny, Rachel kneeling beside Devin, covered in blood. They gently moved Rachel aside, their actions swift and professional as they began evaluating Devin's condition, applying pressure bandages, calling out vital signs, preparing a backboard.

As they carefully lifted Devin onto the stretcher, his eyelids fluttered open weakly. His gaze, unfocused and clouded with pain, found Rachel's tear-streaked face. A single word, rough and strained, escaped his lips: "Rach..." Then, his eyes rolled back, and he lost consciousness again. Rachel watched, her heart suspended between terror and a tiny, fragile ember of hope, as they wheeled him away, the flashing red and blue lights consuming him as they disappeared into the waiting ambulance, leaving her alone amidst the carnage, the silence, and the uncertain dawn breaking over the ruined warehouse.

# Epilogue

Two days after the violent events at the Mercury International Container Terminal, morning light slanted weakly through the privacy blinds of a Philadelphia hospital room. The quiet hum of monitors and the faint, sharp scent of antiseptic formed the room's atmosphere. Devin lay in the adjustable electric bed, his torso and back heavily bandaged beneath a thin hospital gown. IV lines ran from a pole beside him, delivering fluids and pain medication. His face was pale, marked by exhaustion and pain, but his green eyes were open, lucid, fixed on the neutral-toned wall opposite his bed.

Manny slumped in an upholstered visitor chair nearby, the fatigue of the past week visibly aging him. Rachel sat closer to the bed, her own weariness apparent, but her hazel-green eyes, as she gently held Devin's free hand, shone with a profound relief. Annabelle occupied another chair, her expression composed, though the shadow of recent grief and stress lingered; a bandage was visible on her shoulder beneath her blouse. Standing near the window, occasionally looking out at the distant Philadelphia skyline, was Cass, her usual professional demeanor softened by an undeniable exhaustion.

The quiet was broken by Cass clearing her throat softly. "Devin," she began, her voice low but clear, "we need to update you."

Devin shifted slightly, a wince tightening his features. "Go ahead," he murmured, his voice rough.

Cass nodded, her gaze steady. "Forensics confirmed Viktor is deceased. Killed at the scene by Akimitsu." A collective, almost inaudible exhalation passed through the room. "Kate Richards... Katerina Mikhailova," Cass corrected herself, the name still tasting unfamiliar, "is alive, just. She's in a medically induced coma here, sustained severe injuries during the fight with you, Devin. Her prognosis is guarded. Federal agents are posted outside her room."

Manny picked up the report, his voice heavy. "Akimitsu is alive as well, critical condition, under heavy guard after Rachel shot him. Once stable enough, he'll be transferred to a federal detention facility. And Brad Ewing..." Manny paused, glancing briefly at Devin, "...is confirmed deceased. Killed by you, Devin, during the confrontation at the dealership. EAG legal is liaising with the Pennsylvania authorities regarding the circumstances. It's being handled."

"And Kaitlyn?" Devin asked, his voice barely above a whisper.

"Physically okay," Cass answered. "She provided a full statement to Lehighton PD and federal investigators about what she knew of Brad's activities. She's cooperating completely. She's... shattered. Seems she was largely unaware of the worst of it, but she has a difficult path ahead."

A somber quiet settled in the room, filled with the unspoken weight of confirmed betrayals and violent ends.

Cass broke it again, shifting to the wider consequences. "Grand Central..." Cass's voice took on a hard edge. "As we feared after Viktor's threat... it was a catastrophe. Reports confirm the device detonated remotely after panic ensued. Mass casualties... NYPD and federal agencies are still processing the scene and the investigation. It's... grim."

Annabelle closed her eyes, a tear escaping and tracing a path down her cheek. "All those innocent people..." she whispered.

The room fell silent again, the enormity of the loss pressing down on them. Manny cleared his throat, the sound rough. "We lost good people," he said, his voice thick with unshed grief. He listed them, each name a heavy weight: "The EAG personnel... the team members at the Mercury warehouse... the three ambushed on Jamestown road..." His voice trailed off, the tally too great.

"Frank is still critical back in New York, but doctors say he's stable for now," Cass updated quietly. "Thomas is recovering well from his shoulder wound, already pushing for desk duty. Deuce... made it through surgery here in Philly after Kate stabbed him, but it was very close. He's stable but remains critical in the ICU. And your shoulder is healing well, Annabelle?"

Annabelle nodded, touching her bandaged shoulder. "I'll be fine. I just need to be here."

Rachel squeezed Devin's hand gently. "There's... something else," she said, her voice hesitant. She looked at Devin, drawing a breath. "I spoke with my dad yesterday." She paused. "He submitted his resignation."

Effective immediately. He knows he crossed lines, even if he believed his reasons were valid. He has a lot to answer for, legally and... personally."

The news hung in the air, another consequence of Viktor's destructive influence.

"What about EAG?" Devin asked, his gaze shifting to Cass.

"Challenging," Cass admitted, her voice laced with weary pragmatism. "HQ is a wreck, structurally unsound, likely a total loss based on initial engineering assessments. The Brooklyn field office's digital infrastructure was severely compromised; Ethan and his team are working nonstop on recovery and hardening security, but it's a monumental task. DC is operational, but the federal oversight is... intense, to say the least."

She paused, choosing her words carefully. "Devin, the fallout from Kate's betrayal and Viktor's campaign is significant. The FBI, DHS, even congressional committees are looking at us under a microscope. They're scrutinizing everything: our vetting protocols that allowed Katerina Mikhailova to infiltrate us at the highest level for so long, the security failures that led to the bombing of our own headquarters, and our proximity to the events culminating in the Grand Central attack. The fact that our Head of Security was the daughter of a major international terrorist who orchestrated such devastation... it's a reputational nightmare."

Cass continued, "They're asking hard questions: How could a premier security firm be so deeply compromised? What was EAG's role, however unwitting, in the chain of events that led to such a massive loss of civilian life at GCT? The very public nature of our headquarters' destruction doesn't help – it paints a picture of a company that couldn't even secure itself, let alone its clients. We're facing a crisis of confidence, both from the government and potentially from our client base. We need to rebuild, Devin. Not just the buildings and the networks, but trust. Vet everyone, top to bottom. Implement new, almost draconian safeguards. We have to prove EAG can be a shield, not a sieve."

Despite the pain radiating from his back, a flicker of determination showed in Devin's eyes. "We will," he stated, his voice low but firm. "We'll rebuild. The right way. Stronger. Cleaner."

A more peaceful quiet settled over the room. Cass gave a subtle nod to Manny. Annabelle rose. "I think I'll go get some coffee," she murmured, giving Devin's arm a gentle squeeze before she, Cass, and Manny filed quietly out, leaving Devin and Rachel alone, the rhythmic beeping of the vital signs monitor a steady counterpoint to the room's subdued atmosphere.

Rachel leaned closer, her hand still holding Devin's. The morning light caught the lines of fatigue around her eyes, but also the quiet relief, the deep affection.

"You survived..." she whispered, her voice husky with emotion, a correction to her earlier words in the warehouse.

Devin turned his head slowly on the pillow, meeting her gaze. A faint, tired smile touched his lips. He squeezed her hand, a weak pressure that spoke volumes. The room felt insulated from the outside world – the trauma, the losses, the betrayals swirling like a storm kept at bay, yet anchored by the simple, profound connection between them. The larger fight was far from concluded, the future of Echelon Axiom uncertain, the scars, both visible and hidden, deep. But in the quiet holding of hands, in the shared glance of survivors, lay the resilient strength of their bond, a fragile promise against whatever the future held.

Made in the USA
Columbia, SC
15 June 2025

59237338R00217